Content Warning
Contains Major Spoilers

This book does NOT contain any instances of abuse or assault. If that is your sole concern, you can carry on without reading the rest of the warning.

This book does contain mature themes, discussions around the inability to have children, brief mentions of cancer and subsequent surgery. This book also contains a touch of Daddy Kink. Which should be obvious.

Your health is important. You are important. Get your annual checkup.

VII

Prologue – Kendra

"I think I went too heavy on the nuts."

I stop chewing, still hunched over my bowl, and lift my eyes to my laptop screen. "I can't with you," I say with my mouth full of noodles.

"What?" Dad pauses, then rolls his eyes. "Get your mind out of the gutter, Kenny."

I shake my head as I finish chewing.

Dad and I have been doing this tradition for about two years now—cooking the same dish over a video call once a month and eating together. We did it on my thirtieth birthday, when he wasn't able to make the trip from Colorado to Delaware, then decided it was a fun way to catch up.

"It's good though. I'll just do less chopped peanuts next time." Dad nods to his plate.

"Yeah." I swirl my noodles in the sauce. "Feels a little dangerous to be able to make my own pad thai. I'm gonna eat this all the time."

Dad hums. "Maybe you can lure a date over with all these new cooking skills."

"Lure?" I snort. "I'm not trying to trick a man into dating me."

"You could leave a trail of those ravioli we made last month down your sidewalk." He gestures, completely serious. "Then put a bowl of sauce in the middle of your living room."

I blink at the man on my screen. "I'd have to put a giant box over the bowl and prop it up with a stick. So when my dream man crawls across my floor with ravioli falling out of his pockets, I can kick the stick away and trap him."

Dad gives me a blank look. "Now you're being ridiculous."

I crack up. "Yeah, I'm the problem."

He nods.

My fork is halfway to my mouth when someone knocks on the door.

"Hold on." I set my noodles down and push back from my little dining table.

"You expecting anyone?" Dad's voice switches to a parental tone.

"No," I call back over my shoulder, unconcerned.

My apartment building has always felt really safe—with locked front doors and a security guard on duty—so I'm not worried about whoever's at the door.

For all I know, it's Lizzy, my roommate. She often knocks when her hands are full rather than getting her keys out.

We used to work together, and when she offered me her spare room last year, I snagged it. It was closer to the office and cheaper than living alone.

A few months ago, she quit our company for a different job, so now I see her even less. And as someone who likes privacy, it's been pretty much ideal.

I flip the deadbolt and pull the door open.

"Hey—" My smile falters.

It's not Lizzy.

It's the guy from the rental office downstairs.

"Um, hi." I lift a hand in an awkward wave, and he presses a folded piece of paper against my palm.

My fingers close around it automatically.

"Sorry." He clears his throat. "We can't give you any more warnings. You need to be out by the end of the month."

"What?" I look down at the paper in my hand, then back up at him. "What warnings? What are you talking about?"

"You've had four months. Even when you pay up on the rent, you still gotta go." He shrugs. Fucking shrugs. Then turns away and walks down the hall.

I step back into my apartment, letting the door swing shut.

I don't understand.

What the hell is he talking about?

My hands start to shake as I unfold the paper.

They shake even more when I read the words.

He said it.

I heard him say it.

But seeing it...

Eviction Notice

I shake my head.

This doesn't make sense.

I've been paying rent.

I've been...

Embarrassment and shame make my throat feel tight.

I've been paying my roommate.

I've been giving money directly to Lizzy for half the rent.

She already lived here.

She told me she had the rent set up on auto pay. That it came right out of her account.

So I just gave her money.

Cash.

The paper vibrates in my trembling fingers.

She kept my money, but she didn't use it to pay rent.

My eyes lift from the letter, and I look down the short hall toward her bedroom.

She said she quit her job at the office. Said she got a better one. But that was five months ago.

It's been four months.

My heart thuds loudly in my chest.

No one at work ever asks about her.

No one ever said anything about her quitting to me.

Because maybe she didn't actually quit.

Maybe she was fired.

And maybe, probably, she's a fucking liar.

"Kenny?" Dad's voice cuts through the buzzing in my head.

My legs feel heavy as I force myself to walk back to the table.

I drop into the chair.

"You okay?" Dad's expression is full of sympathy, and it makes my throat feel even tighter.

"She... She wasn't paying the rent." The admission tastes like ash.

"I'm sorry, Kenny. That's... messed up."

I place my hands palm down on the table next to my dinner. "The letter says we need to be out by the end of the month." I swallow and will myself not to cry. "That's only ten days away. And... I think that means they'll come after us for the money, right? Like for the unpaid rent that I already paid?"

"Are you on the lease?"

I nod. "And I paid her cash. She said that would be easiest."

Anger pours itself into the concoction of emotions filling my chest.

If I'd paid her with checks or a transfer or... anything but cash, I'd have a record of it.

But I have nothing.

"Shit," Dad sighs. "If you're both on the lease, I bet there's a way for you to just pay back your half."

I press my lips together, embarrassed that I'm in this situation. But I know I need to be honest if I want the best advice.

"I can't afford that," I say quietly. I'm thirty-two years old, and this eviction is going to completely ruin me. "I could maybe scrape the money together, but it would be everything I have. And if I need to be out in ten days, I'll need that money for a deposit and first month's rent at a new place." The tangle of dread builds with each passing moment. "And I'll need to hire people to help me move."

Not to mention, no one will rent to me with this on my record.

My breath starts coming out in pants.

Is this hyperventilating?

"Kenny, it'll be okay." Dad leans close to the screen. "I can give you money."

I shake my head. "No. Thank you, but no. I can't do that."

I don't know my dad's financial situation, so I can't accept that much cash.

He purses his lips. "If you won't accept money, then there's only one other option."

"What's that?"

"You move here. Live with me."

I wait for the punchline.

But there isn't one.

He's serious.

I start to shake my head again.

Dad and I get along well, but we've never lived together.

Never ever.

He's always lived across the country from me.

Sure, he'd visit for a month every summer when I was growing up. We'd talk on the phone. And we do these dinners now. But living together...

In Colorado.

And not just in Colorado.

In the mountains.

It's been a long time since I've visited, but he's been in the same house for as long as I can remember. And it's *rural*.

"I can't just move to Colorado."

"Why not?" he asks, like he really doesn't see the problem.

"I have a job here."

"Quit."

My brows lift. "Just quit? And then what?"

Dad starts to nod before I even finish talking. "Work for me."

"Work... for you." I shake my head. "I appreciate you're trying to help, but I'm not handy. I can't build furniture."

He huffs a laugh. "I love you, Kenny. But I will never hand you a power tool ever again."

I roll my eyes. *You saw through one electrical cord, and the world will never let you forget.*

"I need help with the admin shit. Tracking orders, dealing with shipping and invoices. Honestly, business has been blowing up the last few years, and I need the help. I'd rather have you do it than have to hire some stranger."

"Are you serious?"

"Yeah. And the more I think about it, the more serious I am."

"What about all my stuff?" As I say it, I think about how much I got rid of when I moved in with Lizzy. I puff out a breath. "Really, it's just my bedroom set and clothes. Some knickknack shit, but not much else."

"You can put it in storage, and we can deal with it later," Dad suggests, tilting his head. "Or you can sell it. The guest room has a decent mattress, and I can clear out the closet. Been meaning to do that for years anyway."

I can't believe I'm considering this.

Really considering this.

But what options do I realistically have?

I don't have any friends with spare bedrooms. I don't want to take out a loan just to live. And Mom moved to France six years ago, so even if I wanted to, living with her isn't an option.

My shoulders sag as I watch Dad's expression turn hopeful.

I want to ask him how much he'll pay me, but I think this is one of those *beggars can't be choosers* situations.

I've been working in corporate America for a decade.

I've been screwing up my sleep schedule just as long to go in early and stay late.

I've been a personal assistant to someone for years, doing the majority of their work and making five times less than they do.

I've been at the same pay since I started.
And I have *fuck all* to show for it.
I look at the man on my screen.
And I cry a little on the inside.
Then I say something I never thought I would. "Guess I'm moving to Colorado."

Chapter 1

Kendra

"Yeah, sorry. I just don't want to drive in the dark." I tap my fingers on the steering wheel. "I'll leave early tomorrow and be there by lunch."

Dad lets out a breath that makes me feel a little bad. "I understand. Safety first."

"I'll let you know when I'm like twenty minutes away so you can get the streamers and balloons set up."

Dad chuckles, as I'd hoped. "Yeah, yeah. I'll put the strobe lights away until then."

"Good plan. Night, Dad."

"Night, Kenny."

The call disconnects, and I slump back in my seat.

It'll be easy to message him when I'm twenty minutes away tomorrow, because I'm twenty minutes away right now.

But I wasn't lying about the dark. It's already pitch black. And there are no streetlights out here in the mountains. So, when I saw the sign a mile back about a motel up ahead, I made a game-day decision to have one more night of freedom.

One more night alone.

One more night of independence before I, a fully grown adult, move into my dad's house.

I grab my backpack and wallet off my passenger seat and climb out of my car. Glad I put some fresh clothes in my bag just in case.

Bumping my door shut with my hip, I slip my arms through the straps of my pack, arching my back with a groan.

As much as I might be dreading this next phase of my life, I'm ready to be done driving.

I roll my neck out.

Before me is a two-story motel, nicely lit, painted a dark red with bright white railings.

It's about as classic as they come. And this one even includes what looks like a dive bar, front and center.

A cliff looms behind the building, giving the motel an impossibly dark backdrop.

With my thumbs hooked in my backpack straps, I do a slow turn.

A handful of cars sit in the parking lot beside mine, but the two-lane highway is empty.

I take a deep inhale of the crisp air.

And even though the sun has set, I can tell that the opposite side of the highway boasts a stunning view of the Rockies.

I'll hand it to Dad—this is a beautiful state. So at least there's that.

Pushing thoughts of my new home out of my mind, I straighten my spine and stride toward the sign for Rocky Ridge Inn.

Chapter 2

Luther

"No." My sister holds her hands up, stopping me from coming behind the bar. "You're not even supposed to be here tonight."

I narrow my eyes at her. "Says who?"

"Says HR." She throws her thumb over her shoulder, indicating Steve, the stuffed muskie mounted on the wall.

"Steve would never dare to tell me, the owner of said bar, what I can and cannot do."

"Fine." Jessie huffs and shakes her head. "But if you're going to insist on being here, I'm going to insist you sit on the patron side of the counter. But, and this is just a suggestion, maybe relax a little. Pretend like you're actually taking the day off like you said you would."

I heave out a breath, as though that's a hardship, and back away from the space that Jessie has claimed as her own.

She's right, of course. I said I wasn't going to come in tonight.

But then I couldn't decide what to watch on TV, and I... well, I didn't know what to do with myself.

And rather than address the underlying factor of my inability to just *relax*, I drove the few minutes here.

Two couples sit at the other end of the bar, so I slide onto a vacant stool at this end, leaving plenty of space between us.

They aren't arguing or doing anything exciting, so I don't need to eavesdrop.

Jessie sets a lowball glass filled with dark liquid in front of me. "Drink it."

"So fucking bossy," I grumble under my breath.

I sniff the drink.

Smells like a whiskey cola.

I don't have a *usual* drink. There are too many good options in the world to always drink the same thing. But this is one of my favorites. Especially since we use a local Colorado soda company that makes for superior cocktails.

I take a long sip.

Then down half the glass.

Lowering the drink, I look around the bar.

Jessie has the music set to classic rock tonight, loud enough for those who want to sit and listen, but not so loud you have to shout to be heard over it.

It's a weeknight, so the tables are about a third full, plus the other folks at the bar, but it's not too rowdy.

Some weekends, we fill every seat and then some, but if Jessie won't let me help her, then I'll sit here and take in the chill evening.

As I take another drink, Diego steps out from the kitchen door—along the back wall behind the bar, a dozen steps from where I'm sitting—with a trio of plates balanced on his arm.

He gives me a nod, and I tip my glass toward him.

Diego runs the kitchen and is in charge of the menu. It's a small menu, consisting of three options—a burger, a chicken sandwich, and a veggie wrap. But he changes the flavors each week, hooking our regulars to come try whatever is new.

On busier nights, we'd have two working the bar and two working the grill, but since it's chill, it's just him and Jessie on the clock.

I'm about to turn my attention to the baseball game playing on the TV above the liquor bottles when the back door opens.

The door is on the other end of the bar, mirror location of the kitchen door, and it leads out to the paved area between here and the motel building.

It's pretty much only used by guests of the motel.

Out of habit, my gaze moves toward the guest coming in for a late dinner. Or a drink.

Nothing exciting.

But then the dim overhead lights shine off the newcomer's dark hair.

And my attention is snagged.

It's a woman.

I sit up straighter.

The woman is fucking gorgeous.

Her hair hangs perfectly straight, long enough to brush her shoulders.

Her bare shoulders.

She's wearing a white tank top, and the fabric is stretched tight over full-size tits.

I swallow.

I want to face-plant into her chest.

The bar is blocking my view, so I can't see below her waist. But her body is soft.

Curvy.

Edible.

And way too young for me.

I lift my glass to my lips and swallow the rest of my drink.

The woman's gaze is busy taking in her surroundings, so she doesn't notice me perving.

And before she can catch me staring, I face forward.

I couldn't see the color of her eyes, but the rounded slopes of her cheeks are burned into my mind.

Society likes to make it seem as though men don't like thick, curvy women, but that's not true.

Not for me.

Not one fucking bit.

I like to watch my women bounce. Like to watch my fingers indent into soft flesh.

I like tits that can suffocate me.

I shift in my seat. And I remind myself that I also like to act professionally at my place of business.

I glance back over to the woman.

Our eyes connect for a split second before she drops her gaze.

Was she looking at me?

I watch her roll her lips together as she looks over the open tables again, and I understand her dilemma. Either she sits at a table alone, or she sits between me and the group at the bar.

Hiding my hand behind my empty glass, I cross my fingers.

Pretty fucking please sit by me.

Chapter 3

Kendra

I twist the toe of my sandal on the scarred vinyl floor as I feel my cheeks heat.

He caught me looking.

The urge to turn on my heel and head back to my room is tempting.

Very tempting.

But it's too early to go to sleep. And the thought of sitting in my motel room, sober, thinking about tomorrow, keeps me where I am.

I want to get drunk.

And if getting drunk also includes getting laid by some hot-as-fuck lumberjack... that would also be acceptable.

Forcing my head up, I lift one foot, then the next, determined to sit at the bar.

Four empty stools stand between the pair of couples closest to me and the hot older man at the far end. As I approach the empty seats, I have a decision to make—put one seat between me and hottie, or put one seat between me and the couples.

I keep my gaze on the bar, not looking up to see if the guy is watching me.

Playing it super cool, I stop between the four empty stools.

I could take the one to my right. Putting me closer to the couples.

Or...

I brace one hand on the bar, one on the wooden seat—closer to the hot man—and I boost myself up.

My feet dangle as I lean forward, resting my elbows on the bar.

Immediately, I realize this isn't a very flattering position. But just as quickly, I push the self-deprecating thoughts away.

Hot guy or no hot guy, I'm not spending the night sitting with good posture, sucking my stomach in.

Fuck that.

I lower my chin into my palm and look over the liquors displayed behind the bar.

A woman stops before me. Her dark brunette hair is twisted up and held in place with a clip at the back of her head, casual to match her jeans, T-shirt, and black apron.

Her mouth pulls into a smile. "What can I get you, hon?"

Her energy has me smiling back as my eyes snag on a short, square, clear bottle. "How about a tequila shot?"

She lifts a brow. "Celebrating or something else?"

A sound close to a laugh catches in my throat. "Something else."

Remembering the reason I'm here, I sit up.

Tonight is for letting go.

Embracing the bold, I turn my head toward the silver fox. "You want to join me in taking a shot?"

I don't meet his eyes until I get the words out, and I'm glad for it. Because up close... *Christ.*

Up close, this man is *doing things* to me.

His chiseled jaw is covered in a trimmed gray beard, and his matching hair is tussled, like he's been running his hands through it.

But it's his eyes.

Mountain Daddy

Those rich brown eyes are looking right into mine.

"You want me to take a tequila shot with you, Doll?"

Doll.

I flatten my palms on the bar for balance.

Yeah, Daddy. I want you to take a shot with me. Off me. Whatever.

I nod. "Seems like something I shouldn't do alone."

He turns his attention to the bartender. "You heard the lady. Two shots of tequila."

The bartender's gaze bounces back and forth between me and the man. "Anything else?"

The man looks back at me. "Two Coronas?"

"Okay, Papi," I breathe.

Wait.

No.

I did not just say that.

My mouth snaps shut just as his opens.

I thought my blush was bad before.

I inhale, ready to apologize, but then he drags his tongue across his teeth, and my brain short-circuits.

"Okay..." The bartender drags the word out before rapping her knuckles on the wood between us. "Two beers and two shots."

"Thanks." I reach toward my pocket, where my room key and credit card are.

But the man holds a hand up, stopping me. "Put it on my tab, Jessie."

"What? No." I look at Jessie, the bartender.

But she's backing away, hands up. "You two can sort it out while I get those drinks."

Slowly, the man and I turn to face each other.

God, he's handsome.

And built.

My throat works on a swallow.

Given the opportunity, I'd cling to those shoulders like my life depended on it.

Wow. I need to snap out of this.

I hold my left hand out in front of me, palm up, and keep my fisted right hand an inch above my open palm. "Play you for the bill."

Chapter 4

Luther

The side of my mouth twitches, trying to smile, but I keep my features serious.

I sit up straighter. And if I roll my shoulders back, it's for posture. Not to make my chest look more impressive.

"One round or best of three?" I ask the beautiful woman with beautiful green eyes as I mimic her hand position—readying myself for a game of rock paper scissors.

She tilts her head to the side, her hair fanning out with the movement.

I want to reach out so badly. Want to run my fingers through it.

But I hold myself still and wait for her answer.

Her eyes drop to my mouth before moving back up to meet my gaze. "One and done."

I can't help but do what she did, lowering my gaze to her plump lips for a beat. "Deal."

I know we're talking about the game. But I also hope we're talking about tonight.

Because I don't sleep with guests of the Inn, but...

Maybe it's her body.

Maybe it's her mouth.
Maybe it's the way she fucking called me *Papi*.
My blood simmers at the memory.
Yeah, Baby Doll, I'll be your Daddy.
Maybe it's all of it.
Maybe it's just *her*.
But either way, I aim to break some rules tonight.
She lifts her fisted hand.
I do the same.
Together, we tap our fists into our palms.
Once.
Twice.
On the third time, I extend my pointer and middle finger at the same time she flattens her hand.
I let my smile win.
It's unnecessary, but I extend my arm so my finger scissors are over the empty seat between us.
My pretty little loser only hesitates for a moment before she reaches her flat hand out.
I mime cutting her paper, letting my fingers press against hers.
Her lips purse like she's fighting off a grin.
"Sorry for your loss," I tell her seriously.
She huffs. "Not sure I'm losing when you're paying."
My brows furrow as I notice how cold her hand is.
I twist my wrist and gently grip her fingers in mine. "You're freezing."
Her chest rises with a deep inhale, but I force my eyes to stay on her face rather than looking to see if she's cold all over. Because if I see nipples...
I clear my throat and brace my elbow on the bar while I drop the hand that touched hers onto my thigh.
She clutches her hands together and sets them on her lap, lifting a shoulder. "I run cold. But the tequila should warm me up."
I give her a slow nod.

I could warm you up is right on the tip of my tongue. But even if I've been out of the game for a while, I'm pretty sure corny pickup lines don't work any better now than they did twenty years ago. So I offer something else instead. "Dinner would warm you up even more. Have you eaten?"

She looks suspicious. "They do food here?"

They.

Part of me feels a little bad not admitting that I'm the *they* she's referring to. But it's not like she asked me if I own the place, so it's not like I'm actually lying.

"They do. Small menu, but delicious." I tell her the truth. "You like burgers?"

She nods once.

Jessie appears with two beers in one hand and two shots in the other. "You decide whose tab I'm opening?"

Jessie took ten times longer than she normally would to get our drinks ready, and I'm not sure how to feel about my little sister wingman-ing me.

But... I'll take any help I can get.

"That'd be me. And add a pair of burgers to the bill. Please." I toss the last word on, not wanting to appear rude.

The woman didn't say if she'd already eaten or not, but she didn't shut me down either.

Jessie nods, then disappears through the door leading to the kitchen.

The woman taps her nails on the bar top, the pretty bluish paint drawing my attention. "So, you know the bartender by name, and you have the menu memorized... shall I assume you're a regular here?"

I smirk. "I'm often told, by Jessie herself, that I'm here too much."

"It's true," Jessie says as she walks back out of the kitchen and passes behind us with a pair of plates.

The woman hums, distracted by the plates.

I don't blame her.

We're not quite a dive bar, but it's fair for a newcomer to assume we probably only serve frozen pizza.

"As a regular, I'm confident you haven't been in here before." I wait for the woman's eyes to return to mine. "So, are you new to the area or passing through?"

Chapter 5

Kendra

Isn't that the fucking question?

"Passing through." It's a partial lie since I am moving here. But *here* is still twenty minutes away.

And I can avoid this particular flannel-themed wet dream in the future if it means I can have him tonight.

The man holds his hand out. "Luther."

I noticed how large his hands were the first time we touched.

I noticed their roughness.

Noticed their warmth.

I slide my palm against his. "Kendra."

His fingers close around mine, firmer this time. "Hi, Kendra."

Good god.

His deep voice saying my name... It melts my insides.

"Hi, Luther." His name comes out breathy.

His grip tightens on my hand. "I've never met a Kendra before." He keeps his eyes on mine.

Why is my heart beating so fast?

"I've never met a Luther before," I admit.

I feel like I've heard that name in a movie as the bad guy, but who needs superheroes if this is what the villains look like?

He keeps watching me. Eyes locked with mine.
And I can feel it in my chest.
I can feel the intensity.
The desire.
It thrums against my bones.

His fingers tighten around mine, just a little, then he loosens them.

The slide is slow, skin against skin, as he drags his hand away from mine.

I try to fight the shiver, but it's impossible.
Goose bumps break out up and down my arms.
His fingertips skim against my palm.
My nipples harden.
Then the contact is broken.
My lips part, and I fill my lungs.
This man, Luther, had me holding my breath.

"Grab your shot, Doll," Luther tells me as he reaches for his own.

I feel like I'm already drunk, but I do as I'm told and pick up the shot glass.

Salt rims the edge, and a lime wedge sticks out of the beer bottle.

I pluck the lime out of the bottle, and Luther does the same.
He holds his glass out. "Salud."
I raise my glass with a smirk. "Cheers."
Then I lick the rim.
There's no way to avoid it.
It's part of the drink.

But the act feels lewd. Pornographic. And I accept that my blush is going to be permanent tonight.

I can't take it.

I know literally nothing about this man, but the tension between us is so thick it's hard to inhale.

I press the glass to my lips and tip it back.

The tequila is smooth, but it still burns a path down my throat.

As I swallow, I pull the glass away from my mouth and replace it with the lime.

Luther leans forward. Toward me. Like he can't help himself.

Chapter 6

Luther

Her pink lips close around the piece of fruit, and my dick fucking twitches.

Kendra closes her eyes as she sucks the juice out of the lime.

I nearly groan.

But instead of fisting her hair and dragging her to me, like I want to, I quickly lick the salt, then slam my shot.

When her eyes reopen, I'm biting into my lime.

Her gaze darts to my empty glass, and I swear I see disappointment cross her features.

I glance at my glass too, wondering if she wanted to watch me the way I watched her.

Guess we'll have to order another round.

We set our glasses down at the same time.

"Are we drinking to celebrate or drinking to forget?" Halfway through my question, the music turns up.

Kendra furrows her brow adorably. "Sorry, what?"

We literally never change the volume of the music in here.

Jessie is getting a raise.

Kendra bites her lip as she glances up at the speakers in the ceiling.

Then she slides her beer toward me. She grips the edge of the bar, steps on the brass footrail running the length of it, and slides over onto what has been the empty seat between us.

Jessie is immediately getting a raise.

Already facing her, I reach down and grip the seat of her stool.

My thumb slides between her jean-clad ass cheek and the wooden seat.

I'm not copping a feel.

I'm pulling her closer.

She doesn't protest. And I don't stop until my knees are touching the outside of her thigh.

It's unnecessary.

She could've heard me from where she was. But I'm old. And she doesn't need to know my hearing is fine.

I release my grip but rest my arm on the back of my seat. "I was asking if we're drinking to celebrate or... the opposite of celebrating."

Kendra tries to turn toward me. But my legs are in the way.

I'm about to move back, but then one of her hands lands on my knee—the knee closest to the bar, the one blocking her from turning.

Her touch feels like a live wire.

She applies pressure, pushing my knee toward the bar. "Just move for a second."

I follow her direction and spread my legs.

I'm not so hard I'm tenting my jeans, but I'm not *not* hard.

When I've made enough space, Kendra twists to face me, putting her knees between mine.

This girl is bold.

And I fucking love it.

So I'll be bold back.

I close my knees around hers, and I can almost hear her quick little inhale at the contact.

I won't touch her more than this. Not yet.

But she started it.

She picks up her beer. "As for your question." *Question? I asked a question?* "I'm drinking for something in between."

Oh, right. Between celebration and not celebrating.

Her answer could mean a lot of things, but my mind instantly jumps to divorce.

She's probably thirtyish, but that's enough time for a marriage to start and end.

I pick up my beer. "To the good and the bad."

She smirks. "For better or worse."

As we drink, I look at her left hand resting on her lap, for signs of a recently removed wedding band. But there's no tan line or indentation.

Hmm.

Kendra takes another drink, then looks at the label on the bottle. "This your usual order?"

I shake my head. "I honestly don't remember the last time I had one. But it seemed like the best fit for a tequila shot." I tip my head toward the empty shot glasses. "That your usual order?"

She lets out a huff of laughter. "I don't think I've had a tequila shot in years. Probably not since my twenty-first birthday."

I bite my cheek. Then I ask. Because I feel like I need to know before I take this any further. "And that was how long ago?"

Kendra's smile is wide. And it's perfection. "You're not supposed to ask a woman's age. You know that, right?"

"I know that." I give in to my own urge to smile. "But I also need to know you're at least thirty."

She gives me a small head shake. But not like she's disagreeing, more like she's trying not to laugh at me. "Rest easy, old man. I'm thirty-two."

"Well, that's a relief." I smirk. "And you call me whatever name you want, Baby Doll. But I like it when you say Daddy."

Her mouth opens. Closes.

Glass clinks on the bar, drawing our attention. "Second round now, or wait?"

We turn our heads toward Jessie's voice.

"Now, please," Kendra answers before I can.

"And two waters," I add.

Kendra looks at me and mouths, *Okay, Daddy.*

I narrow my eyes at her.

Her eyes move to my mouth.

And because I can't stop myself, I lower my hand to her knee. Her bare knee.

This girl is a brat hidden behind a sweet girl exterior.

And fuck me, the idea of using these nicknames when we're stripped down to nothing has me more excited for something, *anything*, than I've been in a long time.

Chapter 7

Kendra

A warm palm settles on my knee.

And the heat of it sends a bolt of electricity up my leg. Straight to my core.

I squeeze my thighs together.

If his touch doesn't end me, I'll likely expire of embarrassment. If not tonight, then tomorrow when I remember all the things I've said and done.

Calling him Papi. Boldly touching his leg. Him telling me he prefers *Daddy*, and then me saying it. Doesn't matter that I did it silently.

I've never felt so confident.

Never dared to act like this with a stranger.

I take another drink of my beer.

I've also never had such a perfect opportunity to explore this side of myself.

A hot as hell man.

A bar in the middle of nowhere.

A place I can avoid forever, if I want to.

If there's ever an ideal setup to have a legitimate one-night stand… this is it.

I don't have to ask what he wants out of his future.

I don't have to worry about my heart getting broken.

I bite my lip as excitement thrums through me.

Luther's fingers flex, and his thumb traces a circle on the inside of my knee.

It's nothing.

But it's making my core throb.

Jessie sets a new pair of shot glasses on the bar.

We pick them up, his hand not leaving my knee.

Luther holds my gaze as he lifts the small glass to his mouth.

I lift mine, but then I pause as he slowly licks a path across the rim.

The white salt crystals look harsh against the pink of his tongue.

Jesus shot-taking Christ.

My pussy throbs.

He swallows down the liquid.

I swallow nothing.

Then he sets the empty glass down, reaches over to the cocktail napkin, and lifts the lime wedge I sucked on after the first shot.

I watch, mouth going dry, as he lifts the lime to his mouth and bites down on it.

My eyes dart back to the bar, to the third shot glass holding two lime wedges.

He didn't need to take mine.

Even if there weren't new ones, he could've taken a drink of his beer as a chaser.

But he chose my lime.

He discards the rind back on the napkin, then picks up one of the fresh wedges and hands it to me. Proving he knew it was an option.

I take it, our fingertips brushing.

Someone shouts from the kitchen.

"Our dinner is ready," Luther states, then he nods to my shot.

Chapter 8

Luther

Watching Kendra lick the salt off her shot glass a second time might send me into cardiac arrest. But we all got to die somehow. And death by Brat is okay with me.

Her eyes close as she tips the liquor into her mouth.

My gaze trails down to watch her throat work on a swallow.

If I get to touch her tonight, I don't think I'll be able to have her lips anywhere near my length without embarrassing myself.

But maybe she's staying more than one night.

Hopefully.

Because this girl sucking my cock sounds like a great plan for tomorrow.

But I won't get ahead of myself.

One moment at a time with my Kendra Doll.

When she lowers the shot glass, I take it out of her hand, letting my fingers graze hers again.

She doesn't pull away, and she holds my gaze as she lifts the lime and presses it between her lips.

I'm fifty-six. I've been around the block.

I'm... experienced.

But in all my years, I've never felt an attraction as instant as this.

It's thick.

Heavy.

Electric.

And I know I'm not alone in feeling it.

Kendra lowers her lime wedge.

I hold my hand out.

She drops her eyes and hesitates just a moment before she sets the fruit on my palm.

I can't help myself. I put it between my teeth.

The need to consume anything that's been in her tempting-as-fuck mouth is too much to deny.

And this girl inspires me to indulge.

Movement has me turning my head, and I watch Diego step out of the kitchen, two plates in his hands. "Jessie, what table for the burgers?"

I follow where he's looking and spot Jessie at the other end of the bar, making a round of mixed drinks.

She lifts a brow as she tips her head in my direction. "Those are for *Luther*."

She says my first name with emphasis.

No one calls me that.

I'm not even sure Diego knows it's my real name.

That suspicion is confirmed a moment later.

He turns my way and glances around. When I'm the only man he sees, a look of confusion crosses his features.

Before he can ask *Who the fuck is Luther?*, I drop the lime on the napkin with the other ones and hold my hand out. "Thanks, Diego."

I can sense the question he's dying to ask. But he just hands me a plate.

Then he glances over at my feminine companion, and his mouth splits into a wide grin.

I set the plate in front of Kendra and hold my hand back out for the second.

"Anything else I can get for you or your friend, *Luther*?" His tone is filled with entertainment.

I reach out and graze my fingers against Kendra's elbow, catching her attention. "Need anything?"

She rolls her lips together, shaking her head before turning to Diego. "Looks perfect."

I didn't think it was possible for him to grin any wider, but Diego does. "That's what I like to hear. You two enjoy."

Then the bastard winks at me.

I roll my eyes as Kendra snickers beside me.

"He's a pain in the ass," I sigh.

Kendra smiles. "I dunno, I think he's cute."

I narrow my eyes. "Eat your food."

My sister says the same thing about Diego, that *he's cute*. But she also says he's a player and more family than dating material. Which is good. Because if one of my employees got involved with my sister, I'd have to cut their hands off.

Kendra's humor doesn't fade as she places her hand back on my knee.

I let her push my legs apart, un-trapping hers.

Untangled, we both face forward. But our stools are still close enough that our elbows bump together as we reach for our food.

"Wow," Kendra says under her breath as she looks at her plate.

I hum. "It's a Korean BBQ burger with gochujang carrots."

"Gotta admit, this isn't what I expected to find... in the middle of nowhere." She tilts her head as she gives me a once-over. "Neither were you."

Chapter 9

Kendra

I wasn't sure it was possible for Luther's eyes to get any more heated. But they do. And I have to look away.

I pick up my burger.

Luther picks up his.

And together, we sit side by side and eat our dinner.

Baseball is on the TV behind the bar. It's some West Coast game in extra innings. And the perfect distraction.

Luther's shoulder bumps against mine.

My elbow brushes his.

Luther takes a drink out of my beer.

I take it from his hand and press the opening of the bottle to my lips.

He watches me drink.

Luther orders us two more waters.

I order two more shots.

My tongue lingers as I lick the salt off the glass.

Luther's jaw clenches as he watches me.

And I push my plate away.

The guy from the kitchen shows up and sets down two peppermints before taking our empty dishes.

Luther shakes his head.

I tear one of the little wrappers open and place the mint in my mouth.

Luther does the same.

I turn to face the man beside me. The music is still loud, so I lean in, placing a hand on his thigh. "I'll be right back."

Keeping my hand braced on him, I notice how solid he feels as I slide off my stool.

I focus my eyes on the ground, watching where I'm walking, as I circle the bar and exit through the door I came in.

I feel more keyed up than I've ever been, but in reality, we weren't making a scene. Yes, the shared limes and closeness were flirty, but it's not like we were making out. So, I don't know why I feel so watched.

The fresh air washes over me as I step outside, and I fill my lungs with it.

I have to pee, and since my room is like twenty feet away, I decided going there was the better option.

Silently, I cross the strip of pavement between the bar and the motel.

I can't believe I'm doing this.

I repeat that line to myself over and over while I enter my room.

Like the bar and food, my room is nicer than I expected.

It's just a single room. But the bedding is white and fluffy, and the king mattress is comfy.

When I first checked in, I flopped onto the bed and was tempted to just stay there.

I'm glad I didn't.

After reapplying deodorant, spritzing some perfume, and smoothing down my outfit, I pocket one key card and palm the spare.

My heart is vibrating inside my ribcage while I walk back across the little alley to the bar. But I don't stop.

I don't stop at the door.

I don't stop until I'm behind the stool I'd been sitting in.

Luther watches me the whole way, and now that I'm close, he turns in his seat.

I swallow.

I embrace the bold.

And I set my extra room key on his thigh.

Luther's eyes drop to it.

Then slowly, so slowly, he lifts them back up to meet mine.

"Room two." My voice is low. Quiet. A little shaky.

But my body is on fire.

I want this man so damn bad.

I've never been like this. Never this reckless. Never, ever so forward.

I take a step back.

Then another.

It's up to him now.

I turn.

I'm a little unsteady.

A little buzzed.

But I know what I'm doing.

I know what I need.

And what I need is a night of escape before the next phase of my life begins.

I need a night with Luther.

Chapter 10

Luther

With my eyes locked on Kendra's ass, I place my palm over the keycard on my thigh.

This woman is young enough to... well, she's fucking young enough.

But she's into it.

She asked me to share a shot with her.

She called me Papi.

She moved onto the stool next to me.

She placed her hand on my leg first.

She may have ordered the extra drinks, but the desire was in her gaze from the beginning.

And I may have had a drink before she got here, but I'm bigger. I can take it.

And...

I lift my hand and look down.

Room two.

She just invited me to spend the night with her.

Or, at the very least, she invited me to have sex with her. But I'm not driving home tonight, so after I fuck my little Kendra Doll, I'll spend the rest of the night in her bed, with her body pressed against mine.

When Kendra disappears out the door, I down the rest of my water, then stand.

But instead of following her, I head to the men's room.

After doing my thing, I wash my hands, twice, making sure they smell like our sandalwood soap and not burgers, then I step back out into the bar.

My bar.

Striding toward the back door, I can feel Jessie's eyes on me.

Just when I think she'll let it go, she calls out, "Where you heading, *Luther*?"

I don't look her way. "Good night, Jessie."

I hear her laugh, but then I'm pushing through the door, and my mind is solely on room two.

Chapter 11

Kendra

I make it all the way to my door before I look over my shoulder.

The alleyway is empty.

No Luther.

Not yet.

I pull the keycard out of my pocket and unlock my room.

Stepping inside, I kick my sandals off and pace across the carpet.

I slow my steps as I turn around at the far end of the room and face the door.

The small lamp next to the bed is on, but that's it.

One dim glow, sending shadows around the room.

I stop at the foot of the bed and press a hand to my chest.

Calm down, Kendra.

I close my eyes and take a deep breath.

Calm. Down.

I exhale.

Either he'll walk through that door, or he won't.

I inhale again.

Calm.

Mountain Daddy

I exhale.
And then I hear the lock click. And the door opens.

Chapter 12

Luther

Her eyes open as the door clicks shut behind me.
I flip the deadbolt.
She lowers her hand from her chest to her side.
I toe off my shoes and reach for my belt.
She watches me.
And I yank my belt free with a snap. "Strip."
I wasn't going to demand anything of her.
I wasn't going to walk in tearing my clothes off.
But the way she looks standing there.
The way her eyes lock on mine.
I can't help myself.
I take a slow step toward Kendra as I unbutton my jeans and pull the zipper down.
Kendra's gaze drops to the front of my pants.
I leave my jeans open and work on my flannel.
When I undo the last button on my shirt, she lifts her gaze from my waistband.
And her mouth opens.
Her voice is a whisper. "Fuck me."
"I plan to." I shrug the shirt off my shoulders, letting it fall to the ground. "Take your clothes off, Doll. Now."

Her eyes stay on my chest and mine stay on hers as she grips the bottom of her tank top and pulls it up over her head.

I groan.

God willing, tonight, twenty years from now, I'm going to smother myself with those tits.

I'll die a happy, horny man.

Kendra's fingers fumble with her shorts.

"Relax, Baby." I make a shushing sound. "Just do as I tell you and relax."

Her chest rises and falls with a breath, her shoulders relaxing ever so slightly.

I shove my jeans down my hips at the same time she pushes her shorts down.

Her white panties match her white bra. But they're so thin I can see the outline of her pussy lips just as easily as I can see the outline of her beaded nipples.

I palm myself through my boxer briefs. "Are you nervous because I'm someone new, or do you want to stop?"

Her eyes snap up and meet mine. "I don't want to stop. It's just, you're..." She takes a step toward me, leaving her shorts on the floor. "So hot. And it's been... a while."

The corner of my mouth pulls up. "Not sure anyone's called me hot before."

She huffs out a breath. "Maybe not to your face. But they've thought it."

I hum. "As for it being... a while." I take a step closer to her. "Does that mean you'd like me to be gentle?"

"No." Kendra shakes her head. "No, that's not what I want."

I grin. "That's my girl."

Two more strides and I close the distance between us.

I reach for her as she reaches for me.

My palms frame her face. Her hands grip my bare sides.

Her hands are still cool to the touch, and it sends a shiver up my spine.

I love it. Because I know what my purpose is.

Heat her up.

Using my hold on her face, I tilt her head back. And I drop my mouth to hers.

Our eyes close as our lips meet. And we groan.

Kendra leans into me. Into my touch. Until the length of her body is pressed against mine.

She's so soft.

So perfect.

And warm in all the right places.

I slide one of my hands around from her cheek to the back of her head.

Gentle isn't what she wants.

I grip her hair. And tug her head back farther.

Kendra's fingers curl against my sides.

Dragging my cheek across hers, letting my beard scratch across her skin, I bring my mouth to her ear. "I don't like it gentle either."

Chapter 13

Kendra

Holy. Fuck.

My core floods with heat. And my lips part on a gasp.

But before I can beg for more, Luther's mouth crashes down on mine again.

I don't like it gentle either.

I've never been with a man like this.

Never had anyone talk to me the way he does.

But now…

Now, I'm not sure I can ever go back.

I arch into Luther's hold and swipe my tongue across his lips.

Luther makes a sound deep in his chest as his tongue tangles with mine.

There's a mild taste of mint, but mostly, he tastes like sex.

Like a good fucking time.

Like the best decision I've made in a long time.

His hand tightens in my hair.

And I smile against his lips as I drag my nails down his sides.

There's no space between us.

But I want to feel every inch of him.

I want to press my palms against his abs.

Because this man has *abs*.

I try to slide my hands between us.

Luther lets go of my hair, and I think he's going to step back, to let me touch him.

But he slaps his hands down against my ass.

The sting is minimal, even though the sound is loud.

"Luther!" I gasp.

Instead of replying, he closes his mouth down on my neck, right where it meets my shoulder.

As his teeth graze my skin, he palms my ass with both hands.

My ass is big.

And so are his hands.

I moan.

"You can call me Luther." His tongue drags across my skin, soothing his bite. "Or you can call me something else. Either way, you're mine for the night, Kendra Doll."

And then he slides his hand down, wedging his grip between my legs.

My blood sizzles.

My arms reach up.

And he lifts me.

My thighs part.

My legs wrap around his waist.

I hold him around the neck.

And I revel in his strength.

I don't think anyone has picked me up as an adult.

Then, as I flex my legs around his hips, I feel it.

His arousal.

His hardness.

Pressing against me.

Right. There.

Right where I need him.

He pulls me in tighter, grinding his dick against my center.

"Oh god." I rock my hips.

It's so good.

He feels so good.

And I'm so turned on.
He uses his grip to rock me faster.
Rougher.
And the friction.
The two layers of underwear between us.
It only amplifies it.
And...
Oh shit.
I...
I dig my nails into his back and bury my face in his shoulder.
"Fuck," Luther growls into my hair. "Are you that ready for me, Baby? Are you gonna come for me? Just like this?"
I open my mouth to answer, but he doesn't stop, and I'm nearing the cliff at a sprint.
It's too soon.
Too fast.
But it's been so long.
And he feels so good.
My lips press against his bare skin, and I breathe.
I just breathe as this man bounces me in his hold, rubbing his cock against my clit.
I arch into it.
I trust him not to drop me.
I...
One of his hands slides farther between my legs.
One of his fingers rubs against my entrance, over my panties.
He applies pressure.
I soak the material.
He pulls my panties to the side.
"Let go." A finger pushes inside me. "Come for Daddy."
I tip over the edge.
His finger shoves in deeper.
I shake.
He curses.
A second finger joins the first.

I cry. Or scream.

And then I'm falling.

Literally falling.

And I don't even tense.

My back hits the mattress, and Luther lands on top of me.

His arm is still under me. His fingers are still buried in my pussy. And his cock is still pressed against me, the pressure enough for another jolt of pleasure to rock through me.

"God damn," he grits out, then his mouth is on mine again.

He drags his fingers out of me and around my hip, leaving a damp trail on my skin.

I whimper at the loss.

He swallows the sound.

Then he's gone.

His weight leaving me completely.

My eyes snap open, and I see him kneeling between my thighs.

"Hips up." He grips the waistband of my underwear.

Following his command is harder than it should be because I still feel shaky, but I manage.

He drags the material down my legs, and his nostrils flare.

Luther shifts backward, climbing off the bed as he goes.

He drops my panties to the floor and *slowly* pushes his boxer briefs down. "Take your tits out. I want to suck on them while I'm fucking you."

If I wasn't so focused on his striptease, I'd let my eyes roll back at his words.

My bra is soft. Just enough material to keep the girls in place. And I don't feel like struggling to unhook the band while lying in bed. So, I reach up and push the straps off my shoulders, then pull my arms free.

The material is still covering my breasts.

And his boxer briefs are still covering his cock.

"I'll show you when you show me," I pant.

I watch his tongue push against the inside of his cheek.

Then he slides his hand down and grips his cock.

He strokes it.

The material can't accommodate him.

It's straining.

Finally. Fucking finally. He stretches the waistband and pulls his dick free.

My core clenches.

It's perfect.

Thick and straight, and I need it inside me.

I pull the front of my bra down, freeing my tits.

"Play with them." He drops his boxer briefs to the floor and climbs back on the bed.

I press my tits together.

My thumbs and forefingers pinch my nipples. Rolling the tight nubs.

"I'm gonna fuck those tits." He roughly strokes himself again. "I'll fuck this tight little pussy first. Make you come on my cock. Then I'm putting my dick between those tits, and I'm gonna come all over your neck."

I pinch my nipples harder. "Yes, please."

"In three minutes."

I blink. "Wh-what?"

Luther releases his grip on his cock and bends forward. "Watch the clock, Kendra. Tell me when the time's up."

"I don't—" Luther drops his mouth to my pussy in an open-mouth kiss.

The sensation has my back arching, lifting off the mattress.

A muscled arm drops across my lower belly, holding me down.

His mouth doesn't stop.

He doesn't stop.

His tongue presses inside me. Then drags up my slit.

When he reaches my clit, his lips close around the bundle of nerves. And he sucks.

My body can't stay still. But Luther doesn't let me move.

His arm presses down harder. Holding me in place as I writhe.

And it's...

His other arm hooks around my thigh and pulls it away from the side of his head, spreading me open.

"What's the time?" he asks against my flesh.

Who can read a clock at a time like this?

He drags his tongue roughly over my clit. "Time, Kendra."

"I... I don't know." I tug at my nipples. "I didn't look."

He makes a sound of disapproval. "Brat." Then he licks me again.

And again.

Lower.

The tip of his tongue touches *that spot*. Grazing over my ass before dragging up the length of my core.

When he reaches my clit again, I think I might come.

I let go of my tits and reach down to grip his hair.

Lifting my head off the mattress, I look down and find him looking up.

With my hands in his hair, his tongue extended, twirling around my bundle of nerves, and his gaze locked on mine, I forget what I was going to say.

My breathing picks up.

My legs start to tremble.

And then Luther raises his head, breaking the contact between us.

"No, don't stop. I'll be good." I try to push his head back down. "I'll count the minutes. I promise."

His lips glisten as he smirks at me, his head not budging, no matter how hard I try to shove him back down. "I don't think you will." He pushes himself up, forcing me to let go of his hair, and sits back on his knees. "Plus, I told you that your second orgasm would happen with my dick stuffed inside you."

I look down between us, and yes, I'm okay with that.

Luther reaches for a pillow, and with a hand under my ass, he lifts me and shoves the pillow under my hips.

Raising me to just the right height.

I drop my knees open.

"You're soaking wet. But I still need you to relax." Luther rubs a hand across my lower belly.

The touch is warm and gentle. And even though I'm ready to burst again, I do as he says. My muscles softening.

I lift my head to watch as he lines up the tip of his cock with my entrance.

He's thick.

Wide.

Luther lets out a low groan as he pushes the head inside me.

And the stretch is immediate.

Then he drops forward, catching his weight on one hand while the other stays between us. Only he's not rubbing softly anymore.

His palm is just above my pussy. And he's pressing down.

The pressure has my eyes meeting his.

He holds my gaze for a heartbeat. "Not gentle."

Then he slams forward. Filling me with his entire length in one thrust.

I arch my neck and claw at his shoulders.

And he doesn't give me any time.

Luther drags his cock out and shoves it back in.

Over and over.

And his hand keeps pressing down on my belly.

And... god... I feel him everywhere.

I feel so full.

I feel like my entire insides are filled with him.

I feel like I'm about to come even quicker than the first time.

"You there, Baby?" Luther grunts above me.

I nod.

I'm so close.

I've never felt like this.

Never been so bossed around.

Never gotten off so quickly.

"Feed me one." His voice is so rough I barely understand him.

I blink up into Luther's hooded eyes.

He nods to my chest.

Then I remember his words from earlier.

I want to suck on them while I'm fucking you.

I drop my hand from his shoulder and grip my breast.

He lowers his head. And when his lips close around my nipple, my entire body clenches.

He moans against my flesh, sucking harder.

The sight is vulgar.

It's the hottest fucking thing I've ever experienced.

And it's only for tonight.

I reach up with my free hand and grip his hair, trying to breathe as his cock continues to pump in and out of me.

He hums.

And I fight to breathe. "Do I taste good, Daddy?"

He bites my nipple.

His hips pound into me. Harder.

His cock stretches me more with every thrust.

Then the hand on my belly shifts.

And his fingers are back on my clit.

His lips suck my nipple.

His dick pushes into me.

And I combust.

An orgasm stronger than the one before it rolls through me.

I try to wrap my arms around Luther, but he's leaning back. Out of my reach.

My body shudders.

He strums my clit again.

And just when it's about to be too sensitive, his hands leave my body.

Luther pulls all the way out and shoves my legs down.

My strength gives out, and my legs drop.

"Push 'em together." Luther crawls up my body, and I do as he says.

I push my breasts together.

His cock is slippery from being inside me, and it slides between my tits easily.

Luther groans. And I watch in awe as he moves above me.

His body is defined.

His muscles bunch and flex with every thrust.

I want to drag my nails through his chest hair.

I want to do so much with this man.

One night might not be enough.

I lift my eyes. And meet his.

He's watching me.

He's fucking my tits, watching me as I stare at his incredible body.

He holds my gaze and shoves his hips forward as far as they'll go.

And I tip my head forward, lowering my chin to my chest and opening my mouth.

"Fuck," he growls as he pushes his hips forward a little farther, and I close my lips around the head of his cock.

He reaches down and twines his fingers in my hair, close to the scalp.

The pressure is perfection.

"You want to swallow, Kendra Doll? Is that what you want?"

It's been a long time since I've done this.

But I want to try.

So I open and let him slide out of my mouth. "Yes, Daddy."

"Christ," he growls and rocks his hips, shoving his tip back between my lips. "Where'd you fucking come from?" His cock nearly leaves my mouth with every thrust.

I hum.

He shifts his grip on my hair until his palm is against the back of my head. Holding me in place. "So perfect. So fucking perfect." His movements are getting choppy. I know he's close. I'm so ready for him to be close. "Now be my good girl and start swallowing."

My body is still buzzing, and his deep voice dances over my bare skin.

And I swallow.

His abs contract, and his shoulders hunch forward.

And I keep swallowing as his cock pulses against my tongue.

I don't think about what I'm doing.

I don't hesitate.

I just suck and watch him lose control.

And the sounds he makes...

I'm taking those with me.

I'm remembering them forever.

The hand behind my head flexes, pulling my hair, then it disappears, and I collapse, boneless, against the mattress.

Wow.

"Fucking hell, woman," Luther half pants, half groans.

My chest is heaving as Luther drops down beside me.

And while we lie there, struggling for oxygen, I smile at the ceiling.

Because what a fucking night.

Chapter 14

Luther

I roll my head to the side and look at her.

Tits bare. Soft skin on display. Smile on her lips.

I smile too. "I'm glad I decided to come in tonight."

Kendra rolls her head toward me. "I'm glad I decided to stop in tonight."

A lock of hair falls across her cheek.

I reach out and, letting my fingertip ghost over her skin, brush it off her face.

She holds my gaze, and I figure I might as well tell her now. "I'm staying here tonight."

The side of her mouth pulls up. "You have a room too?"

"Brat."

"I guess I'll allow it." Kendra lets out a dramatic sigh. "But fair warning, I'm about seven minutes away from falling asleep."

I grin. "I might make it eight."

She chuckles, then rolls away from me and climbs off the bed.

The bedside lamp doesn't let off a lot of light, but there's enough for me to see *enough*.

Except it's not enough.

I don't want to be done with Kendra.

Sleeping beside her isn't enough.
One fuck isn't enough.
But it's all I have.
She's just passing through.
She's too young for me.
She's fucking perfect for me.
I stare at the ceiling.

How unfair for the universe to give me Kendra. But to only give her to me for one night.

She steps out of the bathroom wearing little pajama shorts and a thin tank top.

It's not lingerie. It's cotton. But it's just as sexy as her walking around naked.

With one arm propped behind my head, I watch her cross the room.

I don't hide my perusal of her. And it's only fair since she's taking me in the same way.

I pulled my boxer briefs back on, but I'm still naked from the waist up. And with the covers down around my hips—so she can climb into bed with me—I still have a lot on display.

She's still eyeing me when she stops on her side of the bed.

I narrow my eyes. "What?"

She shakes her head. "I'm normally not this shallow, but seriously, you could..."

"Model?" I suggest, completely joking, as she says, "Make porn."

Her answer is not at all what I'm expecting, and a loud bark of laughter jumps out of my chest. "You're ridiculous. Get in bed."

She hesitates, and I suddenly don't feel like laughing.

"What is it?" I ask.

She lifts her shoulders, holds them there for a second, then drops them. "I know this should be a *before*, not an *after* topic, but I just wanted to say that you don't have to worry about me getting pregnant. And I haven't been with anyone since my last doctor's visit, so you don't have to worry about... *that* either."

I feel like such an idiot.

I lower my arm so I can twist toward her. "I'm sorry. I'm old enough to know better. I was just so caught up in you... I wasn't thinking. But tonight was the first time in probably twenty years that I haven't used a condom. You've got nothing to worry about from me either."

She rolls her lips together. "Yeah, you really are old enough."

I shake my head. "You really are a brat." Relaxing onto my back, I stretch out my arm closest to her. "Come here."

Finally, she climbs into bed.

As she scoots closer to me, I reach out with my other hand and turn off the lamp.

Darkness settles around us as Kendra settles her cheek on my shoulder.

I pull the blanket up to her chin.

Her hand settles on my chest.

"Luther?" she whispers into the room.

"Yeah, Baby?"

"Thank you for tonight."

I curl my arm around her back, holding her tighter against my side. "You don't have to thank me for the best night..."

Best night in a long time.

Best night ever? In all my years?

Kendra's shoulders relax under my arm.

And... she's asleep.

Just like that.

She told me she was minutes from falling asleep. And she was right.

I said I was right behind her, but the truth is I sleep like shit.

And being somewhere new, anywhere that's not my bed, I'm even less likely to fall asleep.

I lean my head forward and kiss the top of her head. Then I press my nose to her hair. Wanting to memorize her scent.

At least tonight, when sleep eludes me, I can spend the time soaking up Kendra's presence.

I WAKE ON A DEEP INHALE.

It takes me two blinks to remember where I am. And who I'm with.

Kendra.

She's turned some in her sleep, curling into my side.

I lift my head to look at the clock.

Seven.

I don't think I woke up once.

I don't even remember falling asleep.

My eyes move back to Kendra.

I want to stay.

I need to pee.

I want to come back to bed after.

Want to go back to sleep and wake up together.

Ask her to breakfast.

But it would only prolong this niggling depressive feeling.

Kendra allowed me to stay the night, and that's what I've done.

I won't ask for more.

I gently press a kiss to her forehead, then slide out of bed.

She stirs, adjusting the blankets around her.

I force myself to turn away.

"Bye, Daddy."

Kendra's whispered words halt me.

But when I look back, her eyes are already closing, and she's hugging the pillow I'd been using.

"Bye, Kendra Doll."

Chapter 15

Kendra

GPS says I'm only five minutes away.

It's been a long time since I've been out here, since Dad's been the one traveling to see me for most of the last decade, but I still recognize it. And I don't feel as bummed as I expected to feel.

I'm still not thrilled about moving in with my parent after being on my own since I was eighteen.

And it's a little extra nerve-racking since I've never lived with my dad before. But he's chill. So I have to believe he's not going to be hard to live with.

Air flows in through my open window, and I let the scent of the forest surround me.

It's a beautiful day.

The sun is out.

The high elevation means it's not too hot.

And the scenery is stunning.

So no, I'm not bummed about moving here.

I'm not bummed.

I'm just a little sad. For a reason I didn't plan for.

Luther.

I sigh as I slow for a turn in the road.

When I first spotted Luther sitting at the bar, my mind instantly flashed with visions of what he'd look like over me.

What he might look like naked.

But I never thought it would actually happen.

And my god, did it happen.

I feel myself smile as I think about all the positions we experienced in just one night.

I've never experienced anything like that.

Like him.

Never been manhandled like that.

Never knew I'd want to be.

Part of me is kicking myself for not getting his number. And part of me feels a little guilty for lying and telling him I was only passing through.

But the other part of me recognizes that I don't need to complicate my life any more than it already is. And picking up a fuck buddy, or boyfriend, or whatever he'd be, on my very first night in town would definitely be a complication to my new start.

But what a great fuck buddy he'd be.

When Luther climbed out of my bed this morning, I felt the loss immediately.

But then I reminded myself that I knew exactly what I was getting into, and his leaving was part of that. So I hugged the pillow that smelled like him, and I fell back asleep, accepting the experience for what it was.

But who knows. Maybe, once I'm settled, I'll go back to Rocky Ridge Inn and see if he's around.

I take my foot off the gas as I approach my dad's driveway.

We're up in the mountains. An hour away from a major city. Twenty or so minutes away from a little town called Lonely. Rural. But somehow, this cute little neighborhood is tucked away in the trees.

The lots are bigger than town lots, and every house is surrounded by mature trees, so you can be in your yard and not see anyone.

It seems a little goofy, having all these houses near each other when there's so much unoccupied land out here, but it helps to not feel so isolated.

Even though no one's on the road behind me, I flip my blinker on, then turn across the quiet paved road into the gravel driveway.

I coast, letting my car slow as I reach the turn in the driveway.

Movement pulls my attention to the side, and I see a blur of red fur disappear into the trees.

"Hey, Buddy." I smile. Foxes are so cute.

Once I take the turn, I spot the house.

It's a single-story, three-bedroom, two-bathroom structure with a covered front porch, a larger back deck, and an attached two-car garage.

But none of that is what has me grinning.

It's the dork on the front porch, holding a row of printer paper taped together, reading *Welcome Home Kenny*, like I've been away on a trip.

I wave my hand out my open window as I stop in front of the house.

I put my vehicle into park and turn off the engine before taking a deep breath and climbing out.

"Welcome home!" Dad shakes the banner as he says it.

"You shouldn't have."

He laughs as he drops one end of the paper, letting the banner droop. "I had to test out the new at-home company printer/scanner/something else-er."

I don't know how much I'll need to actually print or scan anything once I get his website up to modern times, but I don't want to rain on his parade.

And I love that he's all about me working from home rather than out of the warehouse where he works. So I'll pretend to scan shit all day if I have to.

He holds his arms out as he hurries down the steps.

Dad has the same dark hair as I do—only his is graying, and he keeps it short. But that's where our similarities start and finish.

He's a solid six feet tall.

I'm five and a half.

He has a slender build.

I... don't.

The only thing bigger than my tits is my ass.

He could spend the summer outside in a tent.

I couldn't.

But as he hugs me, I know we're similar where it counts.

"Thanks for letting me stay here," I tell him as I hug him back.

"I've already told ya. You're always welcome here. Stay as long as you want." He pats my back, then releases me. "Plus, I'm hoping you'll love the job so much that you'll keep working for me, even when you've saved up enough to move out."

"Dad—" It's not like I don't want that too, but I need us to have realistic expectations.

"I know, I know. We'll play it by ear. And since we never discussed it, I might as well tell you now that the starting pay is eighty thousand a year." He says it so matter-of-factly that it takes a second before my brain retains the information.

Eighty fucking thousand?

"American dollars?" I ask.

Dad snorts, like I was making a joke.

But I wasn't joking. That's more than I was making at my corporate job.

"Now." Dad claps his hands together, crinkling the paper still in his grip. "I see you brought a few things."

We both turn and look at my hatchback, every window filled with boxes.

To be fair, I wedged a lot more into my car than I thought I would.

All my clothes, my favorite kitchen items, all my bedding and pillows, and other random things from over the years.

I sold whatever furniture I owned the morning I left, with only one end table unclaimed and left on the sidewalk.

"Let's get you unloaded, then we can have lunch."

"What's for lunch?" I fold my arms like it's a negotiation.

Dad mimics my position. "Hot dogs and mac and cheese."

"Powder or sauce?"

He scoffs. "Saucy sauce, obviously."

I drop my arms. "You have a deal."

Then I snicker. Because really? Hot dogs and mac and cheese?

"What's so funny? It's your favorite meal."

I'm about to argue *Yeah, when I was five*, but it actually sounds amazing.

"Nothing funny." I step forward and brace for boxes to fall as I open the rear door.

Chapter 16

Luther

Jessie's elbow bumps against mine as she makes a drink unnecessarily close to me. For the third time tonight.

I finally turn to her. "What?"

She lifts her brows. "Nothing. Right, Diego?"

I look over my shoulder, finding our cook leaning against the wall next to the kitchen door.

He holds his hands up. "We don't got any questions, boss. None about that pretty girl you were cozied up with."

Jessie nods. "Definitely no questions about how you two disappeared at the same time."

"Or how your truck was still here when we closed down..." Diego shakes his head. "No questions."

I release a long sigh. "When you're not being dumb, you two are smart. I'm sure you can figure it out."

Jessie hands the drink to a guy across the bar, then crosses her arms. "We get the basics. But we want to know details."

I make a face at her. "Ew."

Diego snickers.

"Not like that. Come on, that's gross." Jessie pulls the towel from her apron and tries to snap me with it, but I jump out of range.

"You started it," I say, super maturely.

There's a pause, then Jessie throws her hands up. "Well?"

"Well, what?" I throw my own hands up, mirroring her position.

"Well, did you get her number? Is she still here? Are you going to see her again?" My sister pesters me.

"She was real pretty." Diego helpfully reminds me.

I glare at him.

He mimes zipping his lips.

I give up, knowing they won't stop. "She's gorgeous. I really fucking liked her. But she's gone. No number. No last name. Just passing through."

"That's a bummer," someone says from behind me.

We all turn to find Doug, one of the regulars, posted up at the bar.

"Have these two been yapping at you about my business?" I gesture to Jessie and Diego.

Doug shakes his head. "Didn't have to. I was here."

"Last night?" I ask.

Doug always sits at the bar. I would've noticed.

I think.

"I grabbed a table. You and your lady friend looked ready to combust, and I didn't want to dampen the mood."

"Oh. Well, appreciate that." Living out here, most of our guests are regulars. I just hadn't thought about it.

In fact, after Kendra walked into the bar, I don't think I thought of anything but her.

Which wasn't very professional of me.

Then I remember that I own this fucking place. And whatever grief I might get from customers is worth it.

Just about anything is worth the night I had with Kendra.

And I'd give just about anything to have another.

Chapter 17

Kendra

"Don't forget about breakfast in the morning." Dad reminds me as he walks past my open office door.

"Yeah, yeah." I wave an arm. "My alarm is set."

"See you in the morning."

"Night," I call out as he disappears.

Dad went all out getting the house ready for me.

I don't remember what he used to use this room for, but it's the perfect at-home office now.

The walls are a rich forest green; the wood floors are worn but smooth, like the rest of the house, and tucked under the window, looking out at the forest behind the house, is a beautiful desk—handmade by my father. There's also a matching bookshelf, a pink office chair—which hasn't been my favorite color since I was seven, but it's the thought that counts—and a cute Tiffany-style lamp on the corner of the desk.

Oh, and we can't forget about the printer-scanner, which is on a little side table tucked into the corner.

All in all, it's a cute and functional office.

I put my headphones back on and hit play, ready to finish the last five minutes of this YouTube tutorial.

My business administration degree is helping a little, but had I known I'd end up here, doing this, I would've gone to school to become a web developer.

As it is, I'll probably have to hire someone to design a whole new website. But I've managed to make some decent upgrades already.

And the branding could probably use an overhaul.

The name, Joe's Custom Furniture, is lame, but accurate. And Dad's managed to take some great photos of his finished pieces, so I have a surprising amount to work with.

Considering it's Friday night and I've only been at it for one week, I'd say I'm doing a pretty good job.

The video continues, demonstrating how to use the automated tracking software for shipping orders, and by the time the tutorial is done, I accept I'll need to watch it again on Monday. Because my mind has strayed.

Strayed to the one topic that keeps pulling my attention.

Luther.

I can't stop thinking about him.

And I can't stop wondering if it's a good or terrible idea to try to sneak away to the Inn this weekend.

Closing my laptop, I push back from the desk.

I turn the lights off as I exit the room, then head down the hall to my bedroom.

Dad's bedroom, with an attached bathroom, is on the opposite side of the house. With the combined kitchen, living, and dining room between us.

My side of the house has a short hall with the office first, then the guest bathroom, a.k.a. my bathroom, then my bedroom. So basically, I have my own wing of the house.

It's about as ideal a layout as I could ask for.

I wasn't lying. I did set my alarm for tomorrow morning, but I'm not thrilled about it.

Which makes me feel like an asshole, because Dad has been nothing but accommodating.

But I'm not interested in getting up early to have breakfast with him and his old man bestie before they go out fishing for the day.

I want to sleep in.

I want to spend my Saturday rotting in bed.

But I'll get up, and I'll make the pancakes, because I know it's important to my dad.

And it'll be fine. I'm great at first impressions and can small talk with the best of them.

Fingers crossed this Rocky guy isn't a bore.

Chapter 18

Luther

I shove my truck door closed, then place my hands on my lower back and stretch.

Per usual, I didn't get a great night's sleep. But this time, it was possibly more of my own doing than Mother Nature's. I just can't stop thinking about *that night*.

Can't stop thinking about *that girl*.

Can't stop thinking about the image of *her* with her tits squished around my dick and her lips around my tip.

Can't stop myself from jerking off to the memory of her.

And when I lay in bed last night, another hour going by with sleep eluding me, I jerked off again.

None of that was helped by my old ass waking up at six.

I was half tempted to rub one out again this morning, but with my luck, I'd actually pass out and miss breakfast with Joe.

And his kid.

I sigh and start across the driveway toward my best friend's front door.

Nothing against his daughter, Kenny, but I'm tired, horny, and grouchy, and that's not the ideal mood to be in to make a good first impression.

But I know Joe's excited to have her living here, so I blow out a breath and work on adjusting my attitude.

I remember him saying something about roommates and stealing her money. And for how long we've been friends, it's hard to believe I've never met her, but here we are.

Shrugging off the guilt of not knowing more about my friend's kid, I stride up the few steps to the front porch.

Chapter 19

Kendra

I hear the rumble of a vehicle outside as I shuffle down the hall to the bathroom.

Shit.

Hurrying, I step into the bathroom and shut the door behind me.

What is it with old men and showing up early?

I go through the motions of freshening up for the day as quickly as I can. After slapping on some tinted face sunscreen, scented body lotion, and deodorant, I pull my hair up into a short, bouncy ponytail.

As I'm brushing my teeth, I take in my reflection.

Neck up, I look good enough. Neck down, I'm in the same skimpy pajamas I wore the night I slept with Luther, which consists of a strappy tank—that does nothing to support the tits—and matching shorts.

When I turn my electric toothbrush off, I swear I can hear voices.

Double shit.

I need to get back down to my bedroom before anyone sees me.

If I were thinking, I would've brought a change of clothes with me. But I wasn't thinking.

Because it's Saturday morning. And I should still be in bed.

Taking a deep inhale, I open the door.

Chapter 20

Luther

"Kenny should be out of her room soon," Joe says as he picks up the full carafe of coffee and starts to fill the trio of mugs set out on the counter.

"Kay. I'm gonna hit the head quick."

Joe hums, showing he heard me, as I walk farther into the living space.

I turn down the hall, and I'm two paces away from the bathroom when the door opens.

If I were thinking, I would've brought a change of clothes with me. But I wasn't thinking.

Because it's Saturday morning. And I should still be in bed.

Taking a deep inhale, I open the door.

Chapter 20

Luther

"Kenny should be out of her room soon," Joe says as he picks up the full carafe of coffee and starts to fill the trio of mugs set out on the counter.

"Kay. I'm gonna hit the head quick."

Joe hums, showing he heard me, as I walk farther into the living space.

I turn down the hall, and I'm two paces away from the bathroom when the door opens.

Chapter 21

Kendra

I step into the hallway, and a shadow falls over me as I nearly crash into a body.

A tall, broad, clad-in-flannel body.

I stumble to a halt, and large hands grip my shoulders, steadying me.

Warm hands. Against my bare shoulders.

Slowly, with my heart crawling up my throat, I lift my gaze.

Familiar brown eyes stare back into mine.

"Oh my god," I breathe, not believing what I'm seeing.

Luther takes a step closer, sliding one of his hands across my shoulder to my throat.

His fingers tighten slightly as he uses his hold on me to tip my head back, forcing me to keep my eyes on his.

"What the fuck do you think you're doing?" Luther's voice is just as quiet as mine. But his is full of... anger?

"What?" I can't make sense of this.

I reach up and grip his forearm with both hands. But not to push him away. I don't want him to step away. I just need something to hold on to.

Luther leans down into my space. "You think you can just hop out of my bed and into Joe's?" He hisses the accusation.

"Hop into…?" I finally comprehend what he said and nearly gag.

This time, I do shove at his arm.

But he doesn't budge. And I ignore the heat building in my core at having his hand around my throat like this.

"I am not sleeping with…" I can't say it. I can't say my dad's name.

"And yet here you are…" He drags his eyes down my body. "In the same slutty pajamas."

"Slutty?" I'd laugh, but I'm too busy trying to stay quiet.

And why did the word slutty make my thighs clench?

Luther's lips thin as his jaw clenches. "I don't care what you did. You're done with him. I'm—"

"Kenny, that you?" Dad's voice cuts off whatever Luther was going to say. And I see it.

I see the moment he realizes who I really am.

Who I am to Joe.

But Luther doesn't step back.

He doesn't release me.

His fingers flex once around my neck. "Kenny?"

The understanding hits him the same as it just hit me.

And I literally *have to* fuck with him.

"That's right, Daddy." I lean into his hold, increasing the pressure of his palm against my throat. "But I prefer it when you call me Baby."

A low rumble vibrates through his chest. "Dammit, woman."

He releases his hold on me, but instead of snatching his hand away, he drags it down my chest. And his fingertips leave a scorching trail from my collarbone to my cleavage.

My already hard nipples pulse with the touch.

Then I hear footsteps.

I take a step back.

"I'll be ready in a minute," I call out, hoping to stop my dad from rounding the end of the hall.

Luther, or whatever the fuck his name is, stays where he is, his big body blocking the hallway and any view my dad might have of our indecent introduction.

Chapter 22

LUTHER

As soon as *Joe's fucking daughter* disappears into her bedroom, I step into the bathroom and shut the door.

Then I lean against it.

Kendra is Kenny.

Kenny, my best friend's daughter.

I groan and thud my head back against the door.

I can't believe I fucked Joe's daughter.

I can't believe I fucked his daughter without even knowing it.

I'm the worst friend in the world.

How did I not put it together?

Has he really only ever called her Kenny? Did I really not know her real name?

I try to think if he has any photos of her in his living room. But Joe is a simple man. I don't think he has photos of anything in his house.

Even as I berate myself, my body is still reacting to having her so close again.

To having my hands on her again.

I drag a hand down my face. Then all the way down my body to palm my dick.

I found my girl.

And now I know exactly where to find her. Every night.
I squeeze my dick tighter.

When I first saw Kendra stepping into the hall, my gut reaction was earth-shifting relief.

In our one night together, she imprinted herself into my being. And I was not doing well with the idea of never seeing her again.

Then, instead of using logic or reason—like the fact I was coming here to meet my friend's daughter, Kenny—my brain jumped straight to the conclusion that she was here as Joe's mistress.

I shake my head at my stupidity.

Kendra. Kenny. It's so simple. It should've been so easy to make that connection.

But I didn't.

I didn't make that connection at all.

Like, not even fucking kind of.

So, are you new to the area or passing through?

Just passing through.

I drop my hands to my sides.

The night I met Kendra, she said she was just passing through.

Pretty little liar.

I'll make her pay for that later.

Groaning, I step away from the door and start to undo my pants.

Taking a piss shouldn't feel so vulgar. But wrapping my fingers around my cock with my perfect little dream girl on the other side of the wall…

Nope.

Not going there.

Not thinking about it.

I'm here for breakfast with my friend and his daughter.

I will not jerk off in the bathroom.

I hesitate, then shake my head.

I will not.

Chapter 23

Kendra

Oh my god. Oh my god. Oh my god.

I stand in front of my mirrored closet doors and overthink my outfit.

My bed is strewn with nearly every piece of clothing I own, as I've already tried on every reasonable option.

It's breakfast. At home.

I grit my teeth and let out a quiet shriek of stress.

If I delay any longer, my dad will come looking for me, making sure I didn't fall back asleep.

I wish.

I wish falling back asleep was my biggest problem this morning.

But no.

My biggest problem is the fact that I slept with my dad's best friend.

And we didn't just *sleep together*.

We fucked.

In the span of one evening, we did almost everything two people can do.

And, heaven help me, I want to do it all again.

Chapter 24

Luther

Act cool.

Act natural.

Act like you haven't had your dick inside your friend's daughter.

I clear my throat as I enter the kitchen.

Joe's distracted, doing something on his phone, so I use the time to pick up one of the two remaining coffee mugs.

They're both filled with plain black coffee, which is how I take mine, but I'm curious if Kendra adds anything to hers.

Kenny, I remind myself.

I can't fuck up and call her Kendra when she walks out here. Not until she introduces herself as that.

Will she introduce herself as Kendra?

Will she ask why I introduced myself as Luther?

Do I even have a good answer?

I don't even know what inspired me to do that in the first place. Everyone calls me Rocky. But when I met her...

When I met her, it felt different.

I didn't want her to treat me like everyone else.

I wanted it to be different for her too.

Taking a sip of my coffee, I glance toward the hallway.

It should go without saying that we're never going to tell Joe about this.

Not ever.

Before Joe can look up from his phone, worried he might see some guilty expression on my face, I interrupt whatever he's doing and ask about our fishing spot for today.

"Uh-huh. I called Fisher last night," he tells me as he puts his phone in his pocket. "Says it's still *flush with fish*."

He uses the tone he reserves whenever he's mimicking people younger than him, and I wonder if I sound as old as he does.

Joe has a few years on me. But not many.

Then I hear the unmistakable click of a door opening, and I stop listening to Joe.

I can't hear any footsteps, but I imagine Kendra walking down the hall barefoot. Like she was a few minutes ago. When I had my hand around her neck.

I clear my throat.

And then she appears.

I get one moment to take her in.

One moment before Joe realizes she's here.

And Christ. Her new outfit is hardly less revealing than her pajamas.

She's in cut-off jean shorts and a T-shirt. But the shorts are barely past her ass cheeks and the shirt is so thin and soft looking that it settles on every curve of her body. Not to mention, the white material is practically see-through, showing off the red sports bra she's wearing underneath.

And with tits like hers, the tight material of her bra does hardly anything to diminish their plumpness.

I grind my teeth.

She's asking for a fucking spanking walking out here like that.

"Kenny! There you are!" Joe practically shouts when he sees her, as though they don't live under the same roof.

"Morning." Kendra's smile shows a lot of teeth, and I feel slightly better knowing she's feeling as awkward as I am.

And now I know exactly where to find her. Every night.
I squeeze my dick tighter.

When I first saw Kendra stepping into the hall, my gut reaction was earth-shifting relief.

In our one night together, she imprinted herself into my being. And I was not doing well with the idea of never seeing her again.

Then, instead of using logic or reason—like the fact I was coming here to meet my friend's daughter, Kenny—my brain jumped straight to the conclusion that she was here as Joe's mistress.

I shake my head at my stupidity.

Kendra. Kenny. It's so simple. It should've been so easy to make that connection.

But I didn't.

I didn't make that connection at all.

Like, not even fucking kind of.

So, are you new to the area or passing through?

Just passing through.

I drop my hands to my sides.

The night I met Kendra, she said she was just passing through.

Pretty little liar.

I'll make her pay for that later.

Groaning, I step away from the door and start to undo my pants.

Taking a piss shouldn't feel so vulgar. But wrapping my fingers around my cock with my perfect little dream girl on the other side of the wall...

Nope.

Not going there.

Not thinking about it.

I'm here for breakfast with my friend and his daughter.

I will not jerk off in the bathroom.

I hesitate, then shake my head.

I will not.

Chapter 23

Kendra

Oh my god. Oh my god. Oh my god.

I stand in front of my mirrored closet doors and overthink my outfit.

My bed is strewn with nearly every piece of clothing I own, as I've already tried on every reasonable option.

It's breakfast. At home.

I grit my teeth and let out a quiet shriek of stress.

If I delay any longer, my dad will come looking for me, making sure I didn't fall back asleep.

I wish.

I wish falling back asleep was my biggest problem this morning.

But no.

My biggest problem is the fact that I slept with my dad's best friend.

And we didn't just *sleep together*.

We fucked.

In the span of one evening, we did almost everything two people can do.

And, heaven help me, I want to do it all again.

Then I remember her calling me Daddy. Again. And I clear my throat. Again.

Joe crosses to Kendra and places a hand on her back before turning to face me. "Rocky, I'd like you to meet my little girl, Kenny. Or Kendra if she's in trouble."

Sweet Jesus, he's making this worse by the second.

With her dad's attention on me, Kendra widens her eyes at me as her cheeks turn pink.

I tip my head in her direction. "Nice to meet you, *Kenny*." I pause just long enough to emphasize her name. "I've heard a lot about you."

She inclines her chin. "Same. I've heard so much I feel like I already know you." *This little minx.* "Though I've always wondered, is Rocky a nickname, or did your parents really name you that?"

Joe chokes on a laugh, and I can't stop my smirk. "Nickname." I step forward and hold out my hand. She takes it. "Name's Luther Rockford. But most people call me Rocky."

She's giving me a look like I gave her the wrong name on purpose. But I lift a brow in reply. Luther is my real name. And it's not like I kept my identity from her on purpose. Or at least not for the reason she's thinking. Maybe a part of me didn't want her to know I was the owner of Rocky Ridge Inn while we were sitting in the bar. But I had no fucking clue she was Joe's kid. And there's no fucking way she can think my reaction this morning was fake.

She flexes her fingers around mine. "Kendra Abbott. No one but my dad calls me Kenny."

I shift closer.

"Yeah, yeah, and I'm Joe, and no one has ever given me a cool nickname." Joe mock complains, and Kendra rolls her eyes.

My best friend's voice reminds me we're not alone. And that I can't press my body against Kendra's to make a point.

I flex my fingers, then let go of her hand.

Remembering the coffee still in my left hand, I move back to the counter and pick up the last mug, holding it out to Kendra. "You take it black?"

Kendra takes it but shakes her head. "I'll drink it that way if I must, but it's not my thing."

I watch her ass as she moves to the fridge. Then I force my gaze up as she takes out a carton of flavored creamer.

She pours a healthy amount into her coffee, and I read the flavor on the label.

Hazelnut. Good to know.

I lean my hip against the wall as Kendra and Joe talk breakfast. Joe asking what he can do to help. Kendra insisting that he'll help the most by sitting at the table.

They're having an innocent discussion. I'm staring at Kendra's thighs. Thinking about how they felt wrapped around my head.

I shift.

Fucking hell. I need Joe out of here so Kendra and I can have a word.

When Joe gives up the fight and moves to the dining table, I push off the wall and grab the coffee carafe.

I hold it up toward my friend. "Top you off?"

Joe slides his mug toward me, and I fill it up.

The more he drinks, the quicker he'll have to go.

Putting the carafe back, I select the dining chair that will have me facing the kitchen, where Kendra is currently sipping her coffee. And watching me.

Chapter 25

Kendra

I spill flour on the counter.

I have to pick eggshell out of my batter.

I burn the first pancake.

I flip the next one too early.

Closing my eyes, I place my palms on the counter and give myself a second to calm down.

Settled, I turn around and find *Luther* fighting a smile as he watches me struggle.

Ass.

I pick up my bowl of batter and slowly ladle a scoop onto the griddle.

I repeat the process, filling the pan, trying not to think about the man at my back.

Not just any man. *Rocky.*

I stare down as the batter starts to bubble.

This feels like an old sitcom.

Mistaken identity. Forbidden lover.

I glance over my shoulder as I reach for the bag of white chocolate chips.

Luther is lounging, one arm hooked over the back of his chair, the other resting in his lap.

It's casual. Relaxed.

Hot as fuck.

Flannel shouldn't be hot as fuck.

But honestly, that man could be wearing burlap and I'd still risk the rug burns to climb him. Because I know what's underneath. And I know he knows just how to use all those muscles.

I turn back to our food and sprinkle this batch of pancakes with the chocolate chips and smashed raspberries. Then I flip them.

I will not think about my dad's best friend's chest hair during breakfast.

Distracting myself with the task, I make two more batches—one with dark chocolate and blueberries, and the other with milk chocolate and banana slices—all while a package of breakfast sausages cooks in the oven.

Luther comes into the kitchen once, to make another pot of coffee, proving he knows his way around this house, but I pretend I don't notice.

"Smells good," Dad calls out as he stands. "I'm gonna hit the little boy's room before we eat."

I flip the final pancake. "You have two minutes."

Dad salutes in my direction, then disappears down the short hallway leading to his room.

Luther stands.

And my heart rate spikes.

I turn and face him fully, shifting back until my butt bumps against the cabinet beside the stove.

I lift my chin. "Rocky."

His fingers tap against his thighs as he consumes the space between us.

And as soon as he's close enough, he reaches up and grips my chin.

His front presses against mine, and he shakes his head. "You don't call me that."

His fingers feel hot against my skin. "Why not? Didn't you say most people call you that?"

I don't know why I'm pushing him. I don't actually want to call him Rocky.

He shifts closer, leaning more of his weight against me, his free hand reaching around and flattening against my spine. "You aren't most people, Kendra Doll."

His words shouldn't hit so hard.

They shouldn't mean so much.

We've only spent one night together. Didn't even know who we were with, not in a real-life context. But it's still the nicest thing anyone has said to me in... a long time.

My body arches into his, and even though I know it's a bad idea to push this further, I grip his sides. "My dad will be back any moment."

He moves his hand from my chin to my throat. "We can't tell him about this."

"No shit." I try to huff, but it just comes out breathy as I think about his use of the word *this*.

As in *current*.

Ongoing.

Luther is thinking the same thing I am.

We're going to do it again.

"Such a—" A squeak in the floorboards interrupts whatever Luther was going to say, and he steps back just as I lift my hands to shove him away.

"Can you take the sausages to the table?" I ask louder than necessary as I quickly spin around and start to remove the final pancakes.

They're a little more done than I'd usually cook them but not so far gone that I'll need to explain myself.

Luther opens a drawer on the other side of the stove and takes out a pair of hot mitts, and I move out of the way so he can take the pan of sausages out of the oven.

Dad grabs two of the platters of pancakes, and I take the third.

The table is already set with plates, butter, and maple syrup, so now, with the rest of the food, the surface of the round table is nearly covered.

Four chairs circle the table, and since Dad and his bestie choose seats next to each other, I had to decide between sitting next to my dad and across from Luther. Or next to Luther and across from my dad.

I was tempted to sit beside Luther, but next to my dad seemed like the more socially acceptable choice. Considering Luther and I *just met*.

Plus, being directly across from Luther comes with its own perks. Like eye candy.

The first few minutes are filled with silence as we eat.

Luther shovels another forkful of the raspberry pancakes into his mouth, finishing the short stack in what had to be four bites. Then he sets his fork down and lifts his head to spear me with a look. "What the hell did you put in these?"

I try not to grin like an idiot. *He already likes my pussy. It shouldn't matter so much that he likes my cooking too.*

Dad reaches out and slaps Luther's shoulder. "Told you my girl has talents."

I watch Luther's jaw work, and I know his mind is swimming around in the gutter. Because *same*.

"Thanks, Dad." I fork up some of my own food, pretending this isn't the strangest breakfast ever. Eating with my one-night stand and my dad.

Luther serves himself another stack of pancakes, the blueberry ones this time. And as I listen to my dad tell me about a phone call he had yesterday, I watch Luther eat.

He's a little slower this time, but he still finishes his second round of pancakes in under a minute.

When he's done, he once again lifts his gaze to meet mine.

Dad is still gabbing, eyes on his mug as he pours himself more coffee, so I point to the final platter and mouth, *My favorite,* before Dad looks up.

Luther uses the spatula to slide three of the banana pancakes onto his plate.

Before he cuts into them, I reach out and nudge the butter, then the maple syrup toward him.

Taking the hint, he cuts a square of butter off the stick and drops it on his stack.

Dad looks at the table, watching the silent interaction, but he doesn't stop talking and doesn't seem to find our behavior suspicious.

I make the proper noise in response to Dad's story, but my attention stays on Luther as he lifts his fork.

His lips part.

A drip of syrup falls onto his plate.

I wish I was that plate.

And then he puts the fluffy goodness into his mouth.

He pulls the clean fork out from between his lips, and his eyes close as he starts to chew.

I take a drink of my coffee to help my suddenly dry throat.

Then Luther startles everyone when he groans. Loudly.

Dad jerks his head in Luther's direction. "Damn, Rocky. Keep it in your pants, would you? My daughter's here."

I choke on my coffee.

Luther chokes on his pancakes.

And Dad just shrugs when I widen my eyes at him. "Sorry, but he started it with that R-rated noise he was making."

My cheeks heat because Dad's not wrong. I've heard Luther's groans, and that was the same sound he made in the motel room.

But still, I can't pass up an opportunity to harass my dad. "So… you know what Luther's R-rated sounds are like? Is there something you two want to tell me? Is that what this breakfast is all about?"

Dad sputters for a moment before throwing his head back with a laugh.

Luther lays a hand on my dad's shoulder with a wicked grin aimed my way. "That's right, Kendra. I'm your daddy now too."

I gape.

He. Didn't.

My dad waves his hands around, taking my expression the wrong way. "No. We're not—" He's laughing so hard he can't finish his sentence. "Rocky and I ain't like that. Not that there would be anything wrong with that." He gives me a knowing look.

I roll my eyes. "Thanks, Dad, but I'm not gay. I like men."

It's so hard not to glance at Luther as I say the last word. Because I've dated. I've been with guys. But like I told Luther last weekend, it's been a while. And I don't think any of them actually count as *men*. Not compared to Luther.

"I'm just saying." Dad lifts his shoulders, then shoots a glare at Luther. "And it's a safe rule of thumb to just ignore anything Rocky says. He likes to start shit."

"I have no idea what you're talking about," the flannel-wearing hottie says as he serves himself another banana pancake before sliding the last one onto my plate.

I look down, staring at the caramelized bananas.

It's a simple thing. A chivalrous thing. But it's more than that.

It's the same thing he did at the Inn when he ordered us those burgers.

He's not trying to limit me. Not giving me different food than what he eats.

Not telling me to eat less. Have less. Be less.

And it's shit like this that makes him even hotter.

Dad thumbs his fist against his chest. "I never really thought about what it'd be like having the two of you together, but I'm starting to think it won't be dull." He serves himself the last of the blueberry pancakes. "But back to my original point."

"There's a point?" I ask.

Luther snorts.

"Back to my original point," Dad repeats loudly. "I believe

Rocky was moaning and groaning in an effort to say he likes your cooking."

Luther tips his head toward me. "That's exactly what I was trying to say. Everything you've made is delicious."

Heat flares in my chest.

"Thank you." I hold Luther's gaze as I say it. Meaning it.

"And that's not for nothing," Dad adds, and I see a slight wince pass over Luther's features. "I don't know if you noticed it, but you would've driven past the restaurant Rocky owns on your way here."

I slowly turn my head to face my dad. "Restaurant?"

"It's attached to a place called The Rocky Ridge Inn. He owns it." Dad tilts his head. "Come to think of it, I don't know if the restaurant has a name or not. We just call the whole place *the Inn*." Dad rattles on. And I slowly turn my head back to look at Luther.

"How. Interesting." I keep my expression neutral.

I'm not actually mad. We were together for one night with no plans to see each other again.

He didn't need to tell me he owned the motel we met in. And I didn't need to tell him I was actually only going twenty minutes away rather than *passing through*.

But I also don't need to let him off the hook quite so easily.

My dad hums his oblivious agreement. "Food's real good too. We'll have to go some night."

"That'd be fun." My tone is just sarcastic enough for Luther to stifle a reaction, but Dad doesn't notice.

"Come to think of it." Dad snaps his fingers. "Ashley will be back in, what, just a couple weeks?"

Luther replies with a slow nod.

My eyes narrow. "Who's Ashley?"

If this motherfucker just made me an accomplice to adultery, I'm going to ruin him.

Luther inhales, his shoulders straightening as he prepares to answer. "My daughter."

Oh.

My sudden flash of anger dissipates.

Not a cheater. Just single dad vibes... I dig it.

"You'll like her," Dad says with confidence. "She's about your age."

I choke again.

Chapter 26

Luther

I'm going to kill Joe.

He has no idea that he's doing it, but each sentence that falls out of his mouth digs my grave just a little bit deeper.

"Ashley is six years younger than Kendra," I say it like it's a fact I already knew. But that's only because I did the math when Kendra told me her age last weekend.

"Is she really?" Joe cocks his head as he thinks it through.

"Practically a decade." I pretend to joke, but I do believe in rounding up.

And fuck if I didn't wish I had told Kendra about Ashley myself. In private.

It's not a big deal. At least, I hope it isn't to Kendra.

I had a kid twenty-six years ago, just before I turned thirty. That kid is an adult now, who lives a few hours away. Her mom and I split up before she was even one, and Ashley knows that I date.

When I look at Kendra, she's biting her lip... trying not to laugh.

Relief chases away my anxiety.

This fucking brat.

Chapter 27

Kendra

"A kid. A restaurant. A motel." I lift my mug and cradle it in my hands.

Dad lifts a finger to interrupt, and I almost laugh at the exasperation on Luther's face. "I think it's like six hotels."

I pull an impressed expression. "Damn. A real hotelier."

Luther leans back in his chair. "Hardly that. Just needed something to do after I sold my construction company."

Dad sighs as he rubs his full stomach. "One of these years, I'll get him to take me to his place in Vail for a romantic weekend."

"Next anniversary," Luther replies.

"We have an anniversary?"

Luther shakes his head. "This is why I don't take you."

I bite down on the tip of my tongue because these two are too much.

Dad scoots his chair back. "You got plans today, Kenny? Want to come fishing with us?"

"Oh, god no," I blurt out. Because no. Stuck in a boat with these two, or standing in a river, or however the fuck they fish, sounds like the absolute worst way to spend my day. "Sorry, I mean, no, thank you."

Dad just laughs as he stands. "Fine, fine."

Before he can pick up his plate, I hold my hand out. "I'll clean up. You guys go play with your rods."

Chapter 28

Luther

Driving here. Launching the boat. Sitting on the water. Eating cold salami sandwiches for lunch.

I don't remember any of it.

If you asked me how many fish I caught and threw back, I couldn't answer.

If the details in Joe's stories meant the difference between me going to prison and me walking free... lock me up, because I couldn't repeat a single word.

But if someone asked me to describe every stitch of clothing Kendra was wearing this morning, it would be the easiest thing in the world.

With her father a few feet away, securing the boat to the trailer, I close my eyes and picture how she looked stepping out of the hallway.

Her bare toes were painted the same light bluish-purple color as her fingernails.

I can't remember looking at her toes the night her legs were wrapped around me.

Maybe they were already that color.

Maybe she painted them herself.

Maybe she sat on her bed in her underwear, one heel pressing into the mattress as she bit her lip to concentrate—

"Ready?" Joe's voice cuts into my fantasy.

Wait, fantasy?

Am I into feet?

"Ready," I reply in a totally normal voice.

Climbing into the passenger seat of Joe's truck, my mind wanders back to Kendra's outfit and how I could see her bra through her shirt. Proving I really could recall every stitch of clothing she was wearing... except for her panties.

And that's how I spend an entire car ride with my best friend, wondering what color panties his daughter is currently wearing.

I'm disgusting.

And the worst part of this gross, guilty feeling... I know I'm going to pursue her.

Maybe not as a *relationship*, because I don't know how that would work. With the age gap. My adult child. Kendra's whole life ahead of her...

But I know I'm going to sleep with her again.

There's no doubt about it.

Just... when?

And how?

Joe slows as he starts to turn into his driveway.

"I have to pee," I say like I'm a fucking toddler.

Joe side-eyes me. "Well, can you hold it until I park the truck? Or do I need to let you out now so you can take a leak in the grass?"

I gesture out the windshield. "Carry on."

"Appreciate it." He shakes his head as he pulls up in front of his garage.

While he unhooks the trailer, I carry my fishing pole over to my truck. And while Joe is busy, I open my driver's door.

With my body blocking my actions, I reach into the center console and find what I need.

And after Joe gets the boat situated, I slide the matchbook into my pocket, then follow him into the house.

Chapter 29

Kendra

When I see that Luther is coming up to the house too, I hurry away from the window and drop onto the couch.

The TV is still streaming my favorite home renovation show, and since it's an episode I've seen before, it's easy to pretend I've been watching.

I keep my eyes forward, my back to the front door, when I hear it open. "Hey, Dad."

"Hey, Kiddo."

"Have fun fishing?" I turn sideways on the couch as I ask it, so I can look back. Then I do my best to act surprised. "Oh, hey, Luther."

His lips purse, like he knows I'm faking it, but he still dips his chin. "Kendra." Then he heads down the hall. The one leading to my room.

"He has to pee." Dad helpfully interjects.

"Good to know." I joke. Then I wonder... "How far away does he live?"

"Rocky?" Dad tips his head from side to side. "Twenty, give or take. He's over by the Inn."

"By the Inn, not *at* the Inn."

Dad nods. "Correct. Though it could be kinda fun to live at a motel. Or at least one with a restaurant attached."

"Would be nice to have a chef on call," I agree, though I wouldn't want to actually live in a motel.

This creaky house alerts us to Luther's arrival, and we both look that way.

Luther stops at the edge of the living room, narrowing his eyes at us. "Were you talking about me?"

Dad says no at the same time I say yes.

"Okay." Luther drags out the word before turning his attention to me. "Kendra, it was nice to meet you."

"You too." I roll my lips together.

"Thank you for breakfast. It was delicious."

"Anytime," I say before I can think about what I'm implying.

He gives me the smallest smirk before nodding to my dad. "Joe." Then... he's leaving.

I want to stop him.

Want to ask him if he'd like to sit on the couch with me. Stay a while.

But obviously I can't do that.

So I watch him walk away.

And I watch him pause. Watch him look back over his shoulder at me, one last time, before he disappears out the door.

I stay sitting, not wanting to run down the hall the moment Luther leaves. But that look he gave me... I have a feeling...

And I only have to wait long enough for Dad to put his melted ice packs in the freezer before he tells me he's going to take a shower.

As soon as he disappears, I climb off the couch.

I've had all afternoon to sit here and think about my dad's best friend. To wonder what will happen next. Wonder what I'll have to do to see him again.

I mean, I know he'll come back over.

I didn't know Luther was really Rocky when I slept with him.

But now that I know, I know Rocky's the guy my dad is always talking about.

I'm pretty sure they go fishing every month.

Pretty sure they see each other most weekends for some meal or another.

So I know I'll see Luther again, probably soon. I just don't know how to get him alone.

As my feet lead me down the hall, I wonder, for the hundredth time, if I'm a terrible daughter.

Because I feel like a good daughter would let the guilt win.

A good daughter would bury the one-night stand deep down inside, pretend it never happened, and make sure it never happened again.

But as I step into my bathroom, as I see the matchbook sitting on the counter, I accept I'm not a good daughter.

I pick up the matchbook, rubbing my thumb over the simple Rocky Ridge Inn logo before turning it over.

No, I'm not a good daughter at all. Because Luther wrote his number on the back of the matches, and instead of lighting the whole thing on fire, I take out my phone and save the digits.

"SEE YOU IN THE MORNING," DAD YAWNS AS HE RISES from the couch.

"Not too early."

"Oh, to be young."

Following his lead, I turn off the TV and head to my bedroom.

With the door shut firmly behind me, I climb onto my bed and stare at my phone.

Do I call him?

Text him?
I bite down on my lip.
Calling shouldn't feel so intimidating. But it does.
And texting...

Oh my god, Kendra. He's older, not ancient. This isn't a number for a rotary phone.

Chapter 30

Luther

My phone chimes with a text, and I'm already grinning when I grab it off my nightstand.

Normally, I'd be asleep by now, but I was holding out hope that my little Kendra Doll would use the number I gave her. So here I am, book in lap, up past my bedtime, thinking about a girl.

> Unknown: You know how to text, Old Man?

My grin grows.

> Me: I know how to do a lot of things, Baby.

Before she replies, I save her number in my phone.

I debate for a moment what name to put her under. It's unlikely Joe will ever be looking at my phone at the same time Kendra texts me, but on the off chance it could happen, I don't want him seeing his daughter's name.

> Baby Doll: Skilled with his hands and technology. Color me impressed.

> Me: Skilled with more than just my hands. Or do you need a reminder?

I reach down and adjust my dick through my sleep pants. It's been literal decades since I've felt this damn horny.

> Baby Doll: My memory is a little foggy... I think a reminder will be necessary.

> Me: I think that can be arranged.

> Baby Doll: Promises. Promises.

> Me: I always keep my promises.

> Baby Doll: I'll hold you to that.

I groan, thinking of all the things I'll do to her the next time I get my hands on her.

> Me: Before you go dream of me, I need you to answer a question.

> Baby Doll: Bold assumption.

I'm smiling at my phone like an idiot, but I don't care.

> Me: Am I wrong?

> Baby Doll: I hope not. I'd love for you to finish what you started in my dreams last night.

"Jesus." I reach down and grip my dick again.

> Me: Details, Baby. Give me details.

> Baby Doll: I think I prefer your imagination running wild.

> Me: Brat.

Baby Doll: So you say. Now what's your question?

I hesitate for only a second before I hit send.

Me: What color were your panties today?

Chapter 31

Kendra

I stare at my phone for a long second.

Then I look at the clothes hamper in the corner of my room.

I'm not sure why he's asking.

And I'm not sure why I'm so willing to answer.

But...

I climb off the bed and pad over to the hamper, lifting the lid.

Before I can overthink it, I take a picture of the red thong lying on top of my clothes and hit send.

Chapter 32

Luther

It's been one week.

One whole week since I've seen my obsession.

One week of jerking off to a photo of her panties.

But that ends today.

Even if it's just a touch. A fingertip down the back of her arm. I'm not leaving until I've touched some part of Kendra.

And if I can steal a kiss… well, a kiss would be ideal.

Joe's driveway is already full of vehicles.

Mostly pickup trucks. Mostly ones I recognize since we know all the same people.

Joe thought it'd be fun to host a barbeque as a way for his employees and friends to meet Kendra all in one go. And best-friend perks mean I still got an invite, even though Kendra and I have already met.

Finding a spot in the grass, I shift my truck into park and turn off the engine.

My pulse skips as I sit in the quiet truck. And I soak it in.

It's been a long time since I've felt so… *excited* about someone, even the guilt isn't enough to ruin it.

Maybe that makes me a bad friend. *I'm actually positive it makes me a terrible friend.* But I need to experience more of her.

More of Kendra.

Grabbing the small plant off the passenger seat, I climb out of my truck.

Voices from the backyard float around to where I'm at, but I still head for the front door, taking the shortcut.

I let myself in and find a few people filling up plates of food from the spread on the table.

Recognizing each other, we exchange polite greetings, but I don't slow my stride as I head for the sliding glass doors at the back of the house.

Joe's on the deck, standing in front of the grill, waving a pair of tongs around as he tells a story.

Before I open the door, I scan the crowd scattered around the yard.

I just want to see...

I find her in a blink.

In a fucking slutty little sundress.

I shake my head.

She's too much of a goddamn temptation as it is. But dressed like that...

Kendra is across the yard, standing there with her floral-printed skirt fluttering a couple inches above her knees.

And it's not that it's too short. It's just that I can't stop my blood from simmering at the sight of that much of her bare skin.

I can't even get started on the top half of her dress...

I swallow and reach for the door handle.

The straps holding up her dress are so thin I know they aren't hiding a bra. Meaning her tits are bare under that tight flowery material.

Her large, soft tits.

I want to suck the material into my mouth. I want to make it wet. *I want to make her wet.* I want to watch the damp cotton cling to her nipples.

A utensil clatters to the floor behind me. And I open the door.

"Rocky!" Joe turns toward the sound of the door opening, then greets me with drunken enthusiasm.

He's such a lightweight that I'd guess he's probably only had two beers, but he doesn't have to drive anywhere, so good for him.

Plus... A drunk Joe is less likely to pay attention to details. *Like how close his friend is going to stand to his daughter.* So... good for me.

"Hey, man." I clap him on the back.

"Hey back." Joe sways. "Your sister come with you?"

I shake my head. "Nah, she's working the bar today."

Which is a damn miracle. For me. Because I have yet to tell Jessie that I found my *one-night stand girl*.

And I certainly haven't told her my *one-night stand girl* is Joe's new live-in offspring.

Joe grins and nods to my hand. "Did you bring me flowers?"

The guy Joe was talking to laughs.

"This is how those rumors get started." I shake my head. "It's a succulent, not a flower." I lift the little plant. "And it's for Kendra, not you."

My sister is a plant person, so I know a bit, but I'd never heard of this *string of pearls* before. I really just bought it because the little pot the plant was in reminded me of Kendra's nail polish. It's not the same exact color—more blue than the periwinkle Kendra wears. *I looked up the name of it.* But the color was close enough to make me pause.

Plus, this is a welcome party, so a gift shouldn't seem too out of place.

A welcome party because she lives here now.

My gaze lifts past Joe. And I lock eyes with *her*.

My girl.

"I'll be back," I say as I slap Joe on the back again. Then I walk away, not giving him a chance to protest or come with me.

The deck is low, and I descend the short staircase to the lawn in two steps.

Kendra looks away first, moving her attention back to the two guys in front of her—a pair of carpenters from Joe's shop—but it just gives me more time to take her in.

She's summer perfection.

The beauty to my beast.

My worn jeans and gray T-shirt are a stark contrast to her girliness.

I shift the plant in my grip.

Act normal. Act like an adult who has control over his body.

I come to a stop at Kendra's side.

"Rocky." The carpenters greet me in unison.

I nod my acknowledgment before I dip my chin, looking down at the woman whose shoulder is inches away from my arm. "Kendra."

The side of her mouth pulls up, the smallest amount. "Luther."

One of the guys makes a sound of surprise. "Wait, what?"

I glance at him before holding out the plant for Kendra. "Not sure you still deserve this after outing me like that."

"Let's not get ahead of ourselves." Kendra takes the pot out of my hand. "It was an honest mistake."

I watch her trail a finger down one of the bauble-like strands.

And I feel a ridiculous amount of pride at my color choice when I see her nails are still that pretty purple-y blue.

"Hold up." The guy holds a hand up. "Is your name really Luther?"

I turn to him, letting my body shift a little closer to Kendra. "It is, but only she gets to call me that."

The guy still looks confused, but his friend narrows his eyes. I may have played my hand too loudly, but I don't care. What'll these guys do? Go tell their boss that his friend was acting *too friendly* with his daughter? No. They won't say shit.

"Did you eat already?" I ask the woman, who is still gently touching her new plant.

She lifts her head. "I could snack."

I gently press my hand to the center of her back. "I'll go with you."

My palm is against her bare skin, above the zipper running up the back of her dress, and the connection practically sizzles.

I rub my thumb back, then forth, over her spine, then I drop my hand.

Smiles and hellos are shared as we walk across the yard back to the house.

The party started about an hour ago, but I arrived exactly as planned.

By now, Kendra's had a chance to meet most everyone. Meaning she should be free to spend some time talking with a *friend*.

Chapter 33

Kendra

Holding the little plant to my chest, I walk up the steps of the deck ahead of Luther.

He brought me a plant.

It's not flowers. Not even potted flowers. But a little green bubble-looking plant in a pretty blue pot.

It's kind of bizarre. And oddly perfect.

"There she is!" Dad calls out as we pass. "Enjoy your succubus!"

I pause. And blink.

Luther's warm hand presses into my back again. "It's a succulent, you fool."

Dad nods. "That's what I said."

I look up at Luther and mouth, *Wow.*

He sighs. "Men."

A laugh bursts out of me, and I feel Luther's fingers flex against my back as his gaze drops to my mouth.

I press my lips together, trying to bite down on my wide smile.

My dad didn't specifically say Luther was coming today, but I assumed he'd be in attendance.

And with that assumption, I dressed with Luther in mind.

Then I waited.

And waited.

And about ten minutes ago, I accepted that maybe he wouldn't show up.

He has a life. *Businesses. A kid of his own.* Maybe he was busy.

Which was fine.

I'd almost convinced myself that it was for the best.

That without Luther nearby, I wouldn't feel so... riled.

I wouldn't be drenched in sexual tension.

Wouldn't be distracted with thoughts of ripping his clothes off.

But then I turned my head. And he was there.

Luther was there with his eyes locked on mine.

And my body lit up.

Inhaling, I focus on the spot where his thumb is touching the bare skin of my back. And I focus on not tripping.

I reach for the door handle, but Luther leans past me, wrapping the fingers of his free hand around the pull.

I watch his forearm flex as he pulls the sliding door open, and I drag my eyes away from the sight as I step into the house.

The kitchen is empty, and when Luther shuts the door behind us, silence fills the room.

I turn to face him.

"Thank you for the succulent." I lift the little pot. "You really didn't need to."

"You're welcome." He takes a step toward me. "It reminded me of you."

I lift a brow, glancing down at the interesting plant. "Oh?"

He dips his chin. "Matches your nails. Kind of."

I look at the pale blue ceramic and then at the periwinkle paint on my fingernails.

I smile. "It kind of does."

The shade is close enough. In the same color family, at least. And honestly, it shows that—in the two times we've met—he's paid closer attention to me than... well, all my past boyfriends combined.

Not that he's my boyfriend.
And not that I want him to be.
No. I just want to fuck him again.

My inner self rolls her eyes at me. But I ignore her. What does she know?

Luther takes another step closer, putting us inappropriately close. But his size hides me from anyone outside looking in.

"Luther," I say quietly.

He lifts a hand toward my cheek. "Baby—"

Down the hall, the bathroom door opens.

I step back.

Luther drops his hand.

"Thanks for the plant." I speak louder than necessary. "I'll put it on my desk."

"Ah, yes, your new work-from-home office."

"It's coming together." I turn my head, hoping the move looks casual, so I can see who's coming down the hall.

The woman spots me as she enters the living room and beams. "Oh, I'd love to see your setup. I was tempted to go in there and show myself around, but that felt rude." She laughs, and I can't recall her name, but I think she owns a few of the stores that sell Dad's furniture.

"Hi, Susan." Luther smiles at the woman, drawing her attention.

Her smile grows even wider.

Okay, Susan. Settle down.

Bristling just a little, I let the two of them chitchat while we all walk into my office together.

Susan remarks on the pieces my dad made for the room.

Luther makes a comment about how it's a better use of the space than the clutter my dad had in here before.

Susan throws her head back with a laugh, and when she places her hand on Luther's arm, I use a little more force than necessary to set my new plant on the corner of my desk.

Luther clears his throat. And when I lift my gaze to meet his, I can see the humor in his eyes.

Oh, he thinks this is funny?

Well, there are way more men than women here, and I'm wearing the flirtiest thing I own.

I roll my shoulders back.

Susan is still talking, eyes all over Luther, so she doesn't notice.

But he does.

With his eyes on my cleavage, I take a deep breath, stretching the fabric to its limit.

His lids lower.

The cups of my dress are padded, pushing my tits up even more. The padding also makes it so no one can see my nipples. Which is good. Because even if Susan is annoying, my body is still reacting to Luther's nearness.

I take another breath, this one to calm my inner bitch. Susan doesn't deserve my shitty thoughts. She's reacting like any straight woman would around Luther.

Doesn't mean I won't pay Luther back for this.

Chapter 34

Luther

There's a look in Kendra's eyes, and I don't know if I should be excited or worried.

"Sorry, I've been talking your ear off." Susan lifts her hands.

When it looks like she might try to touch me again, I take a step to the side and hold my arm out toward the door. "No apologies necessary. I'm afraid I'm the one who sidetracked the woman of the hour with my little gift. Kendra was just about to get a plate of food with me."

Susan smiles at the plant. "Oh yes, the pearl necklace."

Kendra lets out a cough that sounds suspiciously like a laugh.

"Uh, string of pearls, actually." I correct her, shooting a narrow-eyed look at Kendra.

Her lips are pressed together in a move I recognize as her trying not to laugh.

Susan says something else about plants as she moves out of Kendra's office, but I'm not listening.

Kendra steps past me, but before she can cross the threshold, I reach out and hook my arm around her chest, my palm flat against her bare cleavage.

I stand with my front to her back as I lean down to speak

against her ear. "What do you know about *pearl necklaces*, Kendra Doll?"

I shift until my pinkie finger presses between her breasts, and the warmth nearly makes me groan.

Her skin is so soft and perfect under my touch.

My free hand circles her waist, holding her steady.

She tilts her head back to look at me. "I know I wouldn't mind you giving me one."

"Christ." I apply pressure against her chest as I lean into her, squeezing our bodies together.

"The real question is, how do you know about them, Old Man?" She's trying for *innocence*, but it's not working.

It's not working at all.

I drag my hand up her chest until my palm is covering the front of her throat. "I might be a generation older than you, Brat, but I've been single for a long time."

I can feel her pulse jumping under my hold, but she still lifts a brow like she's unaffected. "And?"

"And I watch porn, Kendra," I whisper as new voices float in from the kitchen. "Or, I should say, *I did*." I slide my hand up her stomach until I'm cupping her breast. "Now I have a dirty little secret to fantasize about when I stroke my dick at night."

Kendra moans.

And I step back, releasing my hold on her.

Chapter 35

Kendra

Lust courses through my body as I work to steady myself.

My core is throbbing, and I'm tempted to go to my room to rub one out.

Very tempted.

But as good as a self-made orgasm would feel right now, revenge will feel better.

Chapter 36

Luther

Without looking back, Kendra straightens her shoulders and saunters out of her office.

I reach down and adjust my dick. And I wonder if working her up will turn out to be a wonderful or terrible idea.

Chapter 37

Kendra

My skirt swooshes around my thighs as I walk down the hall, and it's just enough to *sort of* cool me off.

"Oh, this is her." Susan waves me toward the table when I enter the kitchen.

There's no suspicion in her tone, and I have to imagine these new people distracted her because there's no good reason why Luther and I weren't right behind her.

"Hello." I lift a hand to the couple beside Susan.

The man is probably somewhere between mine and Luther's age, and he's handsome as hell. A real tall, dark, and brooding type.

The woman at his side is closer to my age, pretty, with braided hair and a baby strapped to her chest in a green carrier.

"Hi." The woman holds her hand out, and I take it. "I'm Courtney. That's Sterling." She nods toward the hot guy. "And this is Ursa, our little baby bear." She runs a hand over the baby's shockingly thick dark hair.

"Nice to meet you all. I'm Kendra, Joe's kid, obviously." I grin down at the baby. "She's adorable."

Courtney huffs good-naturedly. "She's gonna run the house."

The man, Sterling, drapes an arm over Courtney's shoulders, and for a moment, my heart squeezes.

Then I remember my mission, and I turn to the other two people. Both men.

"Kendra." I hold my hand out to the younger of the two.

The guy, maybe my age, gives me a wide smile as his palm connects with mine. "Fisher. Nice to meet you."

I match his smile. His energy is bright and easy.

Nothing like the serious, overwhelming energy pouring off the man who just stopped at my side.

"Fisher." Luther's voice is so serious and loud that the younger man almost jumps.

"Hey, Rocky."

The second man introduces himself as Simpson. And as we all gather plates of food, I find out they all work together at some lodge near here.

Not my jam, but glad they all seem to love it.

When our group steps out onto the back deck, Dad makes a big commotion of saying hello to everyone. And it's another ten minutes before Dad serves us all brats from the grill, and we find seats around an unlit firepit in the backyard.

Dad added extra folding chairs to accompany the usual wooden chairs that live in a circle around the pit.

Everyone shuffles around. And I make sure to catch Luther's eye as I take the chair next to Fisher.

Chapter 38

Luther

I'm torn between a laugh and a growl when Kendra seats herself next to fucking Fisher.

My humor dies when Susan takes the chair on Kendra's other side.

Not cool, Susan.

I hesitate, trying to decide whether I want to take the chair directly across from Kendra or the one on the other side of Fisher so I can hear what they're saying.

Then Kendra crosses her legs, and I beeline for the seat across from hers.

If she's going to flash anyone with that short skirt, it's going to be me.

Torture.

The last hour has been actual torture.

No offense to Simpson's stories, but I've been staring at

Kendra's bare thighs for a fucking lifetime as she leans against her armrest, talking to a man who is arguably more age appropriate.

I've finished my food.

Finished the beer Sterling gave me.

Squished my napkin into an unrecognizable ball.

I watched Kendra rock a fucking baby in her lap when Courtney went to the bathroom.

Watched Kendra laugh at something Fisher said.

And I'm about ready to call in a bomb threat simply to get her alone.

My phone alerts me to a new text.

Grateful for the distraction, I pull it out of my pocket.

> Baby Doll: Remember that last picture I sent you?

Remember?

I look at that photo every night. Imagining the sounds she'd make as I dragged that thong off her body with my fucking teeth.

I raise my eyes from my phone.

Hers are already on mine.

Another text comes through.

> Baby Doll: That's the only thing I'm wearing under this dress.

My eyes drop to her lap, like I can see through her dress. Like I can see that red scrap of fabric wedged against her slit.

I move my gaze over to Fisher.

Kendra is wearing nothing but a formfitting dress and a thong, and he suddenly feels way too close.

Another text.

> Baby Doll: Do you know if Fisher is single?

Chapter 39

Kendra

It's so hard to keep a straight face.

I'm not interested in Fisher. Maybe if I hadn't already met Luther. But even then...

I watch Luther's jaw clench.

Take in the way his muscles are bunched under his T-shirt.

Picture the way his thick thighs look in those jeans...

No. Even if I hadn't met Luther until today, he still would've stolen all my attention.

My phone vibrates on my lap.

> Papi: Make an excuse to go to the house.
>
> Papi: Alone.
>
> Papi: Now.

My heart rate thrums against my bones.
There are so many people here.
My dad is here.
This party is for me.
I can't disappear.
Not for long.

I uncross my legs and slide forward so I'm sitting on the edge of my chair. "I'm gonna go plug my phone in and grab another drink. Want anything?" I ask Fisher.

I should ask the group as a whole, but I don't want to take the chance that anyone will try to join me.

Fisher says he's good, and before he can offer to help, I stand and slip between our chairs, heading toward the house.

My legs feel shaky, and I have to work to keep my breathing under control.

No one stops me. And Dad is sitting down, talking, his back to me, so I make it to the house without interruption.

I slow as I cross the deck, not sure how quickly Luther will be able to follow.

But as I close my hand around the handle, I watch my reflection in the glass. And I see the man approaching.

Chapter 40

Luther

I stop with my chest inches from her back. "Open the door, Kendra."

I hear her exhale before she slides the door open.

The kitchen is empty.

And when she steps inside, I follow.

I shut the door behind me.

But I don't look back.

I don't do anything to make it look like I'm about to do something bad.

Something so bad. But so fucking good.

"Luther?" she says quietly.

She knows what I want.

She knows.

But the question is where.

I place my hand against the center of her spine.

The bathroom is off limits.

We can't risk coming out together. And this is real life, so I can't hide behind the shower curtain while she walks out first.

Her bedroom...

People might not notice that her door was closed. No one would walk in.

I apply pressure against Kendra's back, and she moves toward the hallway. But then I spot the closed bathroom door.

We could probably hurry past to her room.

I guide Kendra into taking one more step.

But then I hear the toilet flush.

Cutting it too close.

I slide my hand up to the back of Kendra's neck and tighten my hold.

She lets me steer her.

We cut across the living room.

Kendra lengthens her stride.

She doesn't want us to get caught either.

She wants to escape with me.

She fucking *wants me.*

I hear the bathroom door open.

Footsteps sound in the hall.

"Hurry," I whisper.

Kendra sees where we're going. She reaches her hand out.

My pulse is racing.

The person coming down the hall is a moment away from seeing us.

Kendra yanks the door open.

And I follow her into the garage.

I push the door closed behind me. But I don't let it click. I silently leave it resting against the latch. The result of some careless person who came into the garage to grab some beer.

It's dim. The row of windows in the top panel of the garage door lets in just enough of the late afternoon sun to illuminate the fridge a few yards away.

Kendra looks at me over her shoulder.

I expect a remark. Maybe a raised brow.

But her gaze is full of need.

Need for me to touch her.

For me to tell her what to do.

What I want.

I tighten my grip on her neck and turn her again until she's facing the back wall.

She sees my destination.

Three steps later, she's reaching out again, this time opening the door to the cramped laundry room.

The room is tiny. Barely room for both of us.

The washer and dryer are side by side, backed up against the wall that separates the living room from the garage.

I've been in the house when these are going, so I know this wall isn't soundproofed.

"You need to be quiet." I whisper the demand as I shut the door, trapping us in the dark.

In the dark, there's only touch.

Kendra turns to face me, causing my palm to drag around her neck until I'm holding her by the throat.

Hands press against my chest.

Her fingers feel cool through the thin cotton of my shirt.

I grip her waist with my free hand. "Tell me you can be quiet."

"I can be quiet, Daddy," she whispers.

My cock throbs.

It's been a week.

A week since I've heard her call me that.

Another week since I've been inside her.

With my hold on her neck, I tip her head back. "No kissing."

"What? Why?" Her disappointment fans my ego.

"Because," I growl.

I use my hold to turn her so her back is to me and her front is to the dryer.

I slide my hand on her waist around to her stomach. "Because the next time you put your lips on me, you're wrapping them around my dick." I slide my hand lower, cupping her sex through her dress. "And when you put that hot little mouth on my cock, I'm going to fuck it."

She moans, arching into me.

"Dirty little brat." I press my hand up under her chin until she's resting her head back against my shoulder. Then I speak against her ear. "You want that? You want to walk out there with puffy red lips and tear tracks down your cheeks? You want everyone to know what a slutty little Daddy's girl you are?"

I close my teeth over her earlobe. Biting just hard enough to hold her still as I let go of her throat and move my hand down to her cleavage.

Her dress is tight.

But not so tight I can't get my fingers between the material and her tits.

Her breathing spikes.

I lick over the bite mark in her flesh before I release her ear. "The perfect fucking handful."

I palm her breast and spread my fingers, then bring them together until her nipple is pinched between two of my fingers, applying even more pressure with my other palm against her mound.

Kendra arches her ass against me, and there's no hiding the fact that I'm hard.

So damn hard.

"Luther."

I exhale against her skin. "When we fuck in this house, you call me Daddy. Now reach back and take my dick out."

She does as she's told.

And the feeling of her hands fumbling with the button on my jeans has my cock fucking dripping.

While she works, I use my fingers to scrunch up the front hem of her dress. And she pulls my zipper down just as my fingers reach her panties.

Her red thong.

I can't see it. But I don't need to.

Her skirt drapes over my wrist, but now the only thing between my hand and her hot pussy is a thin scrap of lace.

I rub.

The material is already wet. Soaked through.

"Hurry up, Baby." I press my fingers against her clit. "We have to be quick. And you better get my cock inside you before you come."

Her chest is heaving.

I pinch her nipple. And I feel her pussy clench.

Finally, she hooks her fingers around the top band of my boxer briefs and tugs them down, freeing my length.

I pull her panties to the side. She pulls up the back of her dress. And the darkness amplifies the feeling of my bare cock slapping against her uncovered entrance.

I drag my middle finger up her slit. She's so slick.

When my fingertip circles her clit, she slaps her hands down on the top of the dryer.

I rub her clit as I bend my knees. "Reach between your legs and put me in."

"Fuck," she gasps.

I shove my finger into her channel. "Exactly."

Kendra bends forward, and I slide my hand out of the top of her dress.

I don't want to. I want to always have my hands on her tits. But I'm going to need this hand to hold her steady. To hold her body against mine.

Reaching down between her legs, her fingers close around my cock. I shift, helping her line me up with her hole.

And then voices that aren't ours fill the garage.

Kendra freezes.

It's not her dad. Not anyone coming to do laundry. Just a couple people looking for extra drinks.

I push my hips forward.

Kendra's pussy swallows the tip of my dick.

I hear her inhale.

Kendra clenches around me.

I thrust halfway in.

Kendra's cunt is so hot it practically burns me.

I circle my free arm around her waist.

Kendra presses back onto me, and I picture her palms flat on the dryer.

I start to rub her clit again.

Kendra holds her breath.

I curl against her, putting my lips to her ear.

The voices are still in the garage.

The people are still feet away.

"Breathe and relax." I pull almost all the way out. "You can take me. You've done it before."

Her pussy flutters.

I rub circles around her clit.

Her body tightens.

I still my fingers.

Her breaths are quiet but heavy in the dark room.

I flatten my hand, my palm against her clit, my fingers spread around the spot where my cock is notched into her entrance.

Her muscles relax around me.

I shove all the way in.

The heat.

The fucking heat and tightness.

My brain glitches.

I can't hear anything.

Can't see anything.

I can only feel.

I can only feel *her*.

Everywhere.

I pull out.

I thrust forward.

I stop just short of our bodies slapping together.

I'm just aware enough to stay quiet.

To breathe through my open mouth.

I tighten my arm around her waist.

Kendra is vibrating.

Her legs are shaking.

A door slams.

I pause. Blinking in the dark. Swallowing to clear my hearing.

Silence.

We're alone again.

"Hurry up." My fingers are frantic over her bundle of nerves. "Hurry up and come before we get caught." I roll my hips. "Unless you want to get caught with my cock buried in this greedy little pussy." I shove deeper. "Then everyone will know that I'm your Daddy now."

She whimpers.

I pull back, then slam forward.

She tenses.

I rock my hips against her ass.

She lets out a strangled sound.

I squeeze her body to mine.

And when my fingers slip over her clit again, Kendra breaks.

She clenches her thighs together.

She bends forward.

She lets out a soft whine as she pulses around me.

As she comes on my cock.

I close my eyes.

I throw my head back.

And I explode.

My cock pulses over and over, and I empty my balls inside my best friend's daughter.

Chapter 41

Kendra

My body trembles as Luther pumps me full of his release.

I wasn't sure anything could top our first time.

But god. Fucking. Damn. This man gets hotter by the second.

My core flutters around him.

If having a Daddy kink is wrong, I will never be right.

Luther's fingers brush over my clit once more, and my pussy clenches.

He grunts, shoving his hips forward, rocking against me.

Then he pulls his hand free from my heat and wraps his arms around me, pulling my body against his in a bear hug, with his dick still buried inside me.

I blink into the darkness.

And I grin.

He must hear something in my breathing because he holds me tighter, dropping his chin to my shoulder. "You okay?"

"Okay?" A puff of laughter leaves my lips. "I think you just fucked my soul into another dimension. In a garage laundry room."

I can feel him shake his head. "Possibly not the most romantic location."

"Romance is overrated."

Luther inhales, like he might argue, but I shut him up by clenching my core around him again.

His exhale becomes a hiss. "You better keep clenching, Brat. Or you're gonna have to walk through the house with my cum dripping down your legs."

"What—"

Luther loosens his hold on me and steps back, his cock slipping free.

It makes sense then. And I have to keep clenching, like he said, because I can already feel the mess of us trying to escape.

"Luther." I try to keep the humor out of my tone as I attempt to scold him.

Lips press against my bare shoulder.

I can't with this man.

As I swoon, my body relaxes. Which is a mistake, because then I have to clench even harder.

"Hold your hand out." Luther's quiet voice caresses my skin, and I struggle to keep my damn muscles flexed.

"Why?"

"Baby, just do as you're told."

Without any light, I don't have to pretend I don't want him bossing me around.

Without any light, I can bite my lip and let my lids lower without anyone seeing.

Without any light, I pull my palm off the dryer and hold it up.

Luther's body presses against my back.

He places his hand on my shoulder, then slides it down the length of my arm, leaving tingles in his wake, until his hand is gripping my wrist.

Holding my hand still, he reaches around from the other side and sets something in my palm.

I close my fingers around the soft fabric.

"It's a clean kerchief." He releases my wrist.

Not wasting time, I tug my skirt up, and, like a lady, I pull my thong to the side and use Luther's *clean kerchief* to catch the evidence of our rendezvous.

When I finish and straighten, I feel Luther's arm against mine. "I'll take that."

I ball the fabric in my fist. "No, you will not. This is mine now."

He hums. "Have it your way."

I tuck the dirty cloth into my dress pocket. "So, what's the plan now?" I keep my voice to a whisper.

"I'll open the door, then we hurry to the fridge and grab an armful of drinks. If anyone walks in, they won't think twice."

Not having a better plan, I turn toward the door.

At my side, I cross my fingers, hoping we don't run into anybody specifically looking for us. Because we were relatively quick just now, but we still disappeared for a questionable amount of time.

"Ready?" Luther asks.

I nod. "Ready."

A moment of silence passes before Luther pulls the door open, and I step past him into the garage that now feels brightly lit.

It's blissfully empty and remains that way while we cross in front of my dad's truck to the fridge.

There's a cooler out back with beers and sodas, but we grab a pair of bottles with each hand.

While Luther shuts the fridge door, I lift the chilled bottles and press them to my cheeks.

"Warm?" Luther smirks at me.

"A touch." I lower them so the glass is against my neck.

"Just a touch?" He takes a step toward me. "Maybe I need to try harder next time."

I shuffle back and to the side. "Hands to yourself, Old Man."

He lunges, and I let out a shriek as I rush away from him.

The laugh behind me is rich and so full of playfulness it makes my racing heart squeeze.

I cannot fall for this man.
We're just having fun.

I can feel Luther right behind me as I reach the door, and my pulse soars from his chase.

I pull in a breath to call for a truce when the door in front of me swings open.

The movement is so sudden it has me lurching back a step as I let out a yelp.

I slam back into Luther's chest, but he's an immovable object, so the collision stops me from falling.

"Sorry," the man—one of our neighbors—laughs as he holds his hands up. "Just looking for some beer."

Luther lifts his bottle-filled hands on either side of me. "How many you want?"

The neighbor's smile is wide, hinting that he's had a few. "Two, please."

Luther's arm extends over my shoulder, and neighbor guy takes the offered bottles.

"Much obliged." He nods, then turns back into the house, showing zero suspicion over the fact I'm still slumped against Luther's chest.

I look over my shoulder at Luther, brows raised.

He uses his newly empty hand to grab a pair of bottles out of mine. "Never question good luck, Baby Doll."

I nod. "Won't argue." Then I reach forward and catch the door before it can swing shut.

Back inside, I set the beers I'm still holding on the counter and scurry off to the bathroom.

When I'm done, and no one is visible in the hall, I hurry to my room and trade my thong for a new pair of ass-covering undies.

Feeling a little more put together, I roll out my shoulders and head back to the kitchen.

Luther's eyes catch mine when I step into the room, and he lifts a paper plate toward me. "Dessert?"

Rolling my lips together, I nod.

The plate has a slice of cake, a brownie, and two chocolate chip cookies.

It's so much.

Too much.

And on the counter beside him is a second plate filled with the same exact items.

"You sure that's enough?" My voice is quieter than I intended, trying to make a joke, but it comes out shy.

"I recently worked up an appetite." He winks at me.

Winks.

And my gluttonous pussy throbs.

If you're going to fuck me, then feed me, you might as well wife me.

I take the plate from Luther's hand.

He picks up a pair of beers. "You want one of these or something else?"

At his question, I notice the scent of coffee in the air.

Looking over, I see that someone started a pot. "I think I'll do coffee, actually." Balancing my plate of dessert in one hand, I open the cupboard and grab a mug. "Do you want one?"

Luther shakes his head as I pour my coffee. "If I have caffeine this late, I'll be up all night."

Shaking off the shyness from a moment ago, I snort. "Sometimes I forget how old you are, then you go and say something like that."

Luther narrows his eyes, and I lift my mug in a mock cheer.

We're still looking at each other when the back door opens.

"My favorites!" Dad's voice booms through the kitchen.

I startle so badly coffee sloshes onto my fingers.

I hiss. "Fuck."

Before I can do more than curse, Luther is taking the mug and plate out of my hands, somehow having already put his own things down.

"Shit, sorry, Kenny." Dad rushes over.

"I'm fine. It was just a little hot." It was more than a little hot, but at least I know the coffee is fresh.

"Here." Luther steps to the sink and turns the faucet on.

"I'm fine."

"Kendra, come here." His voice is stern, and it sends heat rolling through me that has nothing to do with burning my hand.

Dad is pulling an absurd number of paper towels off the roll, not paying attention to the way Luther is bossing me around.

I follow him and stick my hand under the cold running water. "Happy?"

Luther ignores my attitude, gripping my wrist and rotating my hand under the stream.

"How's it look?" Dad sounds a bit less drunk than he did a moment ago, but he still doesn't say anything about his best friend touching me.

"A little pink, but not bad," Luther answers for me.

I sigh. "I'm fine."

Luther does that humming sound I love so much, then holds my wrist for another few seconds before he turns the water off.

"Thank you." I catch his eyes as I say it.

Dad shoves eight thousand paper towels into my hands. "You're welcome."

Luther clears his throat to cover what sounds like a laugh.

Taking the towels, I rip one off, then fold the rest and set them on the counter.

"Are you two mother hens done?" I ask, using the same single towel to wipe off the sides and bottom of my coffee mug.

They both grunt in reply.

I roll my eyes.

Dad reaches past Luther and grabs the brownie off his plate.

Luther snatches it out of Dad's hand before he can put it in his mouth. "Get your own."

Dad huffs. "Sharing is caring."

"I like you, but not a brownie amount."

Dad slaps his hand to his chest with a gasp.

Luther hands one of the unclaimed beers to my dad as a consolation prize. "You cool with me crashing on your couch tonight?"

Brownie slight forgotten, Dad opens the beer and slips the cap into his pocket with a shrug. "It's your back."

Wait, what?

Luther is staying over?

I eye the man. He's not drunk. Not even kind of. There's no reason at all he can't drive himself home.

Luther catches me looking and lifts his beer to his lips, taking a sip.

This man is drinking simply for the excuse to stay.

I slide my gaze over to the couch, and my mind conjures up the image of Luther sprawled there. On his back. One arm behind his head. One foot extended over the armrest, the other leg hanging off the couch, foot on the ground, because he doesn't fit.

I bet he'd be shirtless, his jeans open but not off.

I look away.

"If you two will excuse me, I'm going to go enjoy my dessert outside." I pick up the plate Luther put together for me.

"I'll join you," Luther says, like that wasn't the plan all along.

Dad says something about having to pee, and we leave him inside as we head out.

My feet hit the grass before I see that the chairs we had been sitting in are now occupied by new bodies.

"What a shame," Luther says with mock sadness. "Guess you can't sit by your new boyfriend anymore."

I make a contemplative sound. "Think he'd let me sit in his lap?"

"You're never going to find out." The words rumble out of Luther.

I smile to myself.

The late afternoon sun is lowering behind the tall pines surrounding the yard. Some people have left, others seem to be settled in.

Luther steps up beside me. "Who do you want to sit by?"

I scan the groups before looking up at the man who just fucked me senseless, bent over a dryer. The same man who just cared for my burned fingers while holding my wrist so incredibly gently. And I give him my honest answer. "Just you."

Chapter 42

Luther

Two words.

Seven letters.

And they hit me like lightning strikes.

Electricity and a bit of fear course through my body.

I pull in a breath, my chest expanding with the charged air.

"Alright, Baby." My words are quiet. Gruff. "Just us." I swallow. "Wait here."

Turning around, I leave my dessert and beer on the deck railing, then cut through the house into the garage.

One minute later, I'm back outside.

Kendra is where I left her, sipping her coffee and holding her plate of sweets in front of her.

She takes in the item tucked under my arm as I grab my food.

"We're sharing one chair?"

"You said you wanted to sit on someone's lap." I start walking.

A large oak tree stands at the edge of the yard, the wide green leaves creating the perfect spot of additional shade. It's close enough that it won't look like we're trying to be separate, but far enough that we won't be overheard.

My girl follows me across the lawn, and with my back to everyone, I let myself smile.

I can't believe we just had sex.
Here.
Behind an unlocked door.
With all these people nearby.

There's a tightness in my stomach. My conscience reminding me that this is messed up. That I shouldn't be fucking my friend's daughter, who is twenty-four years younger than me.

I shouldn't.

I shouldn't stay the night.

I should walk away now. Before it's too late.

Before feelings get involved.

Just you.

That tightness travels up to my throat. And my inner voice tells me it's too late.

Because I already have feelings for Kendra.

Chapter 43

Kendra

My cheeks still feel warm from telling Luther I wanted to sit with just him. But as I watch him open what is essentially a two-person camping chair, I can't stop this feeling of levity.

The frame folds out into two connected chairs. An armrest on either side with built-in cupholders, but there's no center armrest.

We really are sharing one chair.

Luther gives it a shake, making sure it's on flat land, then he gestures for me to sit first.

I do, taking the left side so Luther will be on my right when he sits.

It's a typical camping canvas chair. Not amazing but comfortable enough.

My mug doesn't fit in the cupholder, but holding the handle, I rest the bottom on the armrest while I set my plate on my lap.

Luther joins me, and the frame gives a creak.

Luther is a big guy. Tall and broad and built. And I'm not a small woman.

Sure, next to Luther, I feel dainty, but I've never been light. And I don't want to be a part of a chair collapse.

Not seeming to care, the large man beside me relaxes into the seat, lifting the leg closest to me and crossing his ankle over his opposite knee.

His thigh is practically resting on top of mine, and I have to adjust my plate so he doesn't smoosh my things.

I look up at Luther. "You sure this is meant for two adults?"

He nods. "I've sat in this with Joe. It's solid."

"Sounds romantic." I wiggle my brows.

Luther snorts. "It wasn't. The man thought he'd save space on packing by getting this thing." He puts his beer bottle into the cupholder on his armrest, then moves his plate over to his right hand, leaving the hand closest to me empty. "We were checking out a new campsite that was only accessible by four-wheelers, so we had to pack the minimum. But if that moron had told me he was bringing a love seat, I would've brought my own damn chair."

"So it was just the two of you, in the woods, sitting shoulder to shoulder?" I can't stop my laugh.

"Pretty much." Luther shakes his head before lifting a cookie to his mouth and biting off half of it.

My chuckles die as I break off a piece of my cookie and examine it. "We shouldn't keep doing this."

There's a long pause where I think Luther isn't going to answer. But after another moment, he heaves out a breath. "We probably shouldn't."

Staying silent, I break off another piece of cookie, piling it next to the first.

"But there are two problems with that." Luther's tone is gentle.

I tip my head to meet his eyes. "Yeah?"

"Yeah." He dips his chin. "First, I don't always do what I should."

Butterflies flap their wings inside my ribs.

We both know this is a bad idea.

The worst.

But neither of us wants to stop.

And he's admitting it.

"And the second?" I whisper, thinking about him with his hands on me. Remembering the feel of him inside me. Replaying the words he whispered to me in the dark.

"The second..." He looks down as he shifts.

I look down.

And it takes me a second.

Just a second to see it.

Luther put his brownie on my plate.

I snap my gaze back up to meet his.

"The second problem is..." He lifts a shoulder. "I like you a brownie amount."

Chapter 44

Luther

"Joe still doesn't know?"

Kendra shakes her head, grinning up at me. "Nope. My mom thought I was here. He thought I was there. Best lie I ever pulled off."

The expression on her face is... joy. And dammit, I want to kiss her, want to taste her smile.

I lean toward her.

Kendra nudges my side with her elbow, widening her eyes at me. "Behave yourself."

I halt my movement, but I don't back away. "Says the girl who secretly spent her eighteenth birthday in Mexico."

She shushes me. "If you out me for this, I'll never forgive you."

Her tone holds zero threat, but I still place my hand over my heart. "Joe won't learn it from me."

"Promise?"

"I always keep my promises."

Kendra hums. "I'm holding you to that."

I dip my head. "I have my own request."

She narrows her eyes. "Which is?"

"I want to be there when you tell him about Cabo."

Kendra snickers.

It's the cutest sound.

Cutest sound?

I'm seriously losing it over this girl.

But knowing I'm falling doesn't do anything to lessen my momentum.

Knowing I'm fucked doesn't slow my drop.

"WHAT ARE YOU TWO LAUGHING ABOUT?" JOE STOPS IN front of us, blinking a few times before lifting a hand and pointing his finger. "Hey! You said that chair was dumb."

Joe isn't shit faced. He's what I would call a happy day drunk, even if it's pushing nighttime.

"The chair *was* dumb." I argue. "But it's fine if I don't have to share it with your hairy ass."

"You know that I don't have—" Joe's eyes cut to Kendra, and he purses his lips. "Ya know what? I'm not going to respond to that."

"Yeah. Appreciate that." Kendra's expression is amused disgust.

Our desserts are gone. Our drinks are gone. And I believe the last of the guests just left.

"That everyone?" I ask Joe.

"Yeah," he yawns.

Kendra uncrosses her legs and sits forward in our chair. "Thanks for putting this all together."

"It was fun, wasn't it?" Joe yawns again.

While he rubs his eyes, Kendra places her palm on my thigh, then she presses into me as she pushes against my leg to stand.

Her hand leaves me just as Joe drops his. But that second of connection stays seared into my jeans.

"Go to bed. I'll put the rest of the food away." Kendra smooths down the front of her dress.

That damn dress.

I stand and collapse the chair. Holding it one-handed, I follow them to the house.

By the time I put the chair in the garage—only glancing at the laundry room a thousand times—I step back into the house and hear Kendra convince Joe to go to bed.

"Fine, fine. Good night." Joe turns to me. "You remember where the couch stuff is?"

I nod.

Then Joe heads to his room, and it's just us.

Just me and Kendra.

Chapter 45

Kendra

We work together in silence. Putting the leftovers into containers, washing the coffee pot, wiping down the counters.

There's a tension between us.

And not just the sexual tension that has been there since we first locked eyes across the bar.

The feeling right now is more than that. It's different.

It's the need to touch.

I *have to* touch Luther.

And I'm not a toucher.

I don't mind hugs. Handshakes are fine. But I've never been a cuddler.

The thought of leaning against someone never appealed to me.

But Luther... All I want to do is curl up on the couch with him. Sit with him. Be with him.

Okay, yes, I want to have lots and lots of filthy, dirty sex with him too. But... he steadies me.

He can be a bit of a freak. But still, I feel grounded around him.

Grounded.

Sparks light in my belly as I think about him grounding me in another way.

Heat fills my cheeks.

I have a feeling I'd enjoy any punishment Luther would dole out.

"That's everything." Luther starts the dishwasher, then turns to face me.

I pull my lower lip into my mouth, my teeth pressing into the skin.

There are so many things I want to do right now.

But instead of doing any of them, I tell Luther good night, then I turn and walk away.

I TURN OFF THE LIGHT AND OPEN THE BATHROOM DOOR with a click.

Dressed in pajama shorts and a loose tank top, I step into the unlit hall.

The house is quiet.

Dark.

But I still see the man as he peels away from the wall.

His large shape is overwhelming in the dark.

My heart rate jumps.

But not from fear. From expectation.

Luther reaches out, his hand cupping the side of my neck. "*This* is good night, Kendra."

Holding me still, using his thumb under my chin to keep my head tilted back, Luther kisses me.

His lips press against mine.

Firmly.

Electricity zips through my body as I reach for him.

And when my palms land on his chest, his mouth opens.

Luther slides his tongue against the seam of my lips, and I slide my hands to his sides... To his back.

He groans, and I part my lips for him.

His fingers flex against my neck, and he glides his other hand over my shoulder to the center of my back, pulling me in close.

It's my turn to groan as I push up on my toes, chasing to deepen the kiss. Slipping my tongue past his lips.

My hands turn into claws against his back.

His hand slides down my back, like he's going to grip my ass.

I curl my hands in the fabric of his shirt and push him away.

Luther loosens his hold on me, letting me put a few inches of space between our bodies, as he lowers his forehead to mine.

"I don't want to stop," I whisper in the dark.

His breaths come out heavy, his body affected just as much as mine is. "I know, Baby."

We both want more.

"Go to bed." Luther's words puff against my lips, then he steps back.

Chapter 46

Luther

I've given her twenty minutes.

Given myself twenty minutes to calm down. To get my body under control.

With a pillow and rumpled blanket on the couch, I leave the bathroom light on but shut the door.

If Joe comes out to the kitchen for anything in the middle of the night and sees the couch empty, it will look like I got up to use the bathroom, nothing more.

Decoy set, I open Kendra's bedroom door.

The lights are off, but she left her curtains open, allowing moonlight to spill into the room.

Blankets rustle. "Luther?"

"Yeah, Baby."

I close the door and undo my jeans, letting them drop to the floor.

I pause with my hands on the hem of my shirt, wondering if I should leave it on. But if Joe catches me sleeping in bed with his daughter, without pants on, I hardly think the status of my shirt will make a difference.

I pull my shirt off.

"What are you doing?" Kendra rolls to face me.

"Just sleeping."

Tugging down the blanket, I climb into Kendra's bed.

Once I'm on my back, I hold out the arm closest to her.

Kendra doesn't need me to ask. She moves into her spot—head on my shoulder, leg thrown over my thigh—and I hug her to my side.

A chilly hand lands on my bare stomach, and I tense.

She starts to slide it off, but I drop my free hand on top of hers and hold it still. "Keep your ice fingers in one spot."

Kendra snickers.

I hold her tighter.

"Thanks for keeping me company today." Her words are quiet as they skitter across my chest. "Everyone was super nice, but it was a bit overwhelming."

I try to be smooth as I turn my head so I can press my nose to her hair.

This girl.

She makes me feel needed in a way I've never experienced.

But what's even better than feeling needed is feeling wanted. And she makes me feel that too.

I breathe against her. "You don't have to thank me."

Her warmed fingers slide over my stomach until her arm is draped across my waist. "I do. Today was really fun."

"It was." I agree.

Her exhale tickles my chest hair. "I was planning to go, ya know?"

Kendra's body is relaxing against mine, her words getting harder to hear.

She's falling asleep.

"Planning to go where? The party?" I rub my thumb against her arm.

"Back to the Inn."

My breath catches.

Back to the Inn.

She was going to come back to me.

"When?" I whisper.

"That morning. With the pancakes." I feel her yawn.

There's a part of me that hadn't let go of the stress I felt, thinking I'd never see her again.

A part of me still feels like it's stuck in a spiral of panic. Like these last couple weeks might turn out to be a dream. That I'll wake up, and I'll never find the Kendra Baby I met in the bar.

But she's here.

Curled against me.

Once again ready to fall asleep in my arms.

Once again rocking my world.

Even if her dad hadn't turned out to be my best friend, she still would've come back to me.

I allow my anxiety to unravel its hold on me.

My thumb traces another circle.

"I was looking into private investigators," I admit.

I was ready to hire one. I just needed to convince myself it wasn't creepy to go through the credit card records for her motel room to find her full name.

I would've done it. Probably would've done it that same weekend.

"We'd have found each other," I tell her. Meaning it.

Her breathing is getting slower. "What if it ends badly?"

My throat feels tight as I swallow. "It won't."

"Promise?" Kendra's whisper slides into my heart.

"I promise, Baby Doll." I press my lips to her hair. "Go to sleep."

Kendra relaxes into me.

And as I follow her into dreamland, I hope I told her the truth.

Chapter 47

Kendra

When I wake up alone, I stare at my nightstand. And the brownie sitting on the surface.

Chapter 48

Kendra

Papi: I think I did something wrong.

I CRINGE AT A PHOTO OF WHAT I THINK ARE SUPPOSED to be pancakes.

Me: That's a crime against food.

Papi: I think my pan was too hot.

Me: What are the black parts?

Papi: Bananas.

Me: Oh dear.

Papi: Guess I'll need you to teach me. In person.

Papi: Soon.

> Papi: How's your day going, Baby?

I SLUMP BACK IN MY CHAIR, EMAIL FORGOTTEN.
It's the simplest text. But it feels intimate. Relationship-y.

> Me: It's pretty good. Low-key. You?

> Papi: Good day. Just got a little better.

🦊

> Me: Do you go to the Inn every night?

> Papi: You better not be going tonight.

I NARROW MY EYES AT MY PHONE.

> Me: Why not?

I mean, I know we're keeping this thing between us on the down-low. But still.

> Papi: Because I'm not there.

> Papi: And if I miss a chance to see you, I'm going to be pissed.

> Papi: And if anyone hits on you, you need to tell me. I'll ban them.

His meathead attitude should annoy me, but it doesn't feel overbearing. It feels cute.

I don't know where he is if he's not at the Inn, but riling him up more seems appropriate.

> Me: Don't worry, Daddy. I'm not coming without you.

I slap a hand over my mouth.
I can't believe I sent that.

> Papi: Dammit, Doll. I'm in public.

I laugh.

> Me: Sorry.

> Papi: You're not sorry.

> Me: I'm not sorry.

> Papi: So... you're not going to the Inn?

> Me: Not if you're not there. Dad is out with someone tonight, so I was wondering if you were working or...?

> Papi: Who's he out with?

> Me: Don't know. Some friend.

> Papi: Of course that asshole would finally leave the house when I'm out of town.

I bite my lip.
He left town? For how long?

> Me: Oh? Go somewhere fun?

> Papi: Denver. Ashley's college graduation ceremony starts in a few minutes, and afterward, we're going out to dinner. So I got a hotel for the night.

Seriously though, I can't with this man. He's such a good dad, and that makes him even hotter.

Last weekend, when we were sitting in that ridiculous two-person chair, he told me all about Ashley.

About taking her to soccer games when she was little. The at-home hair dye mishaps. The time she went to prom, and how he waited for her date outside, in the front yard, chopping wood with an axe.

And he told me about Ashley starting college courses when she was twenty-two, majoring in computer sciences. How he didn't rush her into starting straight out of high school. Because how can we expect eighteen-year-olds to know what career they want? Because how could they possibly know that when they don't even know themselves?

The way I fucking swooned.

Responsibility is sexy.

> Me: Sounds like a fun time.
>
> Me: She'll love having you there.

> Papi: You home?

MY PULSE SKIPS.

> Me: Yes.

> Papi: I'll be there in ten.

I look down at myself.

Working from home is great. But it's—I look at the clock—almost noon. And I'm still in my pajamas.

Usually I'm more put together than this, but I stayed up way

too late last night, lying in bed thinking about Luther.
 Fantasizing about him.
 Worrying about how much I like him.
 And now I'm paying the price.
 Pushing back from my desk, I get to my feet and run to my room.

Chapter 49

Luther

I couldn't even guess how many times I've driven here and parked in this spot at the edge of the driveway. But today it's different.

Because Kendra is here.

And Joe isn't.

After turning off my truck, I grab the two to-go containers off my passenger seat and shove open my door.

I get that I can't take Kendra out on a date. Not anywhere nearby, at least. So we'll have lunch here.

And if I'm lucky, she'll let me have her for dessert.

As I slam my truck door shut behind me, the front door opens. And Kendra steps out.

She's in jean shorts that show off every inch of her soft thighs.

Soft, delicious thighs.

Maybe after lunch, before Joe comes home, we can watch TV. Kendra can sit at one end of the couch, and I can lie across the couch with my head pillowed in her lap.

I trail my gaze up her body, taking in the silky blue tank top and the hint of a lacy white bra beneath.

I take a step toward her.

She takes a step toward me.

The breeze blows her loose hair around her shoulders.

I slide my tongue out to wet my lips.

And we both stop when we hear tires on gravel.

Shit.

Turning away from my beauty queen, I watch as Joe's truck appears in the driveway.

So much for lap pillows.

Fucker.

I force my shoulders to relax as I remind myself that Joe's my friend. Even if he does feel like a cockblocking enemy at the moment.

Kendra and I both stay where we are, waiting, while Joe pulls his truck into the garage—signaling that he plans to be home for the rest of the day. Which is bullshit because I specifically remember him telling me that he had meetings all day with suppliers. Meetings at the shop, not at fucking home.

"Hey." He lifts a hand as he steps out into the driveway, stopping between Kendra and me. "What's going on? Did I forget about something?"

He's smiling. Head nowhere near the gutter.

I work to keep a normal smile on my face. "Just dropping off some lunch." I lift the containers holding the pair of burgers I brought from the Inn.

"Oh, nice." He eyes my hands. "You didn't bring one for yourself?" Joe asks, sounding surprised.

Yeah, I'm surprised too, motherfucker. One of these was supposed to be mine.

"Nah, I had one earlier." I lie, stomach on the verge of growling. "Just a thank-you for feeding me last weekend."

Joe closes the distance between us, taking the food from my hands.

He presses his nose to the boxes and inhales. "Smells damn good. Compliments to Diego." Joe shimmies his shoulders. "My lucky day. You must've forgotten, but I was supposed to be stuck in meetings all damn day."

I furrow my brows, pretending to think. "Oh, right."

"Rescheduled for tomorrow." Joe shrugs, like he hasn't ruined my life.

Glancing over, I see Kendra fighting a smile.

She thinks this is funny.

I really need to figure out a punishment for her.

"I can split mine if you'd like," Kendra offers, letting me hear her voice for the first time today.

"I'm not going to take your food. I'm trying to feed you. Guys." I awkwardly tack on the last word.

"No, she's right." Joe gestures toward the house. "You can have a third of each of ours. Then it'll be even."

"How are you gonna cut a burger into thirds?" I ask to be annoying. Because no matter what I just said, I'd do just about anything to stay. Especially since everyone is forgetting that I claimed to have already eaten.

Joe tips his head as he walks to the front steps. "Just gotta measure a hundred-and-twenty-degree angle from the center of the bun."

"You bustin' out a carpenter's square for this?" I joke.

Joe pauses. "That's not a bad idea. I have one in the garage." He starts to turn around.

"You're not putting some dusty-ass tool on my burger." Kendra stops him. "We'll eyeball it."

"Fine, fine," Joe sighs as he climbs the front steps. "But don't come crying to me when you end up with the smallest two-thirds."

Chapter 50

Kendra

Turning off my bedroom light, I crawl into bed.
Settled on my back, I grab my phone off my nightstand.

> Me: Thanks again for lunch today. It was a nice surprise.

It really was. Even if it didn't go as he'd planned.

> Papi: Your dad sucks.

A loud laugh pops out of my chest.
I'm still grinning when my phone notifies me of a video call.
I only hesitate a moment before answering.
With the lights off, my image is a black rectangle.
But Luther...
Mounted to the wall behind him is a beautiful piece of wood, with a bark-covered live edge along the top. It's stunning. And it looks like a headboard.
Which means he's sitting in bed.
Shirtless.

With fucking glasses on.

I can't with this man.

I hang up.

My phone rings again.

I let him hear my groan while I accept the call.

"Did you hang up on me?"

"Yes," I tell him. "Because I can't with you."

He narrows his eyes. Behind his *glasses*. "I'm literally just sitting here."

"Exactly."

"I can't see you. Turn a light on."

"No." I answer like the brat he accuses me of being.

"Baby, I might be down to my tighty-whities, but if you deny me this, I will get in my truck, drive over there, and break in."

"Break in?" I have a lot to learn about Luther Rockford, but I can't picture him busting a window on his bestie's house.

He lifts his chin. "Fine, I'd use my spare key. But same thing."

Heat that I've come to associate with Luther's nearness swirls in my belly.

Knowing he has a key to the house.

Knowing he could just walk in at any moment...

"Turn a light on, Kendra." His voice is gruffer. More serious.

I sigh loud enough for him to hear it, then shuffle around until I'm also sitting up against my headboard. Mine is a classic shaker style, matching my dressers and made by my dad.

I hold the phone out, hoping it's at a flattering angle, while I reach over and turn on my bedside lamp.

It's not a bright light, and I'm still mostly in shadows, but it's enough.

"There's my pretty girl."

His words are a purr, and they settle over my skin like a fuzzy blanket.

He's not the first man to call me pretty, but his compliments feel so much more genuine than anything I've heard before. It doesn't feel like he's saying them to get laid. I feel like he's saying them because he can't stop himself.

"How was your evening?" His question is soft.

I blink, bringing myself back to the moment. "It was nice. Read a book on the deck with a glass of wine."

"Sounds relaxing."

I bite my cheek as I look at him.

His shoulders are broad and rounded with muscle. His mostly white beard and graying hair do nothing to diminish his appeal.

And his chest hair...

Also graying, in the absolute best way.

I'm seriously tempted to take a screenshot of him like this. I'd save it to my favorites so whenever I was feeling down or bored, I could pull it up. Because no matter how long this thing between us lasts, right now, at this point in time, this man, this specimen of masculinity, is mine.

Just mine.

I swallow.

And remind myself he's more than a hot body.

He's a goofball.

"Are you really wearing tighty-whities?" I ask, causing the side of his mouth to pull up.

"I'll show you mine if you show me yours."

I press my lips together. *Goofball.*

"Fine." I agree. "But I'm not getting up to turn more lights on."

I didn't get dressed for bed thinking I'd see Luther tonight. But it just so happens that I am wearing the skimpiest pajamas I own.

My shorts are *short*. And the ribbed fabric is formfitting, hugging my hips and ass. It's technically full coverage, but the thin fabric hides nothing.

And the top... Well, the top is more of a bralette than an actual shirt.

It's not modest.

And it's not padded. Meaning my nipples are *right there*, saying hello with a perky salute.

There's a matching cardigan that makes the top half family friendly, but I'd still have to pull sweatpants on over these shorts before I wore them around anyone.

Anyone other than Luther.

Using my free hand, I push the blankets off my lap.

Usually, I'd be self-conscious of showing so much of myself. But as the thought flitters into my mind, Luther pulls the phone closer to his face. A reminder that he likes everything about my body.

Slowly, I tilt my phone.

Inch by inch, I show him more.

My cleavage.

My tits.

And I revel in the sound he makes, knowing he can see through my *shirt*. And knowing he likes it.

I keep my legs pressed together but lift my knees, pressing my feet into the mattress. And then I tilt the phone farther. So Luther can see.

He sucks in a breath.

And I know he can see it. The outline of my...

The proof I'm not wearing anything under my shorts.

I let the view linger.

And even through the phone, even though he doesn't say anything, my body reacts to his gaze.

Heat pools between my thighs.

I pull in a deep breath.

Then I tilt the phone back up, showing my flushed face.

Luther closes his eyes and tips his head back, his skull thudding against the beautiful headboard.

"You okay, Old Man?" I sort of laugh. Sort of whisper.

"I should've gone first," he groans.

"Why's that?" I tease, dying to see for myself.

Luther's eyes open, catching mine through the screen. "You know exactly what you do to me, Doll."

My lips part, ready to reply, but then my throat dries up because Luther is tilting his phone.

The lights in his room are on, illuminating every part of him.

The hand not holding his phone settles on his chest, between his pecs.

And what wonderful pecs they are.

I've laid my head there twice, and both times, I fell asleep within moments.

His hand, and my view, move lower. To his abs.

Freaking *abs*.

Lower still. To that trail of hair.

And whoever named it was right. *It does cause me happiness.*

Lower.

My breath hitches.

They aren't white undies like Luther claimed. They're gray boxer briefs.

And there's something inside them trying to get out.

Luther palms his cock through the cotton. Squeezing.

I feel the flex of his fingers in my core.

And when I notice the dark spot, the wet spot, where the tip of his dick is, I think I whimper.

"You can't make those sounds." Luther grunts as he rubs his palm down his dick.

"You can't possibly expect me to see you like this and stay quiet." There's no point in playing it cool.

"Kendra—"

"Show me." I reach up and palm my breast, angling the phone so Luther can see.

Luther's abs flex. "Ask nicely."

"Please," I beg quietly. "Please, Daddy. Show me your cock."

I swear my phone rattles with Luther's growl.

His hand releases his length, then slips under the band of his boxer briefs.

My breaths are coming out as pants as I watch him grip his dick, skin on skin this time.

The cotton blocks my view, but with the next stroke, the head of his dick peeks out from the top of his waistband.

My lips part.

His fist moves under the fabric.

I pinch my nipple.

Then Luther curses. And not the sexy kind.

His hand pulls free of his underwear.

"What are you doing?" I practically gasp at his audacity.

"Sorry." He lifts his hand to his phone. "Let me send this to voicemail."

"Who's calling?" I glance at the time.

It's just after ten. Not that late. But late enough that no one should be calling my man.

"My mother." Luther sounds so disgusted; I have to laugh.

I also have to let go of my boob. "Is it an emergency? Or does she always call this late?"

He shakes his head. "Not an emergency. Now, where were—" Luther drops his head back again. "God dammit. Hold on, now my sister is calling."

While he rejects the second call, I lean over and reach into the top drawer of my nightstand.

"Sorry, these impatient fools are asking questions about next weekend," Luther grumbles as he types out a text.

"What's next weekend."

"Ashley's college graduation party. It's not until next Saturday, and they have all the details on their fucking invite. They're just too lazy to look. Not to mention, I'm usually asleep by now, so why they're even trying to call this late, I have no idea." He shakes his head, meeting my eyes again when he's done typing. "Tell me you'll come."

I know he's asking me as *me*, his Kendra.

I also know I'll be there as Joe's kid. But it doesn't matter, I'll be there.

"I'll come," I tell him. "Go deal with your family. And don't worry about me. I'll come tonight too." Grinning, I lift my hot pink vibrator into view. "Night, Luther."

His mouth opens.

I hang up the call.

Chapter 51

Kendra

At five to noon, I step out onto the front patio.

Luther texted me this morning, telling me to be ready to go at noon. He didn't say where or for what, but if he steps foot inside this house, we won't be going anywhere. We will only be going to my bedroom. And if I get Luther into bed, there's a good chance we'll still be there at the end of the day when my dad comes home.

Which would be bad.

Not even a minute later, I hear his tires on the driveway.

I start down the stairs and walk up to his passenger door as he slows to a stop in front of the house.

Through the window, I can see him reach for his seat belt like he's going to get out to open the door for me, but I grab the handle before he can do any of that.

"You should've waited for me," he says as soon as my door is open, his eyes jumping all over me, taking in my torn jeans and light blue tank top.

I climb into the truck. "I could've waited." I don't sit on the seat—I kneel on it. Leaning over the console, I place my hands on his shoulders. "But then I wouldn't be doing this."

Luther doesn't wait for me to reach him. He grips my waist and leans into me, pressing his mouth to mine.

His lips are warm.
And god, I missed him.
I wrap my arms around his neck.
He glides his hands up my sides until his thumbs press against the underside of my breasts.
We breathe each other in.
And it feels like it does every time.
It feels like the first time.
Feels like we've been doing this for years.
Like the best thing ever.
It feels like it will hurt when it's over.
"What if it ends badly?"
"It won't."
"Promise?"
"I promise, Baby Doll."

Chapter 52

Luther

Kendra sighs against my lips as she pulls her mouth away from mine.

"Hi, Baby Doll."

"Hi, Luther."

I love the way she says my name.

"You look nice." I run a hand down her back.

It's been a long time since I've thought about what my favorite color is. But if someone were to ask me now, my answer would be blue. Any shade. Or maybe periwinkle, since she's still wearing it on her fingernails.

"Thank you." Kendra leans back, putting space between us, dragging her hands over my shoulders and down my chest as she does. "I like your shirt."

I release her sides and place my hands over hers, warming her fingers as I hold her hands against my body. "I thought you might." I was absolutely thinking of her while I pulled this pale blue flannel off its hanger.

Her smirk is filled with satisfaction, and it reminds me of the smile on her face when she hung up on me last night. Reminds me of that damn vibrator.

Kendra sinks back into her seat, breaking our contact, but she's still facing me.

I turn to face her, then grip the side of her neck, my thumb aligned with her jaw. "You've been a bad girl."

She sucks in a breath, and I swear her eyes dilate.

"Tell me what you did wrong," I demand.

Her fingers curl around my forearm. "I didn't let you watch."

I close my eyes. "Dammit, Kendra."

"Was that not the answer?" I can hear the smile in her tone.

Opening my eyes, I see I was correct. And it's that smile of hers, the one she does when she's truly happy, that sinks into my bones.

I shake my head. "That wasn't the answer I was looking for, but it's correct."

She snickers. "I'll warn you now. If you keep up the touching and the dirty talk, we're going to have to blow off whatever plan you have and go inside. To my room."

I groan, dropping my free hand down over my growing erection.

She glances at my lap, then lifts a brow.

I tighten my hold on her neck and drag the pad of my thumb down the front of her throat before I let her go and sit back in my seat. "If sexual frustration is how I die... at least there are worse ways to go."

Kendra settles back into her seat. "So dramatic."

I press my feet to the floor, lifting my hips so I can better adjust my jeans. "Yeah, well, you try getting comfortable with a hard-on stuck in your pants."

Kendra lets out a loud laugh, and I can't fight my smile.

"You think that's funny?"

She nods, pulling her seat belt across her body. "I'm just glad no one can tell I'm turned on."

My gaze drops to her lap. "Are you telling me that your panties are wet?"

When I look back up, there's a devilish gleam in her eyes. "Guess we'll never know."

I buckle my seat belt. "You don't need to tell me. I'll have my hand in your shorts before this outing is over."

"Promise?"

I shift the truck into drive.

Chapter 53

Kendra

Twenty minutes later, I read the sign as Luther turns off the road. "Black Mountain Lodge. If you're planning on us spending the night here, I feel like we should have packed a bag or something."

We pass a fancy-looking gate, and I wonder what kind of lodge this is and what we could possibly be doing here in the middle of the day.

"Sadly, I don't have an overnight planned." Luther shakes his head. "I feel like I'm back in high school, sneaking around to avoid my girlfriend's dad."

His attention is on the winding driveway, so I don't think he even realizes what he said. Or rather how it sounded.

My girlfriend's dad.
Girlfriend.
Is that what I am? His girlfriend?
Just in secret?

"Did you ever get caught?" I ask, curious what a teenage Luther would've been like.

During the ride over here, we talked about nothing.

What I did this morning at work.

What's on the menu at the Inn right now.

Nothing. And that's what makes this feel so right.

I flex my fingers around Luther's.

We weren't even out of my neighborhood before Luther placed his hand on the center console, palm up.

He didn't say anything. No demand. Just the open hand.

So, I did what any sane person would do. I set my palm against his.

And he's been holding my hand since.

He squeezes my fingers back.

"I had some close calls but was never caught. One of my buddies, though, he got walked in on. Had to run down the street naked, his girl's dad running after him, screaming his head off." Luther chuckles, and I have a suspicion.

"Please don't tell me that was my dad."

Luther grins. "I can't lie to you, Baby."

"Ew." I try to pull my hand away so I can rub that image out of my eyes, but Luther just holds my hand tighter.

"You shouldn't've asked."

"Next time I won't." I pretend to gag.

The forest ahead of us thins, and we start to drive past buildings. Cabins, a pair of campground bathrooms. More cabins on the other side of the drive.

Then I see another sign. This one is temporary, set up like you'd see on a sidewalk outside a shop.

An arrow points farther into the woods, and two words have me forgetting all about Luther's story. "Bake sale?"

Chapter 54

Luther

We meet at the front of the truck—Kendra looking around at the towering pines, me resisting the urge to take her hand in mine.

I want to. I want to so badly.

But we're still too close to home.

And the more I think about it, the more I think this might be a dumb idea.

Possibly the dumbest.

The owners know me better than they know Joe, so I know they wouldn't go blab about me bringing Kendra here. But it's not just Sterling and Courtney here. There are all the employees. And whoever else might be stopping by to buy stuff.

My steps start to slow.

"Black Mountain Lodge," Kendra mumbles while subconsciously matching my new pace. "Why does that sound familiar?"

"You met the owners during that barbeque."

She cocks her head, brows furrowing as she tries to remember.

It's fucking adorable.

I reach up and rest my palm on the back of her neck.

"Kendra?" A male voice stops me from pulling my girl in for a kiss.

We both look up, spotting the man as he cuts through the forest to join us on the path.

"Fisher?" Kendra sounds confused.

And I amend my previous thought.

It would be even more adorable if she didn't remember Fisher at all.

It's fine.

Kendra just has a good memory.

I'm not jealous.

She was practically in my lap, kissing me like her life depended on it not too long ago.

"Good to see you again." Fisher's smile is wide.

Totally fine.

Then he opens his arms, like he's going to hug her.

Never mind. This is not fine.

Totally *not fine.*

Kendra lifts a foot, like she's going to step away from me. Like she's going to hug this other man in front of me.

I tighten my hold on the back of her neck.

She clears her throat like she's trying to cover a laugh. But she puts her foot back down where it was.

"Nice to see you too." She holds out her hand.

His eyes lock on to where I'm gripping Kendra as they shake hands.

"You guys here for the bake sale?" he asks as he releases her hand.

"Sure are." I release my hold on Kendra and step forward, putting myself between him and my girl and grabbing his hand before he can lower it. "Good to see you, kid."

I pull him in, like men do, and slap my other hand against his back.

It might be a little rougher than necessary... But is it, though?

"Don't let us keep you." I dip my chin as I step back.

Run along, Fisher Boy. This girl is taken.

He purses his lips as he steps back, like he's fighting a grin. "You two have a nice time."

Kendra waves. "Thanks. See you around."

Fisher hops back a few steps before he turns and walks back into the woods.

The guys out here are a different breed. I like the outdoors and all that. But I also like a weekend on the couch.

"He's such a nice guy." Kendra's tone is light, but she keeps her head down, not making eye contact.

I grip the back of her neck again and start walking her forward. "Just keep racking up the punishments, Brat."

She snickers. "I have no idea what you're talking about."

"Uh-huh."

Kendra leans into my side. "You didn't have to rough him up like that."

I scoff. "Yes, I did."

She shakes her head.

Ahead of us, another cabin comes into view that's a little different from the rest.

In front of the building is a concrete pad covered with picnic tables. A few people are seated at them, eating and talking, but I recognize them.

I guide Kendra to the front door, which is propped open with a brick, and she steps through.

The air is scented with buttery pastry and sugar, and my mouth starts to water as I follow Kendra inside.

This is where the staff and guests of the Lodge usually eat, so the inside has just as many picnic tables as there are outside, but right now, half of them are covered in baked goods.

Courtney and Cook are behind the stainless-steel island in the back half of the room, bagging up items for a customer. But Sterling is on this side of the counter.

And he's grinning.

I shudder. Sterling does *not* grin.

Creepy smile still on his face, the man crosses the floor, stopping in front of us.

"Rocky." He nods to me. Then he holds out a hand to Kendra. "Sterling Black. I know we met the other weekend, but in case you forgot."

Kendra smiles as she shakes his hand. "Appreciate that, but I remember you guys."

She's just good with names. Has nothing to do with the fact that these men are attractive.

"Courtney will be happy to hear that." Sterling lets go of her hand. "She's been asking me how long she should wait before asking you to lunch."

"Sterling," Courtney snaps, clearly catching our conversation.

Sterling just laughs. "What?"

Kendra glances up at me with a questioning look on her face, like she's asking permission.

I nod.

And her answering smile is fucking gorgeous.

With her happiness on her face, Kendra, my beautiful girl, leans into me to look around Sterling. "Lunch would be awesome."

Courtney lets out a sound of excitement, and Kendra presses her hand to my side before stepping away and walking toward the counter.

"So..." Sterling shoves his hands in his pockets as he rocks back on his heels.

"So, what?"

"So... you're messing around with your friend's kid." Sterling can hardly contain his humor.

"And you messed around with your employee."

Sterling smirks. "Yeah, but I married her. Joe know you're fucking his daughter?"

"Watch it," I snap, then take a breath to settle myself. "And what do you think?" My blood has been simmering with possessiveness all day, and these guys aren't helping.

"I think this is gonna be fun to watch."

"You're a dick." Shaking my head, I walk past Sterling to where Kendra is talking to his wife.

Courtney is telling Kendra about the animal shelter they raise money for, and I can't help myself. I place my palm against her lower back.

Kendra's shoulders relax at the contact.

A second later, Sterling stops beside me with a snicker.

"Dick," I huff under my breath so only he can hear me.

He lets his shoulder bump mine. "Honey." He catches his wife's attention. "Hook this fine couple up with some pies."

Fine couple.

I jab my elbow out, aiming for his ribs, but he jumps out of reach.

Courtney asks what we'd like, and I tell her we'd like something savory for lunch, along with some sweets to take home.

Courtney nods and puts two of her Havarti and ham hand pies and two mini apple pies on a pair of metal plates for us to eat here as our lunch. Then she puts what has to be half a dozen more mini pies into a bag, along with a short stack of Funfetti cookies.

"Oh, um, could I buy a brownie too?" Kendra asks quietly.

She sounds a little… embarrassed?

Then I remember.

I remember and my chest suddenly feels tight.

I like you a brownie amount.

I curl my fingers into the material of her shirt, holding her in place beside me.

I like this girl more than a brownie amount.

Chapter 55

Kendra

"These are amazing." I hold my hand in front of my mouth as I chew while I speak.

Luther grunts in agreement, his mouth also full.

I take another bite of the savory pie.

It's rich and flaky and may be my new favorite food.

"Please tell me this bake sale happens every day." I'm sure it doesn't, but seriously, I could eat this on repeat.

"Every other month, give or take." Luther lifts a shoulder. "Whenever Courtney and Cook have time to spare."

I hum and take another bite.

"Care if we join you?" Courtney asks from beside the table, and I jolt. "Sorry." She grimaces.

"No, sorry, I was too focused on my food." I lift my paper napkin and wipe it across my mouth, sure I have crumbs on my face. "This is seriously so good."

"Thanks," she laughs as she climbs onto the bench next to me.

Sterling sits across from Courtney on the other side of the picnic table, next to Luther.

The men's shoulders are touching, and I fight down a laugh

when Luther rolls his eyes and moves a few inches down the bench, away from Sterling.

"So have you been to any of the restaurants in town?" Courtney asks me.

I glance over at Luther, and he smirks.

"Just, uh, the Inn." I'm not sure if she's talking about Lonely or one of the other small towns around here, but I haven't been to any of them yet.

Courtney bites her lip, and the look on her face says she knows more than she's saying.

"What?" I prompt, my cheeks already blushing.

Courtney gives me a guilty smile. "His sister was here earlier this morning. She said Rocky met someone at the bar recently, but I didn't realize that was you."

"Wait, whose sister was here? Luther's?"

He told his sister about us?

"Luther?" Courtney scrunches her face up.

"Rocky," Sterling supplies, tipping his head toward my man.

Courtney looks stunned. "Huh?"

"Last name Rockford." Sterling continues, not fazed by his wife's shock.

"Well. Fuck me." Courtney huffs, picking up her cookie.

Before I can ask Luther more about his sister, Sterling's phone dings with a text.

Chapter 56

Luther

"Uh, Luther?" Sterling types something into his phone.

"What?" I eye him warily, his tone putting me on edge.

"Remember that favor I owe you?" he asks.

"Yeah." I nod slowly.

This can't be good.

"You're cashing it in now." He starts to stand.

"Why?" I swing my leg over the bench and follow him up.

"Fisher just texted me. Joe's here."

We all turn to look at Kendra.

Her eyes widen. "Well, that's not good."

Same page.

And dammit, now I owe Fisher one.

The girls stand at the same time.

"I'm gonna need this backstory, but you can come hide out with me at the house. I have to go relieve Simpson from babysitting duty, anyway," Courtney offers to Kendra.

Kendra nods. "That would be awesome." She turns to me and shrugs, at a loss for better options. "Text me when he's gone?"

Her eyes are still wide, but her expression is more disbelief than frantic.

Glad one of us gets to run and hide.

"Take your food," I tell her before she can step away from the table.

Kendra reaches for her plate but pauses and reaches into the bag.

She pulls the brownie out and sets it on my plate.

The fucking brownie.

Her gaze flits up to meet mine. And she whispers, "Good luck."

Then she's rushing away with Courtney. Out the door and into the woods.

Chapter 57

Kendra

I follow Courtney down a different path through the forest.

We can hear voices, but I can't see anyone, so I hope that means they can't see me.

It's almost funny that we, fully grown adults, are running around, hiding from my dad.

Almost.

We come out into a clearing, and I recognize the A-frame cabin at the end of the driveway.

I see my dad's empty truck, but no one is in sight.

Guilt is the reason this is only almost funny.

I know Luther and I aren't technically doing anything wrong, but we aren't being honest either.

Though truthfully, there's nothing to tell.

My dad doesn't want to know that we're sleeping together. And even though this feels like more than that... unless it turns into a forever thing, then there's no point in telling Dad.

What he doesn't know won't gross him out.

I keep following Courtney, and once I pay attention again, I realize we're circling around behind the house.

Okay, back door, makes sense.

Except Courtney walks past the back deck.

And I'm too distracted with the sudden sight of a lake hidden back here that I don't notice the vehicle until Courtney pats the seat beside her. "Hop in."

I climb into the passenger side of the golf cart on steroids. It's not a four-wheeler because we're sitting side by side, but this thing is definitely meant for tougher terrain than a golf course.

Courtney turns it on, and I take in the scenery as we drive along the lakeshore. Then she turns onto a path, taking us deeper into the forest.

The engine isn't super loud, but it's loud enough that we don't talk.

I should probably ask where we're going since I assumed the house back there was the house we were headed to. But I'm along for the ride now. Courtney doesn't feel like the serial killer type. And if she turns out to be... Luther will avenge me.

A minute later, the trees open up and we're at the back of a different house.

This one is huge. And beautiful.

"We just finished building it last summer," Courtney tells me as she slows, circling us up around the side of the house. "It's all on the same property as the Lodge, but with the way the main road turns, the driveways are pretty far apart from each other. So this is the easiest way to go back and forth."

"Handy."

Courtney comes to a stop in front of one of the garage doors and turns off the engine. "Here we are."

I follow her out of the vehicle and up the front steps.

She stops. "You're not allergic to dogs, are you?"

I smile. "No. Why?"

She smiles back. "I have a few."

She has six.

Chapter 58

Luther

"Rocky?"

I lift my head at the sound of Joe's voice and plaster on my best surprised expression. "Hey."

"Fancy seeing you here." He drops onto the bench across from me.

I hold up the last bite of my ham and cheese pastry. "Couldn't resist the opportunity." I know Joe likes coming here too. But today was supposed to be safe because he was supposed to be busy. "Don't you have meetings today?"

He nods, dragging my paper bag across the table so he can peek inside. "Had two this morning, and I'm heading back after this for another with my stain supplier."

"Fun." This acting casual shit is harder than I thought it would be. Because no, none of this is fun. Joe said he had meetings all day, and I believed him.

If I happen to be lying to him while I think that... well, we're not talking about me.

"Living the grind." He shrugs. "You planning to eat this all yourself?"

He starts to shove his hand into the bag, and I reach out and snatch it back to my side of the table. "I'm bringing it to the Inn. Jessie asked me to get her some stuff."

He looks like he doesn't believe me, but it's not like he knows Jessie was already here.

Jessie. My sister.

Another detail I still need to tell Kendra about.

Joe takes his phone out of his pocket and types something. And I instantly regret my lie.

What if saying that made him think about bringing something home for Kendra before he goes back to the shop?

He makes a noise.

"Something wrong?" I try to get a peek at his screen.

"No. I was just seeing if Kenny wanted anything. But apparently, she's not feeling great, so she's going to nap for the lunch hour."

I try not to show my relief.

I'm certain Kendra felt bad lying, but it's a good answer.

I TAKE IN THE HOME BEFORE ME AS I PULL UP TO THE new Black household.

It's nice. Exactly the sort of place I'd expect them to build.

Shaking the residual tension out of my shoulders, I turn off my truck and climb out.

Joe and I walked back to our vehicles together, but I pretended to answer a call so I could wait for him to leave first. Then I waited another five minutes to make sure he was long gone and used that time to text Kendra to let her know I was finally coming to get her.

She texted me back, saying to let myself in, which feels weird since I haven't been to this house before. But then I remembered the baby. And since I've lived that life, I'll follow instructions and do it quietly. I won't be the oaf that wakes the baby. Nothing set my rage on fire like someone waking up Ashley after I'd finally gotten her down for a nap.

I love my daughter. And raising her full-time as a single dad was my choice, one I refuse to regret. But I'm also glad that life is behind me. I'm old now. I have the house to myself. And the only reason I'm waking up in the middle of the night is to pee.

I pause when I reach the front door.

Thinking about those days...

Kendra and I really need to have a talk about... everything.

About Joe. About what she wants in life. What she wants her future to be. If that includes Colorado. If it includes me...

I take a calming breath.

We didn't do anything wrong that first night we met. We were consenting adults enjoying each other. If we'd known the truth about our real identities...? I don't know if it would've changed anything. The attraction between us is real. And if the first time I'd seen her had been in Joe's hallway, Kendra stepping out of the bathroom in her little pajamas. Her big bright eyes blinking up at me... I'd still have gotten hard.

And I'd still have put my hands on her.

So, we were inevitable.

But where we go from here...

I shake the worry from my head and open the door as quietly as I can.

We can talk later.

The house has an open-concept main floor, so it only takes a few steps until I'm in the living area. Only a few steps until I spot Kendra. Sitting on the couch with a sleeping baby sprawled across her chest.

Her eyes find mine, and she lights up.

And she looks so perfect.

So happy.

S.J. Tilly

It's like getting a glimpse into her future.
But it's not a future I can give her.
And I don't know what to do about that.

Chapter 59

Kendra

I'M SO HAPPY TO SEE LUTHER.

This tiny human might look sweet and sleepy now, but she's been a damn demon creature for the last fifteen minutes. And that was *after* she barfed breast milk all over me.

I still want to gag just thinking about it. But thankfully, Courtney had laid a blanket over me before she handed me her little grizzly bear cub, so the blanket took most of the damage.

When Ursa finally passed out, Courtney took the reprieve to run upstairs and change, since her shirt took a hit of blowback.

I resist shuddering, holding as still as I can, because if this gremlin wakes up and starts crying, I might start crying too.

It's been a long time since I've come to terms with the fact that I won't have children, so I don't really think about it much. And even before that, I never really thought about it. Was never really a baby person.

They're great for some people.

I can understand the concept of desiring them.

But the reality... No, thank you, sir. Not my thing.

And days like today are the perfect reminder that I enjoy my life just how it is.

I have a new job I like.

I have a good relationship with my dad.

I like living out here in the mountains.

And... Luther.

I like Luther.

"Hi," I whisper to the man as he steps into the room.

The side of his mouth pulls up, but the smile doesn't reach his eyes.

My own lips pull down. "Everything go okay with my dad?"

While I was busy over here getting yarfed on, Luther was stuck pretending to act normal while my dad surely talked his ear off.

Luther nods as he crosses the room, taking a seat beside me on the couch.

"You sure it went okay?" I'm still whispering, but I have to ask again because he seems off.

He nods again. "Yeah, just sulking because we keep getting interrupted."

I huff a laugh. "Maybe next time we go hang out in the middle of the woods."

He purses his lips. "That's not a bad idea."

Chapter 60

Kendra

"Uh, you sure this is a road?"

He hums. "Technically... yes."

I eye Luther as the truck continues to bump along *the road* that is actually just a pair of tire tracks worn into the dirt, heading through a field, toward the forest. "Is this where you reveal you're going to murder me so no one will ever know what we did? Because I'm telling you now, I will haunt you. Hard."

As I'd hoped, Luther smiles. "How exactly do you haunt someone *hard*?"

I sigh. "So much to teach you." I turn in my seat so I'm facing him. We're still bouncing down *the road*, but we're going about ten miles an hour, and there is literally no one and nothing out here, so I'm not worried about an accident. "It's like those episodes of *Ghost Hunters* where—"

"Episodes of what?"

I blink at him. "*Ghost Hunters*. The TV show."

"I gathered that much." He lifts a brow as he glances at me.

"You're so uncultured."

Luther laughs. Really laughs. And the heaviness that had been filling the truck vanishes.

I don't know what happened back at the bake sale, but when Luther came to get me, something wasn't right.

I didn't want to press it. I'd already asked him, twice, if everything was okay. And he said it was, so I left it alone.

Luther knows he can talk to me.

Or at least he should know.

Later. We can have a serious talk later. For now, we'll talk about ghosts.

"So, you're saying if I murder you, you'll fling knives out of kitchen drawers."

I cross my arms. "You're acting like that wouldn't be terrifying. You could lose a toe, Luther. Do you have any idea how much you need your toes for balance? You'd have to go to physical therapy."

Luther shakes his head. "The way your brain works..."

"Pretty amazing, I know."

He turns his head to look at me. "You are pretty amazing."

I stare at him.

It's a simple compliment. Just repeating what I said. But, like everything Luther says, it sounds like he means it.

There's nothing empty in his words.

Not ever.

I feel my smile soften. "You're not too bad yourself."

Luther smirks, then tips his head, gesturing toward the windshield.

I look. And my mouth drops open.

I don't know how long we were driving through the woods. But we're not in the woods anymore.

"Holy shit." I lean forward until my seat belt is taut across my chest. "Where are we?"

Instead of answering, Luther does a U-turn so the view is behind us, then he turns the engine off. "Come on."

I climb out and walk to meet Luther at the rear of the truck, but I keep my eyes on the scenery.

"It's so pretty," I whisper.

The mountains are everywhere out here. I literally live in them. But this is different.

The ground we're standing on is flat, but a few yards away, the land slopes steeply down into a valley. And the earth dropping away creates the perfect vista.

Bright blue skies.

Soaring mountain tops.

Birds floating on the wind.

Pine trees and aspens as far as the eye can see.

Just... wow.

Luther clasps his hand in mine, drawing my attention away from the view.

I let him guide me over, then he releases my hand and grips my hips, lifting me so I'm sitting on the open tailgate.

I spread my knees, and Luther steps between them.

"Sorry about today." He reaches up and tucks a piece of my hair behind my ear. "I—"

I shake my head and place my hands on his chest. "Don't apologize. We got to spend time together. There's a bag of mini pies in your truck. And if I'm guessing correctly... I'm about to have my first outdoor sexual experience."

He leans closer, not stopping until our lips are just inches apart. "You're guessing correctly."

The smile reaches his eyes this time, and it's an even better sight than the mountains behind him.

I slide my hands up his chest, over his shoulders. "I love it when I'm right."

He hums, then leans in a little more, lips brushing against mine. "Kiss me."

My body replies.

I arch my neck and press my mouth against his.

The first kiss is soft.

Gentle.

Luther cups my face, his palms warm against my cheeks.

He pulls back just enough to speak. "Open for me, Kendra."

His words are a warm breath against my lips. And even if we didn't speak the same language, I'd still know what he was asking for.

I open.

And this time, it's less gentle.

Luther slides his tongue into my mouth.

I moan.

He groans.

I cling to his shoulder with one hand while I slide the other up the back of his neck, dragging my nails against his scalp until I'm gripping his hair.

He groans again.

He wraps his arms around me, hands against my back, holding me steady.

I shift, widening my thighs.

Luther fills the space with his body. Pressing into me.

His teeth scrape across my bottom lip.

I tug on his hair.

He smiles against my lips. "Brat."

"So you keep saying." I release his hair and slide my hands back to his chest. "And you keep promising this punishment." I undo the top button on his shirt. "But..." I pop the next button free. "You keep rewarding me instead."

"How am I rewarding you, Baby?"

"Pie." The next button goes. "Compliments." The next. "Kisses."

His fingers flex as he grips my hips. He tugs me to him, closing the last inch until our bodies are flush.

Two layers of denim are between us, but that doesn't stop the heat from pooling where his hard length presses against my core.

All the buttons undone, I grip his shirt and pull the two sides of his flannel apart, revealing the bare muscles beneath.

I slide my fingers down his stomach.

"I'll punish you next time." He speaks the words into my mouth.

I swallow them.

I moan against him, and his abs flex beneath my touch.

"Next time," I agree.

I drop my hands to his belt.

His hands go to the hem of my shirt.

I tug at the leather.

He starts to lift my tank top.

And then a throat clears. "I just *know* you're not about to fuck in my park. In broad daylight."

I freeze.

My eyes snap open wide.

Luther opens his slower.

Then he sighs, his breath warm on my lips.

Luther tugs the hem of my shirt down before he straightens and turns toward the man.

"You suck, you know that?" Luther's tone is full of annoyance but no real anger.

"How about a thank-you," the other man replies. "Wouldn't you like to make it to retirement without indecent exposure on your record?"

I bite down on a laugh over his dig about retirement as I slowly turn to face the man who interrupted us.

Then I narrow my eyes. Because *god damn*, what are they feeding the men out here? Why are they all so fucking hot?

This *park ranger* is in the typical uniform of dark green pants and a tan button-down short-sleeve shirt. But with tattoos covering both arms, shaggy dark hair under a worn baseball hat, and... *Does he have two different colored eyes?*... He doesn't look like a park ranger. He looks like a bad boy playing at being a park ranger.

Then I notice the gun on his hip.

Okay, so not playing.

"You could've just walked past." Luther rests one hand on my knee and gestures at the vast amount of land around us with the other.

"Not gonna do that." The man turns his mismatched eyes on me. "You good?"

"Me?" I glance between the men. "Like, do I know this guy?" I point at Luther.

The ranger nods.

I nod back, setting my hand on top of Luther's on my knee. "I know this guy."

"Dude," Luther says flatly, holding his free hand out, palm up.

The man lifts a shoulder, not at all apologetic.

And then the men stare at each other.

Luther drops his arm. "You gonna stand here until we leave?"

"Yep." The man crosses his arms.

This grump seems like kind of a dick, but it comes off funny.

But looking at the men's serious expressions, I wonder if maybe I'm the only one who's feeling the humor.

Luther tried to bring me lunch. My dad showed up and thought it was for him.

Luther tried to take me to a bake sale. My dad showed up, and I had to hide in someone's house.

Luther tried to give outdoor sexy times. A grumpy park ranger catches us before we can begin.

I look around, verifying that we're still in the middle of nowhere. Not a person or road or manmade structure in sight. And still, someone interrupted us.

I snicker.

Luther turns his head to look at me.

I lift my hand to my mouth and place my fingers against my lips.

Luther heaves out a breath, then grips my waist and drags me off the tailgate, setting my feet on the ground. "Kendra, this is Ethan. Ethan, Kendra."

I wave at Ethan. "Sorry about the, um... trespassing?"

"Not your fault, I'm sure." He dips his chin.

Luther rolls his eyes and places his hand on my back, guiding me around to the passenger side.

I debate if I should say goodbye to Ethan, but it's like Luther can read my mind and doesn't like it, because he increases the pressure on my back.

Reaching past me, Luther pulls my door open. "Get in the truck, Baby Doll."

I do as he says.

Once I'm settled in my seat, Luther shuts my door.

Through the side mirror, I watch him walk to the back of the truck, where he shuts the tailgate and says something I can't make out to Ethan.

A few seconds later, Luther opens his door.

"... little young for you, yeah?"

"Fuck off." Luther climbs into the truck and reaches into the back seat, pulling a mini pie from the paper bag.

Then he chucks it at Ethan.

"Luther," I hiss, even as Ethan catches the pie.

It breaks under the impact, and I can see some of the gooey cherry filling seep out, but Ethan doesn't act mad.

He lifts his hand, like he might lick the pie filling off his fingers, and I decide to focus my attention forward.

"I hope that attracts a bear," Luther calls out before he slams his door shut.

I snort. "Friend of yours?"

Luther starts the truck. "Seat belt."

Chapter 61

Luther

Jessie looks at me. Again.

I set down the glass I was washing and turn to face her. "What?"

She lifts her shoulders. "Didn't say anything."

"You're *not saying anything* louder than a..." I trail off, unable to think of something loud.

Jessie widens her eyes at me. "Good one."

"Shut up." I grab the glass and start washing it again.

"You okay? You seem a little... tense?" she says with a teasing tone, so I ignore her.

I'm not okay.

It's been days since I've seen Kendra. Since our day of interruptions that ended at Lonely Peak State Park.

My balls feel perpetually blue, no matter how much I jerk off.

And it's getting harder to ignore the guilt.

And the guilt isn't just about hiding the sex from Joe. It's about hiding my emotions too.

If I were experiencing these strong feelings for anyone else, I'd talk to Joe about it. We'd sit here, at my bar, and talk it out.

He'd tell me to keep seeing her.

He'd tell me to keep having fun and let what happens happen.

But if he knew it was his daughter we were talking about... He'd punch me.

I'm sure of it.

"Marching band," I blurt out, with a little more volume than I meant to.

Now Jessie is looking at me like I've completely lost the plot.

Probably because I have.

She slowly sets down the rag she's holding. "You wanna talk about it?"

"Talk about what?"

Jessie sighs. "About your little one-night stand with Joe's kid."

My shoulders drop. "Who told you?"

I know she's a good sister when she doesn't laugh at me. I can tell she wants to. Know she will eventually. But I'm pretty sure she can see how not well I'm doing.

"One of the guys from the Lodge." She doesn't name names, but the list of suspects is short. "I wasn't sure I believed them, but the description of the girl and your reaction just now..." She puffs out her cheeks, still fighting that laugh. "Man, Rock, that must've been a mind fuck."

I don't want to talk to my sister about my sex life. But with Joe unavailable for the task, I need someone to talk to.

"You have no idea." I put the twice-cleaned glass back in the sink and drag my damp hand over my face. "I went over there for breakfast the next week before fishing, and... there she was."

Jessie sucks in a breath. "Oh fuck." Then she laughs. "Sorry. Sorry."

I wave her off. "Just get it out of your system."

She tries to school her features. "So, what? You walked in, and she was just sitting at the table?"

"Not exactly." I don't know if that scenario would've been better or worse. "I literally ran into her as she was coming out of the bathroom."

"Bet that took you back a step."

I recall the moment and let out a deranged chuckle. "I accused her of sleeping with Joe."

Jessie's burst of laughter is so loud it draws the attention of half the bar.

She slaps her hand over her mouth and steps closer, lowering her voice. "You didn't."

"I did."

"Did she slap you?"

My mouth slowly pulls up into a smirk.

She didn't slap me.

She clung to me as I held her in place with my hand on her throat.

I might be fucked in the head, but I kind of want to role-play that moment. Only in the replay, I can shove her back into the bathroom and pound into her over the sink.

I'm definitely fucked in the head.

"What's this?" Jessie gestures toward my face. "I don't like it."

I drop my smirk. "She didn't slap me."

Jessie's still giving me a narrow look. "Okay. And then what? You just pretended like you didn't know each other."

"Pretty much." I also put my hands on her the second I got Joe out of the room, but she doesn't need to know that.

She purses her lips while she nods. "And that's what's eating you up? You feel bad about sleeping with her?"

I chew on my lip.

Jessie thinks it was just the once.

Just the one-night stand.

I blow out a breath. "You really want to know about this?"

Her nod is way too enthusiastic. "I don't need to know what happened in the motel room, but the aftermath? Hell yeah, I want to know. This is better than *Dawns of Agony*."

I give her a look for comparing my life to a soap opera. "Fine. You want to know? I'll tell you." Jessie suddenly looks unsure. But too bad for her. "We pretended we didn't know each other. Joe has no idea. But I gave her my number. We snuck off for a... rendezvous during the welcome barbecue thing Joe hosted. I slept in her bed that night. Every day since, we've texted, talked, or video called. I brought her lunch. Got caught by Joe and had to pretend the second meal was for him. I took her to the bake sale a few days ago. Almost got caught by Joe. She had to go hide with Courtney." Jessie's eyes widen as I go. "I took her to Lonely Peak, got caught by the fucking ranger. And today's, what, Thursday? And I'm hosting Ashley's grad party Saturday, so I should be thinking about that. But instead, I'm thinking about Kendra. Who, by the way, I already invited to the party. So when you see her there, you need to pretend like you haven't met."

Jessie whistles. "Damn, Bro. You're in *deep*."

I slump against the bar. "What do I do?"

"What do you want to do?"

I answer her honestly. "I want to keep seeing Kendra."

She watches me but doesn't act surprised by my answer. "You gonna tell Joe?"

Slowly, I shake my head. "No. Not yet. I... I need to know where this is going. If it's a forever thing, then I'll tell him. But..."

"But?" She lifts a brow, prompting me.

"I'm too old for her."

Jessie snorts.

I narrow my eyes. "What?"

"You were too old for her when she first stepped foot in this bar, ya fucking creep. But it didn't stop you then, so why should it stop you now?"

She has a point, but... "That was just supposed to be a one-time thing." My fucking chest hurts as I say it. One time was never going to be enough with Kendra.

"You have things in common?"

Jessie's question catches me off guard, but I nod.

Surprisingly, we do.

She might not be into fishing and the outdoor shit I do, but that day—sitting in the two-person chair—we talked about so much. Movies, music, politics, food, space travel, houseplants. We talked about her job, her ideas, and I fell even more...

My throat dries up.

I feel my spine stiffen.

Oh fuck.

"What?" Jessie steps closer to me. "What just happened?"

I love her.

I lift my hand and rub it against my chest.

"Are you having a heart attack? Oh my god!" Jessie reaches into her apron like she's going for her phone.

"I'm not having a heart attack." My voice is a little croaky.

"You sure?"

It feels like I am. But it's not a heart attack.

It's fucking love.

The front door opens, and we both look over.

It's Jessie's replacement.

Jessie lifts her hand in a wave but speaks to me. "If you want me to stay..."

I shake my head.

I don't remember why she needed to leave work early tonight, but my misery doesn't need company.

"You sure?" She's looking at me warily.

"I'm sure."

Then my phone notifies me of a text.

I take it out of my pocket.

> Baby Doll: My dad just left. For the night.

> Me: As in overnight?

My blood starts to sizzle.

And oh, how quickly my guilt can turn into lust.

> Baby Doll: Overnight.

> Me: Pack a bag. I'm leaving the Inn now.

Baby Doll: A bag?

Me: I'm bringing you to my house.

Sliding my phone back in my pocket, I take a step back. "See you Saturday."

"Where you off to?" Jessie lifts her brows.

"Saturday," I reply, then turn around and stride out of my bar.

Chapter 62

Kendra

I lock the door behind me, then set my backpack on the front steps.

We'll only get one night. Barely twelve hours since the sun is already setting and I need to beat my dad home tomorrow morning.

I didn't even ask where he was going.

I mean, it's a date. It has to be.

And am I curious? Yes.

But was I willing to ask questions, risking that, in turn, he would ask me about my dating life? No.

We can both have our secrets.

The night air cools my bare legs.

I'm back in the pajamas I wore during our interrupted video call.

The see-through bralette top and the barely-there shorts both cling to me like a second skin. But I put a navy blue cardigan on over the gray material, covering the fact that I'm hardly dressed and partially masking the fact that, like last time, I'm not wearing anything underneath.

I feel sexy.

And turned on.

We've texted since the debacle at the park. And I've had my hand between my legs every night thinking of him. But there's been too much teasing and too many failed attempts.

I need the real thing.

I need Luther.

Headlights flash in the driveway.

He's here.

Chapter 63

Luther

Kendra walks down her front steps, backpack in hand, legs on display. All that skin flashing in the beam of my headlights.

By the time I put the truck in park, she's already opening the passenger door.

Instead of chastising her, I reach across, take the backpack from her hands, and set it on the back seat.

She climbs into the seat in silence. And I look.

I look at her shiny hair, hanging down to her shoulders.

I look at the cardigan that can't hide her nipples.

I look at her lap.

At the outline of her pussy in those fucking shorts.

She shuts her door, and the overhead light turns off. Leaving us in the dark.

I swallow and shift the truck back into drive.

Chapter 64

Kendra

I shift in my seat.

We haven't spoken.

The radio isn't on.

There's only the noise of the tires rolling down the road.

And the noise of lust pounding through my veins.

I press my thighs together, aware I'm about to soak through my shorts, and stare out through the windshield, watching the light dwindle around us.

I feel like my skin is vibrating.

I feel like it's my first time.

Chapter 65

Luther

My fingers tighten around the steering wheel.
I might be having that heart attack now.
Or maybe it's just Kendra's nearness.
Maybe it's just the scent of her.
I swallow.
My hands ache to touch her.
But we're almost home.
And I won't touch her until she's under my roof.

Chapter 66

Kendra

I'm about ready to undo my seat belt and crawl into Luther's lap when he slows.

We've been driving for fifteen minutes on another country highway, but we're not turning onto another road.

We're turning down a driveway.

My core clenches.

We're here.

It's another minute until I see the house.

And holy fuck.

My mouth drops open.

It's not a house.

It's a freaking log-style mansion.

The house is surrounded by tall pines that block out the setting sun, draping the property in shadows.

But lights glow along the last length of the driveway and up the path leading to the front steps.

And lights glow from inside too, illuminating the two stories of windows.

It's... stunning.

It's out of a damn magazine.

I glance over at Luther. He glances at me, still not speaking, and lifts a shoulder.

Just a casual *Yeah, I'm loaded.*

I remember my dad saying he owned a bunch of hotels, but I was picturing motels with dive bars like the Inn.

This house was built in a whole different tax bracket.

Luther presses a button on the truck visor, and one of the three garage doors opens.

Chapter 67

Luther

I close the garage door after I turn off the engine.

I grab Kendra's bag and open my door. And by the time I reach the passenger side, Kendra is sliding out of the truck.

The overhead lights are on night mode, filling the garage with a dim glow.

I hold out my hand to Kendra.

She slides her palm against mine.

Her fingers are cool, and I wrap mine around hers.

I'll warm you up soon, Baby.

Kendra walks beside me through the garage, past my old Bronco, past the empty spot where Ashley parks when she's home.

I open the door that leads into the mudroom and let go of Kendra's hand long enough for her to step inside first, and for me to kick off my boots, then I take her hand again.

We walk down the hallway, past my home office. Past a laundry room. And into the great room.

Kendra's head swivels around, taking in the oversized furniture and the massive windows that look out on the deck over the backyard.

We cut past the kitchen with the ten-foot island.

And my pulse doubles when we reach the staircase.

We walk up, side by side, our fingers still entwined.

To the right, at the top of the stairs, is a loft area, Ashley's room and her bathroom.

But to the left...

I flex my fingers around Kendra's as I turn her to the left.

We pass through a set of double doors into the owner's suite. Into my room.

I left my bedside lamps on—I always do—and it's the perfect mood lighting for what I have planned.

The lofted ceilings are crisscrossed with large wood beams.

The stone fireplace climbs the wall across from the bed.

The wood floors are covered in fur rugs. *Faux fur, because I'm not a monster.*

Across from the doors we just walked through are windows. Lots of windows. And a glass door leading out to my private balcony.

There's a hot tub downstairs on the main deck. But I'm thinking I need to put another one up here.

No swimsuits allowed.

I watch Kendra turn her head toward the bed.

It's an Alaskan King.

Too big for one man.

But perfect for fucking a feisty brat.

Only we aren't starting in the bed.

Letting go of Kendra's hand, I drop her backpack at the foot of the bed, then cross the room to my leather armchair.

I'm still standing, but when she takes a step forward, I hold up my hand. "Stay."

She stops.

I reach down and undo the button on my jeans.

She watches.

And my cock swells at her attention.

I pull my zipper down.

She wets her lips.

"On your knees." My command comes out as a growl.

Kendra lifts her gaze from my jeans.

I think she might protest. Might say something.

But with her eyes on mine, she lowers.

I could come from that sight alone.

Kneeling, she lifts her hands to the front of her cardigan.

When she pauses, I nod, and she undoes the first button. Then the rest.

She shrugs the cardigan off, letting it drop to the floor beside her.

I clench my jaw because she's in the same outfit as the night we did the video call. The one that barely counts as clothing.

We watch each other. Eyes roaming.

Her face is flushed.

Her chest is rising and falling with heavy breaths.

And her nipples are begging for attention.

I lower myself into the chair.

Kendra wets her lips again. Like she's starving.

"It's time for your punishment, Brat." I palm my hardening cock. "You ready?"

"Yes, Daddy."

I groan. "Good." Then I lean back in the chair and spread my legs. "Hands and knees, Baby Doll."

She bends forward onto all fours, palms on the ground.

I take her in.

The way she has to tip her head up to keep her eyes on mine.

The way her heavy tits strain against the thin material trying to hold them in.

The way her back arches, the way her ass looks.

The way it'd look with my hands gripping it.

I squeeze my dick once more, then place my hands on the armrests. "Crawl to me."

Chapter 68

Kendra

My core clenches around nothing.
Crawl to me.
I shift one hand forward.
One knee.
And then I'm crawling.
I'm crawling across a fur-covered floor toward the sexiest man I've ever seen.
Luther watches me.
His eyes are on mine.
His mouth is open.
His chest is heaving.
And I don't feel demeaned at all.
On my hands and knees, I feel alive. Invincible.
I feel powerful.
And the look on his face, the appreciation, makes me feel like a fucking queen.

Chapter 69

Luther

She stops at my feet.

And I make her wait for the next command.

I make her wait because I'm having trouble forming words.

Because she's on the floor. She's at my mercy. But it still feels like she holds all the power.

Because she does.

She always will.

But... I know my girl. And I know she wants this as much as I do.

"Sit up and take your top off."

Kendra pulls in a shaky breath, then she sits back on her heels.

As she reaches for her skimpy top, I undo the buttons on my shirt.

Her tits bounce as they're freed from the material, and she drops the top to the floor.

Her hands move to the waistband of her shorts, but I shake my head.

She freezes in place.

"Play with your tits."

Kendra slides her hands up her sides until she's cupping her breasts.

She cups them. Squeezes them. She pinches her nipples.

My cock throbs, but after letting my shirt fall open, I grip the armrests of my chair.

I'm here for the show.

"Does that feel good?" I grit out.

Kendra nods with a moan.

"Use your words."

"It feels good." She presses her tits together while still rolling her nipples between her fingers. "But I want your hands—"

"I didn't ask what you wanted." I grip the armrests harder.

She bites down on her lip, and her eyes start to close.

"Stop."

She stills.

"Hands down."

Kendra drops her hands to her sides, but I watch her fingers twitch, like she wants to touch herself more.

"Are you wet?"

She nods. "So wet."

"Try that again."

She blinks at me, those pretty green eyes sparkling in the dim light. "I'm so wet, Daddy."

I flex my jaw.

I'm going to blow the second she fucking touches me.

"Turn around." My voice is gravel.

Kendra shifts around until her back is to me.

"Hands on the floor."

Like a good little girl, she bends forward onto all fours.

Chapter 70

Kendra

My body is *thrumming*.

I'm so primed.

I've never come just from nipple play, but I was fucking close.

My fingers sink into the soft fur rug.

The chair creaks, signaling Luther adjusting his position.

"Spread your knees."

Every one of his commands sends a pulse of heat between my legs.

I shift my knees wider.

Fabric shifts.

Then a palm is pressing up between my legs.

I jump at the contact.

But a second hand lands on the center of my back, keeping me in place.

"Hold fucking still." His voice is strained.

I focus on breathing.

Focus on not moving.

Luther must be on the edge of his seat, leaning forward.

The pressure increases on my back as the palm between my legs cups my sex.

He rubs.

He moves his hand forward and back, rubbing me through my thin shorts.

Luther lets out a sound like a tortured moan at the same time one of his fingers presses harder, wedging the thin fabric between my pussy lips.

He wiggles his finger.

I try to arch into his hold.

The hand on my back disappears, then smacks down on my ass cheek.

It's not too hard. It's just hard enough.

I moan.

"Quiet." He spanks me again.

I bite my tongue to keep from moaning again as his hand soothes circles against my ass.

The hand between my legs slides back and away.

I pull in a breath. Ready for his next command.

But he doesn't say anything.

Instead, he pulls my shorts down.

Chapter 71

Luther

I tug the material down her hips.

I can't help myself.

I need to see more of her.

All of her.

I smooth my hands over her perfect ass cheeks.

I dig my fingers into the soft flesh.

I grip her. And I spread her.

She makes another sound.

I let go of one cheek and spank it.

Her ass jiggles.

My balls squeeze.

I reach down and slide my fingers over her wet slit. And I swallow down the sound that tries to climb out of my throat.

She's soaked.

I could feel it through her shorts.

But skin on skin, she's so fucking slippery.

I push two fingers inside her.

Her neck arches.

I shove them in deeper, my other hand kneading and squeezing her ass.

I curl my fingers inside her, gathering her wetness as I pull them out of her channel.

Her hips shift like she's trying to get me to touch her clit.

With my fingers just inside her entrance, I spank her with my other hand.

She squeaks, and I feel her clench against my fingertips.

"This is your punishment, Baby. You're not getting my fingers on your clit. But you can have them somewhere else." I pull my hand up and back toward me.

But I don't lift my fingers from her skin.

I drag them up between us.

Between her cheeks.

Until my shine-covered fingers reach her pretty pink asshole.

Kendra gasps.

I grip her ass cheek with my free hand, spreading her best I can one-handed, then I flatten my fingers against her rear entrance. And I rub.

Chapter 72

Kendra

He...
Holy shit.
Oh my god.
Holy fuck.
My body tenses.
My pussy pulses.
And Luther spanks my ass again.
I clench.
He spanks me again.
"Relax." His fingers keep rubbing me... there. "Have you ever taken a dick here, Baby Doll? Have you ever had your ass filled?"
I shake my head.
I shake my head again.
This. This is why you date experienced men.
None of my exes have ever so much as hinted at wanting to...
The tip of his finger presses into me.
"Words."
I open my mouth, but he pushes his finger deeper.
His other hand spanks me again. And this time, when my body reacts, squeezing my muscles around him, it's more intense.
He doesn't go deeper.

But he jiggles his finger.

And this time, my body tenses for a different reason.

I'm going to come.

Is that even possible?

"I've never..." I pant. "I'm going to..."

His hand stills.

"You don't get to come yet, Brat." He pulls his fingertip free from my body. "Turn around."

Staying on all fours, with my shorts around my thighs, I shuffle around to face him.

I'm so close to losing it that a breeze against my clit will probably be enough to get me off.

And I don't know how to feel about it.

I'm buzzing.

My body is lit up.

But my nerves are frazzled.

I'm frustrated.

My nipples ache.

My clit aches.

And now even my ass feels empty.

I lift my gaze to Luther's.

I'm finally understanding this punishment thing.

His eyes are fiery but full of understanding.

"You're doing so well."

His praise caresses me. And I take a full breath of air.

He's shirtless now. His flannel on the ground beside the chair.

"Shorts off."

Keeping my gaze on his, I shift onto my knees and shimmy my shorts down, lifting one knee at a time until I can toss them to the side.

He wipes his finger clean on the thigh of his jeans as he watches me.

When I'm completely naked, Luther leans back in his chair. "Take my pants off."

I swallow. "Yes, Daddy."

My pulse jumps as I reach out and grip the top of his jeans.

Then, looking up into his eyes, I work my fingers under the band of his boxer briefs, pausing, waiting for permission to pull them off with his jeans.

Luther dips his chin as he sets his hands on the armrests.

He lifts his hips, helping me.

His cock is tenting the front of his jeans, and when I work the material down, it jerks free.

My mouth waters.

But he hasn't told me what to do. So I pull his pants the rest of the way off, then sit back.

Wearing absolutely nothing, he spreads his knees. "Closer."

I move closer.

"Hands on my thighs."

I'm trembling as I do what he says, my palms pressing down on his muscled thighs.

"You're going to suck my cock."

Electricity sparkles across my skin, and I lean forward.

His hand leaves the armrest, snapping out to grip me by the throat. "I didn't say to start."

I swallow, his fingers feeling like fire against my skin.

I'm so fucking primed I'm about to start rubbing myself against him.

Rub my nipples against his knees. Grind my pussy against his fucking shin.

I don't even care what part of him gets me off. I just need it.

Now.

I whimper.

He leans forward, bending down.

I think he's going to kiss me.

My eyes start to close.

His thumb presses against the side of my throat, and my eyes open again.

He's inches away.

"You're going to suck my cock," he repeats. "You're not going to touch yourself. You're going to work your mouth on my dick until I'm ready to come. Then, when I tell you to, you're going to climb up here, straddle my lap, and swallow my cock with that sweet slit." He leans in closer. "And when I'm filling you, that's when you can come. And that's when you can kiss me." He releases my neck and leans back. "Start."

Chapter 73

Luther

Kendra's fingers dig into my thighs as she leans down.

I hold my breath.

Her lips close around my dick.

My head tips back, and I groan.

She goes deeper.

I grip the armrest harder.

I want to grab her hair. Want to push her face down. Want to control the pace.

But I want her to do the work.

I want her to show me how good she is at sucking cock.

She swirls her tongue around my head.

I tip my head forward. Needing to watch.

She's looking up at me.

Eyes only for me.

Just for fucking me.

I won't do the work for her. But...

"Deeper."

Kendra blinks. Then she slides her mouth down my length. Taking me deeper.

I bump against the back of her throat.

I feel her muscles work.

She pulls off a little.

"Is that all you can take?"

Kendra sucks on the head of my cock, blinking up at me, tears forming at the corners of her eyes.

"Can you deep throat, Baby?"

She gives her head a small shake, keeping my dick in her mouth.

Excitement fills my chest.

"That's okay," I tell her soothingly. "When you're being good, I'll teach you how. I'll teach you how to fit my cock down your throat while I teach you how to take my dick in your ass." My stomach muscles clench at the idea. The way her little hole was squeezing my fingertip, it's going to take work.

Kendra makes a sound around my cock.

"You like that idea?"

She nods, taking me as deep as she can again.

My fingers feel like they're going to tear through the leather beneath them.

"Be a good girl and I'll teach you."

My breathing is coming out faster. I'm getting so close. And I need Kendra just as ready.

"That's it. Take as much as you can." She bobs her head. "Get my dick nice and wet."

She hums.

My balls tighten.

"One more time, Doll. Take me as deep as you can one more time."

She does.

My dick presses all the way back.

Her throat muscles convulse.

"That's my girl. Hold it there." She looks so fucking pretty like this, I can hardly catch my breath. "One more second."

Her throat muscles pulse once more.

She blinks.

Two tears roll down her cheeks.

And I'm done.

I reach out and hook my hands under her arms, then I lift her, and my dick slides out of her mouth.

Kendra is trembling. Literally vibrating. And I have one second to worry that I took it too far. But then she's helping me, scrambling onto my lap, her knees on either side of my hips.

She reaches down between us, gripping the base of my dick and aiming the tip at her entrance.

Then she drops.

Her legs giving out.

Impaling herself.

Chapter 74

Kendra

Luther's groan rumbles through me as I stretch around him.

It was so much, so fast. But I'm so wet that he slid right in.

I use what's left of my strength to lift my hips, then I drop back down.

I squeeze my core around his length.

Luther curses. Grips my hips. And his fingers dig into my flesh as he rocks me in his lap.

I brace my free hand against Luther's chest to hold myself up, then with the hand that's still down between us, I reach for my clit.

The first brush has my body tensing.

Luther grunts as he rocks me rougher.

"You ready, Baby?"

"I'm ready, Daddy." I'm practically crying.

He slides one of his hands around to my ass.

And then his finger is there again. Rubbing. Circling.

I roll my hips.

"Wait for me." He thrusts his hips up below me, shoving deeper. "You wait for me."

Mountain Daddy

The tip of his finger pushes into me.
I tense.
And he starts to pulse inside me.
Pleasure explodes around me.
And I lean forward, sealing my mouth over his, as I come.

Chapter 75

Luther

Lips crash against mine, and she cries into our kiss.

My tongue tangles with hers.

I push my finger farther into her ass. I dig my fingers into her hip.

Kendra shakes as her pussy continues to dance around my cock.

And my balls squeeze painfully as I fill her with all of my release.

Chapter 76

Kendra

Luther wraps his arms around me as our kiss slows.

We're both naked. Covered in a sheen of sweat. Chests heaving.

I can already feel the mess forming between us.

And I've never felt happier.

He presses his lips against mine one last time, then he relaxes back into the chair.

I blink at him, clearing my blurry vision.

Luther's eyes are focused on mine. "You okay?"

A grin cracks across my face, and I drag my hands over his shoulders, pressing my palms to his chest. "I'm great. Are you okay?"

His mouth pulls into a smile. "I think that orgasm might've shaved a few years off my life, but it was worth it."

I huff a laugh, which makes my muscles clench.

Luther groans as his body twitches in response.

"Sorry," I chuckle again.

He slides his hands to my hips, holding me still.

He grips me much gentler than before, and I wonder if I'm going to have handprints on my skin tomorrow.

I kind of hope I will.

"I think we need a shower." Luther's thumbs trace circles on my skin, making me shiver. Causing my muscles to clench, again. "Dammit, woman."

I press my lips together and widen my eyes, knowing if I try to talk, I'll laugh, making it worse. So I nod, agreeing to the shower.

Taking a slow breath, I gather my composure.

Luther pats my ass. "You gotta get up first, Baby."

I look down between us. "It's gonna be messy."

Luther shrugs. "Leather is easy to clean."

I make a face.

He's not wrong, but the visual of cleaning *sex mess* off a chair is... gross.

Moving my hands back to his shoulders, I try to lift my hips. But my quads shake, and I barely budge.

That's it. I give up trying, accepting my new existence. Stuffed with cock.

Luther is biting his lip, trying not to laugh.

"I think you'll have to toss me over the side of the chair," I tell him seriously.

Luther lifts a big shoulder, then lifts me—his dick sliding free—and shifts his weight like he's going to seriously tip me onto the floor.

"Luther!" I screech, clawing at his shoulders.

The laugh that comes out of him is the loudest I've ever heard.

He drops me back onto his lap, his dick under my ass but no longer inside me. And while I try to clench my core muscles for all I'm worth, he continues to laugh.

"You're impossible." I slide one of my hands down, cupping my vagina, trying to keep the mess from going everywhere.

Bareback sex is hot. But the aftermath is real.

"Your face." He's still fucking laughing.

I glare at him. "I'm showering without you." I pull my hand up and slap it, and the mess, against his chest.

He smiles harder. "That's right, Baby. Mark me as yours."

I roll my eyes, refusing to find him cute right now. "Most of that is yours."

He shrugs, unbothered. "Yeah, but it's your handprint."

Considering I was having the same thought about bruising, I can't really judge.

Damage done, I shuffle backward off his lap.

Luther keeps his hands on my sides, helping me balance, until I'm finally standing.

Lounged back, nude, covered in sex, Luther looks as comfortable as I've ever seen him.

And standing here, nude, dripping sex, I feel as comfortable as I've ever felt.

Insecurities... Body-image issues... Who are they?

While Luther lazily takes me in, I turn and walk toward the open door in the front corner of the room, snagging my backpack as I go.

I'm thinking about how beautiful the bedroom is, how I can't wait to climb into that massive bed, when I reach the bathroom.

There are four light switches, so I flip on the first one, and a soft golden glow illuminates from behind the matching mirrors over the double vanity.

And I stop.

His entire house has been impressive. But this bathroom is stunning.

A forest lover's spa.

The ceiling boasts exposed wood beams. Dark green glass tile on the walls of the giant glass-enclosed shower. Marble counters...

Luther enters behind me, his footsteps the only sound in the room.

He stops beside me and drags his hand across my bare ass. "Let's clean up."

While Luther starts the shower, I grab a hair tie out of my bag and pull my hair up into a ponytail.

As the water warms up, Luther opens a cabinet and grabs a

pair of fluffy green towels, and I prepare myself for the most luxurious shower ever.

Chapter 77

Luther

"You hungry?" I ask Kendra as she steps out of the bathroom.

I'm sitting on the foot of the bed—chair already cleaned—wearing a pair of gray sleep pants and a white T-shirt. And Kendra is dressed in gray sweatpants and a white tank top.

I smirk at our matching outfits.

Kendra nods in response to my question, even as she lifts a hand to cover a yawn.

"Or do you just want to go to sleep?" I smile at how cute she looks.

Kendra drops her hand. "I'm fifty percent hungry. Fifty percent tired."

"How about leftover pizza in bed?" I offer, feeling the same.

She perks up. "That sounds amazing, actually."

I hold out my hands.

Kendra rolls her eyes as she crosses the room and takes my outstretched hands in hers.

I groan as she helps me stand.

"Need me to get you some Aspercreme, Old Man?"

She's teasing me, but I'm tempted to say yes. "If you're offering to apply it."

Kendra swats at my stomach, and I catch her hand.

She's not going to get lost walking with me to the kitchen, but I still slide my palm down until our fingers are entwined.

For the last few days, I've spent so much time thinking about Kendra, about what I should do, what's right, that I forgot how good I feel when I'm around her.

I know nothing has changed in our situation. But we're adults.

And as long as we keep what's between us private until we decide what to do, then we aren't hurting anyone.

With Kendra's hand in mine, we step out of my bedroom and into the hall.

A door slams from somewhere downstairs.

I push Kendra behind me, putting myself between her and whoever just—

A voice cuts through my fight mode.

A voice I'd recognize anywhere.

"Dad, I'm home!"

Chapter 78

Kendra

My heart is racing.

Because Luther's daughter is here.

But also because Luther's hand is still gripping the front of my shirt from when he shoved me behind him.

He didn't even hesitate.

We heard the door downstairs, and Luther dropped my hand, grabbed my shirt, and put himself directly between me and the danger.

The *danger* turned out to be his daughter, but damn.

Be still my fucking heart.

"Dad?"

The voice sounds closer.

Luther releases his grip and turns to face me.

His eyes are wide, his *oh fuck* expression matching my own.

"Bedroom," he whispers as he grips my shoulders, turning me around.

I try to keep my steps silent as I rush back through the double doors.

With my flight mode on and activated, I dart to the side, into the bathroom.

My racing heartbeat is the only sound I can hear, but I make sure to breathe quietly.

After a moment, I slowly turn around and peek back into the bedroom.

It's empty.

And the double doors are closed.

Chapter 79

Luther

I want to say something. Reassure Kendra.

But there isn't time.

Pulling the doors to my bedroom closed, I leave them just short of latched so they don't make any noise.

Then I take two long, quick strides down the hall toward the stairs. "Ash?"

I take another step, putting distance between myself and the woman hiding in my room, when my daughter appears at the top of the stairs.

"Hey, Dad." She drops her duffel onto the ground but keeps her backpack on.

I wasn't expecting her tonight. And she was about thirty minutes away from witnessing something she'd never be able to unsee. But no part of me is mad at her for coming home.

I tap my chin. "It's weird because I didn't think today was Friday…"

Ashley rolls her eyes as she walks her five-foot-ten frame toward me.

Her hair is a darker purple than the last time I saw her and hangs halfway down her back.

I pull her into a hug.

"Becks said she'd take my shift at work tomorrow so I could come home for an extra night," she says, referring to the tea shop she works at.

"That was nice of her." It was nice. But a heads-up would also be nice. I nod toward the duffel. "That all you brought?"

"I still have a suitcase in my car."

I'm not surprised. She's never packed light in her life.

Resigned to the situation, I start down the steps. "I'll bring it up."

Chapter 80

Kendra

I SET MY PHONE ON MY CHEST AS I LISTEN.

Footsteps. Door hinge opening. Door clicking shut.

"Where're you hiding, Baby?" Luther's quiet voice has me releasing my breath.

"Over here." I stick my arm straight up, but I'm not sure if my fingers show over the top of the mattress.

Lifting my head off the pillow, I watch Luther round the foot of the bed.

His gaze holds mine before glancing at the pile of furry rugs beneath me. "Why are you on the floor?"

"It felt weird to stay in the bathroom." I spent ten minutes doing just that, poking through his drawers and using his deodorant when I realized I forgot to pack mine. "And I didn't want to be on the bed, in case, you know... So, this seemed like a good solution."

He nods. "Solid assessment. But I can tell you right now, Ashley would never just walk into my room. I'm not sure she's ever even set foot in here."

That sounds unlikely, but when I think about it, I can't think of a single reason I'd ever walk into my dad's room.

"So..." I sit up, crossing my legs. "This is a pickle."

We can't let Ashley see me.

Even if we were serious enough that Luther would feel comfortable telling her, she knows my dad. And I'll be back here on Saturday *with* my dad.

So no, she can't know I'm here. We can't involve other people in our lies.

And if that means I have to hide all night, then I'll hide all night.

Luther sighs and lowers himself to the floor in front of me. "She was supposed to come home tomorrow."

"I heard." I admit to eavesdropping. "At least we got interrupted *afterward*."

Luther snorts. "No shit. That would've—Fuck." He leans back and shoves his hands into his pants pockets. "Shit, I bent them."

"Bent what?"

Luther holds up two Ziploc bags filled with slices of cold pizza. And I have to hold my hand over my mouth to keep from laughing.

"I can bring up more, or something else..." He grimaces, *unbending* the slices.

I drop my hand and take the bags from him with a smile. "This is perfect, thank you. I assume you're going to stay up for a bit."

Luther's expression is apologetic. "I'm sorry."

"You have nothing to apologize for. Our luck is just... not great," I say at the same time Luther says, "Cursed."

I reach out and poke his chest. "I'll be fine."

He grips my finger. "I have a water glass next to the sink in the bathroom. The tap water is good."

"Luther, I'll be fine," I tell him again. "I already tried to see if I could get an Uber out here, but there aren't any available."

He starts shaking his head before I even finish. "You're not getting into a stranger's car."

"There aren't any. It's not an option."

He shakes his head again. "Even if it was. I'll drive you home. We just have to wait and go early in the morning."

"Works for me." I open one of the bags and pull out a slice of pizza. "You're super certain Ashley won't come in?"

"I'm certain."

I nod. "Okay, but fair warning, if you're gone for more than an hour, there's a one-hundred-percent chance I'll be asleep in your bed when you come back."

His look softens. "And I'm super certain that I'll like finding you there."

Chapter 81

Luther

"I'm calling it a night." I stand from the couch with a groan.

Ashley shoves her hand into the bowl of popcorn on her lap. "'Kay. You want me to help with anything tomorrow?"

I roll out my shoulders. "You can come with me to the grocery store. Diego gave me a list of what I need to buy."

She perks up. "Diego is cooking?"

I nod.

"What's he making?"

"Come with me to the store and find out." I pick up our dirty plates and head to the kitchen. The pan from the nachos we made is still sitting on the stovetop, but I ignore it, leaving it for tomorrow.

Ashley turns to look at me over the back of the couch. "You don't want to go shopping early, do you?"

I huff. "As though you'd be awake." I have to give her crap because it's what I do, but I'm happy to take the opening. "I have to run out for a bit in the morning, so I might be gone when you get up, but we can go around noon and grab lunch while we're out."

"Sounds good. Night, Dad." She turns back around to face

the TV and the rest of the treehouse-building episode we were watching.

"Night." With Ashley's back to me, I snag two packets of Pop-Tarts out of the pantry, along with a bag of peanut butter–filled pretzels. I don't know if Kendra is still awake, but the thought of her being hungry has me reaching for a pair of granola bars. Keeping my body angled so Ashley won't see my pile of treats, I call back over my shoulder. "Don't stay up too late."

Her *Yeah, yeah* follows me as I climb the stairs.

What a fucking night.

The lights are off in the bedroom when I push my doors open. And I'm careful to be quiet as I close them behind me.

I consider locking them, but I'm still just as certain that it would take an actual house fire for Ashley to come in here. I'll risk her finding me asleep next to a woman rather than locking her out during an emergency.

Shaking the idea of a fucking fire out of my head, I carry my stash of food into the bathroom and leave it on the counter.

I quickly get ready for bed, brushing my teeth and ditching my clothes so I'm left in a pair of boxer briefs.

The drapes are still open, so the moonlight illuminates my way to the bed—and the sleeping woman under the covers.

I take a moment, standing there.

Kendra's curled up on her side, hugging one of my pillows, with the blankets pulled up to her nose.

If it were any brighter in here, I'd take a photo. Saving this memory forever.

Instead, I climb into bed.

Carefully, I pull the pillow free from Kendra's grip and slide my body into the space.

She makes a humming sound in her sleep as I drag her against my chest.

I press a kiss to the top of her head, shushing her.

And it feels so right.

It all feels so fucking right, having both my girls under my roof.

My daughter safe in my house.

My woman safe in my arms.

And I want to keep this.

This feeling.

This sense of peace.

I want to keep it so fucking bad that it breaks my heart.

"Wake up, Baby." I gently shake Kendra's shoulder.

She grumbles something but doesn't move.

"I don't want to get up either." I yawn and tighten my hold on her. "But if we don't go now, then we're gonna have to lower you from the balcony with tied-together blankets."

"That only works in the movies." Kendra tips her head back and cracks an eye open to look at me. "But nice of you to offer. After the chair, I figured you'd just toss me over the railing."

I grin. "I'd never. And certainly not after you took directions so well." I flex my fingers against her side. "Who knew you had it in you."

The hand on my chest shifts, and she tugs on my chest hair.

"Watch it." I slap my hand down, trapping hers with a tsk. "It's too early for punishments."

She huffs.

The alarm on my phone that I snoozed a few minutes ago starts up again.

Groaning, I release her hand and reach over to turn it off.

"What time is it?" Kendra rolls onto her back beside me.

"Little after five."

"Five?" She says it like it's the most absurd thing she's ever heard.

"Uh-huh."

She groans but starts to sit up. "At least I can go back to sleep when I get home."

I think about crawling into bed with her at her place... then I remember it's *Joe's place*. And we don't know what time he's coming back.

Defeated, we both get up.

With minimal talking, we head into the bathroom and brush our teeth together, finally utilizing my double vanity.

I pull on jeans and a flannel while Kendra stays in her sweatpants. Then we exit my room.

We're both silent as we walk down the hall. And even though I'm sure she's sound asleep, I still keep my eyes on Ashley's closed bedroom door.

The stairs are quiet under our feet, and we make it to the mudroom without incident.

I have to toe Ashley's shoes out of the way before I can step into my boots. And as I bend down to lace them, I can't stop the ache in my chest.

It's early Friday morning, and I'll get to see Kendra tomorrow afternoon when she comes over for the party. It'll be here before I know it.

But when she's here, I won't get to touch her.

I can't.

And we can't have another laundry room moment.

We really can't.

But...

Standing, I reach out and grip Kendra by the shoulders.

She only has one of her sandals on, and she nearly stumbles as I pull her to me, but when I hug her to me, she wraps her arms around my waist.

After the party.

After the party, we'll figure our shit out.

Chapter 82

Kendra

"Wait, am I supposed to bring something?"

Dad looks at me, then down to the envelope in his hand. "It's just some cash. Isn't that what people do for graduations?"

"Well, yeah. But..." I heave out a breath, not believing I didn't think about it until this moment. "Did you already seal the envelope?"

Dad nods slowly as he pulls a face. "Probably should've let you sign the card too, huh?"

I drop my head back with a groan. "Just give me a minute."

In my bedroom, I drag one of my cardboard boxes out of the closet and rip it open.

If I can make it through today without stress sweating through every item of clothing I have on, it will be a fucking miracle.

First, I woke up with a jolt in the middle of a nightmare. I don't remember the details, but my heart rate told me it wasn't good.

Then, I spent a literal hour trying to decide what to wear to my secret boyfriend's daughter's college grad party.

I finally settled on a pair of flowy dark green linen pants and a snug black tank top. My hair is down, and I'm wearing my favorite pair of comfy black leather sandals.

Appropriate for summer. Cute but not sexy.

And the colors hopefully won't show the sweat that's already gathering.

Finally spotting what I'm looking for, I grab the painted tin box.

Unlatching the box, I take the stationary to my nightstand and pull out one of the handmade cards and a matching brown paper envelope.

The bright floral design might not be on theme for a twenty-six-year-old woman I've never met, but these are the only cards I have.

I pull my cobalt-blue pen out of the tin, open the card, and stare.

This is why people spend too much money on store-bought greeting cards. Because trying to decide what to write in a blank card, to a person you don't know, whose dad you're fucking, is… horrible.

I lower the pen to the paper three separate times before I settle on simple.

Congrats!
From,
Kendra Abbott

My mouth pulls into a frown.

It looks so dumb. The signature is three times longer than the message.

Whatever. Too late now.

I drop the pen back in the tin and carry the card to my office, where I keep my purse.

Taking a hundred dollars out of my wallet, I figure the cash will make up for the lackluster card.

I lick the envelope and seal the card and cash inside.

I groan again when I look at the blank envelope.

Gritting my teeth, I go back to my room, find the pen, and write *Ashley* on the front of the envelope.

Why does this also look dumb?

I drop the pen, again, and with stress filling every inch of my body, I head back to the kitchen.

"Did I spell her name right?" I hold the envelope up.

Dad looks at it, looks at the envelope in his hand, and shrugs. "That's how I spelled it."

I press a palm to my forehead. "Dad."

"What?" He lifts his hands. "Rocky talks about her all the time, but he doesn't spell her name when he says it."

I groan. "If this is wrong…"

Dad shrugs again. "The cash still spends the same."

I let my cheeks puff out with my exhale. "True. Alright, let's go."

Dad eyes me as he opens the door leading into the garage. "You okay?"

I follow him, keeping my gaze firmly away from the laundry room. "I'm good."

He stops next to his truck, not getting in. "You sure? Because you're acting stressed out."

Cool. Glad that's translating.

"I'm fine. I just…"

I'm stressed because I've been sleeping with your best friend behind your back.

Today I'm meeting his daughter, who is only six years younger than me, and I have this bone-deep need for her to like me.

I'm terrified that she won't like me and that Luther will call this all off.

Instead of that, I go with a partial truth, knowing Dad won't drop it until I give him an answer. "I want Ashley to like me. You and Luther are such good friends, it… it would be awkward if we didn't get along."

Dad sets his hand on my shoulder. "Of course you'll get along. You get along with everyone." He smiles and drops his hand. "And if Ashley doesn't like you, we'll fight them."

A laugh pops out of me. "Them?"

He nods. "Yeah. Father versus daughter."

"Versus?" I laugh again.

"Yep. I'll take Ashley, you get *Luther*." He says Luther in a high-pitched voice, mimicking me.

I scoff. "You're such a chickenshit."

"Have you seen the man? He eats workouts for breakfast." Dad reaches for his door handle. "I ain't fightin' him."

Walking around the truck to the passenger side, I bite down on my smile.

I'm still stressed, but I have *seen the man*. And he does indeed look like he eats workouts for breakfast.

Chapter 83

Luther

THE WEATHER IS PERFECT.

The overhead garage doors are open.

The vehicles are parked in the grass, and the garage is filled with borrowed tables. Two are covered with the food Diego has been prepping all morning, and the rest have tacky gold plastic tablecloths.

Gold has nothing to do with Ashley's school, but it's her favorite color, and when we went to the party store yesterday, she insisted.

They match the gold balloons tied to the mailbox and the gold streamers hanging from the rafters.

It's basically a re-creation of her high school graduation, and it has me feeling all sorts of nostalgia I wasn't prepared for.

My daughter walks past me, headed for the food, but I snag her arm and pull her in for a hug.

"What is wrong with you?" She laughs as she twists out of my hold.

"I'm just proud of you." I reach for her head like I'm going to ruffle her hair, and she skips out of reach.

"I appreciate that, but you've told me a thousand times

already." She holds her hands out, warding me off, as she walks backward.

"Your point?"

Ashley rolls her eyes as she spins toward the dessert table.

I turn my attention to the driveway.

The party is an open house from noon to four.

It's one.

Kendra should be here soon.

"Brownie?" Ashley holds one out for me.

I take it, smiling to myself. "Thanks."

We take bites at the same time.

Then we make matching sounds of appreciation.

As we eat, I look around at the crowd. About a dozen people linger in the driveway and yard, standing or using the scattering of camping chairs. And just as many sit around the tables in the garage.

My sister is one of the people in the garage, and she's been giving me the side-eye since she got here—when I quietly reminded her to pretend she hasn't met Kendra before.

Ashley brushes her hands together. "Those are good."

I shove the rest of my brownie into my mouth. "Yep."

"You sure you don't mind if my friends stay? They just texted to say they're about an hour away."

Some of Ashley's college friends surprised her this morning, saying they were driving the few hours here for her party, and I told her they could stay the night. Going back tonight would be too much driving. And I suspect if they know they can stay, they'll partake in the coolers of beer and hard cider.

"As long as they don't mind sleeping on couches and floors." I give Ashley a pointed look. "And as long as you're not trying to sneak a boy into your room."

"Boy." Ashley snorts. "And no, hand on the bar top, I'm not interested in any of my friends that way."

"Good."

She's twenty-six. She's dated. I've met a few of her boyfriends. But... not in my house.

Ashley makes a noise of excitement, her attention moving past me. "Oh my god, is that Joe's daughter? She's so pretty."

I force my head to turn slowly. Force my features to stay the same.

But when I see her, my heartbeat falters.

She's so fucking pretty.

As she walks toward us, Kendra's pants shift against her thighs with every step.

Her tank top is modest, but it's clinging to her every curve.

She clearly doesn't understand that no matter what she wears, she's always going to look like a goddess of desire.

And her loose hair... My fingers twitch, itching to grip it.

I swallow. "That's her."

Kendra's eyes are hidden behind sunglasses, making it impossible to tell exactly where she's looking.

It's a smart play. If no one could see where I was looking, I'd be staring at her tits.

Joe raises his hand. "Happy graduation!"

Ashley waves back, then rushes forward.

Chapter 84

Kendra

I hold my breath as a girl, who has to be Ashley, hurries toward us.

We meet right at the threshold of the garage. And as much as I want to keep hiding behind my sunglasses, I push them up onto the top of my head.

My dad holds his arms out, and Ashley goes right to him, giving him a hug in greeting.

And that's when I realize Luther's daughter is tall. Like... way taller than I am.

My dad is just about six feet tall, and she's practically the same height.

I glance down to see if she's rocking six-inch heels, but no. Her sandals have maybe an inch-thick platform sole, but that's it.

Her jean shorts are tattered but expensive looking, and her purple hair is beautiful against her sparkly gold tank top.

She's stunning and not at all what I expected.

Not that Luther wouldn't have beautiful children. She just looks nothing like him.

Must look like her mom.

I blink.

How have I never asked about her mom?

"How's that big old brain feeling?" Dad asks as he releases her.

Ashley laughs and taps a finger to the side of her head. "The brain is happy finals are over and that we never have to take another test, ever."

Dad nods. "It's a good feeling. I'm proud of you, kid."

She beams.

And guilt claws at my stomach.

Then she turns her attention to me, giant smile still in place.

Even though we're only an arm's length away from each other, Ashley lifts her hand, giving me a wave. "Hi."

"Hello." I wave back, feeling so incredibly awkward.

There's a beat of uncomfortable silence before she shrugs. "Sorry, I'm a hugger."

By the time I register her words, she's stepping into me and pulling me into a hug.

After a second, I gently hug her back, the card in my hand crinkling with the motion. "It's, um, nice to meet you."

I can barely see over her shoulder, but I still widen my eyes at Luther as he walks up behind her.

His jaw twitches, and I can't tell if he's amused or as stressed out as I am.

"Totally same." Ashley gives me a squeeze before she lets me go and steps back.

Luther stops beside her, in front of my dad.

"Welcome to the party." Luther's voice settles some of my nerves.

Dad reaches out and slaps him on the shoulder.

"Thanks for having us." I try to say it as normal as possible, but I still feel overwhelmed with awkwardness.

Dad says something about the weather, and I open my mouth to tell Ashley I like her hair, but when I glance at her, I find her looking down.

At my feet.

I glance down, wondering if I stepped in something.

But I don't...

My heart stops.

My sandals.

The same sandals I was wearing the other night when I was here.

When I left them by the door.

When I got trapped in Luther's bedroom because Ashley came home early.

I swallow and look away, not wanting to meet her eyes.

She saw them.

She had to.

My pulse revs. And the stress sweat comes back with a vengeance.

Why didn't I think of that?

Will she ask me about them?

Do I try to think of a lie?

"Alright, what smells so good?" Dad rubs his stomach.

"Diego's cooking." Luther steps to the side, making a path for my dad. "I'm sure we have too much, so please help yourself to multiple servings."

Dad nods as he heads toward the food tables. "Can do."

Who could eat at a time like this?

Before my body can decide between puking and passing out, Ashley hooks her arm in mine, startling me.

I glance up, waiting for her to drag me out back, but she just follows my dad. "I'm so excited you're here. Joe's always talking about you."

Ahead of us, Dad grins over his shoulder. "I didn't even pay her to say that." Then he pretends to sneakily hand Ashley the card he brought.

Ashley laughs as she takes it.

Taking the opening, I hold out the card I brought as well.

"Aww, thanks, you guys." Ashley holds the cards against her chest with her free hand, our arms still hooked together.

"Ashley, let the woman get some food. You can smother her with your affection later." Luther holds a plate out for me.

Ashley huffs but drops my arm. "Okay, food first."

I take the plate, and Dad and I take our time loading up on savory items, while Luther and Ashley go to the dessert table.

As I grab a fork and napkin, I tell myself that I imagined her staring at my sandals. That it was night when she got home and the lights were on low. She probably didn't even see them.

She was probably just looking at my nail polish. I did put on a fresh coat last night. And maybe she loves periwinkle just as much as her dad does.

While I try to convince myself of this, I look around for a place to sit.

I step toward the closest table, and I smile at the woman sitting there.

Then I pause. Because I recognize the woman.

And it takes me a beat. But then I remember. And I can feel the color drain from my face.

It's the woman from the Inn.

The bartender.

Sweet guilt-laden Jesus, I'm not going to survive today.

Why didn't I think about this possibility? Of course Luther's employees would be invited.

And didn't he just say Diego made the food? Is he here too?

I only saw him for a moment, so maybe he won't remember me.

I think about the bartender. I saw her for a lot more than a moment.

But maybe her memory isn't great. Maybe she won't remember me.

Pretty fucking please, don't remember me.

The woman's eyes lock with mine, and that's all it takes for me to know she remembers everything.

I'm going to be sick.

A warm palm presses against the center of my back.

He shouldn't.

Not with everyone around.

But...

I lean into him, just the smallest bit.

Luther steps up next to me, his side pressing against my shoulder. "Kendra, this is my sister, Jessie. Jessie, this is Kendra, Joe's daughter."

I feel like my eyes are about to fall out of my head.

I'm fucking sorry, did he just say sister?

Luther increases the pressure on my back, like he's worried I might just drop my plate and run.

Honestly, it's a good option.

Jessie stands and holds her hand out to me over the table. "Nice to meet you, Kendra. So funny because I've heard Joe talk about you, but he always calls you Kenny."

Setting my plate on the table, I shake her hand, when what I really want to shake is Luther. With my hands around his throat.

"So funny." I try to laugh, but it sounds like a choke.

That day at the bake sale, Courtney mentioned something about Luther's sister being there before us, but then my dad showed up, and then the park ranger showed up, and then I completely forgot about it.

I forgot about it. But Luther sure as shit shouldn't have.

I glance up at Luther, and he gives me an apologetic expression.

"Men." Jessie provides, reading the situation correctly.

I huff. "Seriously."

"Sorry," Luther whispers.

We ignore him as I take the seat across from Jessie, and we both sit.

I want to say something, but I don't know what I can say here, in the open.

I feel terrible that we're including Jessie in our lie. She mentioned my dad talking about me, but maybe it's more of a passing-by type of friendship. Like she just knows him because her brother is friends with him.

Maybe.

Hopefully.

Universe, please just give me this.

On fucking cue, Dad sets his plate next to Jessie's and drops into the folding chair, bumping his elbow into hers. "Hey, Jess, how's it going?"

Well, that was the shortest-lived delusion ever.

Luther sets a bottle of beer next to my plate as he takes the seat next to me, across from Dad.

"Thanks," I murmur, torn between wanting to strangle him and wanting to curl up in his lap.

"Can I sit by you?" His daughter's voice startles me, again, as she sets a plate of dessert on my other side.

"Of course." I smile, and I know I show too many teeth.

Flustered, I reach for the beer.

Before I can wrap my fingers around it, Luther's hand reaches it first.

That idea of strangling is suddenly even more likely, but then I watch as he twists the top off for me.

Oh.

"Thank you," I say as I take the open bottle from him.

"Mine too." Dad pushes his beer across the table toward Luther.

"Open your own." Luther shakes his head.

"The caps hurt my hands," Dad complains, pushing the beer even closer to Luther.

Sighing, Jessie leans forward, grabs the bottle, twists off the top, flicks the cap at Luther, then hands the bottle to my dad.

Dad flutters his lashes at Jessie. "I think I'm in love."

She rolls her eyes at him.

"I think you're an idiot," Luther grumbles as he opens his own beer.

Ashley laughs.

And I bite my lip. If I laugh right now, it will one thousand percent turn into full-blown hysteria.

"So, are you liking Colorado?" Ashley turns sideways in her

chair to talk to me. "Have you been anywhere cool? What's your favorite part?"

I blink at her.

Luther stage whispers from my other side, "She's a bit of an extrovert."

My smile feels less forced this time. "I haven't really gotten out and about yet, but everywhere is just so pretty," I tell Ashley truthfully.

She starts to tell me about her favorite places to go, and as she talks, I notice that the cards my dad and I gave her are blessedly nowhere in sight.

She probably put them wherever the rest of the gifts are. But she could've lit my hundred dollars on fire for all I care. I just don't want to be around when she reads the lamest card in history.

Eventually, Dad butts in with questions, and the conversation flows to Ashley's classes.

Finally free from attention, I slump into my seat.

Which is when I spot Luther's plate. And the fact it's heaping with nothing but brownies.

"THEY'RE HERE!" ASHLEY HOPS UP OUT OF HER CHAIR, and we all turn our heads to see a group of twentysomethings—three girls and two guys—walking up the driveway.

She mentioned earlier that some of her friends from school were coming. And seeing her excitement over their arrival, I'm glad they did.

My hope for today was that Ashley wouldn't hate me, but I hadn't really given any thought to whether or not *I* would like *her*. But it didn't take the past hour for me to decide. I think it's probably impossible to not like Ashley. She's sweet and funny and seems like a genuinely nice person.

And yes, I'm still peeved at Luther for not telling me that his sister was our bartender. But seeing how kind of a human he raised... that's made up for it, more than a little.

"Guess I should say hi to the people who are going to be sleeping under my roof tonight." Luther groans as he pushes himself up to standing.

Ashley and her friends are already walking through the garage, so Luther doesn't go far.

As they approach, I watch in amusement as all of Ashley's friends stare at him.

Even the guys.

One of the girls whispers something to Ashley, and she replies by pretending to gag.

I bite down on a snicker.

I get it.

If one of my friend's dads looked like Luther... I'd be inviting myself to sleepovers as often as possible.

"DRINKS?" I ASK AS I STAND FROM THE COUCH.

The weather took a turn about an hour after Ashley's friends showed up. We were able to drag all the outside chairs into the garage before the rain started. But the drop in temperature sent everyone inside.

Somehow, I ended up in the living room with Luther, Ashley, and her friends. All of us easily fit on the two large couches and pair of armchairs.

I don't know where my dad is, but he was chatting with Jessie last I saw, and I'm trying my best to avoid her.

Which I feel bad about. Because she seems cool. But I still feel guilty about her having to lie for us. And the hard cider I just had is sitting so nicely in my system that I'm afraid I'll say something I shouldn't, outing the fact that we've met before.

Maybe this next drink will be a mistake, but the alcohol is helping the stress-sweat situation, and my dad is the one driving home, so... I'll take the gamble.

Luther drains the rest of his beer. "If you don't mind."

I hold my hand out for his empty. "I don't mind."

I haven't paid attention to how many Luther has had, but the way he's looking up at me says he's had a few.

My fingers open and close, and he presses the glass to my palm.

Ashley's sitting on the other side of Luther, and when I lift my brows in question, she shakes her head.

"Anyone else?" I ask, and one of the guys nods.

"I'll take a beer, but I can help." He starts to get up from his couch.

"Don't worry, I got it."

"You sure?" he asks, still perched on the front of his seat.

"Positive." I smile.

He's nice, but I don't remember his name.

I think Luther and I have done a good job of acting casual around each other, but I can feel the possessiveness radiating off Luther, and letting another man close to me might make him unreasonable.

Excusing myself, I make a quick detour to the powder room, then grab two beers and a cider from the garage before heading back into the living room.

No one has moved, so my spot on the end of the couch next to Luther is still open.

I give the beer to the other guy first and sit back in my spot, tucking one leg underneath me.

"Here you go." I hold the beer out for Luther.

He sits up from his reclined position, taking the bottle. "Thanks, Baby."

My heart stops.
He just called me Baby.
In front of his daughter.

"Goats." Luther coughs the word while he pats his chest, like he swallowed something wrong. "You can hire them to eat your lawn."

I cannot with this man.

It's the worst recovery in the history of recoveries.

I'd laugh if I didn't instead want to spontaneously combust and die.

The side conversations that had been going on are now quiet. And I don't know if it's because they heard him call me Baby, or if his dramatic chest thumping caught their attention.

Pretending none of this is happening, I open my can of cider and bring it to my lips as I lift my gaze.

Ashley is on the other side of Luther, so I can't see her expression, but one of the girls on the couch across from ours is smirking at me.

When we lock eyes, she mouths, *Lucky.*

Chapter 85

Luther

I make it halfway through the beer Kendra brought me before I need to get up.

Sitting forward, I turn my head toward Kendra. "I'll be right back," I tell her quietly.

She nods. "'Kay."

I want to touch her so fucking bad.

Even just a squeeze of her knee.

But I control myself and keep my hands to myself as I stand.

Wanting to use my own bathroom, I cross the great room and head up the stairs.

I internally berate myself with each step, not believing how badly I messed up by calling Kendra *Baby*.

I could feel Ashley's narrowed gaze on the side of my face the whole time but pretended not to notice.

I don't use pet names. Not ever. So her friends might not have thought too much about it, but Ashley would know better.

Shaking my head, I round the top of the stairs and notice my bedroom doors are closed.

I don't remember closing them.

My face scrunches at the thought of someone sneaking up

here to fool around, but when I swing the doors open, I find the room empty.

No one—

My gaze snags on something red.

I cross the room and stop beside my bed. And I grin down at the red thong sitting on top of my pillow.

Kendra must've snuck up and left it here when the party was still outside.

Setting my beer on my nightstand, I pick up the thong and hang it off one finger as I take a photo for my Brat.

Then I slide the panties into my pocket.

Chapter 86

Kendra

My phone buzzes, and I slide it out of my pocket.

It's a photo from *Papi*.

I open the text and immediately close it when an image of my thong fills my screen.

"So..." Ashley's voice sounds from beside me, and I jump, flattening my phone to my chest. I was so distracted I didn't notice her moving into Luther's spot. "I have a question."

I glance around, my stress immediately back up to peak levels. But the girl who said *lucky* seems to be the only one paying attention to us.

I turn back to Ashley. "Um, okay."

She shifts. "Are you and my dad, ya know, together?" She lifts her brows and tilts her head as she says *together*.

I open my mouth. Close it. Swallow.

I want to shake my head. Deny it. Tell her it's wild for her to even ask such a thing.

But I can't seem to do it.

Can't seem to deny *him*.

"I..." With no answer to give her, I trail off.

Ashley scoots closer and lowers her voice. "I saw your shoes here."

My stomach drops, and the cider inside it swirls.

Mayday!

"I didn't really think anything about it at the time. Figured they were Aunt Jessie's or something. But I recognized them when you got here. They were *your* sandals. You were here."

"I—" I bite my lip.

"Don't freak out." She moves even closer, until our knees are touching, both of us turned toward one another. "I want you guys to date."

She... what?

I don't understand.

"Why would you want that?" I ask just as quietly.

"So you are?" She squeals, then hunches forward, going back to being quiet. "You're really dating?"

I puff out my cheeks, then give her the smallest nod.

When she starts to bounce in her seat, I'm the one to lean closer. "It's new. And my dad doesn't know."

She gasps. "This is so scandalous." I can't stop my smile at her reactions. Then she mimes zipping her lips. "He won't hear it from me."

I appreciate her immediate answer, but I feel bad about adding yet another person to our growing mountain of lies. "It really doesn't bother you?"

"The twenty-year age gap? No."

"Twenty-four," I correct her.

She snorts. "Even better. Now when I tell Dad I have a boyfriend who's ten years older than me, he can't say shit."

When I was twenty-six, I thought I knew everything, but now that age suddenly seems so young.

"Is it serious?" I ask her, feeling instantly protective.

Ashley beams. "Yeah. He's great. Is it serious with you two?"

I don't have a good answer for her.

It feels serious. But we haven't really talked about it. Haven't talked about a future between us at all.

I lift a shoulder, confirming without saying.

She leans in more, until our noses are inches apart. "Do you love him?"

The question slides over me like molasses.

Do I love him?

The man who brings me food.

The man who cares for and provides for his family.

The man who can make me laugh and swoon and melt all in one night.

Do I love the man who makes me feel desired?

The man who makes me feel loved, even if I don't dare ask him for the words.

Do I love Luther?

I lift my shoulder again.

"Oh my god." She squeals as she reaches for my arms. "I can't believe it!"

"Can't believe what?" Luther's deep voice startles us both.

Ashley shrieks.

I jump.

Luther slaps the hand not holding his beer against his chest. "Jesus, Ashley, are you trying to fucking kill me?"

"Are you?" Ashley has both of her hands pressed to her chest. "Don't sneak up on people."

Luther huffs. "You're the one not paying attention. Now move over."

THIRTY MINUTES AND THE REST OF MY CIDER LATER, I feel like I'm going to crawl out of my skin.

I'm a bit tipsy. And all I want to do is cuddle with Luther.

I want to press my face against his neck.

I want to breathe him in.

I want his arms around me.

I want his words in my ear and his dick in my—

"This is where all the cool kids are hanging out, huh?" Dad stops beside the couch.

"Clearly. So go away," Luther replies, then finishes his beer.

Dad puts his hands on his hips. "I was going to offer to help clean up, but not with that attitude."

Luther waves him off. "Not necessary."

I glance toward the kitchen and the counters that are covered with trays of food.

Luther sees me looking and shakes his head. "I'm not putting you to work."

I sigh. "If you say so."

"I say so." Luther leans forward, sets his bottle on the coffee table, then stands.

Turning, he holds his hands out, one for me and one for Ashley.

It's the perfect cover. The only way for me to touch him without it seeming out of place.

I place my palm against his, and he bends his arms, his biceps bulging under his sleeves, as he helps us up at the same time.

His fingers flex around mine.

I squeeze his back.

And then we let go.

"Thank you so much for the cards." Ashley slips past Luther to hug my dad. Then she turns to me. "So great to meet you." She wraps me in a tight hug and lowers her voice to a barely audible whisper. "I'll give you time to tell my dad I know."

"Okay," I whisper back.

I don't really know if I want to be the one to tell him, but I guess it's better than her blindsiding him with it. Like she did to me.

"Congrats again," I tell Ashley as we break our hug.

"Thanks." She flicks her hair back with a smirk.

My dad holds his hand out to Luther. "Until next time."

Luther grunts as he shakes his hand.

And then it's time for us to say goodbye.

Am I supposed to shake his hand?

Is it weird if we hug? Ashley gave my dad a hug goodbye...

I want to hug Luther. I want it more than anything. But we've never hugged in front of my dad before.

"Joe, let me give you a bag of cookies to take home," Ashley says brightly, walking toward the kitchen. Pulling my dad's attention with her.

She really is my new favorite human.

Luther's palm settles on my back.

I think he's going to keep it there. Walk me to the door.

But then his hand slides around to my side, and he turns me as he tugs me into his body.

My arms go around his waist as his circle my back.

And I inhale, pulling that perfect scent of his into my lungs as I get the hug I was just hoping for.

I feel his mouth press against my hair, and my heart throbs.

Then he's letting me go.

I drop my arms as I step back, not daring to look at Ashley's friends as I do.

"I'll text you later." Luther's eyes bore into mine, and I know he wants more too.

I take another step back. "Have a good night."

Bye, Baby, he mouths silently.

I bite my lip, then turn and walk away.

Chapter 87

Luther

> Me: You did not have to give Ashley money.

I SHAKE MY HEAD JUST THINKING ABOUT IT.

After what I put Kendra through today...

Meeting Ashley. The surprise of Jessie being my sister—which was a stupid but honest mistake. I've been so caught up in Kendra I forgot all about that little detail.

But I'll thank the gods for the lady at poker night who gave my mom a cold. If I'd added her to today's lineup, Kendra would've run for the hills.

But instead, she gave my kid money.

My phone vibrates.

> Baby Doll: I remember being a broke college student.

I lean back in my chair, the worn leather molding to my shoulders.

> Me: I paid for her school. She doesn't have a single loan.

Baby Doll: That's really sweet of you.

Me: Thanks, Baby. But I wasn't fishing for compliments.

Me: Let me properly thank you for your generosity by taking you out for coffee this week. Wednesday?

Baby Doll: In public? Is that a good idea?

She's not wrong to worry. But I need to feel like I'm doing something to actually woo her.

I need one normal interaction where we don't have to hide and we don't have to pretend.

Me: There's a coffee shop called BeanBag about fifty minutes from here. I think you'd like it.

Baby Doll: I'll meet you there.

Setting my phone down, I pull her thong out of my pocket and run the material between my fingers.

Chapter 88

Kendra

Stepping out of my car, I realize that it's warmer down here than it is at home—higher up the mountain.

I pause for a moment, considering if I should take off my lightweight navy cardigan, but I decide to leave it. The shop could be cold inside.

Hiking my backpack onto my shoulder, I shut my car door and turn toward BeanBag Coffee.

When I plugged it into my GPS last night, to see if Luther's estimated time was correct, there were lots of hits for BeanBag. But the closest one was forty-nine minutes away, and I confirmed the address with him.

I'm early to our three o'clock meet time, and I brought my laptop so I could do some work while I waited.

But apparently, Luther got here even earlier since I can see his truck parked in the next row over.

All the same, I keep my backpack with me. Maybe I'll stay a bit after he leaves, enjoy the change of scenery.

I cut across the lot, and my traitorous sandals crunch a twig on the pavement.

I take a deep breath, careful to keep my expression neutral in case Luther's watching me through the wall of tinted windows.

I haven't decided when I'll tell him that Ashley knows about us.

I'll tell him eventually. I just don't know if today is the right time.

Our luck has been so bad already. We just need to catch a break for a minute.

The scent of coffee wafts around me as I open the door. And there's a wooden tinkling sound as I step inside.

Looking up, I see a small rain stick hanging next to the door, and it flips back over when the door closes. It's a satisfying sound and a much more earthy welcome than a metallic bell.

The place has a cabin feel to it. Wooden tables and chairs, large leather armchairs, and a fireplace that isn't currently crackling, but I can imagine that it would be in the winter.

A few of the tables have occupants. But only one of them has my man.

A bright kind of excitement fills my chest as I look at Luther from across the coffee shop.

He's watching me.

Staring.

And I feel like I can breathe again.

I feel settled.

Luther stands, but I stay where I am.

I didn't even realize how off-kilter I've felt until now.

His long strides close the distance in just a few seconds.

A few seconds for me to take him in.

To appreciate how his thighs look in those jeans. How his forearms look with the sleeves of his gray flannel rolled up. How his chest looks with the top buttons of his shirt undone.

He's such a fucking Daddy, it's unreal.

I clench my thighs, wishing I'd worn a skirt rather than shorts.

Not that we should have sex in a coffee shop restroom. But...

Luther stops before me, a smirk forming on his lips.

I open my mouth to ask him what he's smiling about, but he stops my question. With a kiss.

Warm hands grab me.

One against the side of my neck, the other on my hip, holding me in place while his lips press against mine.

My eyes close. And I reach for him. My fingers clinging to the material at his sides.

I want to wrap my arms around his neck.

I want to drag him to the floor.

I want to do so much.

But we're in public.

And even if we're away from people we know, we still live in a mostly civil society, so we can't dry hump each other.

We pull away at the same time, but Luther doesn't drop the hand he has against my neck.

"Hi, Baby Doll." His voice is desire and gravel.

I bite my lip. Knowing what I want to call him.

Knowing I shouldn't. But...

"Hi, Daddy." I keep my voice at a whisper.

Luther runs his tongue along his teeth.

I stare at his mouth.

"Let's get drinks." Luther lifts his chin toward the counter.

I nod.

The barista is about my age, and the way she's trying so hard not to look at us makes me wonder if I whispered as quietly as I thought I did.

I stop at the counter, and Luther stands directly behind me, so close that his front is pressed to my back.

He reaches an arm around me so his forearm is against the top of my chest and his hand is gripping my opposite shoulder.

"You first." I can feel his words vibrate against my back.

I look up at the menu board.

"Sorry, I need just a second," I tell the woman who's finally making eye contact with me.

"Oh, take your time."

There are so many drink options. I want to read all the descriptions, but I also don't want to take forever.

"Do you have a favorite?" I ask, rather than making a panicked decision.

"The, um, salty nut is really good."

I feel Luther huff a laugh at the name.

I smile as I try to find it on the board. "What is it?"

"A salted caramel and hazelnut latte," the barista supplies.

I perk up.

"Hazelnut is your favorite, right?" Luther asks.

I tip my head back to look up at him. "How'd you know that?"

"I saw the creamer you used at your, uh, dad's house." He starts to look sheepish as he explains. "During breakfast."

My brows lift. He's talking about that very first pancake breakfast. "Well, that was perceptive of you."

The side of his mouth goes up. "I have my good days."

I give him a side look, then turn back to the barista. "That would be great, thank you."

She taps the order in. "Iced or hot?"

"I'll... hot actually." The plan is to linger, so I'll get a hot drink to sip.

"And for you?" Her cheeks are pink when she asks Luther for his order.

"Hot black decaf, please. And do you have any bags of those Chilean beans?"

She nods.

"You still have that grinder at home, right?" I can tell from his breath on my cheek that he's tipped his head forward to ask me.

I hum my reply.

Going out on a date was a cute idea, but not if Luther is going to be all rumbly and sweet. It's affecting me too much.

"We'll take two bags of the whole beans," Luther tells the woman.

She gives us a total, and rather than try to argue with Luther over paying, I lean against him as he holds his wallet in front of me and pulls out a couple of bills.

"I'll grab those beans quick, then we'll get the drinks ready," the barista says as she hands Luther his change.

He stretches to the side and drops the leftover cash into the tip jar.

Yet another reason to find this man sexy.

"Thank you for the latte. And the beans." I reach up and wrap my fingers around the arm still around my chest. "I don't know if I've had coffee from Chile."

Luther slides his wallet back into his pocket, then settles his hand over mine, warming up my fingers. "Last year, one of the guys who worked here told me about them. Apparently they come from the same area of Chile that the rain sticks come from."

I think about the pretty sound from when I opened the door. "Interesting."

Luther shrugs. "Or maybe the guy was full of shit. But either way, it's damn good coffee."

When the woman returns with two bags, we untangle from each other, and Luther takes the beans.

I let him lead the way back to where he was sitting in the far corner.

The table is small and round with just two chairs. Perfect for being close.

Luther sets the bags side by side on the edge of the table, then goes back for his plain coffee when the order is called out.

I put my backpack on the floor beside one of the chairs and sit.

We stay quiet as Luther sets his coffee down, then goes back for my latte.

He puts the paper cup in front of me, and I wrap my hands around it while he lowers himself into the other chair.

"How was your day?" Luther's dark eyes stay on mine.

I let a smile pull at my lips. "It was alright."

"Just alright?"

"Well, it's recently gotten better."

The man smirks.

I tell him about my current project at work. We sip our drinks.

He tells me about the rest of his weekend with Ashley. We slide our free hands across the table.

Our fingertips meet, and I slide mine another inch closer.

Luther places his hand on top of mine.

And I have to ask him.

"Luther?"

"Yeah, Baby?"

I hesitate for a moment, then exhale. "Can I ask you about Ashley's mom?"

I expect Luther to pull away.

To move his hand off mine and sit back in his chair.

But he doesn't.

He stays leaned in.

And he doesn't sigh. Doesn't act uncomfortable.

"I'll tell you whatever you want to know," he says, and I know he means it.

"I didn't hear anyone mention her during the grad party. Is, um..." I didn't think this through. I can't really just ask if she's alive, can I? "Is she around?"

"If by *around* you mean living in the US, then yes. But she's not involved in Ashley's life."

His answer brings up so many more questions, but I ask the first one that pops into my brain. "Were you married?"

Luther glances away. Then he slides his hand off mine. "Are you fucking serious?"

"Sorry." My heart starts to pound. "Sorry, I—"

He turns his head back to me, his gaze wide. "No, Baby, it's not—"

"Kenny?" My dad's voice infiltrates my bubble of panic.

My head snaps to the side. "Dad?"

He's halfway across the room, walking straight toward us.

I look down to where my hand is on the table. Where Luther had his hand over mine.

Did Dad see that?

I look at the bags of coffee standing on the edge of the table.

Please let that have blocked his view.

"What are you two doing here?" Dad's eyes are narrowed when he reaches our table.

"Hey, man." Luther somehow sounds completely normal. "I'm just running into everyone today."

Chapter 89

Luther

"You ran into each other here?" Joe's eyes are bouncing between us. And I'm surprised he could even hear my words over the sound of my heart trying to thud out of my chest.

I really need to get my affairs in order because I give it a fifty-fifty chance I survive the year.

"Yup." I pick up my coffee. "Small world." Feigning a casualness I do *not* feel, I take a sip of my drink, then nod at the table next to ours. "Grab a chair."

I slide the bags of coffee beans across the table so they won't be in Joe's way.

Joe looks at Kendra.

She smiles brightly and pats the top of her backpack. "I brought my laptop to do work, but maybe my boss will give me the rest of the day off."

My heart aches.

I hate this.

Hate lying to my friend.

Hate making Kendra lie to him.

Hate involving my sister in the lies.

Guilt fills my throat, making it hard to speak.

I force myself to swallow.

We can't keep doing this.

"Alright," Joe says slowly. "I'm going to order. Need anything else?"

I shake my head, same as Kendra.

Joe's kindness makes me feel even worse.

When he turns away, I meet Kendra's gaze.

And I hate the look shining in her eyes.

"I'm sorry," I whisper.

I'm sorry I thought this was a safe location.

I'm sorry for the stress and guilt.

I'm sorry for making you feel anything other than joy when we're together.

"It's not your fault." She rolls her lips together and glances toward the counter where Joe is ordering his drink. "I just... I'll be right back."

Kendra pushes her chair away from the table and stands.

I want to say something. Tell her we'll figure it out.

But I can feel the turmoil rolling off her, so I don't push the topic. I just nod.

Joe's still busy ordering, so I watch Kendra.

I watch her walk behind her dad.

Watch her pass a pair of women sitting next to a pair of strollers.

Watch a small toy fly out into her path.

Watch Kendra stop and pick it up.

Watch her smile as she says something to the moms.

Watch her hand the toy back to a tiny hand sticking out of the stroller.

I watch my girl interact with a future I can't give her.

That guilt runs down my throat, filling my stomach.

I—

Joe steps into my view, and I realize I was staring after Kendra.

With his eyes on me, he grips a neighboring chair and drags it noisily to our table.

I take another drink of my coffee, giving me something to do other than speak.

Joe lowers himself into the seat and lifts his coffee to his mouth, then pauses like he remembers it's hot.

"Rocky." He sets his coffee down. "Are you trying to seduce my daughter?"

I blink.

If he'd used any other word, I probably would have given myself away. But *seduce*?

I shake my head with a snort. "Seduce? What century is it? Are you ill?"

His shoulders slump, and he heaves out this breath. "Sorry, I... It just looked like—" Joe drags a hand down his face.

And I swallow down more guilt. "Long day?" I ask to change the topic.

Joe drops his hand and lifts his coffee again.

Then he tells me about a mess-up on an order at his shop.

He tells me because I'm his friend and because he took my response as a no.

But I was shaking my head *at him*, not in answer to his question.

If he asked me the right question. If he looked me in the eye and asked me if I'd slept with his daughter.

I'd tell him.

I'd admit to everything.

I'd tell him I was falling for her.

Tell him I've already fallen.

If he was anyone other than her father, I'd talk to him.

I'd ask him what to do.

I'd ask him if it was worth risking my friendship for the possibility of something good.

I'd ask him if he thought I was enough.

If offering myself in exchange for a future with a family was enough.

But he didn't ask the right question.

So I don't tell him anything.

Chapter 90

Kendra

I wash my hands twice before using the restroom, then I wash them again after.

The baby was cute enough, but that rattle thing was somehow both slimy *and* crusty. And if he tosses it in my path again, I will step around it and keep walking.

I pause at the door, not yet able to step out just yet.

When I was trapped in Luther's bedroom that night Ashley came home early, he said our luck was cursed.

And I think it must be.

Think this series of constant close calls is some sort of punishment from the universe.

I blow out my breath.

We're at the point where we need to just do it.

We need to tell my dad.

I close my fingers around the door handle and pull it open.

We won't tell him here. Not right now. Not before we have a strategy.

But soon.

Stepping out of the bathroom, I can't stop my eyes from going straight to Luther.

The way he greeted me today...

I can still feel his hands on me.

His heat on my back as we ordered.

I can still feel the way his voice rumbled against me.

Our luck might be cursed, but it still feels like magic every time we're together.

Squaring my shoulders, I cross the room.

Luther sees me first, and then my dad turns in his chair to watch me.

His smile seems normal.

He seems fine.

Luther shifts, and I watch him pull his phone out of his pocket.

"Sorry," I say to my dad as I reach the table. "Had to go."

He lifts his cup. "We really shouldn't drink so much of this." Then he takes a sip.

I roll my eyes as I take my seat.

Luther slides his chair back from the table. "I gotta go. Jessie's not feeling great, so I need to take over the bar."

Dad cocks his head. "Really?"

"Oh, that sucks." I wrap my hands around my latte so I don't reach for Luther.

I'm not sure if he's telling the truth or if he's making it up as an excuse to leave.

And I'm not sure if I should thank him or be mad.

It'll be less awkward if it's not all three of us. But still.

Luther stands. "Sorry for cutting this short." His eyes meet mine. For just a moment.

"Bye," I say quietly.

Luther nods and grabs his coffee and one of the bags of beans, then he walks away.

My dad watches Luther leave. "Does he seem a little off to you?"

Danger. Danger.

I shrug. "Maybe he's worried about Jessie?"

Dad shakes his head. "She seemed fine when I saw her."

"At the grad party?" I ask. "That was like four days ago."

"Huh? Oh, right."

Speaking of acting off. "Are you okay?"

He sighs. "I think I need pizza."

I laugh. "Oh, is that the diagnosis?"

Dad nods. "Want to stay and finish these here?" He lifts his drink. "Or should we do an early dinner on the couch in our pajamas?"

"Definitely option two."

Chapter 91

Kendra

> Papi: Are you home?

I PICK MY PHONE UP OFF MY DESK.

> Me: Yes.

> Papi: I'll be there in ten.

> Me: Okay.

I set my phone back down.

I haven't spoken to Luther since the coffee shop yesterday. And I just feel... uneasy.

Jittery.

We need to talk. I know we do.

And as much as I know it has to be done, I am *not* looking forward to telling my dad about us.

I stand, needing fresh air.

Chapter 92

Luther

I slow as I turn into the driveway.

My heart has been pounding since I texted Kendra. And I feel like I'm going to throw up.

The house comes into view, and I see her.

Sitting on the front steps, she looks perfect.

And as I put my truck into park, I know I'm doing the right thing.

Opening my door, I get out.

Chapter 93

Kendra

Luther shuts his truck door, and I stand, moving down the rest of the steps.

But he doesn't come to me.

He stays where he is. A few yards away.

And I can feel it.

It's heavy. And thick. And dark.

"Luther," I whisper.

It's a plea.

An unspoken question.

A *please don't do this.*

His shoulders drop. "I'm not right for you."

One sentence.

Five little words.

And every one of them slices through my heart.

He looks down, taking a second, then he lifts his head. And he holds my gaze. "You have your whole life ahead of you, Kendra. You're beautiful and smart. You have so much to offer. And I have nothing to give."

"I... I don't understand." Moisture fills my eyes.

How did I read this thing between us so wrong?

So incredibly wrong.

"I've already lived. I have my daughter. I got to experience raising her. And I wouldn't change it, but I'm not going to have more kids." He shakes his head. "And I can't take that away from you. I won't make you choose."

His voice is steady, and it makes me want to scream.

Why is he doing this?
Why didn't he ask me about kids?
If he asked me, I'd tell him.
I'd tell him everything.
I want to tell him.
I open my mouth. Inhaling.
I can stop him.
Stop this.
But he keeps going.

"Joe's my best friend." Luther's voice finally hitches. "He's my best friend, and he deserves better from me."

I close my mouth.
There it is.
The tears finally fall, streaming down my cheeks.
I can't stop them.
Can't stop the sliced pieces of my heart from slipping between my ribs.
If it was just about kids...
If that was the only thing holding him back...
But it's not.

"I won't tell him. But if you want to, I won't stop you." His features twist as he watches me cry. "I'm sorry."

I lift my shaking hands and press my fingers to my lips.
They're trembling.
Everything is trembling.

"I'm sorry," Luther says quieter this time. "Please say something."

I part my lips to pull in a shaky breath.
Locking eyes at the bar.
His hand on my thigh.

Luther walking through my motel room door.
The first kiss.
The first caress.
My Daddy.
The man sleeping at my side.
Running into Luther in the hallway.
His hand on my throat.
Luther giving me his number.
The first text.
The first phone call.
My Calm.
Hands and mouths and heat and skin.
Him promising that this wouldn't end badly.
His daughter asking me if I love him.
Him telling me he's not right for me.
Him choosing a friend over taking a chance.
Him not choosing me.
His fucking promise.

He takes a step toward me.

I drop my hands. "You promised." I take a step back. "But I understand."

I understand it all too well.

More tears fall.

"Kendra," Luther chokes out.

I shake my head as I turn my back on him. "You should go."

Chapter 94

Kendra – 10 years ago

"You should go." I hold my apartment door open.

My boyfriend looks at me in confusion. "I don't understand. I thought things were good."

"I'm moving, and I... I like you, but I don't want to do long distance."

It's true. I am moving.

But in three weeks. And only thirty minutes away. I just... This is for the best.

"I'm sorry," I add.

My composure is slipping, and I need him to leave.

I need him to leave so I can have my fifth breakdown in as many days.

He lifts his hands, then drops them to his side. "I can't change your mind?"

When I shake my head, he sighs and walks out.

I open the next box and finally find the plates I was looking for.

I've only unpacked about a third of my stuff into the new apartment, but it's only been a few days.

I sent my dad my new address today, and he called immediately, asking why I didn't tell him sooner so he could've come to help.

It took fucking everything I had to keep it together, lying and saying I had help.

He would've come. I knew that. And that's why I didn't tell him.

Because if Dad were here, I'd end up telling him about *it*.

And I... I just don't want to make him worry.

Everything will be fine.

I'm sure of it.

So he doesn't need to know.

Not now.

Maybe someday.

A calendar notification pops up on my laptop screen.

Surgery tomorrow at seven a.m.

"Hi, Kendra. Can you hear me? How are you feeling?"

The voice bobs around me as I blink my eyes open.

"Wha..."

"Kendra, you just had surgery. The tumor removal was successful."

THE NURSE HELPS ME INTO THE WHEELCHAIR, THEN helps me to the main entrance of the hospital.

My friend already has her car pulled up to the front of the hospital.

A hospital that is only a five-minute drive from my apartment.

"You sure you don't want me to stay until your mom comes?" my friend asks as she pulls up to my building.

"I'm sure."

My mom isn't coming.

I never told her either.

TAKING THE FINAL PRESCRIBED PAIN PILL, I SET THE empty bottle down on the bathroom counter.

I tap my fingers against the tile, then I pick up the business card that's been propped against my mirror for a week.

I carry it out to the living room and carefully lower myself onto the couch.

Then I dial the number.

"Hello, this is Doctor Merideth's office."

I swallow. "Hi, um, I think I need to talk to someone."

Chapter 95

Kendra

The door shuts with a thud.
A literal barrier between me and him.
Luther.
The man...
I pull in a gasping breath.
I didn't see that coming.
I should've seen it coming.
I don't look back.
Don't need to see him go.
Luther is leaving.
For good this time.
I walk through the house. Straight through to the back door.
Through the backyard.
Through the grass.
To the edge of the woods.
And then I step through the trees.
I keep going until I can't see the house behind me.
Until there's no one around.
Then I let my legs give way, and I sit in the dirt.
The tears are still falling.

Mountain Daddy

My breathing is still choppy.
But I'm quiet.
Only my inhales give me away.
He didn't choose me.
I close my eyes, and images of Luther fade in and out of the darkness.
Memories.
Feelings.
Wishes.
My spine loosens, one vertebra at a time, and I lie down on my back.
Pine needles catch in my hair.
A branch digs into my side.
But I don't move.
I feel it.
I feel all of it.
That's something I learned from my therapist.
I learned how to feel it.
How to feel the bad, the unknown, the uncomfortable.
Feel it. Let it live. Let it die. Let it go.
Right now, the bad is alive.
It will be alive longer than I want it to be.
But if I don't feel it.
If I don't let myself accept Luther's words, then I'll never move on.
Tears still trail down from the corners of my eyes into my hairline. But they're falling slower.
I fill my lungs all the way.
And I hold my breath.
Then I let it out.
Another breath. Another exhale.
On the next breath, it hits me again. The hurt.
And I let it live.
I let the hurt fill my chest, same as the oxygen.

S.J. Tilly

Because the pain is true. The pain is as alive as I am.
But it won't beat me.
Won't defeat me.
It will just hurt me.

Chapter 96

Luther

The street sign blurs before me.

I squeeze the steering wheel tighter.

I didn't cry when my wife cheated on me.

I didn't cry during our divorce.

I don't remember the last time I cried from sadness.

But my throat aches.

And my heart fucking hurts.

Why does this hurt so much? I did the right thing.

I keep telling myself that.

I did the right thing.

By letting her go, I'm letting her choose whatever future she wants.

By letting her go, I'm not holding her back.

Letting her go was the most chivalrous act I've ever done.

So why does it feel like I just made the worst decision of my life?

Chapter 97

Kendra

A crunch sounds to my right.

I open my eyes.

Another crunch.

I don't know how long I've been lying here, but it's long enough that my tears have dried on my cheeks and my breathing has evened out.

The sun filters through the branches above me, and my body aches as I sit up.

There's another crunch right before a cute pointy face appears.

"Hey, Buddy," I whisper through my still-tight throat.

The fox takes a few steps closer.

I cross my legs and set my hands on my knees.

I want to reach out for him. I'm dying to pet him. But I also know he's a wild animal, and I probably shouldn't let him this close to me.

But I'm not exactly in the best headspace right now, so I continue to talk to the furry guy.

"It's okay." I keep my voice gentle. "I'd love to be your friend. If that's okay with you."

He inches closer, and that's when I notice his limp.

My exhausted heart squeezes inside my chest. "Are you hurt too?"

He comes another step closer, then another, keeping his front foot off the ground.

I thought I was done crying, but I've been wrong about a lot of things recently.

More tears fall as I see the string wrapped around his perfect little furry foot.

"You poor thing." My crying turns to sobbing.

This is too much.

He hobbles closer and lets out a noise that's more like a scratchy shout than a bark.

The sound catches me off guard, and I jump, making him jump.

And it's all just sad and cute, and *oh my god, I am currently not mentally stable enough to tend to an adorable woodland creature while maintaining any sort of dignity.*

He shouts again, creeping closer.

Ready for it, instead of startling, I laugh. "You really are the cutest thing ever, aren't you?"

I hold out my hand, palm up.

My new best friend stretches his neck, sniffing, while I focus on breathing and staying still. "See, I'm okay."

He hobbles closer. And closer, until his bristly chin hair rubs against my fingertips.

I huff a laugh that has him hopping back. "Sorry, sorry." I let out a real laugh this time. "I mean, I'm clearly *not okay*, like, at this moment. But in the general sense of the term... I'm an okay person. I'm just dealing with a little heartbreak," I explain. To the fox.

I reach my hand out a little farther, setting it down on the forest floor between us.

"Can I call you Buddy, or do you have another name you prefer to go by?"

He cough-shouts and takes a hop forward, clearly confirming that Buddy is acceptable.

"Okay, Buddy. Can I see your leg?"

I'd feel ridiculous about talking to a fox, but I swear he understands me.

Buddy shuffles forward, then holds his injured leg higher.

Finally, a male that listens.

The ends of the string are frayed, like he's chewed it. But it's still knotted around his leg, between his ankle and his elbow. Or whatever an elbow is called on a fox.

I lift my gaze to meet his yellow eyes. "I need scissors. I could probably untie those knots with enough time." I glance at my painted nails and refuse to think about Luther. "But I'm afraid it would cause too much tugging, and I don't want to hurt you."

He blinks at me.

"I'm going to get up now, okay? And I need you to follow me."

I get to my feet as slowly as I can, trying not to startle Buddy.

He backs up but doesn't run away. And I take that as a good sign.

"Okay, come on, little dude." I pat my side and take slow steps.

Buddy shouts again. Then follows me.

I can feel dirt and other forest items stuck to my body, but I don't want to scare Buddy by trying to brush it off, so I leave it.

When I reach the yard, I glance back to confirm Buddy is still behind me.

He's just a few feet away.

"Keep following me, okay?" I keep my voice soft.

His little feet are quiet in the grass.

"Now, just wait here for one second." I hold up my hands before I hurry onto the deck, into the house, and down the hall to my bathroom.

Yanking the top drawer open, I pull out my little pair of beauty scissors, then I rush back outside.

I stand on the deck, looking. But I don't see him.

Buddy is gone.

"No." I start to cry all over again. Big hiccupping sobs.

Buddy is hurt.

And he needs help.

And—

A scratchy shout cuts through my tears, and Buddy scurries out from under the deck.

"Dammit, Buddy." I keep crying. "I told you I lied about being okay. You can't play games with me right now."

He sits at the base of the steps.

I pull in a slow breath, needing to gather my composure so I stop embarrassing myself in front of the wildlife.

"Okay..." I exhale. "I can do this."

I move toward Buddy and cautiously descend the stairs, lowering myself to sit in the grass before him.

Buddy watches me as I cross my legs.

And this time when I hold out my hand, I lay the scissors on my palm.

They're small enough that they don't hang off my hand, and I have the pointy end facing me so Buddy won't accidentally poke his nose.

He inches closer and sniffs the metal.

Then he sits again.

I chuckle. "Ready to get this over with, huh?"

My hands want to shake as I reach for his leg, but I will them to be steady.

Buddy is a wild animal, but he's small.

Worst case scenario, he freaks out and bites me, and I have to go to the hospital to get some shots. And when I come home with a bandage on my arm, I'll have to explain to my dad that I was playing nurse to a fox from the woods, and he bit me.

Best case scenario, Buddy holds still, lets me cut the string off, and then he becomes my lifelong companion.

"I promise to do my best," I whisper to Buddy as I reach for his leg.

His fur is thick, but he feels so fragile.

"You're such a good boy." He holds perfectly still. "The best." I slide one side of the thin scissors under the string. "We're almost done." I squeeze the handles of the scissors together. And the string breaks, dropping to the deck.

I slowly lower his leg and watch as Buddy gingerly sets his foot down.

"See? Does it feel better?"

Buddy darts his head down, snaps up the string, and then he shakes it like he's trying to kill it.

A real laugh bubbles out of me.

"Yeah, you tell that string who's boss."

Buddy drops the offending item and shouts again.

I snag the string before he can go back for it and ball it up in my hand.

I don't want him swallowing it.

"Well..." I look at his leg and the indentation in his fur where the string was.

I want to do more, like apply some ointment or something, since I'm pretty sure his skin is rubbed raw in places. But I'm certainly not qualified to treat a fox.

"How about I get you a little snack?"

He bounces once, and this time, his shout is extra loud.

I laugh again. "Alright, just hang tight."

Rushing back inside, I put some lunch meat into a small metal mixing bowl, then I dig through the garage to find a handful of towels.

Buddy is still waiting for me when I step back onto the deck.

"I know they aren't much," I lift the bundle. "But maybe you can take a little rest on them and let that leg heal up."

The towels are old, discards meant for rags, so my dad won't miss them.

I stand in the grass, not sure where to set them down, when Buddy lunges forward and snags the corner of a towel.

He drags it out of my hold and goes under the deck with it.

"Dad's not gonna like this," I say as I drop the rest of the towels where he disappeared. "Now, don't get so lazy that you forget how to hunt." I set the bowl of meat down next to the towels. "This is a one-time thing."

I'm pretty sure we both know this is not *a one-time thing.*

Buddy pops his head out from under the deck, sniffs the meat, then dives face-first into the bowl.

I lower myself to the steps, turning sideways so I can watch him.

The smile fades from my face.

I was expecting something so different from today.

I could tell something was off.

Knew we had to talk. Was nervous about exposing our relationship to my dad.

And the unease I felt was real.

Just for all the wrong reasons.

"Karma, am I right?"

Buddy glances up at me as he swallows another slice of turkey.

Buddy is confused, but I'm right.

I deserved this.

I did the same thing all those years ago. I made the decision to end it with my boyfriend. I didn't give him a choice.

But I knew.

I knew he wanted a family.

I knew I was doing him a kindness by not making him choose between me and something he wanted.

And *I knew* I didn't love him.

I didn't love him, and I wasn't sure I ever would, so I cut him loose.

Unlike then, Luther doesn't know what I want.

He doesn't know what I can and can't have.

He doesn't know how I feel about him.
But maybe he knows something more important than all that.
Maybe he knows that he doesn't love me.
And maybe he knows he never will.

Chapter 98

Luther

The sun is setting by the time I get out of my truck.

I've been sitting here, truck backed into the dark garage, engine off, staring at nothing for... hours.

Her tears.

The way she cried.

Her voice as she said you promised.

I press my hand to my chest.

I did promise.

And I meant it. When I said it, when I told her this wouldn't end badly, I meant it.

But I was wrong.

My boots are loud in the silent garage.

I was so fucking wrong.

Opening the door, I step into my house.

My empty house.

I keep walking.

I walk down the hall, through the main room, and out the back door onto the deck.

I can't be in there.

Not yet.

Not with Kendra's energy lingering in the corners.

"Crawl to me."

"Take your top off."

"Does that feel good?"

"I didn't ask what you wanted."

I close my eyes.

I never asked her what she wanted.

And that was my fatal mistake.

I never asked.

If I'd asked... If that day, before pancakes... If I'd asked her and she'd told me, we could have stopped it then.

It.

Us.

I tip my head back and breathe.

What's that bullshit saying?

It's better to have loved and lost...

I don't think so.

Whoever said that is full of shit.

Whoever said that never really loved someone.

Because if they had, they'd know that there's bliss in the ignorance of not knowing what you can't have.

There's bliss in the lack of hope.

Because for a few weeks... I hoped.

For a few weeks, I pretended she was mine.

For a few weeks...

I breathe.

I wish I'd never...

I breathe again.

Met her.

Seen her.

Touched her.

Tasted her.

Known her.

I try to breathe.

My throat is so tight I have to open my mouth to pull in air.

And with my eyes closed, the thin mountain air feels heavy around me.

I suck in a breath.

And I lean into the pain.

I feel it.

I deserve to feel it.

And as my heartbeat slows, I admit that I'm the one full of shit.

I wouldn't give up my memories of her for all the ignorance in the world.

Because if I can't have her, at least I can still have those.

Chapter 99

Kendra

"What's all this?" Dad's voice startles me, and I almost drop the plate of bacon.

"I need to put a bell on you," I say loudly so Dad can hear me over the music.

He crosses to the counter where my phone is blaring the nineties pop music and hits pause. "What's, uh, going on?" Dad eyes the piles of food I have spread throughout the kitchen.

"It's breakfast for dinner." I set the bacon down next to the sausage links.

"I can see that. And how many other people are coming?"

"Har, har." Then I take in the cheesy scrambled eggs, French toast sticks, hashbrowns, and cinnamon rolls.

Dad lifts his brows at me. "Something you want to talk about?"

I puff out my cheeks.

Clearly, I showed a little too much of my hand with this spread.

I was just trying to distract myself. And I was hungry.

And breakfast food is my favorite thing to make when I'm feeling down, but I couldn't decide what to make since pancakes are my usual go-to, but those remind me of Luther now...

I feel myself start to tear up.

Dad's eyes widen. "Is it your period?"

The scoff that bursts out of me is enough to put my waterworks on hold. "No, but thank you for asking." I don't tell him that I don't get those anymore. Today is certainly not the day for *that* particular conversation.

"Then...?"

"I found a fox."

I wasn't sure I should tell Dad about Buddy. Figured I'd wait and see if he even stuck around first.

But I'm still not really okay at the moment. And if I'm honest with myself, I think it's going to be a while until I'm okay again.

I know I'll get there. Eventually.

But in the meantime, I'm going to need to find other things to talk to my dad about. So it might as well be Buddy.

"Was it... dead?" Dad grimaces.

"Was what...? No!" The tears build in my eyes all over again at the mere thought of finding Buddy dead. "He's fine."

My voice cracks, my tears start to fall, and my dad looks absolutely horrified.

He waves his hands around. "Then why are you crying?"

"Because you asked if he's dead!" I practically yell.

Now that I've started crying, I can't stop.

"I don't even know who *he* is!" Panic fills his voice.

"He's Buddy!"

I use the back of my hands to brush off my face as I try to even out my breathing.

"Kenny." Dad lowers his voice like I'm the wild animal. "You know I love you, right?"

I choke on a laugh. "I know."

"So if you tell me you met a fox named Buddy, then I'll believe you, okay?"

This time I snort. "I didn't make him up."

He nods. "I believe you."

I brush away another tear as I smile. "Dad."

"Yeah?"

I point past him to the back door.

He glances to where I'm pointing, then rears back. "Holy shit."

Buddy, who is sitting just on the other side of the glass door, lets out a scratchy shout.

Dad slowly turns his head back to me. "It's a fox."

I grin. "It's a fox."

"Night."

"Night, Dad," I call over my shoulder as I walk down the hall.

"I was talking to Buddy," he calls back, heading to his room.

I shake my head.

We ate our breakfast for dinner while watching *Indiana Jones*.

It's a favorite from when I was younger and had just the right amount of violence and humor to distract me from my mood.

But as I step into the bathroom, my thoughts are no longer distracted, and I have to focus on getting ready for bed.

I concentrate on brushing my teeth and washing my face.

I take care applying lotion.

I avoid my reflection in the mirror.

And when I enter my bedroom, I push my cute pajamas aside in the drawer and choose my frumpiest pair. Ones Luther has never seen.

Clothing Luther has never touched.

And it's not until I turn my light off…

It's not until I climb into bed. Not until I'm under my covers.

It's not until then that I let myself think of *him*.

Chapter 100

LUTHER

My feet settle against the cool floor as I climb out of bed.

I can't sleep.

Can't settle.

Can't shake this horrible feeling that's crawling all over my skin.

I leave the lights off and walk through the dark house, letting the moonlight guide me downstairs.

To the liquor cabinet.

Chapter 101

Kendra

"Fuck." I squeeze my eyes shut. The sunrise creeping in around the curtains is too much for me to handle.

The pillow against my cheek feels damp, and my throat aches like I've been talking in my sleep.

But it's not from talking. It's from crying.

I was crying in my fucking sleep. Because even in unconsciousness, I can't shake thoughts of him.

And if sleep isn't safe, then I guess I'll get up.

And it'll be better if I'm tired today. I can let the exhaustion distract me.

Staying in my worn sweatpants and oversized T-shirt, I shuffle my way down the hall toward the scent of coffee.

Dad seems to already be gone for the day, and that's for the best.

I can only say I'm crying over Buddy so many times before Dad either gets suspicious or assumes I'm having a complete mental breakdown.

My eyes snag on the bag of coffee beans sitting next to the coffee maker.

The beans Luther bought me.

And my damn eyes start to burn. Again.

Probably am having that breakdown.

I cross the room and pick up the bag.

It's been opened.

I unroll the top and sniff the beans inside. Then I take the carafe off the warmer and sniff the steam floating up from the surface.

Definitely having that breakdown.

With my free hand, I take a mug out of the cupboard and fill it with the special Chilean brew.

For a moment, I consider drinking it black, like Luther does. But I'm already sad. So I take my hazelnut creamer out of the fridge and add some to my coffee.

Then I take the container of leftover breakfast sausage out of the fridge, dropping the lid in the sink.

Carefully, I balance the Tupperware on top of my mug, and I pull the back door open.

Somehow managing not to spill, I bring my goods over to the stairs and take a seat.

"Buddy?" I say quietly, in case he's sleeping, and set the glass dish of sausage on the bottom step.

I know leaving food out isn't a great idea since I don't want to accidentally attract bears. Or mountain lions.

And I know cooked meat isn't the usual diet of a wild fox.

But I literally cannot handle the thought of Buddy going hungry because his foot is injured.

Sighing, I cup my mug with both my hands, and I stare down at the liquid for a long minute before I take a sip.

When I do, I curse.

Of course it's delicious.

Why? Why can't it be terrible?

If it were terrible, I'd happily throw the bag away and never have to drink it again.

But I can't do that. Not with good coffee.

The heaviness that's been looming around me settles on my chest as I stare off at nothing.

How am I going to do this?

Luther is best friends with my dad. They hang out all the time. How am I supposed to stay here and pretend I'm okay being around him?

I think about the possibility of Luther dating someone his age who *doesn't want kids*.

Think about him bringing her over here for dinner.

Think about my dad telling me stories about Luther and his new woman, not knowing he's breaking my heart with every word.

I think about it.

And I truly don't think I could handle it.

Setting my coffee down, I stand and head back inside, leaving the door open an inch as I do.

It only takes me a moment to retrieve my laptop, then I return to my spot on the steps.

I place the laptop on my thighs and open it, spending the next thirty minutes sipping my coffee and searching for corporate assistant jobs in Denver.

A few sound decent. And I apply for them because I need to give myself options. But honestly... I like working for my dad.

Tired of applications, I open a new browser and search for apartments in Denver. With the amount Dad is paying me, I could keep working for him but still move out. And Denver is close enough for a day visit, but it would put a few hours between me and Luther.

A few states would be better, but I won't let this *breakup* rule my future, and I like living in Colorado.

Minutes go by while I scroll apartments, and a streak of red catches my attention.

Looking up from my screen, I spot Buddy darting toward me.

"Hey, Buddy." I smile at his perfect little face.

He smiles back before shouting at me and leaping at the sausages.

My smile grows when I realize he wasn't limping.

"Well, you seem to be feeling better."

Buddy lets out another one of his scratchy shouts. Then downs another sausage.

I laugh. "You must be a growing boy." As I say it, I wonder how old he is.

After opening a new web browser, I start a search for *How to tell how old a fox is*.

In the results is a suggested question for *How long do foxes live*.

I click on it.

I should not have clicked on it.

That sadness inside me folds in on itself. Doubling. Tripling.

"That... That can't be true," I sob.

Unable to help myself, I search more. And the answer is still the same.

Buddy tilts his head, looking at me.

"It's not true." I lie to him. "Foxes can live forever."

Chapter 102

Luther

Jessie gives me the side-eye. Again.

"What?" I sound as exasperated as I feel.

She flicks her wrist so the towel in her hand drapes over her shoulder, then she puts her hands on her hips. "I'm going to ask you what's wrong, and you're going to tell me."

"Noth—"

"And you're not going to say *nothing is wrong*." She says the last part in her mocking man voice. "Something is obviously wrong."

It's been four days and—I glance at the clock—three hours since I told Kendra we were done.

And yes, something is definitely wrong.

I feel like someone died.

I can't sleep.

I'm drinking every night.

I haven't showered in two days.

So, even though we're in a heat wave, I have a beanie pulled down over my hair so no one can tell what a mess it is.

At least here, in the bar, you can't tell if the whiskey you're smelling is from me or the bottles lining the wall.

"I..." I can't make myself say it.

I haven't told Jessie that it's over between me and Kendra. And saying it out loud...

I blindly grab a random bottle off the shelf behind us and a shot glass off the drying rack.

Saying it out loud will be the final nail in the coffin.

And I can't lift that hammer sober.

Eyes on me, Jessie grabs a shot glass for herself and holds it out.

I fill hers, then mine.

Setting the bottle down on the bar—knowing I'll need more than one round—I tap my shot to hers.

We don't say anything as we tip the drinks back, swallowing them in one go.

I set my glass down next to the bottle, and Jessie puts her empty next to mine.

She looks at me cautiously. "If someone died, you'd tell me, right?"

The edge of my mouth pulls up into an ironic smile. "I'd tell you."

This time, she's the one who picks up the bottle, pouring two more shots. "How about we get drunk on the job, you spill your guts, and we make Joe come drive us home."

Joe.

I pick up my glass and down it.

She clicks her full shot to my empty one, then tips it back.

"I appreciate you," I tell my sister.

She's a pain in my ass, but she understands sibling code.

Never get drunk alone when you can get drunk with your sister.

"I—" My phone rings.

Pulling it out of my pocket, I see it's Ashley and accept the call.

I press the phone to my ear. "Hey."

"Hey, Dad."

"What's going on? Everything okay?"

She huffs. "Everything is fine. Why do you sound so... stressed out?"

Jessie snorts. "Because he *is* stressed out."

I narrow my eyes at her. *How good is her damn hearing?*

"Hi, Aunt Jessie," Ashley half shouts into the phone.

"Hey. Ash."

I sigh and put the phone on speaker as I circle around the bar and sit on one of the stools.

It'll start getting busy soon, but we're in that late-afternoon lull, so there's no one but Jessie close enough to hear our conversation.

"What're you up to?" I ask.

"Just driving home from work. We're going out to dinner tonight to celebrate my new raise," Ashley says excitedly.

"A raise? That's awesome," I say as Jessie lets out a whoop. "Just for being your usual amazing self?"

"I mean, yes." She snickers. "But also, because..." I hear her drumroll her hands on her steering wheel. "I got a promotion."

Jessie whoops again, and my first real smile in days pulls across my lips. "That's great, Ash. I'm so proud of you."

"Thanks. My boss told me she'd give me a gift for graduating from college. I figured it would be some bonus money or maybe a day of PTO or something. But she made me assistant manager."

"Damn." Jessie drags the word out.

I point at the pair of glasses. "Pour us a celebratory shot."

Ashley laughs over the phone as Jessie complies.

Jessie and I clink glasses.

"Who are you going to dinner with? Your new subordinates?" I tip my shot back.

"Uh, my boyfriend, actually."

I swallow wrong, choking on the booze as it burns my throat. "Excuse me?"

Jessie grins.

I point a finger at my sister. "Why are you smiling? Did you know about this?" Ashley laughs. "And you—" I point at the phone, the three shots starting to hit me. "Since when do you have a boyfriend?"

Ashley hums. "Since... a little while ago."

"Was it one of the boys who spent the night at my house? You said—"

"It wasn't one of them. Calm down before you hurt yourself. Kurt was out of town that weekend."

"Kurt? What sort of name is Kurt?" Both of the women in my family continue to laugh at me, but I ignore them. "And where was he? What was more important than his girlfriend's graduation party?"

"He was in Oregon helping his mom move into a retirement place."

"Oh." That takes the wind out of my sails. "Well, if you're serious about this guy, bring him by sometime."

"Thanks, Dad." She pauses for a beat. "Maybe we could double date."

I blink at the phone. "Double date?"

"Yeah, with you and Kendra."

I blink at the phone some more, then lift my gaze to Jessie. "Did you tell her?"

She's wide eyed, but it's only humor written all over her face, not guilt.

And not sadness, because I still haven't told her it's over.

"No one told me about Kendra," Ashley answers before Jessie has to.

"Then how...?" I sound off. I can hear it. But hopefully, they'll think it's from surprise. Not heartbreak.

Ashley scoffs. "I could smell the pheromones wafting off you two the minute she walked up the driveway."

Jessie barks out a laugh.

"Pheromones? Seriously? Who raised you?" I try to joke.

"Uh-huh. That and the fact that I recognized her shoes. They were in the entryway the night I got home."

I purse my lips. I even remember kicking Ashley's shoes aside the next morning but didn't consider... "Well. Shit."

Ashley laughs.

And I push the shot glass closer to Jessie.

I can't think about that night.

Can't think about how perfect Kendra was.

How perfectly we fit together.

I can't think about how right it felt to have her sleeping in my bed.

Jessie only fills the glass halfway this time.

"You guys are so cute together." Ashley sounds wistful. "Love looks good on you."

Love.

Pain fills my eyes, and I swallow the shot, then shove the glass back to Jessie.

"Love is..." *Love is a strong word.* "We aren't..." I swallow.

We aren't in love.

We aren't even together.

"Chill, Dad. It's okay, she told me."

I stare at the phone screen.

Ashley hasn't seemed to pick up on my emotions, but I can feel Jessie staring at me.

"She told you what?" I work to keep my voice steady.

"That she loves you."

She loves you.

I press my fist against my chest.

It feels like my heart stopped.

Ashley makes a thoughtful sound. "I mean, she didn't just come out and say it. I kinda questioned her. But she was cool about it, so don't get mad at her for telling me."

"I'm not mad." The sentence comes out as a whisper.

"Oh, shoot. My friend is calling, I gotta take this. Love you, bye."

Ashley ends the call the moment she stops talking, saving me from having to find my voice.

She told you what?
That she loves you.
I stare at the bar top.
Kendra said she loved me at the party.

"I don't know why you're acting so surprised. It's obvious to anyone with eyes how you feel about each other. You're like freaking magnets. Drawn together." Jessie sighs. "I know the whole part about telling Joe is going to be messy, but... she's your other half, Luther. He'll understand."

The pain inside my chest builds.

And builds and builds.

I reach for the bottle, pouring another shot to the brim of the glass.

Lifting it, I make eye contact with Jessie. "I broke up with her. It's over."

I take the shot.

Jessie's mouth drops open. "What? Why the fuck would you do that?"

"I'm not right for her," I croak.

"Bullshit," Jessie snaps, then leans over the bar. "That's total bullshit. You might be a giant dumbass, but you're perfect for that girl."

"I'm not. She deserves better."

"What about what you deserve?" Jessie angrily pours a drink for herself. "Don't we all deserve our person? No matter the risk."

Our person.
My other half.
I push my glass across the counter.
Jessie pours.

Chapter 103

Kendra

"Can I borrow your truck?" I ask, stopping beside the couch.

Dad looks away from the TV. "Sure. You helping someone move?"

"Um, never. I just need the, uh, space."

Dad turns all the way to face me, narrowing his gaze. "Am I going to regret this?"

Fighting the constant urge to cry, I drop onto the open end of the couch. "Foxes in zoos can live up to fifteen years."

Over the past few days, I've spent way too much time researching foxes. And rain sticks.

It hasn't been healthy.

"Okay..." Dad has a worried look on his face.

My next inhale is shaky. "Foxes in the wild only live for three to five years."

I watch Dad swallow and glance toward the back door. "How old is Buddy?"

"I don't know." I press my lips together. Hard.

He looks back toward the door.

I've caught him feeding Buddy more than once. And even though all my research tells me to stop doing it, I know I won't.

"Is that what you want the truck for? You gonna build a zoo?" Dad tries to joke, but I can hear the tremor in his voice.

I don't know why he's never had pets. He clearly has the heart for it.

Then I think about the three-to-five-year answer I found online and how that deadline has hung over my head since I learned about it.

Is this what pet owners feel like? This desperate mix of love and terror?

Is this what it feels like to be a parent?

"I thought..." I take a breath, needing to keep my shit together. If I lose it now, I'll cry all night. "I thought I could buy him a doghouse. I know it's not a whole habitat like at a zoo. But..." I take another breath as I think about the other fact I learned. "Foxes are self-domesticating."

Dad clears his throat. "What does that mean?"

"They want to come inside."

Dad drops his head back and lets out a deep breath. "Well, that feels heartbreaking."

"I know." I half laugh. "And I know we can't just let Buddy into the house. But I thought if we could get him a house..."

Sitting up, Dad picks up the remote and turns off the TV. "I'll come with you."

WITH THE LARGE PLASTIC DOGHOUSE SECURED IN THE truck bed with a pair of straps, Dad slams the tailgate closed.

They had a few styles, but this one is shaped like an adorable little cottage, and sections of the roof pop up as vents, so it won't get too hot inside.

It was the most expensive one the store had, but since Dad

was happy to drive the hour it took to get here, I wasn't surprised when he insisted on paying.

I also won't be surprised when Dad decides to build Buddy a custom house. It's only a matter of time.

I climb into the passenger seat while Dad puts the cart in the corral. And I'm buckling my seat belt when he gets in the truck.

"Hungry?" Dad asks, starting the engine.

"Starving."

Chapter 104

Luther

"We need to switch." Jessie sets a glass of beer in front of me, swaying a little as she steps back.

Since I'm already well and truly drunk, I don't disagree.

My fingers wrap around the cold glass, and I close one eye as I raise it to my mouth, grateful Jessie chose the stout and not a bottled beer that's often served with limes.

Gulping down a third of the glass, I wipe my mouth with the back of my other hand as I set the beer next to my empty plate.

I'm tempted to ask Diego for a second burger, but I'm just as tempted to go lie face down in one of the motel rooms and cry myself to sleep.

She fucking loved me.

Loved. Past tense. Because she certainly doesn't anymore.

"Be right back." I stand from my stool, then grip the edge of the bar top to steady myself.

I'm well aware this isn't a good look for the owner in his own bar, but the locals won't judge me, and the nonlocals don't know I'm the owner. So... I pick up my beer and swallow down another third.

Gotta counteract the food I had. I can't afford to be any sort of sober right now.

The glass thuds against the wood as I set it down harder than I intended.

"Gonna piss," I tell Jessie.

She wrinkles her nose at me, then she starts to snicker. And it makes me feel a little better that she's drunk too.

Diego sticks his head out from the kitchen door. "Smalls said he's on the way."

I blink at him before I remember. "Cool."

Jessie snickers again.

And Diego rolls his eyes before he disappears back into the kitchen.

I don't really care if Jessie is getting drunk with me while on the clock, but I do need a sober person around for closing, which is why Smalls is coming in.

"Jess, do you want a room? I think there's two open." I don't feel like going home tonight, even if Jessie can find someone to drive us.

She tips her head from side to side, then stills like that made her too dizzy. "Probably should. I bet Joe'll be asleep by the time we lock up."

I nod.

He does go to bed pretty early. And we can't really tell him why we got wasted.

"Good thinkin'." I nod again. "I'll get us keys."

Chapter 105

Kendra

It hits me too late.
Way too fucking late.
Dad is taking us to the Inn.

Chapter 106

Jessie

I sway my hips to the classic rock playing from the speakers overhead.

What a night.

I feel awful for Rocky, but it's been a while since I've been this drunk, and I kinda forgot how fun it is.

And I'm purposely forgetting how horrible I'll feel tomorrow.

I sway some more.

This would be more fun if I had someone to dance with.

Across the room from me, the main door opens. And Joe walks in.

I blink.

Is this real?

Did I just manifest my brother's best friend?

I blink again.

He lifts a hand.

I lift my hand in return, my lips pulling up into a grin.

Then someone walks in behind him.

Kendra.

Joe's kid.

Wait.

Not just Joe's kid.

The reason I'm drunk. The woman Rocky is losing his mind over.

I blink again.

Oh fuck, Rocky!

Joe and his daughter start to cross the room while I fidget with my apron.

They're going to sit at the bar.

Of course they will.

Because Joe doesn't know Rocky and Kendra are going through something.

Joe doesn't know anything.

I swallow as my heart hurts for my brother.

Even shit-faced, I know Rocky will keep his secrets. But I can't make him do that.

I can't make him face Kendra.

Not tonight.

Not like this.

As if scripted, Smalls walks in through the back door, right next to the bar.

"Hey, Jessie." The tall, lanky man smiles at me.

He makes it behind the bar just as Joe and Kendra grab stools.

As they all say hi, Joe introduces Smalls to Kendra, and I sidestep toward the end of the bar.

"Hey, guys." I try to greet them casually, hoping to hide the panic I'm currently feeling.

But Joe tilts his head, that adorably curious expression covering his face. "You good?"

I nod. "Super good. Just gotta... do something."

Chapter 107

Luther

Someone crashes into me.

I grunt, reaching out to catch the arm of the person in front of me.

It takes a moment for my vision to cooperate. "Jessie?"

We're standing in the alleyway between the bar and the motel rooms, and I don't know why she's out here.

She pushes at my chest. "Get back."

"Huh?" I look down at her hands. "What are you doing?"

"You have to turn around." She pushes again, but she's so weak it doesn't do anything.

"Your muscles are so puny." I poke at her bicep.

"Focus." She slaps my hand away. "You need to disappear."

My face scrunches up. "What? Why?"

She leans in, lowering her voice. "Because Kendra is here."

The sentence slithers into my brain one word at a time. Kendra. Is. Here.

My eyes lift over Jessie's head to the door just feet away. Here.

Kendra is in my bar.

I take one step forward into Jessie's space.

"She's not alone." Jessie shoves at my chest again.

"Not alone?" Red sparks in my vision.

"Joe is with her."

The jealous rage vanishes as quickly as it appeared.

Joe.

Fuck.

Kendra isn't here looking for me. She's here because Joe wants to be here, for whatever reason, and she couldn't tell him she didn't want to come.

Because I'm certain she didn't want to come.

Jessie drops her hands as she feels the fight leave me. "Go lie down. I'll tell you when they're gone."

I pull the keycards out of my pocket, double-checking the numbers before I hand one to Jessie. "I owe you."

She takes the key for a room on the second floor. "I take payment in the form of airline vouchers."

I huff. But as I stumble back to room number two, I figure I owe my sister a whole vacation.

Because I can't have Kendra see me like this. As a drunk, unshowered mess.

I need Kendra to be okay. I need her to find someone better than me.

And if she sees me looking like hell...

Her heart is too big. She'll know I'm struggling, and she'll know I...

She'll know I love her too.

And I can't let her know that.

I need her to believe me.

I need her to believe she's better off without me.

Chapter 108

Kendra

"Whiskey and ginger ale, please," I tell the tall bartender.

He smiles and turns to my dad.

Jessie ran out of here pretty much the second we sat down, and I have to wonder what she's doing.

Maybe warning Luther that we're here?

His truck is in the lot, so I know he's here. I panicked about it the whole walk in.

But I don't see him.

Dad orders the burger of the week, and I ask for the same.

I didn't hear the description, but if Luther is nearby, it doesn't matter. I won't taste it anyway.

The bartender steps back and calls into the kitchen for two burgers, then he starts on our drinks.

Dad got a root beer since he's driving. But since I'm not driving, I suck down half of my cocktail the moment the bartender slides it in front of me.

Thankfully, Dad is talking to Smalls about some baseball game, so he doesn't notice my sudden thirst.

I'm still darting my gaze around, looking for Luther, when Jessie steps back into the bar.

I try to look casual, unbothered, as she circles back around behind the bar.

"How's it going...?" Jessie sounds like she regrets the question before she's even done asking it.

And I know she knows.

We both glance at my dad, but he's still talking about the game.

I shrug in reply, not able to give her a real answer. "How are you?"

She bites her lip and shrugs herself. The movement makes her step to the side, and she reaches out to grip the bar. "Sorry," she snorts. "I'm a little drunk."

I choke on a laugh.

Dad turns his head. "Miss Jessie, did you just say you're drunk?"

Jessie nods, trying to suppress a smile.

"Does Rocky know?" Dad glances around like he's just realizing his bestie isn't here.

I lift my drink and suck down more.

Her gaze darts to me. "He's, um, drunk too."

"Seriously?" My dad laughs. "Where is he? I want to give him shit."

Jessie shakes her head. "He's asleep. You'll have to wait until tomorrow."

"Asleep here?" Dad keeps asking the right questions.

Jessie nods. "We had a sibling drinking contest. He lost."

Dad huffs. "Lightweight."

I suck down more of my drink.

Sibling drinking contest. I have theories about that.

Jessie leans her elbows on the bar and rests her chin in her hands. "How's Buddy?"

"Good. We just picked him up a doghouse," Dad replies.

Jessie hums. "That's cool. I bet he'll like it."

Air rattles through my straw, and I release it from my lips.

I wonder for a second who told her about Buddy, but it had to be my dad.

Or I guess Dad could've told Luther, and Luther told Jessie, but no one heard it from me.

I befriended the fox the day Luther broke up with me, and I haven't seen him or Jessie since.

I'm not right for you.

I push my glass across the bar, making eye contact with the tall guy.

He nods and starts to make me a second drink.

When he replaces my empty with a full, I pick it up and take a sip.

I feel a touch more relaxed, knowing Luther isn't going to walk in at any moment. But this was too close of a call. And I know it's only a matter of time before Dad has Luther over for one of their bestie breakfasts.

I need to find a way to find out ahead of time. And then I need to find a way for them to do it at Luther's house.

Chapter 109

Luther

"Hey," I answer Joe's call after the first ring.

I'm supposed to leave in ten minutes to meet for breakfast at his place, and I've been pacing a path across the house for the last thirty.

"Hey, man, Kendra isn't feeling well. She said we could still do breakfast, and she'd just stay in her room, but I told her I could meet you somewhere else. Then we don't have to worry about being quiet."

I feel like an even bigger piece of shit as I heave out a breath of relief.

I'm not relieved that Kendra isn't feeling well. I'm almost positive she's fine and just using that as an excuse not to be near me.

And as much as that hurts to admit, I'm not ready to see her either.

Chapter 110

Kendra

I stare at the email.

It's been two weeks since that day I sat on the deck with my laptop.

Two of the companies emailed to say they've filled the position I applied for. Three of the companies haven't sent an update. But one of the companies just messaged me, requesting an interview.

Next Friday.

In Denver.

I bend down and put my plate in the dishwasher. "Oh, I forgot to mention, I'm running to Denver tomorrow."

"Oh yeah?" Dad hands me his plate.

I put it next to mine, then slide the rack closed. "Yeah." I use my foot to shut the dishwasher. "I gotta go to IKEA."

My father literally gasps and slaps his hand to his chest. "You wouldn't."

I let him see me roll my eyes at him. "I'm not going for furniture. They have a mirror I want."

It's not a lie. I saw an ad online for a pretty gold-framed mirror that would look nice on top of my dresser.

And if I happen to be going to a job interview at the same time... well, that's a detail I'll keep to myself.

Even if the idea has my dinner rolling in my stomach.

My shoes click across the marble floor, the sound loud in the quiet lobby.

The building is beautiful.

It's in a nice spot downtown.

There are lots of great apartment complexes nearby.

The emails I've sent back and forth with HR to schedule today have been friendly and welcoming.

And... I hate it.

I hate everything about it.

I hate being back in a city.

I hate the way these shoes feel on my feet.

I hate the way this dress screams *corporate lackey*.

I hate the idea of not seeing my dad all the time.

Hate the thought of telling him I'm leaving.

I stop in front of the elevator bank and press the Up button.

The shiny metal doors slide open, and I step inside.

As the cab rises, I stare at my distorted reflection. "What are you doing?"

I told myself it wouldn't hurt to interview. That I can always say no to an offer.

And on principle, I stand by that. It's always best to have your options open.

But being here, standing here, feeling like I'm back in my old life. Like I'm back out east, ready to spend the day dancing to my boss's tune... It's not me anymore.

I don't know if I've changed that much or if I've just experienced a different way to live.

A more relaxed life.

And I like it.

I more than like it.

I'm good at working from home.

I'm productive.

In the time I've been here, I've accomplished a lot for Joe's Custom Furniture.

And I feel good about that.

I have more passion for my dad's website than I had for all my previous jobs combined.

And I can do my current job anywhere.

I can still move out, so I don't have to be there when his friends come over.

But I don't need to move all the way to Denver.

And, with time, I'll get over Luther.

I'll be okay seeing him.

Eventually.

The elevator doors slide open, and I step out.

Ahead of me is a front desk, and the man sitting behind it smiles at me in welcome.

"Hello." I stop across the counter from him. "I'm here for an interview. But I have to cancel."

I LICK AT THE VANILLA SOFT SERVE, STANDING IN FRONT of a wall of mirrors.

My hair is still down. My makeup is still done. But instead of my dress and heels, I'm in jean shorts, sandals, and a cropped T-shirt that's currently making my tits look great since I'm still in the push-up bra I put on this morning.

I don't know if Dad has plans for tonight, but he often comes home early on Fridays, and there's no way he'd believe I dressed all fancy just for a trip to Ikea. So I was happy when the gas station attendant didn't bat an eye at me entering the bathroom in one outfit and exiting in another. I'm sure they've seen weirder things.

I close my mouth over the top point of the soft serve and let it melt on my tongue before swallowing.

After I changed, I logged in to the job finder website and closed my remaining applications.

It was the right choice.

The mirror I saw online is here and just as pretty in person. It's bigger than I expected, but I should still be able to get it in my car without having to fold the seats down.

Reaching out with my free hand, I feel the shiny frame of the mirror.

This is the right choice too.

Ice cream cone in hand, I take another lick and wander off to find a cart.

Halfway home, my phone rings.

I accept the call, and Dad's voice fills the car. "Kenny, how long till you get here?"

I glance at the ETA on my GPS. "Fifty-seven minutes."

Dad hums. "Okay, that'll work."

"Work for what?" I ask, assuming he's planning dinner.

"The fish fry."

Silence.

"The what?"

"The firefighters' fish fry. It's tonight."

My mouth forms an *O*. As in, *oh, shit*.

I've never attended one of these, but Dad's told me about them since he goes every year.

It's some sort of fundraiser block-party type of thing.

In theory, it could be alright. Except I'm fairly certain every person in the surrounding area will be there.

Every person. Including Luther.

"You don't have to wait for me," I tell him, hoping he'll leave without me while I figure out how to bail.

"Nope, you're driving. It's my turn to get wasted."

I groan, mostly because I don't want to go, but also from hearing Dad say *get wasted*.

"Is there any way I can convince you to let me sit this one out?" I try.

"Nope." He pops the *P*.

I groan again, but I'm extra grateful to my past self for packing the change of clothes.

"Fine," I grumble. "But you're paying."

Dad laughs and tells me to hurry up, then ends the call.

Heaving out a breath, I lift the hand not holding the wheel and cross my fingers.

If I have to go, I hope it's packed.

More people for me to hide behind.

Chapter 111

Luther

I honk the horn.

Jessie steps into view through her living room window and holds up two fingers.

I probably should've gotten out of the truck and gone to her door, but I'm not in the mood.

I'm not in the mood for any of this.

If I weren't the top sponsor for tonight's fundraiser, I wouldn't go.

Really, if Jessie weren't forcing me to be her designated driver, I wouldn't go at all.

But here we are.

I drop my head back against the headrest and stare blankly.

I don't mind staying sober. I haven't had any alcohol since that night Jessie and I took shots at the bar. I just don't want to go, period.

I don't want to make small talk.

I don't want to smile and laugh and act like everything is fine.

Everything is not fine.

Everything's not fine, but I'm going to have to pretend like it is because Kendra will be there.

Kendra.

I wish I knew how she was doing. Like *really doing*. But there's no one for me to ask.

Joe told me about Buddy. And I focus my eyes on the rearview mirror, thinking about the deer antler I have in the bed of my truck.

Joe mentioned that Kendra was really upset over the fox being injured and that she was adamant about taking care of it.

But Kendra has a huge heart.

She's a lover and a giver.

And so I don't know if the stuff with the fox is just about the fox or if it has anything to do with me.

Jessie's front door opens, and she steps out.

I scrunch up my nose as I watch her walk to the passenger door.

"What are you wearing?" I ask as she buckles herself in.

"It's called a dress." She smooths her hands down the striped skirt while eyeing me. "It's called fashion, but clearly, you know nothing about that."

"What's wrong with this?" I look down at my gray flannel and jeans, then I lift my arm and sniff.

"Ew!"

"I was just checking." I drop my arm. "It's clean."

"Uh-huh."

"I took a shower."

She widens her eyes. "Good job."

"Even used deodorant."

Jessie stops listening and reaches for my radio.

Chapter 112

Kendra

Not wanting to carry a purse around all night, I slide my car keys into my front pocket and my phone into my back one.

It ruins the nice silhouette of my ass in these shorts, but I'm not here to catch dates.

Locking the doors, I keep my sunglasses on as I follow Dad onto the sidewalk.

The sun will set long before we leave, but the thin layer of tinted plastic between me and the world is a must. Even more now than it was at the grad party. Because this time I'm trying to hide myself from Luther.

He sees too much.

"Mmm." Dad rubs his belly.

The scent of fried fish floats down the street, and even though my stress levels are creeping up with every step, so is my hunger. The ice cream I had at IKEA was hardly a proper lunch.

"Do you pay by the plate or by the person?"

Dad laughs at my question. "How much are you planning on eating?"

I roll my shoulders out. "Just want to make sure we're getting our money's worth."

"Well." He purses his lips. "I don't actually know. I've never tried getting seconds."

"Amateur." I scoff.

We turn at the end of the block, and the scene unfolds before us.

It was a thirty-minute drive here, and it's exactly as I imagined.

The streets are lined with cars, which is why we had to park a little way down the street, and up ahead is a classic brick fire station.

The giant garage doors are open, and the driveway in front of the station is covered with white party tents, plastic tables, and folding chairs. The fire trucks are parked in the street, blocking traffic from passing through while also being available in case something flammable dares to ignite during the fish fry or the firefighters need to get out.

Dad waves to a group of people seated at one of the tables, and I follow as he heads toward them.

While he introduces me, I try to keep an eye out for the oversized man who regularly haunts my dreams.

I'm not right for you.

I swallow and tuck my hands into my pockets.

Focus on tonight.

Focus on the now.

You can feel the bad later.

I pull in a slow breath through my nose and plaster a small smile on my face.

About half the chairs are filled, but the line for food originates somewhere inside the building and winds around outside, indicating it will be a full house.

I check the line for a familiar frame but don't spot him.

But I do spot a DJ booth already playing music with one of those light bars above it, ready to start strobing as soon as it gets a little darker out.

I'll never get Dad out of here once the dancing starts.

My gaze shifts toward movement on the sidewalk. A family of... six is walking up.

Four kids? Pull out already.

I nudge Dad, wanting to get in line before this herd does.

He looks up but looks past me and lifts his hand. "Over here!"

I look back at the family, wondering if I should've recognized them.

But he's not waving at them.

My heart throbs behind my ribs, and my throat constricts.

It's him.

Luther.

The family breaks off, heading to the back of the line, while Luther and Jessie head right for us.

Be normal.

Act normal.

This is normal.

I lift my hand, my fingers trembling as I wave.

As I smile.

As I pretend that seeing Luther doesn't hurt something deep inside my chest.

Jessie waves back. "Hey guys, how's it going?"

"Good." My cheeks fucking ache as I lie. "How are you two?"

I pray my glasses are dark enough so no one can tell that I'm only looking at Jessie.

"Hungry." Jessie hooks her arm in mine and gestures to the guys. "We're getting in line."

She starts to pull me away. I let her. And I think I might love her.

"Jeez, hold your horses." Dad huffs, then says something I can't hear to Luther.

Jessie talks at me for the first few minutes, filling my silence as we ignore the men behind us. But then Dad asks Jessie something, and she turns around.

The line is slowly shuffling ahead, but I feel conspicuous

facing forward while the rest of my group stands facing each other.

Clenching my jaw, I turn around.

And he's right there.

Was standing directly behind me.

His thick chest is covered in soft gray flannel. And I force myself not to notice that, once again, we practically dressed in matching outfits.

At least with our height difference, I don't have to look into his eyes. I can stare at his chest. His biceps.

My gaze dips to where his sleeves are rolled up, leaving his tanned forearms bare.

I look away.

I shuffle with the line.

I make sounds of agreement so Dad and Jessie think I'm listening.

And I continue to avoid eye contact with Luther.

Jessie distracts my dad the whole way through the line, and I think she might be my new favorite person.

I didn't ask her outright when we were at the Inn, but she knows.

And this confirms it.

"We're up." Dad shoves at my shoulder, turning me to face the food tables.

And the firefighters.

There are two tables. One serving up the freshly fried fish. The other dishing out French fries.

At the close end of the first table is a stack of trays.

I pick up the top one and hold it out toward the very attractive firefighter behind the first table.

"Evening, miss." He grins.

"Good evening," I reply, way too fucking formally. "May I have some fish?"

His grin grows. "You may." He uses a pair of metal tongs to

place three long pieces of the battered and fried fish on my tray. "Thanks for the support."

"Thanks for the, uh, service." *Oh my god, what is wrong with me?* "And the food."

I nod to my tray, then shift down to the next table.

This firefighter is super friendly, just as attractive, but less my type.

"Hey, hon." She greets me with a smile.

"Hello." I lift my tray, then decide I've already made it weird, so I might as well continue. "Thank you too, for, um, being brave."

The woman beams at me.

Dad leans forward, looking around Jessie at me. "Quit holding up the line."

I pretend I can't hear him as the woman across the table scoops up fries for me.

Chapter 113

Luther

Bobby is watching Kendra walk away.

I reach out and bump his arm with the corner of my tray.

His gaze snaps forward, meeting mine. "Oh, hey, Rocky." He glances back toward Kendra. "Who's that?"

"That's an ass beating," I reply dryly.

Next to me, Joe laughs. "That's my Kenny." Then he pats me on the back. "Uncle Rocky here is a little overprotective."

Jessie coughs through a laugh, and I nearly gag. "Please don't call me that."

Joe pats me again, then moves over to get his fries.

Bobby is still looking between us, seeming way too perceptive.

I bump him with my tray again.

Finally through the line, I follow the other three to the last four spots available in the center of one of the long tables.

Joe and Kendra went around to the far side, Joe choosing the seat across from Jessie. Which leaves me to sit across from Kendra.

She still has her sunglasses on, and her head is tilted down, like she's trying to decide what to eat first.

I noticed—because I can't stop myself from noticing everything she does—that she didn't grab lemon wedges or the little paper cups of tartar sauce. So I grabbed extra.

I set my tray down, then take my seat.

She doesn't look up.

I clear my throat. "You forgot these." I pick up one of the cups of sauce and set it on her tray. Then I do the same with two lemon wedges.

"Oh yeah, can't forget that," Joe comments a second before he shoves fish into his mouth.

Kendra lifts her head.

I see my reflection in her lenses. But then she reaches up and takes her glasses off.

I inhale.

I hold my breath.

And her eyes meet mine for the first time in weeks.

My Kendra Doll.

She's so perfect.

She's... not mine anymore.

"Thank you." Her soft words glide past me.

She doesn't mean it.

She's not thankful to me. For me.

I nod anyway. "You're welcome."

Kendra breaks eye contact, picking up the lemon wedge and squeezing it.

Then she jumps.

"Shit," she hisses, dropping the lemon and holding the back of her hand up to her face.

"What'd you do?" Joe turns to her.

"Nothing." She has one eye closed as she reaches for the napkin dispenser in the center of the table. "Just a bit of lemon juice in my eye."

Joe makes a face. "There's a restroom in the back. Need help washing it out?"

I'm already placing my hands on the table, ready to stand.

Kendra shakes her head as she pushes back her chair. "No, you guys eat."

She doesn't look at me, just gets up and walks away, food untouched.

My stomach twists.

The reasonable part of my brain knows that this particular incident wasn't my fault.

But the part of my brain that hates me for letting her go is shouting at me for being such a fuckup.

I gave her that lemon.

Hand selected the wedges that looked the most perfect.

The lemon juice in her eyes is just as much my fault as the sadness blanketing her shoulders.

Chapter 114

Kendra

I do my best to dab at my eye with a wet paper towel, trying to get the stinging to subside while leaving my mascara intact.

But there's nothing to be done about the redness.

Luckily, I had a nice little cry while washing my hands, so at least both my eyes are red, evening out the deranged look.

I sniff.

Why?

Why couldn't I have just left my sunglasses on?

Why did I have to take them off and meet Luther's gaze head-on?

A toilet flushes, and someone steps out of a stall just as the main door opens and two more women walk into the restroom.

I toss my wet paper towel into the trash and move out of the way, catching the door before it closes.

Keeping my eyes down, I avoid looking at anybody as I make my way back to my seat.

I can do this.

I can get through tonight.

Dad shoots me a pained smile as I pull my chair back. "You gonna be alright?"

I shake my head as I sit. "I'll probably need to take Monday off. For recovery."

Dad hums. "I'll need to see a note from a doctor."

I pick up a cold fry and gesture with it. "I'm sure one of these fine folks is an MD."

Dad furrows his brows. "I think you'll need an optometrist."

"Actually." Jessie holds up her own fry. "I think you're looking for an ophthalmologist."

We both look at her.

"What's the difference?" Dad leans his elbows on the table.

Tuning them out, I blink a couple times.

My eye still feels irritated, but I don't want to touch it.

"I'm sorry." Luther's quiet voice rolls across the table.

I force my gaze up from my tray. "It's not your fault."

His jaw moves, like he's biting his cheek.

And then I *really* take him in.

He's handsome, of course.

Still filling out his clothing like it's his job.

But beneath it... He looks miserable.

He's not teasing.

He's not grinning.

His stance is rigid. Bracing.

And I hate it.

I don't want to see him.

I don't want to talk to him.

Not now.

But I also don't want him to look... like this.

"I'm fine," I tell him.

I'm fine.

He dips his chin once. Swallows. Then he looks down at my food. "I squeezed the lemons on your fish while you were in the bathroom. If it's gotten too cold, or if you don't like it, I can get you more."

I look at my tray. At the squished lemon wedges in the corner.

My throat tightens, and my eyes start to sting all over again.
That was...
That was really thoughtful of him.
But I don't have it in me to say the words aloud.
So I don't say anything.

Chapter 115

Luther

Kendra picks at her food, and I know I'm making her uncomfortable.

Another reason to despise myself.

After offering to get a round of drinks, I take my time collecting two beers and two lemonades, hoping she'll eat some while I'm gone.

I need her to eat.

My plan works, and by the time I return with the drinks, half of Kendra's food is gone.

I do my best to engage Joe in conversation, asking about things I know will keep him talking. Like how his garbage day changed to Tuesday.

My plan keeps working. And even though I still feel like shit, I feel a jolt of success when Kendra finishes her last bite.

Chapter 116

Kendra

I reach for Dad's tray, stacking it on my empty one.

"You don't have to do that," Dad says, even as he drops his napkin on the tray.

"It's fine, I want to stretch my legs." I smile over at Jessie as I reach for her tray too. They're both on their second beer. "Want another drink while I'm up?"

She rolls her neck out as she pushes back from the table. "I should stand for a bit too. Joe, you want another?"

Dad shrugs and reclines in the uncomfortable folding chair. "Won't say no."

Jessie asks Luther if he wants another lemonade, and while he's answering her, I stack his tray with the rest and stand.

The cute firefighter is still here, leaning against a wall, talking with a group of people about our age. And I consider going over there. But I'd only be doing it in an effort to make Luther jealous.

And making him jealous is childish.

It wouldn't accomplish anything.

And it wouldn't work.

Because he'd have to still want me.

I blow out a breath as I cut through the tables.

The music has gotten louder, and the tables are half empty now that some of the people have left and some have moved to the dance floor.

Stopping at the trash cans, I sort out the garbage, then set the trays in the provided wash bin.

Jessie is in line at the bar, and a glance across the station shows that my dad and Luther are no longer alone.

Four women.

Four women, appropriate in age, have taken up the empty seats around them.

The chairs Jessie and I were sitting in are still open, but I watch the woman next to Luther lean into him, reaching for his arm.

I look away.

Hopefully Dad will see my sunglasses and grab them before it's time to leave. But even if I lose them, it will still be better than going back to that table.

Chapter 117

Luther

The woman on the other side of the table reaches for the chair across from me like she's going to move into it.

I hold my hand out. "That's Kendra's seat."

She glances around. "Who's Kendra?"

It's hard not to grit my teeth.

How could anyone not know who Kendra is?

She's my fucking reason for existing.

The reason I want to live and die at the same time.

"He's talking about Kenny, my daughter." Joe looks toward the garbage cans and shrugs. "She's around here somewhere."

"Oh, well, I can move when she comes back." The woman slides into Kendra's spot.

And it infuriates me.

That's not her chair.

It's Kendra's.

And it's the only way I get to be near her.

Chapter 118

Kendra

A form swims into view beyond my phone.

I lift my eyes from my screen and watch as Luther lowers into the chair across from me.

I'm in the farthest corner of the farthest tent, sitting mostly in shadows, in the hopes that no one would find me.

Luther sets something on the table between us. "Didn't want you to lose these."

Glancing down, I see my sunglasses.

I drag them closer to me. "Thank you."

"What are you reading?"

His question is its own reminder.

That he listened.

That I told him things.

"A book about a vampire." I set my phone down next to my glasses.

"Does he sparkle?"

The edge of my mouth tries to pull up, knowing Ashley has to be the reason he'd ask that. But I don't have it in me to smile. "He doesn't. But he can smell his fated mate from across the city."

And he would never dump her.

Not for anything.

Not fucking ever.
"You like it?"
I lift a shoulder. "So far."
We look at each other, and it's so uncomfortable because it's all so wrong.
We shouldn't be sitting across the table from each other.
We should be sitting on the same side.
We should be part of the same team.
This... distance. It doesn't feel natural.
And the wrongness of it makes me so sad.
Luther breaks the silence. "I brought an antler for Buddy."
My lips part. But my throat closes.
He brought something for Buddy?
My Buddy?
"What?" I can only manage a whisper.
"It's in the bed of my truck. I found it. Thought he might like it."
My shoulders drop.
Just... release.
I try to ask why, but no sound comes out.
And I feel so frustrated with the whole thing. With all of it. That my eyes fill with emotion.
I blink. Fast.
Luther's features go tight, and he leans forward, putting his arms on the table. "Fuck, Ba—"
"Don't," I breathe.
I've never been the one to command him.
But he listens.
And I press my lips together.
He brought Buddy an antler.
Because he thought he might like it.
A tear breaks free, leaving a trail of sorrow down my cheek.
Luther's voice is low. Pained. "Do you want to talk?"
I shake my head.
And I shake my head a second time when it looks like he

might ask me again. "I don't want to talk to you. I can't." Another tear and then another. "Not yet."

I discreetly brush at my cheeks with my fingertips.

"I'm sorry," Luther whispers, and fuck, it hurts.

"Please stop," I whisper back.

He nods.

And I lower my gaze to the table, fingertips catching more tears as they fall.

"I can drive Joe home if you want to leave." His tone is gentle but resigned. "Or if you want me to go… Whatever you want."

Whatever I want.

It's never been about what I want.

That's not how my life is.

But in this… since I have a choice. I tell him the truth. "I want to leave."

"Okay." He slides his arms off the table.

Holding my glasses and phone, I stand.

Luther rises across from me. "I'll tell him you aren't feeling well."

A sad puff of breath escapes me.

Not feeling well.

I look up and meet his eyes.

And I remind myself that this is us now.

He's not mine.

I'm not his.

I'm not anyone's.

I take a step back. "Bye, Rocky."

Then I turn and leave.

Chapter 119

Luther

Rocky.
   It's what everyone calls me.
   But not her.
   Except that's what I did to us.
   I made us like everyone else.
   And. Fuck. I think I might've made a mistake.

Chapter 120

Kendra

With my Chilean coffee in hand, I step onto the back deck.

Even though I work from home now, and I like my job, there's still something about a Sunday morning.

Not that my mornings were like this back home.

Home.

It feels wrong to call Delaware home.

Sitting on the steps, I take a deep breath while my gaze wanders over to Buddy's doghouse.

Sticks are spread around in the grass just in front of the little house. The tattered corner of a blanket sticks out of the doorway. And I can just see a tuft of fur in the shadows.

My lips pull into a smile as I picture him sleeping, curled around his antler.

Yesterday morning, after sleeping in, Dad and I came out here together to give Buddy the antler Luther found.

The scratchy yowling sounds Buddy made were hilarious.

He was bouncing around, tossing it in the air, tearing around the yard.

His joy was visceral.

And, like I seem to do over everything nowadays, I cried.

I shake my head remembering it.

Dad probably thinks I've been having a weeks-long mental breakdown. And honestly, it might be true.

But yesterday, in that moment, I felt something shift.

I'm happy here.

Even with the hurt. Even with the sad.

I'm happy here.

This is my home now.

And I'm going to find a way to be okay around Luther.

I can't separate him from *home*.

I'm not willing to lose the relationship I'm building with my dad just to avoid him.

And... isn't that the decision Luther made?

Even if he added in some other imaginary reasons, ultimately, he didn't want to lose his friendship with Dad.

He chose my dad over me.

It still hurts.

Still makes me sad.

But if I look at it from a distance, I can't blame him for his priorities.

I can't blame him for not sharing my feelings.

And if it wasn't going to work, then I'm glad it ended when it did.

I'm glad it ended before I handed him my entire heart.

I take another inhale of the fresh morning air.

Today, I'm letting go.

I exhale my breath.

Today, I'm letting the bad die.

I'M ON MY SECOND CUP OF COFFEE WHEN THE BACK door slides open, and Dad's footsteps thump across the wood surface of the deck.

"Morning."

"Morning." I stop reading and set my phone down.

"How's Buddy?" Dad lowers himself into the chair beside mine, groaning as he does it.

"Sleeping."

Dad grunts and takes a sip of his coffee. "Good stuff."

"Yep." I take a sip of my sweeter, creamier version. "Luther knows his beans."

It's the first time I've brought up his name since...

It feels a little forced, but it's a normal thing to say.

It's what someone would say if the coffee came from a friend.

Friend.

That's another pill to swallow.

Dad shakes his head. "You two are so weird."

I look at him, brow raised. "We're weird? Have you met yourself?"

Dad rolls his eyes. "Luther knows his stuff," he says in a high feminine voice, then he switches to a deep tone. "That's Kendra's chair."

I laugh. "You sound ridiculous."

"*You* sound ridiculous."

I shake my head. "And what chair is mine?"

He takes another sip of his coffee, gesturing with his free hand. "At the fish fry, before you bailed."

"Bailed," I repeat dryly.

Dad never really believed I wasn't feeling well. Pretty sure he thought it was a lie because I was bored. Which is still better than him knowing the truth.

He huffs. "Yeah, well, if you'd come back, you'd have saved us from the flock of women trying to flirt with Rocky."

I purse my lips, thinking about those women. How that one reached for him. "Maybe *Luther* liked the attention." I emphasize his name just to be a pest.

Dad scoffs. "Not him. He's no saint, but he's damn close. Been forever since I've seen him interested in anyone."

I hum as I take that in.

On the topic of women, I'm tempted to ask Dad about Ashley's mom—since he's the one who interrupted our conversation back in the coffee shop. But it still feels like something I should hear from Luther himself.

Dad stretches his legs out. "Well, won't have to worry about the clingers tonight." He looks around. "If it stays this nice out, maybe we should eat outside."

I turn my head slowly to look at Dad. "What's happening tonight?"

"Steaks." He grins.

I lift an eyebrow, hoping he can't hear my heart pounding.

"With *Luther*." He uses his high-pitched voice again.

"You're obnoxious." I close my eyes and lean back in the deck chair.

Guess it's time to put my new mindset to the test.

Chapter 121

Luther

I put my truck into park, but I don't turn off the engine.

This feels like a mistake.

Last time I saw Kendra, she cried.

She didn't just cry. *I made her cry.*

I swallow.

Maybe I should go.

Make up some lie.

I...

The front door to Joe's house opens, and the man himself steps out onto the front step.

He lifts his arms in a *What the hell?* gesture.

I hold up a finger, nod, and move my mouth like I'm talking on the phone.

He crosses his arms.

I nod some more. I feel like an idiot. And then I say, to absolutely no one, *Okay, sounds good* and turn off the engine.

Too late for second-guessing now.

Even though second-guessing is all I seem to do anymore.

Chapter 122

Kendra

I LOOK AT MYSELF IN MY MIRROR.

The gold frame looks good propped up on my dresser. And I even dressed it up with some perfume bottles and my potted *string of pearls* plant.

I wasn't willing to throw a live plant away, but looking at it on my desk all day while I was working was just too much.

But in here, next to my new mirror, I can pretend I bought it for myself.

I take another inhale, then shove the air out of my lungs forcefully.

The sound is rough.

Cleansing.

Then I smile at my reflection.

No teeth, just a lift of the lips. Natural.

Believable.

Luther is here.

Dad shouted as much a minute ago. And I shouted back that I'd be right there.

I smooth my hands down the front of my yellow top.

The opposite of blue.

And I tug on the waistband of my dark-wash jeans.

A short rainstorm rolled through this afternoon, cooling everything off and leaving the deck furniture wet, meaning we'll eat inside.

I tuck my hair behind my ears.

"You are good. This will be fine. Luther is a nice guy. He won't say anything out of line. You can be calm around him."

I do one more noisy exhale, then I turn my back on my reflection and open my bedroom door.

I hear their voices, but then I hear the sound of the back door sliding closed as they move out onto the deck.

My shoulders relax.

It's the perfect start.

Stepping out of the hallway, my movement catches the attention of both men.

Dad's mouth is moving, already telling Luther a story. And Luther is nodding, but his attention is on me.

I can feel his eyes take me in.

Can feel the way they always take me in.

I am good.

I inhale.

I lift my hand.

And I smile.

Chapter 123

Luther

She smiles, and I can feel it in my bones.

It's not brittle.

Not pained.

It doesn't look forced.

I exhale, releasing the breath I've been holding.

She looks like herself.

The bright yellow of her shirt contrasts with her dark hair, and her green eyes look like they're sparkling.

She looks healthy. Full of life.

My arms ache to wrap around her.

I want to press my nose to her hair.

I want to hold her.

But I do the next best thing.

I lift my hand and wave back.

Her eyes move to my palm before she lowers hers to her side.

Joe holds a beer out to me.

I reach for it, but he pulls it back. Then he points to the bottle while lifting his brows at Kendra.

She rolls her eyes but crosses to the door leading into the garage.

"I could've gotten my own," I grumble.

If I'd known he was going to make Kendra get it, I would've insisted.

Joe waves me off, turning to the grill. "She'll get one for herself." He pulls the cling wrap off the tray of raw steaks, then looks out into the yard. "Ha, I was wondering if you'd come out for this."

I turn to see who Joe is talking to and spot a pretty little fox standing just a few feet from the bottom of the deck stairs, looking up at us.

I've seen dozens, probably hundreds of foxes. But never one this close or this still.

"Buddy, this is Rocky. Rocky, this is Buddy."

The fox lets out a scratchy noise that makes him sound like he's spent his life smoking a pack a day.

"Hey, Buddy." I keep my voice quiet.

His head tilts, then he darts into the doghouse Joe already told me about.

The deck door slides open behind me. "Should've brought another antler."

Kendra's voice is soft but not timid. And I feel myself holding my breath again as I turn to face her.

"He—" I clear my throat. "He liked it?"

She nods and holds a bottle out to me, another for herself in her other hand. "He loves it."

I take the offered beer and turn my gaze back to the doghouse and the furry muzzle sticking out of the open door. "I'm glad."

The bottle hisses as I twist the top off. And I watch the nose twitch as I lift my beer and take a pull.

The liquid cools my throat.

"You need any help?" Joe asks Kendra.

I turn back to watch the pair.

Kendra shakes her head. "The brussels sprouts are in the oven. I just need to mix up the glaze." My nose scrunches, and Kendra notices. "Is there a problem, Luther?"

Luther.

Not Rocky.

A thin layer of my self-hatred peels away from my heart.

"No problem." I hate brussels sprouts. But I'd rather eat them with every meal for the rest of my life than tell her. "Sounds perfect."

My name will always sound perfect when she says it.

She narrows her eyes, like she's seeing through my lies.

So I distract her. "Here." I hand her my already open bottle.

She takes it in her empty hand, freeing up both of mine.

"You want to trade?" She lifts a brow, looking pointedly down at the beer I've already started.

"No, just don't let go."

With her still holding the base, I grip the neck of the other bottle to steady it, then use my other hand to twist the top off.

The hiss of the beer is muted by the hiss of the first steak landing on the hot grill.

Joe's not watching.

He's reaching for the second steak with his grill tongs.

And Kendra isn't breaking eye contact.

I let go, slipping the bottle cap into my pocket alongside the first, then hold my hand out.

But the bottle Kendra extends toward me is the newly opened one.

And my fingers miss it by a mile as I watch her lift the other one to her mouth.

She swallows.

And so do I.

Lips still pressed against the smooth glass, Kendra smiles.

I don't know if she's fucking with me, flirting with me, or putting a curse on me.

But I find I don't care.

I'll take anything over seeing her cry.

I want her happy.

That was the whole point of me calling things off.

I didn't break my own heart for me. I did it for her.

Because I want her happy.

Jessie's voice echoes in my thoughts, telling me I deserve to be happy too.

But as I take a sip of what was supposed to be Kendra's beer, I feel a shimmer of peace settle over me.

Kendra's happiness will be enough for both of us.

Chapter 124

Kendra

Dinner has been surprisingly okay.

I can still feel the tension dragging my attention across the table, but Luther has been pretty much himself. And we've both done a good job encouraging Dad to fill the silence by prompting him to tell stories.

I put a piece of steak in my mouth and chew.

Another few meals like this and I might be able to pretend my history with Luther never happened.

Might be able to put those memories into a corner of my mind and pretend it was all a daydream.

"How's Ashley?" Dad asks, shoving his empty plate toward the center of the table.

Luther grunts as he swallows a brussels sprout. "Got a raise."

Dad hums. "That's good."

"And a boyfriend."

Dad laughs, but my eyes widen.

She told him?

Luther's gaze catches mine.

Does he know I know?

Did she tell him that she knows about us?

Something twists in my chest.

What if she brought it up after… And Luther had to tell her he broke up with me.

That would've been so uncomfortable. For both of them.

"Have you met him?" Dad asks.

Luther shakes his head. "Not yet."

"Welp, better meet him soon before he becomes the father of your grandbabies."

Luther gapes at him. "Fuck you so much."

I snort.

Dad laughs as he turns to me. "Just gotta get you a boyfriend. Then maybe you can give me grandbabies at the same time."

He doesn't mean anything by it.

It's just a thing parents say.

But it slices through my calm.

I press my lips together.

I'm okay.

Seriously, I'm totally fucking okay.

It's just… I don't want to have this conversation.

I've avoided it for years.

And years and years.

But I knew I'd have to do it eventually.

And… Fuck. I think it has to be now.

I glance at Luther as I dig my teeth into my lip.

He should know too.

Even if it doesn't change anything.

Even if everything between us stays exactly the same.

He should know too.

I set my fork down.

"Dad, I…" I swallow. "I can't have kids."

His mouth opens, but then he closes it. "You don't want to?" he asks slowly.

Rolling my lips together, I wish I could do this without feeling so emotional.

Tears won't help.

I'm okay now. And I need him to understand that part the most.

I lift a shoulder. "I can't."

"What do you mean?" Dad's voice is quiet.

I can feel Luther's eyes on me, but I can't look at him. Not while I say this part. "I mean... I'll never be able to have children. I..." I take a breath. Then I say it. "I had my ovaries removed."

Dad's throat bobs. "When?"

"Ten years ago," I admit, knowing it will hurt him.

Dad blinks, then whispers the next question, like he's scared of the answer. "Why?"

It was a lifetime ago.

I remember it like it was yesterday.

"They—the doctors, they found a tumor."

Dad exhales, like the answer struck him in the chest.

We found a tumor.

We need to remove it as soon as possible.

I try not to think about that day. But it's easier now. Easier than it was.

My dad's eyes shimmer with emotion. "Cancer?"

I lift my shoulder again and nod.

He makes a sound of distress.

"I'm fine." I hurry out. "They got everything, and nothing spread. That's why they took both."

"Kendra." Tears spill down Dad's cheeks.

He never calls me that.

I fight my own battle against my tears.

"I'm okay." I reassure him.

"Why didn't you tell me?" He wipes at his cheeks.

I twist my fingers together in my lap.

I don't have a good answer to this question.

And now that we're here. Now that it's caught up to me. I feel fucking awful.

"I'm sorry," I whisper. "It all happened so fast. And..."

I brush at my cheeks.

There's no real reason.

No excuse.

Dad shakes his head, wiping away his own tears. "No. No, I'm sorry. I shouldn't have asked. Don't apologize."

"I just..." I fucking shrug again.

I hate that he's the one saying sorry when I'm the one who didn't tell him.

"Were you at your mom's?" He sniffs.

His question hurts. I hate that he'd even think I would tell Mom but not him.

And I hate my answer just as much.

But I give him the truth and shake my head. "I never told her."

"You... No one...?" His inhale is choppy.

I never told either of them.

Didn't tell anyone.

Didn't tell my boyfriend.

Never told him the real reason I broke up with him.

Because I knew he wanted kids. He'd talked about it. He wanted several.

And when I knew I'd never have them...

"Please don't be sad." I plead with my dad as tears continue to stream down his face.

"My little girl had cancer, and I didn't even know." His words are choked. Like he's saying it to himself.

I feel like the worst daughter ever.

"I'm sorry," I whisper again. "I... I just wanted to deal with it alone. The surgery... It... The recovery wasn't that bad."

It's the truth. Followed by a lie.

"You're really okay though? It's—" Dad swallows. "The cancer is gone?"

I nod, glad I can give him this. "It's gone."

"You're sure?"

"I'm sure. I go in every year, and I had my checkup three months ago. There's never been any signs of it coming back."

I try to bolster him with the good news, but he still looks like I told him I'm dying.

"Did you go by yourself?"

My shoulders drop.

I did all of it by myself.

Every appointment.

Every follow-up.

Every phone call.

Every medication.

I thought it was what I wanted.

Thought it would be easier to do it alone.

Thought it would be less stressful if I didn't include anyone else in the trauma.

But sitting here, heart hurting over Dad's reaction, I realize I was wrong.

I was wrong to keep it from him.

Wrong to keep it from my mom.

I was even wrong to keep it from my boyfriend.

I didn't love him, and leaving was the right choice, but he deserved the truth.

So does Luther.

Dad rubs his palms over his eyes, and I finally turn my head, meeting Luther's gaze.

His face is pale.

He's sitting so still that he looks... haunted.

But he's watching me.

Hearing every sentence.

Taking in every word.

So I answer the question he should have asked me.

I tell him what he should've known.

"I was never sure if I wanted kids. I was only twenty-two, and I wasn't ready to decide." I take a second to breathe. And then looking into Luther's eyes, I give him the rest of the truth. "But it hurt. Having the choice taken away from me hurt. And it wasn't fair."

Chapter 125

Luther

My heart feels like it's folding in on itself.

Ten years ago, Kendra had cancer.

Ten years ago, Kendra went through surgery alone.

Ten years ago, when my dream girl was only twenty-two, she had to find out she couldn't have children.

Ten years ago, I was already friends with Joe.

Ten years ago, I'd heard of this beautiful woman, but I didn't know her.

Ten years ago, I could have been there for her.

But... I wasn't even there for her now.

She can't have children, and I broke up with her because I thought...

I struggle to breathe.

Barely more than ten days ago, Kendra stood there as I told her she deserved better.

Barely more than ten days ago, I told her she deserved to have a family with someone else.

Barely more than ten days ago, Kendra stood there as I broke my promise, as I broke her trust.

Kendra stood there as I told her it was over between us, all because I made an assumption.

A horribly wrong assumption.

I release my grip on the edge of the table and press my hand against my chest. Wishing I could dig my fingers between my ribs and offer her my tattered heart in apology.

I'm so sorry.

I'm so fucking sorry for failing you.

For failing you in the worst kind of way.

She breaks eye contact, finally looking away from me.

How she can look at me at all...

I press harder against my chest.

"I talked to a therapist for a while," Kendra tells her dad. "She helped me a lot. And, now that I'm older, I feel sure I would've chosen a child-free life."

Joe is still wiping tears away. "You're not just saying that?"

Kendra lets out a watery laugh. "I'm not just saying that. Kids are gross."

Joe drops his hands to his lap, his shoulders sagging, his eyes bloodshot. "You're gross."

Kendra's laugh is brighter this time. "I love you too."

Joe sniffs. "You'll tell me if something happens."

She nods. "I swear it."

"And you'll tell me when you have another doctor's appointment."

I want to demand that she tells me too.

Want to insist that I'll go with her.

Want to promise her that I'll hold her hand the whole time.

I want her to know I'll dedicate my life to protecting her, if only she'll let me.

But what good are my promises?

"I'll tell you," Kendra says before she glances at me, our gazes catching.

"Good." Joe wipes at his eyes again. "Good. And I don't need any stinky grandkids. I have a grand-fox already."

Kendra smiles, eyes shining. "We can make it official and design him a nursery inside."

Joe heaves out a breath. "Guess the least I can do is build him a new house. He'll need it to carry on the family name."

Kendra shakes her head.

Joe lifts a hand and drags it down his face before dropping it back into his lap. "Can I give you a hug?"

Kendra's lips tremble as she nods.

And I look away as they stand.

There's more sniffling.

Joe mumbles something.

Kendra replies with a murmur.

And I feel like I might be ill.

How was I so wrong?

So wrong about literally everything.

I hang my head forward.

What has she been going through these last couple weeks?

How much must she hate me?

It might even be more than I hate myself.

"Quit making it weird. Come join the group hug." Joe's voice is gruff.

I lift my head.

Me?

Joe holds one of his arms out, the other still hugging Kendra.

I look to her.

There's no way she wants me to join.

She probably wants to tell me to leave.

If I were her, I'd never want to see my face again.

If I were her, I would be so full of rage.

Except there's the smallest smile on her lips.

And when I continue to watch her, she dips her chin.

The rope around my throat tightens.

She can't...

Kendra holds her arm out too.

And I don't care if it's a hug of friendship and nothing more. I'll take it.

I'll take any scrap of acceptance Kendra is willing to give me.

I stand so fast my chair tips over.

They both chuckle at the loud noise, but I don't pause as I circle around the table in three steps and wrap them both in a bear hug.

Their bodies shake with humor, so I squeeze them tighter.

Joe shoves at my side, and I smack my hand firmly against his back.

He grunts, and I know it must've stung, but he stops trying to push me away.

And then I feel it.

Kendra's hand at the small of my back. Her fingers tangling in the fabric of my shirt.

It's more than I dared to wish for.

I tighten the arm I have around her, my hand curling around her shoulder, pulling her into me.

I want to tell Joe to get lost.

I need to hug Kendra for longer.

Need to hold her for-fucking-ever.

But this isn't about me.

It never was.

But I still managed to ruin it.

Chapter 126

Kendra

"I'm glad you're okay." Luther's whisper is spoken into my hair as his fingers flex around my shoulder.

I want to turn into him. I want both his arms around me.

Even if it's a mirage, I want him to hold me against his chest and wrap me in his warmth.

But we can't do that when we're sharing this hug with my dad.

And we can't do that because we aren't a *we* anymore.

So instead, I whisper back, "I'm glad too."

Another few seconds slip by, then Dad sighs. Loudly. "I need ice cream."

Three build-your-own ice cream sundaes and an hour-long documentary about penguins later, I set the dirty bowls in the sink.

Emotional exhaustion setting in, I cover my yawn.

"Good night, Kendra." Luther's voice draws my attention to where he's standing with my dad by the front door.

I can feel how badly he wants to say more.

Ever since dinner. Since I told them what happened. I could see it written all over his face.

And I get it.

It was an unexpected turn of events. *For him.*

And I get it.

It's a lot to unpack. Especially after...

And knowing Luther, knowing the type of man he is, I can only imagine how much he's beating himself up right now.

I didn't say it all while he was here to hurt him. No matter how bad I've felt. No matter how many tears I've cried. Hurting him back was never the goal.

But I can't tell him that. Not with my dad here.

Not with the other half of the reason Luther ended things with me standing beside him.

Luther doesn't want to mess around behind his friend's back.

So ultimately, there's nothing else to say.

I still give him a small smile as I take a step toward the hallway. "Good night, Luther."

Chapter 127

Luther

I climb into my truck.
 I turn the engine on.
 I steer down the driveway.
 I turn onto the road.
 And I pull over.
 I park.
 I turn the engine off.
 And I wait.
 I wait. And I stare. And I think.
 I think about what I want.
 I think about everything Kendra said.
 I think about the meaning of the word regret.
 And I wait until forty minutes have passed.
 I open my door.
 I climb out of my truck.
 I walk down the driveway.
 I take Joe's spare house key out of my pocket.
 And I unlock the front door.

Chapter 128

Kendra

A CREAK FILTERS IN FROM THE HALLWAY.

I blink my eyes open.

I'm so tired I could hardly keep my eyes open as I brushed my teeth. But now that I'm in bed, I can't fall asleep.

The creak sounds again.

I lift my head from the pillow.

I heard Luther leave as I was stepping into the bathroom. And by the time I'd come back out, the rest of the lights in the house were off.

I wait.

Then I hear my door handle turn.

I sit up.

The door swings open.

My curtains are pulled shut. It's dark.

But I can see enough of his outline.

My pulse jumps.

"Luther?"

The tall, wide-shouldered man steps into my room and closes the door behind him.

"I'm sorry." His voice is quiet. And broken.

I don't think. I just climb out of bed and go to him.

"I'm so sorry," he breathes.

I knew he was hurting, but his voice...

I can't find my own. So instead, I reach out and place my palm on his chest.

Both his hands close over mine. Encasing it. *Warming it.*

"Looking back on my life, I'd do a lot of things differently. But pushing you away..." Luther pauses, and I can feel his muscles move as he swallows. "Hurting you is the last thing I ever wanted to do. I thought I was... Fuck, Kendra. I don't deserve another chance with you. And I'm not asking..." His fingers squeeze mine. "I just... Can I hug you again? Please?"

I'm glad it's dark.

Glad he can't see me as my features break.

Luther isn't asking for forgiveness.

He doesn't believe I'd give it to him.

He just wants to hug me.

I pull my hand free from his.

And his exhale sounds... defeated.

But then I step into him.

I lean against him.

And I rest my cheek over his heart.

His body hitches, then his arms gently wrap around me.

"I'm glad you're okay." He says the same thing he said before, only this time, his hand cups the back of my head as he holds me against him. "I need you to be okay."

I close my eyes as I lean into him.

The anger and the pain are still there.

My dad is still there.

The situation between us is still there.

But Luther is here too.

He waited, and he came back. Because he wanted a hug.

I inhale his scent.

And I don't know if this next part is a mistake or not, but I need the comfort just as much as he does.

"You can stay."

Chapter 129

Luther

I couldn't have heard her right.

"Stay?"

She nods against me.

I close my eyes as my head tips forward. "Are you sure?"

She nods again. "I'd like you to stay."

I hold her tighter as the rope of despair loosens from around my neck.

If she's letting me stay. If she *wants* me to stay...

Maybe there's hope that I haven't broken everything.

Maybe I'm not too late.

I want to tell her I love her. Want to tell her I've loved her this whole time.

Beg her to believe me.

But that's just it. I need her to believe me when I say it.

And I don't think she would right now.

I poisoned the trust she had in me, and I need to earn it back.

So instead of telling her how much I love her, I press my lips to the top of her head.

Chapter 130

Kendra

I hold my breath as Luther kisses my hair.

It's moments like this... actions like this... that made me fall for him in the first place.

Luther straightens, and his hold on me loosens.

I step back, clearing my throat. "Just sleep. But you can... get comfortable."

Even with my eyes adjusted to the dark, I still can't make out his expression, but I see that he doesn't move.

I sigh. "You don't have to sleep in your jeans, Luther."

When I take another step back, Luther lifts his hands to the front of his shirt.

I wait as he shrugs off his flannel and drops his jeans to the floor.

Then his hand finds mine, and he walks with me to my bed.

He climbs on first, lying where he's lain before. And when he stretches his arm out, I crawl into the opening.

Luther pulls the blankets up to my chin, then wraps his arm around my back, holding me against him.

With my front flush with his side and my head on his chest, I breathe him in.

I listen to his heart as it beats beneath his ribs.

And I relax.

Then, with the man I dream about holding me tight, I finally find sleep.

Chapter 131

Luther

Kendra's body goes soft against mine as sleep pulls her under.

And I hold her tighter.

I cling to her.

I grip the hand she has on my chest in my own.

I'd like you to stay.

This is so much more than I deserve.

She's so much more.

But I tried living without her already, and I was no good at it.

So I might not deserve a second chance, but if she gives it to me, I'm going to take it.

I'm taking it, and I'm never letting it go.

Something warm moves beside me, pulling me out of sleep.

Light filters into the room, and I blink my eyes open, focusing on the woman tucked into my side.

Kendra makes a humming sound, and her fingers twitch under mine.

I run my hand up her side.

She's such a stunning creature.

Beautiful, smart, funny.

Strong, tough, independent.

She doesn't need me.

Maybe never will.

But that's okay.

I don't need her to need me.

I just need her to want me.

I want you to stay.

I close my eyes as I replay her words.

There's so much to make right, but it's a start.

A clatter sounds from somewhere in the house, and my eyes snap back open.

Shit.

My gaze jerks to the door, then back to the early morning sunshine creeping in around the curtains.

Double shit.

I press my lips to Kendra's hair. "Baby, I gotta go."

I have no right to call her that. Especially when I remember the way she reacted the last time I almost called her that.

But she let me spend the night with her. Said she wanted me to. And she wouldn't do that if she hated me all the way.

Pretty sure.

She groans and nuzzles her face against my chest.

No, she doesn't hate me all the way.

I kiss her hair again.

Kendra's eyelids flutter.

I rub my thumb back and forth over her shoulder. "I have to leave," I whisper. "You can go back to sleep. I just wanted to tell you."

Those big green eyes blink up at me.

"Hi." I keep my voice low.

Her cheek lifts in a wary smile. "Hi."

There's another clatter and a muttered curse.

Kendra's eyes widen.

I grimace. "Yeah. I overslept."

She turns her head to look at the clock, seeing that it's after six thirty and knowing this is late for me. "Must've been tired." Her voice is just as quiet.

I was beyond tired last night.

I was wrung out.

Finding out about...

Fucking cancer.

I roll toward Kendra, pushing her onto her side.

"What are you—"

When we're front to front, I wrap both my arms around her and hug her to me.

One of her hands is trapped between us, but the other slides around my side to my back.

"I'm okay, Luther. I swear."

I hold her tighter.

I'm still not.

I don't think I'll ever be able to think about Kendra having cancer without feeling a piece of my heart crumble away.

"I'm sorry." I force the words through my tightening throat. "I'm sorry you had to go through that. And I'm sorry I didn't know. And I'm so fucking sorry, Baby." I have to stop. Have to take a breath. "I'm sorry I'm such an idiot. I should've talked to you. I just... I'm too old. Too jaded. Felt too fucking unworthy to steal your future and keep it as my own. But... I can't let you go. Even though I tried. Even though I should." I curl around her. And she clutches at me. "I'm not... I won't ask you for anything right now. I want to, but I won't. Not yet. Just know that I'm not done. I'll make this up to you. I'll find a way." I press my lips to the side of her neck. "You hear me, Kendra Doll?"

Chapter 132

Kendra

I nod against Luther, my mouth pressed against his shoulder.

"Tell me, Baby." His lips brush against my neck with every word.

And I shouldn't go there.

I shouldn't let myself pretend it's like it was before.

But it's Luther.

And he's here.

And I like doing what he tells me to do.

"I hear you, Daddy." I whisper it *so* quietly.

Barely more than a puff of air.

But I feel Luther harden against me.

His muscles. His body. His... It's all hard.

One hand slides up my spine to cradle the back of my head. "That's my good girl." He holds me to him. "My perfect girl."

My.

Everything isn't just okay. Not after one night.

But I never stopped caring for Luther.

Never stopped...

I swallow.

"You have to go." I flex my fingers against his back once, then drag my hand around to his side.

Luther pulls back enough to look down at me. "Go back to sleep, then text me when you wake up."

I roll my lips together and nod.

The hand on the back of my head moves to the side of my neck. Then he holds me still as he leans in and presses his lips to my forehead.

My stomach clenches, and I narrow my eyes on him.

He pauses as he pulls back. "What?"

"That's playing dirty."

His eyes move to my forehead. Then he leans in and kisses it again, his lips lingering longer this time.

His exhale dances through my hair, then he rolls away from me and out of bed.

I watch him. *His body.*

Luther's muscles bulge as he crosses the room. His abs contract as he bends to pick up his clothes.

I continue to watch as his large hands work their way through his shirt buttons.

And I feel envious that he looks so damn handsome moments after waking up.

Fully dressed, I expect him to put his ear to the door or to ask me to step out and see where my dad's at. But he strides back across the room.

He pauses beside my dresser, reaching a hand out to run his finger across the plant he gave me.

I stay quiet. Until he steps over to my window and unlocks it.

I sit up. "What are you doing?"

"Avoiding Joe." He removes the screen and sets it on the floor. "I'll put that back in the next time I stay over." He turns his head, eyes meeting mine. "Tonight."

I swallow. Feeling like I should tell him he can't. But knowing I want him to.

"Lock this after me, okay?"

"Okay. But..." I glance toward the door. "You can just wait in here for him to leave. So you don't have to...climb out." I gesture to the window.

Luther stays where he is, his tongue dragging over his teeth. "Don't tempt me, Baby. I haven't earned your sweetness yet."

Heat fills my belly. "That's not what I meant."

It's not what I meant.

But also...

Luther reaches for the window. "Plus, I parked in the street like a dumbass. There's no way he wouldn't see my truck. I'll be smarter next time." He slides the window up and sticks his head out, looking toward the back deck. "Don't forget to lock this."

Then he climbs through the opening and drops to the ground on the other side.

Luther slides the window shut from the outside, holding my gaze for an extra beat, before he steps back.

Then the loud, scratchy shouting starts.

Scrambling out of bed, I hurry to the window in time to see Buddy streaking across the lawn after Luther, screaming his furry little head off.

Luther backs away, with his finger to his lips, trying to shush the wild animal.

Buddy doesn't shush. And the noise is *so loud* in the silence of the morning.

Luther turns and runs, disappearing around the side of the house just as I hear my dad shout Buddy's name.

I shove the window open again and stick my head out just in time to see Buddy disappear into the woods.

I fight my laugh but not my smile as I turn my head toward the back deck where Dad is still standing, yelling for his grand-fox.

He spots me. "You hear that fool?"

This time I do laugh. "I think we got ourselves a guard dog."

Dad shakes his head. "What good is chasing off bears if he gives me a heart attack while he does it?"

I snicker. "It was pretty loud."

Dad presses his hand to his chest. "I'm just glad I'd already taken my morning bathroom break."

"Um, ew." I make a face. "I'm going back to bed. But maybe throw Buddy a burger for a job well done."

He nods.

Having planted the idea in Dad's mind, I pull my head back into the house and shut and lock the window.

If Dad gets distracted looking for a treat for Buddy, then maybe he won't try to investigate what Buddy was really chasing.

It ain't no bear.

I crawl back into bed and place my head on the pillow Luther used, thinking about him telling me he'd be back tonight.

I want him to come back.

I want to see him.

My poor, broken heart wants to forgive him.

And my body wants his attention.

But I know I need to be careful.

I can't just lose myself in the comfort of him. We need to talk.

Chapter 133

Luther

> Baby Doll: Good morning. Again.

I DROP ONTO MY COUCH AS A BIT OF TENSION LEAVES my body.

I wasn't sure she would actually message me. Thought maybe she'd take the time apart to realize she doesn't want to talk to me.

I don't want to talk to you. I can't. Not yet.

Guilt worse than anything I've ever felt over lying to Joe clogs my throat.

I don't want to break his trust too. But he was always just an excuse.

An excuse I used to make the decision for Kendra rather than making her choose between me and a future I thought she wanted.

Because if it was left to her, and she chose to leave...

She would've hurt me as much as I hurt her.

My fingers tremble as I type out *I'm sorry.*

I stare at the two inadequate words. Then I delete them.

She deserves my apologies in person.

> Me: Did you sleep more?

> Baby Doll: Yeah. I just woke back up.

More tension drains from my shoulders, but it's just replaced with more guilt.

I think Kendra has been just as miserable as I've been. Which means she probably hasn't been sleeping well either.

> Me: I'm glad you got more rest.

> Baby Doll: Same. But it took a bit to fall back asleep since I'd been laughing so much.

I smile at the screen. Glad I could give her a moment of levity, even if it came at the cost of me running for my life.

> Me: You think it's funny that your little friend chased me off the property?

That damn fox was nipping at my heels the whole way to my fucking truck.

> Baby Doll: Hilarious.

> Baby Doll: You should probably bring him another gift, though. He might not let you back on the property otherwise.

A little piece of hope wedges itself inside me, next to the guilt. She's not telling me not to come back.
She called me Daddy this morning.
I swallow.

> Me: I gave him all the beef jerky that was in my truck.

I shake my head remembering it. That damn fox nearly took

my fingers off when he snapped the meat out of my hand, but I don't tell her that part.

> Baby Doll: I'm sure he appreciated it.

> Me: It was a start. But I still have a lot to atone for.

> Me: I'll make it right.

I watch the phone screen.

Wait.

Wonder what she's thinking.

I didn't mean to change the tone of our messages. But if there's a chance I can undo the wrongs I've done, I need her to understand that I want to. That I *want* to fix this.

If she'll let me.

I still know it's wrong.

Still feel like I'm stealing her away from something else.

Still feel guilt over being in love with my friend's daughter.

But the loss of her...

The loss of her bright presence in my life...

And then finding out I could've lost her for good, before I even knew her...

That broke something inside me.

And the fear swallows me whole all over again.

My chest aches and my eyes burn.

My throat closes.

The image of Kendra in a hospital gown flashes in front of me.

I close my eyes.

I will it away.

Kendra is okay.

She's healthy.

She's fine.

She'll keep being fine.
I open my eyes.

> Baby Doll: Tonight.

> Baby Doll: You can start making it right tonight.

Chapter 134

Luther

The house is dark when I open the front door.
Silent.
I've camped out with Joe before. I know he can sleep through a thunderstorm, but I still take careful steps as I move down the hall to Kendra's door.

It's closed, but not all the way. I just have to press on it, and it opens without a sound.

The lights are off in here too, but unlike last night, the curtains have been left open.

I shut the door behind me, turning the small lock in the center of the handle.

Kendra's under the blankets, on her side, facing the empty half of the bed.

She doesn't stir as I undress.
Doesn't wake as I climb into bed.
And when I settle onto my back, she shifts in her sleep. Moving into me. As though we do it every night.

Drawn together like magnets.

Kendra snuggles against my chest.
Her back rises with a deep inhale.
I hug her to me.

She lets out a hum. "Luther?"
I stroke a hand down her back. "Go back to sleep, Baby."
She hums again. But doesn't say more.
I wrap my fingers around hers on my chest.
And I close my eyes.
I can be this for her.
Be her comfort.
Be her warmth.
I can be anything for her.
If she'll let me.
I fill my lungs with the scent of her.
If Kendra will let me, I'll have coffee with her in the morning.
I parked half a mile down the road, down a dead-end street.
So I can stay.
So we can talk.
And if she'll let me, I'll tell her everything.

Chapter 135

Kendra

When I wake up, the first thing I notice is being surrounded by warmth.

I could get used to this.

I blink my eyes open.

That's a dangerous thought.

I take in the man beside me.

Relaxed in sleep, Luther looks like himself.

Asleep, I can see the difference. I can see how tense he's been the last few times I've seen him.

Hurting you is the last thing I ever wanted to do.

I don't deserve another chance with you.

I stare at the line of his jaw.

He didn't ask for another chance. Just said he didn't deserve one.

I assume he wants one, but assuming things hasn't worked out too well for us.

And what if...

I roll my lips together.

What if he's only here out of pity? Because he feels bad about what I went through?

I don't want that.

I can't have that.

I think I could forgive him for a lot of things. But I couldn't forgive him for being with me for any other reason than wanting me.

I take a slow breath.

No assumptions, Kendra.

Slowly, I extract myself from Luther's hold.

I have a call with a supplier this morning. The perfect excuse to get out of bed.

Because we do need to talk. But if I stay next to a mostly naked Luther much longer, it won't be our mouths that do the talking.

Chapter 136

Luther

Buttoning my shirt, I still can't believe how late I slept.

I figured I'd be tired from sneaking around so late at night, but I didn't think I'd stay asleep past eight.

When I step out into the hall, I can hear the soft cadence of Kendra's voice.

It's coming from her office, through the partially closed door, and I want to peek inside just to see her. But I don't know if she's on the phone or a video call, so I keep walking to the kitchen.

She hasn't made coffee yet, so I figure she couldn't have gotten up too long ago.

Standing in front of the coffee maker, I spot the beans I bought for Kendra on the counter.

I've thought about our date at the coffee shop over and over. Thought about how good she made me feel.

Replayed the look in her eyes when Joe showed up.

It's a day that haunts me. But knowing she's been using the coffee I got her... that she didn't throw it away... It settles something inside me.

And holding on to that bit of calm, I brew us a pot.

The back door slides open, and I turn my head to watch Kendra walk onto the deck, mug of coffee in hand.

"Morning." It's the first time I've used my voice today, and it comes out a little rough.

"Morning." Kendra shuts the door and moves to the chair beside mine.

She's in a pair of soft-looking shorts and a sweatshirt. The morning air is still cool enough to justify the layers.

"Thanks for making coffee." She takes a sip, then rests her head against the back of the chair.

I set my mug on the armrest. "I didn't mean to sleep in so late. I should've made it before your meeting." Kendra turns her head so she's looking at me. I hold her gaze, knowing I need to give her nothing but the truth from now until forever. "I haven't been sleeping well. I haven't been doing well."

"Me either." Her whisper breaks my heart.

"I'm sorry," I whisper back.

Kendra holds up a hand, stopping me from saying more. "Before... Luther..."

I sit forward, hating the pain in her voice.

I want to go to her. I want to close the few feet of space between us. But I don't want to push her.

She swallows and turns in her chair, bringing one foot up onto the seat so she can face me. "Before we... go further. I need you to know that I'm okay. That the cancer stuff is in the past. I've made peace with it."

The cancer stuff.

I press my hand over my heart. It hurts every time.

She watches the movement. "If you're here because you feel bad for me... Then you need to stop. I don't want your affection because of pity."

Pity?
She thinks I'm here because of something as small as pity?
I choke on the idea.
Then I get out of my chair, stopping before her in one step.
I drop to my knees.
Kendra twists forward, and I grip her hips.
"I need you to hear me." Like this, we're eye level. And I make sure her eyes are on mine. "I feel *sorry* that you had to go through that. I feel *anger* that you had to go through that. I feel *horrible, all-consuming fear* knowing that you had to go through that. And I feel *sick* thinking about you doing it alone." I fight to keep my voice steady. "But I don't pity you, Baby Doll. And affection is just one of the things I'll give you if you let me. I'll give you everything I have. If you need a treatment. If you need money for a specialist. If you need to go to the doctor... I'll go with you. But I'll do it because I don't want to be anywhere else, with anyone else. This has nothing to do with pity, Baby. Not at all."

Her eyes shimmer. But she dips her chin, nodding once. "Okay."

"Okay." I watch her watching me. "I was wrong. Everything I said to you... I was wrong about all of it. And I'm sorry. I should've talked to you."

She nods again. "You should've. I would've told you."

"I know." Shame fills me. Because I do know that. If only I'd asked. She would've told me anything.

"But it doesn't change anything about my dad." Kendra leaves her mug on the armrest and twines her fingers together in her lap.

I shuffle closer on my knees until hers are pressed against my chest. "It changes everything. Joe was an excuse I used to make letting you go hurt less." I shake my head. "But it didn't work."

Her brows furrow. "You're not worried about him finding out about..."

She doesn't finish the sentence. Because the description of what's between us is too complicated.

I shake my head. "I'm not worried about him. We'll wait to

tell him. Until we have this sorted. Until..." *Until you love me back.*

"I don't understand." Her eyes plead with me to explain. "You said you weren't right for me. And now that you know..." She lifts that damn shoulder. "Now that you know I can't have kids, you're suddenly okay with... me?"

It hurts. Hearing her say that. But it's what I did. I earned this pain.

"You're still too good for me, Baby Doll." My tone is somber. Because it's true. "But I'm greedy enough not to care. You're too fucking good and too fucking sweet for an old man like me. And I couldn't live with myself if I kept you from a future I thought you wanted. So, instead of talking to you, I let you go." I lower my eyes to her lap. To where she's gripping her hands together so tightly her knuckles are turning white. "I let you go... Because I didn't want to hold you back. Didn't want to make you choose. But I should have asked." I sigh and lift my gaze back to meet hers. "I should've told you."

"Told me what?" She's back to whispering.

I fill my lungs. "I should have told you I can't have children either."

It's the first time I've said it out loud.

First time I've told another person.

"But..." She flattens her hands against her thighs. "What about Ashley?"

I think of my daughter.

Think of the joy she's brought me.

Think about how much I love her.

And I silently beg her forgiveness for saying this next part.

"She's not mine." Admitting it tastes like ash on my tongue.

In every other sense of the word, she is. But biologically, she's not.

"What?" Kendra reaches for me.

Her hands grip my shoulders, steadying us both.

"Her mom..." I sigh. "Sit with me for this part?"

Kendra nods.

Bracing against her chair, I stand, then hold my hands out.

Kendra places her palms in mine, and I help her up. Then I take her chair.

I move her coffee down to the floor of the deck and pat my leg.

Kendra hesitates.

"Sit on my lap."

She blows out a breath, then turns her back to me and sits on my thighs.

Reaching around her, I grip her knees and tug her around until she's sitting sideways.

Keeping one hand on her knee, I wrap my other arm around her back, bracing my palm against her hip, holding her to me.

Kendra leans her head on my shoulder. "Tell me."

"Twenty-seven years ago, I was dating Ashley's mom. It wasn't serious. Or it didn't feel serious to me. But then she told me she was pregnant. We weren't at a point where we'd talked about having kids, but I'd always wanted them. Eventually. So…" I sigh. "I did what I thought I was supposed to do. I asked her to marry me."

It feels so stupid now. The marriage part. Even if Ashley *was* my blood, what did it matter if I was married to her mom or not?

Kendra reaches out and grips my forearm with both her hands.

I flex my fingers on her knee. "We did a courthouse wedding four weeks later, and six months later, Ashley was born." My mouth pulls up into a sad smile. "It was the best and worst time of my life. I had this perfect little baby. This little girl… I took a month off work when she was born. Did as much for her as I could. And when I had to go back to work… it was torture. So I came home early one day. Decided to make it a short week, needing more time with my girl. Except there was a car in my driveway. And when I went inside, my baby was crying in her crib, and her mother was fucking some other guy in our bed."

Kendra tightens her hold on my arm. "Luther..."

I flex my arm around Kendra's back, holding her even closer. "She didn't even hear me. So I walked right back out of the room, packed a bag of Ashley's things, took my daughter to a hotel, and sent divorce papers to my wife."

It's almost funny to think back on it.

I saw another man balls deep in my woman, and I didn't react.

Didn't cry or shout or throw things.

But hearing that fucking firefighter simply ask about Kendra... I was damn near ready to commit homicide.

If it had been her... If I'd caught Kendra with another man... I wouldn't be able to breathe.

But that's the difference.

Kendra would never betray me like that.

She'd never betray me at all.

I tip my cheek against the top of Kendra's head. "I had money, even back then, so I told her I was keeping Ashley full time. We could keep it labeled as joint custody in the courts. I'd pay her child support. But Ashley would never live under her roof again."

"She agreed?" Kendra sounds so full of rage it makes me smile.

I turn my neck and kiss her forehead. "She agreed. Because she knew if she fought me, I'd spend every dollar I had ruining her. And if I did that, she'd never get a dime."

Kendra scoffs. "That bitch better not live around here."

A laugh huffs out of me. "She doesn't. And she doesn't visit."

"Good."

I trace circles on the inside of Kendra's knee with my thumb. "When we got married, Ashley's mom moved into my house. It was all in my name, so I had her out within a week." I think about that little house. How crowded it was with all the toys and kid-sized furniture. "After catching her cheating, I always wondered... Suspected... But Ashley was my child. And I wasn't going to test her paternity. When she was six, I was building the house that I live in now, she was starting school, and for the first time since she was born, I was thinking about dating again. But I knew Ashley was it for me. I didn't need or want more kids. And I didn't want to have to worry about another unplanned pregnancy or questionable parentage. So I decided to get a vasectomy." I fill my lungs with the calming scent of Kendra. "It's all pretty routine. And they don't require you to... *check how things are working* before the procedure. But a part of me wanted to know... Wanted to know if it was even possible for me to be Ashley's father. So I had them test my... stuff." This is another thing I've never told anyone. But it's not as hard as I thought it'd be. "Turns out I didn't need the vasectomy after all. The odds of me being able to reproduce were basically zero."

Kendra sniffs.

I turn my hand palm up on her lap, and she releases my arm so she can grip my hand in both of hers.

Her fingers squeeze mine. "I'm sorry."

I squeeze hers back. "I'm not. It was all pretty fucked up, but in the end, I got the child I always wanted."

It feels wrong saying that to her, but I have to trust Kendra. I have to trust her when she says she's okay not having children.

Kendra sighs, relaxing into me, and I know she didn't take any offense. "Did you ever tell her mom?"

"Never." I shake my head. "As far as she knows, there's a fifty-fifty chance Ashley is mine. Or, well, probably worse odds than that since I doubt it was just the one guy. But no matter what she thinks, in the end, I won. And Ashley won because she didn't have to grow up with a revolving door of stepdads."

Kendra tips her head back, and her eyes are filled with emotion. "I'm still sorry you had to go through that. Ashley... she doesn't know, does she?"

"No one knows. Just you."

Kendra watches me for a moment, like she's deciding something. "Luther?"

"Yeah?"

"I'm still mad at you."

I swallow and nod. "Understandable."

She blows out a breath. "But I'm going to forgive you."

I stare at her.

Just stare.

She sighs. "I had a boyfriend, when I got my diagnosis."

My hold on her tightens. Like this boyfriend from ten years ago might appear and try to take her from me.

Kendra lowers her head back to my shoulder. "We hadn't been together long, but I knew he wanted kids. He'd talked about it before."

"Did he break up with you because you couldn't...?" Anger flashes through my veins.

She shakes her head before I can lose my temper. "I broke up with him. *Because I couldn't.* I just never told him why."

It's what I did.

She did to him what I did to her. Only I was wrong.

Kendra never told me she wanted kids. I just assumed. I saw her interact with children, and I assumed.

I kiss her hair. "I know you already said so, but I'm going to ask one last time."

She sighs. "One last time."

I kiss her hair again. "If you want children, we can find one."

"Find one?" She laughs. "You're not stealing a child for me, Luther."

She tries to lift her head to look at me, but I use my cheek against her head to hold her in place. "I meant adoption, Brat. But if you want me to steal you a baby, I'll steal you a baby."

"You're ridiculous." There's no heat in her tone.

"Ridiculous for you."

We sit together.

The quiet of the morning surrounds us.

I feel her inhale before she speaks. "So, what now?"

Chapter 137

Kendra

"Now..." Luther rubs his hand up and down my thigh. "I make you breakfast."

"Breakfast?" I tilt my head back to look at him.

He nods. "Let me feed you."

My eyes move to his lips.

They're so close.

He's so close.

I want to lean into him.

Remove the inches between us.

I want it so bad.

But I know it's too soon.

So instead of pressing my lips to his, I slide off his lap.

And then my phone rings.

I grab it off the deck railing and recognize the caller.

"It's work," I tell Luther.

"Take it." He stands from the chair. "I'll bring you fresh coffee."

And he does.

Then, twenty minutes later, he sets an egg and cheese sandwich on the desk next to my keyboard.

I mute the call I'm on as the woman on the other end keeps talking. "Sorry, the website is glitching—"

Luther holds up a hand. "Don't apologize." He leans down and presses a kiss to my forehead. "I'll see you tonight."

The smile he gives me is soft.

And it breaks my heart a little.

Then the voice on the phone asks a question.

I look away from Luther to unmute my call, and when I look back up, he's gone.

Chapter 138

Kendra

The bedroom door swings open.

He's here.

I watch as Luther steps into my room and closes the door behind him.

It should be comical, this man in his fifties, sneaking into my bedroom at night, hiding from my dad.

But all I can think about is how sweet it is.

How sweet *he* is.

How he fucked up. How he thought he was doing the right thing.

How it's exactly what I did a decade ago.

I swallow as I think about his story.

About Ashley.

About his ex-wife.

About his own discovery.

I think about how he never told anyone.

I think about how much walking in on my spouse with someone else would ruin me.

I think about how Luther would never.

How he'd never cheat on me.

How he's trying.

How he told me everything.

And as I watch him undress, I exhale.

I let it go.

I let the bad go.

I let the sad go.

I let the anger and the hurt and the doubt... I let it all fucking go.

"I don't want to wait." I say it as I think it.

Luther pauses, stopping at the foot of the bed.

"I don't want to wait, Luther." I sit up, letting the blankets bunch at my waist. "I don't want you to be cautious around me. And I don't want to be guarded around you." The wall I've been struggling to maintain between us crumbles into nothingness. "I just want... you." I breathe the admission.

There's a beat. A second-long pause. Where my heart hangs in the air between us.

Then the blanket is ripped away. And Luther is gripping my ankles.

He yanks me toward him, and I fall onto my back as I slide down the bed.

When my ass reaches the edge of the mattress, Luther drops his hold of me, and my thighs spread, making room for him to step closer.

Luther leans over me, placing a hand on the mattress next to my head. "Say it again."

His voice is a low growl and probably not as quiet as he should be.

But I love it.

"I want you." I reach up and curl my hands over his shoulders. "Don't hurt me again."

"Never." Luther turns his head and presses a kiss to my wrist. "Never again, Baby. I fucking promise." He kisses my wrist again, then leans down, putting our foreheads together. "Tell me you believe me."

"I believe you," I tell him, because I do. "I trust you."

His exhale is sharp. And then his lips are on mine.

Our mouths crash together.

And with his body pressing down against mine, I feel a weight lift from my chest.

I open for him, and he takes every inch of space I offer, his tongue plunging between my lips.

He's heat. And tenderness.

He's...

Emotion tightens around my throat.

Fuck, he's everything.

He's everything I didn't know I needed.

He's everything I didn't think to want.

And he's worth risking the fall.

My hands claw at his back as I try to drag him closer. And I wrap my legs around his waist.

He drops his hips down against me.

And I moan.

He's so hard.

So big. Ready.

"Please." I beg for more. I need him to hurry.

"Please, who?" He rocks his hips against me as his lips brush mine with each syllable.

Warmth builds between my legs.

I lick my tongue across his.

Then I tilt my hips up to meet his. "Please, Daddy."

He groans. "Does my Baby need to be fucked?"

I dig my heels into his lower back. "God, yes."

Luther pulls back, standing to his full height and breaking all contact.

A pitiful sound leaves my throat, but I don't have long to worry.

Luther grips the waistband of my sleep shorts and tugs them and my panties down my legs, dropping them to the floor.

Then he shoves his boxer briefs down.

I left the curtains open again tonight. And the moonlight dances over his muscles.

He reaches down and grips the base of his length.

Needing to be just as naked, I reach for the hem of my shirt and pull it up.

When it's over my head, blocking my view, two hands press my thighs open, and the puff of air on my sensitive skin is my only warning before Luther's tongue licks the length of my pussy.

He does it again.

And again.

And I get stuck in my damn shirt, writhing and trying not to make noise as he continues to eat me out.

Luther groans, and the vibrations are nearly too much.

My thighs clamp down around his head.

He chuckles. With his tongue on my clit.

And I nearly come.

I finally toss my shirt free, and he looks up, his tongue still working me over.

His eyes are full of smiles.

His mouth is full of pussy.

And I have no regrets over welcoming him back into my life.

I reach my hands up and grip my breasts.

Luther moans.

I play with my nipples as I hold his eye contact.

He presses my thighs open and stands.

I lift my knees, opening for him.

He squeezes the base of his cock. "You have to be quiet. Remember?"

I nod. "I remember."

Luther steps forward until his thighs hit the mattress, then he guides the tip of his dick to my entrance.

My breath quickens.

We've done this before.

He's been inside me before.

But this... This time feels different.

The blinders are off.
This is us.
Bare.
Exposed.
Raw.
He's watching me.
Waiting.
"I want you." I remind him. "Take me." I beg him.
A low sound rolls off Luther as he presses into me.
He grips my hip, holding me down. Holding me in place.
I'm so wet, so slick for him, that my clenching muscles aren't enough to slow him down.
He releases his hold of his cock and presses his palm down on my lower stomach.
He presses down and he pushes in.
My back arches.
I'm so full.
It's so perfect.
In and out.
Luther drags himself in and out, and I can't think about anything other than where we're connected.
My body is on fire.
And there's only Luther.
There's only *him*.

Chapter 139

Luther

I rock my hips against her, sinking as deep as I can go.

And it's not enough.

Where we're touching is not enough.

I shove my hips harder against Kendra, and she slides a few inches up the mattress.

I put one knee on the bed, and with my cock buried in her, I use my hips to shove her farther up the bed.

Bracing myself over her, I put my other knee on the bed.

I pull my hips back, my length sliding out of her heat.

Then I slam forward.

The bed frame creaks.

I do it again.

And again.

Kendra arches against the onslaught, her mouth opening in a silent cry, and I drop down, latching on to her exposed neck.

My teeth graze her skin.

She moans.

My hips work.

The bed creaks.

I lick her neck.

She drags her nails over my back.
I fuck her deeper.
The bed creaks.
My hand slides between her body and the mattress to grip her ass.
She clenches around me.
My balls squeeze.
The bed creaks.
"Luther. Fuck. Luther," she pants. And I feel it all the way down my spine.
"That's right, Baby." I flex my fingers against her ass, my fingertip teasing her other hole.
Kendra clings to me.
I grind against her.
And she trembles.
I grind harder.
She whimpers.
Pride swells in my chest.
My girl needed this.
And I'm giving it to her.
I roll my hips again.
It's that perfect angle.
The perfect angle for the base of my cock to rub against her sensitive little clit.
Kendra's breathing changes.
She tenses.
Her hips lift.
I grind harder.
"Take me." I press my mouth to her ear. "Take all of me, Baby Doll. And come on Daddy's dick."
She implodes.
I roll my hips.
And when she presses her mouth to my shoulder to muffle her cry, I follow her over the edge.
Filling her with everything I have.

Chapter 140

Kendra

> Papi: Can you find an excuse to be out for the night?
>
> Papi: I need you here.
>
> Papi: I need you to stay over.

MY CORE THROBS AT HIS QUESTION, STILL SORE FROM last night.

And I wish I could go over there now. Wish I could be the one climbing into his bed, falling asleep under his covers. But there's no way for me to do that without my dad asking a thousand questions.

And I'm not ready to tell him.

Not yet.

> Me: Friday.

THE MATTRESS SHIFTS.

    I blink my eyes open. "Luther?"

    "Hush, Baby." He pulls me to him.

    "I said I'd come over Friday." I nuzzle against his chest.

    "I know what you said. And I'll wait to fuck you until then, but I never said I wasn't coming over." He pulls the blankets up over us, then smooths a hand over my hair. "Go to sleep."

I WAKE UP ALONE.

    And I wonder if I dreamed him.

    If it was all in my head.

    But then I see it.

    Sitting on my nightstand. Wrapped in clear plastic.

    A brownie.

Chapter 141

Kendra

Rain pounds off my windshield, and I slow to a crawl as I search for the turn into Dad's neighborhood.

It's Friday. I'm going over to Luther's tonight. And I can't wait.

He's snuck into my room every night this week, just to sleep beside me.

Then he makes me coffee, kisses me on the forehead, and leaves me to work.

It's been nice. Healing.

But I'm really looking forward to tonight.

It will be good to just be together. Plus, Luther needs to get more rest. Sneaking into my room well past his bedtime can't be good for him, even if he does sleep in when he's at my side.

I turn my windshield wipers up another notch as I turn off the highway.

This seemed like a great idea earlier, to go buy more of the coffee Luther likes. But I hadn't realized a rainstorm was coming.

The sky continues to pour, and I lean closer to the windshield. The visibility is shit.

This weather better let up; otherwise Dad will freak out about me *driving to Denver* and try to convince me to reschedule my *dinner with friends*.

Spotting the driveway, I double-check for oncoming headlights, then turn onto Dad's property.

Not wanting to get my clothes wet, I use the remote Dad gave me and open the garage door.

Finally parked, I turn off the engine, leave one of the bags of coffee on the passenger seat, and grab the other to bring inside.

With the overhead door still open, I stand at the edge of the garage and watch the rain come down.

It's loud, the water pelting off every surface in sight. But it's refreshing.

The temperature has dropped. The air is cool. And the smell of it...

I close my eyes and take a long inhale through my nose.

There's something so invigorating about a downpour in the woods.

A horn blares.

My eyes open.

Tires screech.

I take a step forward.

And a creature lets out a scratchy shout.

My heart stutters.

The shout gets cut off.

And I start to run.

"Buddy!"

The coffee falls from my hands.

I run faster.

It can't be.

Raindrops crash against my face, mixing with my tears and blurring my vision.

"Buddy!" I try to yell, but my voice cracks.

My tennis shoes slap against the wet gravel as my clothes are soaked through.

It can't be.
I round the turn in the driveway.
I can't breathe.
I keep running, but I can't breathe.
He's there.
Lying in the road.
"No." I gasp for breath. "Buddy, no."
I stumble to a stop beside him.
Red fur is matted from the rain.
He looks so small.
"Buddy," I sob.
I drop to my knees.
There's blood on his temple.
And his leg…
It's the leg that had the ribbon wrapped around it when we first met…
It's broken.
I can see that it's broken.
I swallow against the bile rising in my throat.
I reach for him, pausing my trembling hands inches from his fragile body.
I don't want to hurt him more.
And I don't…
I don't know if he's…
He can't be gone.
I glance up at the road. Checking for traffic. Checking for help. But all I can see is Buddy.
"Please…"
I rest my hand on his side.
I try to stop shaking.
I hold my breath.
He can't be.
And I feel his rib cage move.
Alive.

Mountain Daddy

A sound I don't recognize leaves my chest.
He's alive.
As carefully as I can, I scoop him up.
"Just hold on, okay?"
I cradle him to my chest, and I run.

Chapter 142

Luther

"Hey." I answer the phone with a smile.

"—mergency... Buddy." Kendra's distressed voice cracks through the speaker.

My heart drops into my stomach. "Say that again, Baby."

The line cracks.

I stride across my living room.

"Stay on the phone and say it again."

Fucking shitty mountain service.

I grab my truck keys and shove my feet into my boots.

The line clears, and I can hear the sound of rain and windshield wipers.

"Kendra."

"I'm here." Her broken inhale is audible over the background noise.

"What happened, Baby?" I keep my voice as calm as I can while jogging through the garage.

"He... He was hit by a car. His leg..." A sob cuts her off.

I climb into my truck, and I wait until I close my door before I hit the button to open the loud overhead door.

"Where are you?" I turn my engine on.

"I..."

"Take a breath." I shift into drive and roar out of the garage. "I'm coming to you, okay? It will be okay."

I listen as she takes a breath. "O-okay."

I try to think of what's closest to her. "Are you heading to the vet in Lonely?"

"I think so. I just typed emergency vet into my GPS, but..." She hiccups through another sob. "What if they won't help him?"

"They'll help him."

"But he's a wild animal."

"They'll help him." I turn onto the main road. And floor it.

"Promise?" Her plea is so quiet, but I hear it so loud.

She's asking me to promise her something.

She's trusting me to promise her.

After everything.

After what I did.

She'll still believe me if I promise.

"I promise, Baby." I swallow, forcing myself to stay composed. "I need to make a call. What's your ETA?"

"Twenty-two minutes."

"I'll meet you there, okay?"

"Okay."

"Have you called Joe?"

She sniffles. "No."

"I'll call him. You focus on driving. Okay?"

"Okay." My girl sniffs again. "Thank you."

"I'd do anything for you, Baby. That includes Buddy." I swallow down the urge to tell her I love her. But it's not the time. "I'm going to make that call now. Okay?"

"Okay."

"Keep your eyes on the road." I use my commanding tone. "Be careful."

I wait for her whispered okay, then I hang up.

I give myself thirty seconds to just breathe.

Then I search my contacts for the man I need.

It rings twice.

"Rocky." There's no hint of surprise in his voice, even though we've only spoken on the phone maybe once before.

"Ethan, I need a favor."

"I'm not letting you fuck in my park." His tone is so dry I almost crack a smile.

"Oh, I'm gonna fuck in your park, grump-ass. But that's not the favor."

He grunts. "What is it, then?"

I shake my head. He really is the least friendly bastard I know.

"I'm bringing an injured fox to the vet in Lonely."

"You can't bring a wild—"

"It's my girl's. She's practically adopted him, and... dude, I just need you to make this work."

The line is silent, and I worry I've lost signal.

But then I hear his annoyed exhale. "The visitor area needs updates, and our funding just got cut."

"Fine." I press the brakes as I approach a turn.

"It'll be ten grand at least."

"Whatever."

"Maybe fifteen."

"I'll write a check for twenty if you'll shut the fuck up and go make whatever calls you need to."

"Deal."

The line goes dead.

This fox better fucking live.

Figuring I have about five minutes before I lose service for a stretch, I make another call.

It goes to voicemail. Which is probably for the best, because I don't know how to explain why Kendra called me first.

"This is Joe from Joe's Custom Furniture. Leave me a message." There's a long pause, some rustling, because Joe still hasn't fixed his recording, then finally the voicemail clicks on.

"Joe, if you get this in the next twenty minutes, call me, not

Kendra. She's driving. Buddy was hit by a car, and she's bringing him to the clinic in Lonely. I'm already on my way. And I've called in a favor."

Hanging up, I tighten my grip on the steering wheel.

This fox has to fucking live.

Chapter 143

Kendra

Headlights fill my rearview mirror as I slow, the sign for Lonely Peak Vet Clinic just up ahead.

The rain has slowed to a steady stream rather than a downpour, but my body is still tense with stress as I turn into the small parking lot.

The headlights follow me. And as I pull into a parking spot, I look over as the truck parks in the spot next to mine.

Luther's truck.

He's here.

I start crying all over again, choking on an inhale.

I've learned my lesson.

I don't want to do the hard things alone anymore.

And Luther is here, so I don't have to.

Turning off the engine, I push my door open as Luther rounds the back of his truck, meeting me at the side of my car.

I'm soaking wet. A total mess. But Luther doesn't stop walking until our bodies collide and he wraps me in a hug.

Tears fall from my eyes as worry and relief war inside my chest.

Luther presses a kiss to my head, then grips my shoulders and steps back. "It's going to be okay. Okay?"

I swallow and nod. "Okay."

He looks through the rear driver-side window.

Buddy is there, wrapped in a towel I snagged off a shelf in the garage before settling him onto the back seat. His broken leg is sticking out the top of the towel, so there, hopefully, wouldn't be any pressure on it.

"Grab your purse."

Following directions, I turn back to my open door, reach across to the passenger seat, and grab my things. The bag of coffee reminds me that I left the other one lying in the driveway.

I hear the rear door open, and by the time I stand back up, Luther has Buddy in his arms.

The little guy is awake but looks dazed.

"If you bite me, I'm going to be pissed," Luther tells the fox, then looks at me. "Get the doors."

Happy for the task, I push both car doors shut, then hurry ahead to the front door of the vet clinic.

A few other vehicles are in the parking lot, and as I hold the door open for Luther, another pickup turns into the lot.

I was too frantic when I was searching for a vet in my GPS, so I didn't take the time to read if this is really an emergency vet or if it's just a regular vet, but I have to believe Luther when he said they'd take care of Buddy.

Following my boys inside, the cool air sends an instant shiver through my body.

I internally curse myself for not already packing my overnight bag because I'm going to need a doctor, too, if I stay in these wet clothes for hours.

"Afternoon, how can I…" The woman behind the front desk trails off, eyes widening as she looks at Buddy.

"Our dog was hit by a car." Luther doesn't waver. "His leg is broken, and he hit his head."

A whimper catches in my throat.

I don't think I told him about Buddy's head, but Luther must've seen the blood for himself.

My poor Buddy lets out a pitiful sound to match my own.

"Sir, that's, um, not a dog."

I step up next to Luther and tuck my fingers into the crook of his arm. "Please help him."

The woman looks at me, then back at Buddy.

Her eyes are full of sympathy, but I know she's going to deny us.

"Let them in, Brenda." A deep voice sounds behind us.

I turn, and my mouth opens when I see the hot park ranger striding through the door.

"Ethan." Brenda's voice is breathy. And I get it. But I need her to focus.

"Doctor Child is on her way." Ethan steps up to the counter on the other side of Luther. "I'll stay as a representative for wildlife control."

Brenda slides her chair back and stands. "Okay, follow me." We all start to move, but she holds up a hand. "Just Ethan and the fox."

"But..." I press my lips together. I want to argue. But I also don't want to be difficult and have her change her mind.

"It'll be okay," Luther tells me. Then he shifts his hold, and Ethan takes Buddy from his arms.

I cling to Luther as I watch Buddy look up at the new human holding him.

But it's like he knows this is important because he just blinks up at Ethan.

"Be a good boy," I whisper. Both the man and the fox turn their heads to look at me. "We'll be right here."

I swear Buddy nods his head.

Then Ethan turns, and they disappear down the hallway.

Luther tucks his arm against his side, trapping my hand against his body, then he leads me away from the desk to the waiting area behind us.

An older man sits in one of the dozen chairs lining the front corner of the building. The chairs are padded but don't have arms, and they're backed up against the large windows, showcasing the gloomy weather outside.

The man doesn't even look up at us, unconcerned with the scene we created.

Away from the single man, Luther guides me to the stretch of empty chairs that have their backs to the parking lot.

My hand slips free from Luther's warmth as I take the second from the end.

"I'll be right back." Luther smooths a hand over my wet hair, then he steps back.

I stare blankly at the small TV on the wall across from me as I hear the main door open and close.

I drop my purse onto the empty seat next to me, and a few seconds later, the door reopens, and Luther's heavy footsteps cut across the floor.

He crouches before me, a flannel in hand. "Go to the bathroom and switch this for your wet shirt."

I look at the soft fabric in his hands. There's a baseball hat too, with the logo for Rocky Ridge Inn on the front.

He taps the brim with his finger. "I don't have anything warmer in my truck, but it might help."

I lift my gaze to meet his.

How different would the last decade have been if I'd had Luther in my life?

If I hadn't done all the bad alone?

He's been alone too.

For twenty-six years, he kept his secrets to himself.

My heart squeezes.

I want to be there for him too.

I take in his own wet clothing that clings to his body. "What about you?"

Luther shakes his head. "I'm fine."

"Your clothes are wet too."

He shakes his head again. "I run hot. You don't."

"But—"

"Don't argue with me, Baby." He nods toward the pile in his hands. "Do it for me."

Sighing, I take the clothes. "Thank you."

With his hands empty, he lightly rests his palms on my thighs. "Are your knees okay?"

I look down at the wet denim and the streaks of dirt covering my knees.

I swing my feet a little, moving the joints. "They're okay. Just a little sore."

He sighs like he doesn't like that answer, but he doesn't say more.

Luther stands first, then he helps me up.

Now that I'm thinking about them, my knees are a little more sore than I realized. But I keep myself from limping as I cross the lobby to the door labeled *Restroom*.

With the door locked behind me, I peel my shirt off.

My bra is also wet, and I want to take it off, but I don't really want to free-boob it in public. So I grab a handful of paper towels and press them against my bra, soaking up some of the dampness. Then I repeat the process with my hair, squeezing sections at a time until it's as dry as I can get it.

With my skin also dry, I shrug the flannel on, enjoying the way it hangs halfway down my thighs as I button it up.

I wish I had dry pants to change into, but my jeans aren't as soaked as my top half was, so I'll survive.

I don't have a hair tie on me, and my hair isn't really long enough to braid, so I just comb it back with my fingers and pull the hat on.

I grimace at my reflection.

My tits fill out the oversized shirt, but the sleeves hang past my fingers. And the hat covers half my face in shadows.

I look like a mini female version of Luther.

My lips tug into a small smile.

Folding my damp shirt, I hold it away from myself and open the door.

Luther is in the chair next to the one I vacated, leaning forward, elbows on his knees.

His eyes were already on the bathroom door when I opened it, and I hold his gaze as I cross the room.

When I near, he sits up and stretches his arm over the back of my chair.

I collapse into the seat, dropping my shirt onto the chair with my purse.

Luther curls his hand around my shoulder and pulls me into his side.

I lean into him.

Lean *on* him.

He rests his chin on my head. "You look cute."

My smile is hidden from his view. "Thanks. I was just thinking I looked like you."

His hand flexes on my shoulder. "I like that."

I curl my fingers into the long sleeves covering my hands. "Thanks for the shirt."

I'm still a little cold. But nothing like before.

"Stop thanking me. It's nothing."

I pull back enough to look up at Luther from under his hat. "It's not nothing to me."

He reaches across with his free hand and tugs the brim of the hat down.

My eyes still sting from crying so much, but I feel the worry loosen its hold on me.

I lean back into his side.

Headlights flash through the windows behind us as we watch a dog food ad play on the muted TV.

A woman rushes in through the main door, speed walking through the lobby and down the hall without pausing.

She must be the vet.

I shove my hands between my thighs to keep from fidgeting.

Luther's phone rings.

He keeps his hold on me as he shifts around, pulling it from his pocket.

"Hey." He keeps his voice quiet, even though it's still just us and the other guy.

I can hear the muted tones of a man speaking on the other end of the call.

"Yeah, I'm with her." He hums some agreement, and I love the way his chest vibrates with the sound. "The vet just got here. Uh-huh." Luther traces circles on my shoulder with his thumb. "Ethan. Yeah. No. Don't worry about it." Luther lets out a loud sigh. "I said don't worry about it. No. Yes. She's fine. Joe, I swear to fucking god..." I snort at the exasperation in Luther's tone. "Yeah, that's her, laughing at you." I tug my hands free from my thighs and poke Luther in the side. He captures my hand and presses it against the top of his leg. "Bring us coffee. Yeah. Hazelnut. Uh-huh. No, get it hot." Luther sighs. "I'm hanging up."

I can hear my dad say something as Luther pulls the phone away from his ear.

But I can't make it out before Luther hangs up.

"I don't know how you live with that man." Luther slides his phone back into his pocket.

"It wasn't by choice." I half joke. It wasn't by choice, but he's been a surprisingly good roommate. "He's on his way?"

"Yeah."

I don't move.

Not yet.

Luther leans back in his chair and crosses his closest leg over the other, his ankle on his opposite knee and his thigh over the top of mine.

I curl my hands under my chin, my elbows resting on his leg, and relax into him more.

I'll move before my dad gets here.

Chapter 144

Luther

The main door opens, and Joe rushes inside, drink carrier in hand.

I lift the arm not around Kendra's shoulders and hold my finger to my mouth.

I work to keep my muscles relaxed. Because if I act guilty, I'll look guilty. But there's nothing wrong with my friend's daughter falling asleep beside me after an emotionally taxing event.

The fact she's in my clothes, curled into my body, with her mouth pressed against my side... minor details.

And if it plants a seed in Joe's mind... so be it.

He'll be learning the truth soon enough anyway.

He glances at the form next to me, inhales like he's going to say something, then does a double take.

His brows lift in shock, then his eyes narrow as he looks at me.

I speak first, cutting him off but keeping my volume low. "Who's the fourth drink for?"

Joe looks down at the cardboard carrier like he forgot he was holding it. "Uh, Ethan."

I shake my head. "I told you no."

"Yeah, well" is his great comeback.

"What did you get him? Maybe she'll want it." I use my head

to gesture toward the front desk. The woman, Brenda, is currently doing something on her phone and not paying any attention to us.

I didn't tell Joe about the twenty-grand price tag for Ethan's involvement, so I'm sure I sound like a dick, but I don't think the man needs a thank-you drink.

"Vanilla latte." He shrugs. "I played it safe."

Joe gives Kendra one more look, then moves to sit on the other side of me.

When he acts like he's going to sit directly next to me, I shove him with my elbow. "Move over."

He scoffs, offended, as he leaves an empty chair between us. "Gee, sorry for trying to sit next to my best friend."

That old guy left about ten minutes ago, meaning every single seat is open.

I roll my eyes. "You're close enough."

"You let Kenny sit next to you," he grumbles as he twists the to-go cups around to read the names written on the sides.

"Yeah and? She's not a smelly man. And she was cold. It was pouring rain when the accident happened." I add on, answering the question of why she's wearing my clothes.

Joe's shoulders slump like he just remembered why we're here. "He's okay?"

A fox-shaped weight presses down on my chest. "I don't know. No one's come out since—"

I stop talking when I hear footsteps in the hall.

When Ethan comes into view, I squeeze Kendra's shoulder.

I don't want to wake her since she was clearly exhausted if she fell asleep sitting up, but I know she'll want to hear the update with us.

She grumbles something that sounds dangerously close to *Daddy* in her sleep.

I clear my throat and give her shoulder a shake. "Kendra. Wake up—" I clear my throat a second time when I nearly call her *Baby*.

She lifts her head away from my body, and cool air fills the space.

The hat blocks me from seeing her sleepy face, and I hate it.

Joe leans forward, head turned toward Kendra. "Hey, Kenny."

Kendra jumps in her seat, a shriek of surprise leaving her.

Joe jolts, Kendra startling him right back.

He grips the carrier in both hands. "Christ. Don't yell at me."

"Sorry, Dad." Kendra lets out a strangled laugh. "Guess I'm a little out of it."

I let my hand slide off Kendra's shoulder.

Ethan's brows raise when Kendra says *Dad*. I don't think he knows Joe personally, but I know he's seen us together.

And he's seen me trying to *fuck Kendra in his park*.

Thirty, he mouths.

Fuck you, I mouth back.

He shrugs and opens his mouth.

I narrow my eyes and mouth, *Fine*. Then I mouth, *Fuck you*, again because he really is a bastard.

"I wasn't trying to scare you." Joe balances the carrier on his knees so he can slap a hand to his chest. "Didn't Rocky tell you I was coming?"

"Yeah, but I fell asleep."

"Well..." Joe seems to remember Ethan's arrival. He holds the carrier with both hands again and sits up straight. "Hey, man."

Ethan nods to him, and I uncross my legs while Kendra sits up on the edge of her seat.

He wouldn't be milking me for another ten grand if Buddy was fatally injured, but I'm still bracing myself.

"The fox—"

"Buddy," Joe interrupts.

"Buddy..." Ethan says slowly. "Is going to be fine."

The father-daughter duo on either side of me slump back in their seats with loud exhales.

Ethan's lips twitch, but he continues. "He's currently sedated, and Dr. Child is setting his broken leg."

Kendra reaches over to me with her flannel-covered hand.

I think she's forgotten about Joe. But I won't deny her.

Not this. Not anything.

Not ever.

I wrap my fingers around hers, setting our joined hands on my thigh. And I keep my eyes forward, away from Joe.

"Will he have a cast?" Kendra asks, her voice sounding shaky again.

I rub my thumb over the back of her hand.

Ethan nods. "He'll have a hard plastic brace that attaches with Velcro. There's a chance the—Buddy can chew off the straps, but it's better than him chewing on a plaster cast. And it won't matter if he gets this one wet."

"He won't chew it off," Joe says like he knows it for a fact.

Kendra nods in agreement.

They're probably right.

"He had a scrape on his head, but it's small enough that the doc just cleaned it. No stitches needed. She x-rayed his whole body while looking at his leg, and there are no other breaks. No cracked ribs. So the chance of internal organ damage is minimal."

Kendra sniffs, and I rub my thumb over her knuckles again. "He'll really be okay?"

"A broken leg isn't nothing. I'd like him to keep the cast on for at least four weeks. Longer if he'll leave it alone. But if he keeps his weight off it, it should heal back to normal." Ethan sighs. "I feel required to add that wild animals can be dangerous. And—"

"Yeah, yeah." Joe waves off his concern. And again, I think he's probably right. Buddy might be a furry little maniac, but he's not going to bite these two. "Can he have some painkillers or something? Even with the cast, I gotta think that leg will hurt."

Ethan nods. "Yeah. He'll have some meds for a bit. Foxes usually eat things pretty fast, so if you stick the pills into some sort of food, he should take them just fine."

"One of us'll stop for some more meat on the way home," Joe states.

Ethan's jaw works. "He won't be able to hunt with a cast. So, if you want him to stay strong and healthy, you'll have to feed him. And if you do that, he will become dependent on you, and you'll have to continue to feed him. Which"—he holds up a hand to punctuate the importance of this next part—"I do not recommend. Wild animals are not pets." He drops his hand. "But I have a feeling none of that will deter you."

"Thank you," Kendra says earnestly.

I shake my head.

She and Joe will absolutely ignore the last part of Ethan's little speech.

"In normal circumstances, we'd probably keep the animal overnight for observation, but I think Buddy would do best in familiar surroundings. It's gonna be a bit before he's awake enough to go, but we'll send him home tonight. Though I will insist you transport him using one of our travel crates. You can return it next week."

"We can do that. And truly, we really appreciate the help." Joe pulls one of the cups free from the carrier. "I brought this as a thank-you."

Ethan looks uncomfortable accepting the gift. Like he's not used to another man buying him a latte.

I smirk.

He takes a sip, then nods to Joe. "Tastes like thirty grand."

My smirk drops, and I mouth, *Fuck you*. Again.

Ethan dips his chin to Kendra, then turns and heads back down the hall.

"I don't get it," Joe mumbles. "Is that a thing people say?"

Kendra leans forward to look around me. "Is one of those for me?"

"Huh?" Joe's eyes move to our joined hands.

"The coffee." Kendra points at the drinks with her other hand.

When Joe moves his attention to his lap, she slips her fingers free from mine.

I hand Kendra's drink across to her, then take the one Joe hands me.

"I don't know how long *a little while* is. Maybe I should've brought dinner too." Joe sets the empty carrier next to him.

"We can have something delivered," I offer before he can suggest that I leave for food.

I'm not leaving Kendra.

TWO HOURS LATER, WITH THE EMPTY PIZZA BOX jammed into the trash, we get permission to bring Buddy home.

I try to help pay for the procedure, but when Joe insists on covering it, I don't press the issue. I'm already practically paying for Buddy's college tuition.

But I do insist on helping Buddy get settled back at the house.

They decide they have plenty of food for the next couple days, so we all drive straight to the house, leaving the grocery trip for later.

Buddy does fine on the car ride and slowly hobbles into his doghouse after I carry his crate to the backyard.

Kendra brings him fresh water and a chicken breast with a pill hidden inside.

We all watch him eat it. And when we can't stare at a sleeping fox any longer, we head inside.

"What if something comes after him?" Kendra asks, standing in the living room, wringing her hands together.

She's changed out of her stained jeans into sweatpants. But she's still wearing my flannel.

And she looks so fucking cute I want to sit her on my lap again.

"I'm going to sleep on the couch," Joe states as he heads toward his room. "That way, I'll hear him if he needs anything."

He disappears from view.

"Well, shit," I sigh.

I'd already accepted that Kendra wouldn't be coming over tonight, but I was still holding out hope that I could sleep here.

But with Joe sleeping in the living room, that won't be possible.

Even if I could sneak in and out through the window, I can't risk running into him when I have to pee in the middle of the night. And tomorrow's Saturday, so he won't even be leaving in the morning.

"Sorry." Kendra reaches for me, and she closes her fingers around my wrist.

I step closer and lift my other hand, cradling the side of her neck. "Don't apologize, Baby."

I drag my thumb along her jawline.

"I was looking forward to tonight," she whispers up at me.

"Me too." I bend down and press my lips to hers.

Footsteps sound, and I drop my hand.

Joe appears, arms filled with pillows and blankets.

I step to the side, toward the front door. "Keep me posted on the patient."

Joe grunts his reply as he drops his bedding on the couch.

"Thank you. For... everything." Kendra's voice is soft.

I want to remind her that she doesn't need to thank me.

But I nod instead.

Then I turn away from my girl and walk out of the house, even though it's the very last thing I want to do.

Chapter 145

Kendra

My stomach twists when the door closes behind Luther.
    I don't want a barrier between us.
    I don't want anything between us.
    I want him by my side.
    Always.

Chapter 146

Luther

Me: Good night, Beautiful.

Baby Doll: Night, Handsome.

SETTING MY PHONE ON THE NIGHTSTAND, I CLOSE MY eyes and picture my Kendra wearing my flannel.

And the last thought I have before sleep takes me is, *I should've taken a photo.*

Baby Doll: Morning.

Baby Doll: *sends a video of Buddy bouncing around on three legs, scarfing pieces of chicken as Joe tosses them*

Me: He seems in good spirits.

> Baby Doll: I'll say. He greeted us this morning with his scratchy shouts.

> Me: Maybe Joe will sleep in his room tonight...?

> Baby Doll: The man has already told Buddy he'll sleep on the couch all weekend.

> Me: What an asshole.

> Baby Doll: Knock it off. Dad just asked me what's so funny, and I had to lie.

I GRIN TO MYSELF.

> Me: What did you tell him?

> Baby Doll: I said it was a funny video of a duck.

> Me: Why a duck?

> Baby Doll: I don't know! I panicked.

> Baby Doll: Then he wanted to see it, so I had to sneakily pull up Instagram and then pretend I lost the video.

> Me: He's so nosy.

> Baby Doll: You're telling me. Now he's asking me who I'm texting.

> Me: And what did you say?

I know she won't tell him it's me. But a part of me still hopes she does.

> Baby Doll: Ashley.

I choke and slosh the coffee out of my mug.

> Me: Dammit, woman. I just inhaled my coffee.

Baby Doll: Sorry!

Baby Doll: Promise I'm not laughing.

Baby Doll: Hope it wasn't too hot.

> Me: I'll survive.

> Me: Why Ashley?

Baby Doll: I. Don't. Know. I. Panicked.

Baby Doll: I really don't text with her. I'd tell you if I did.

Baby Doll: I don't even have her number.

I think about my last conversation with Ashley.
I think about her knowing about me and Kendra.
I think about Kendra admitting that she loved me.
I close my eyes and beg the universe for that to still be true.

Baby Doll: Sorry. I didn't mean to be weird.

> Me: Don't apologize. You didn't make anything weird.

> Me: I'd be fine with you two talking.

> Me: She likes you.

I worry for a moment if I shouldn't have said that.

Baby Doll: Aww, that makes me feel cool.

I hesitate. Then I hit send.

> Me: I like you too.

I hold my breath.

> Baby Doll: That makes me feel less cool.

I grin.

CHAPTER 147

KENDRA

I ROLL MY LIPS TOGETHER. THEN I HIT SEND.

> Me: I like you too.

I hold my breath.

We promised no more secrets and not telling him... Not telling him that I'm dangerously in love with him feels like the biggest secret I've ever kept.

Not telling him feels like a lie.

But telling him...

Telling him terrifies me.

Because if he doesn't say it back...

I look away from my phone and up at the sky.

If I tell him I love him and Luther doesn't say it back, then it really will be over.

Chapter 148

Luther

I hold the phone to my chest.
I like you too.
"I love you, Baby Doll." It comes out as a whisper.
It's true.
It's so fucking true.
But saying it out loud...
Even alone.
Saying it out loud is the scariest thing I've done.
Because when I tell her.
When I tell Kendra that she has my whole damn heart...
If she doesn't feel the same way...
If she doesn't love me back...
I don't think I can recover from that.
So I'll wait.
I'll wait until she's ready.
I'll wait as long as it fucking takes.
And until then, I'll take whatever she's willing to give me.

Me: Good.

Chapter 149

Luther

> Me: I'm going to injure the man so he's forced to sleep in his fucking bed.

It's been four nights. Four fucking nights of sleeping alone in my bed while Joe cockblocks me.

"You alright?" Jessie, always the perceptive one, leans her hip against the bar.

"Fine," I grunt.

She nods, eyes wide. "Yeah, I can see that."

Last night, when I stayed at the bar late because I had nothing better to do, I told Jessie I was back with Kendra. Even if we haven't made it officially official.

Then I texted Kendra to ask if it was okay to tell Jessie about her cancer.

Kendra said it was fine.

I asked if she was sure.

She said she was positive.

Then I told Jessie.

And when I was done telling her, I locked myself in room two and cried for ten straight minutes.

I swallow down the urge to be sad again.

"I'm fine," I say more convincingly this time.

Jessie nods. "That's good. Because your girl is here."

My head jerks up.

The front door is open, and the midday sun is outlining a perfectly curvy body that I'd recognize anywhere.

I'm striding around the bar before I notice the man holding the door.

Joe.

Fuck.

I slow to a casual pace.

With Joe behind her, Kendra gives me a huge, knowing grin before mouthing, *Hi, Daddy.*

I clench my jaw and project the word *Brat* at her.

Joe steps inside, and the door swings shut.

"What are you two doing here?" I slide my hands into my pockets so I don't accidentally pull Kendra into a hug.

Joe slaps a hand to his stomach. "We're hungry."

"Good timing. I was just about to eat." I am hungry, so it's not a lie. "If we sit at the bar, Jessie can join us."

Joe lifts a hand, waving to my sister. "Hey, Jess."

Jessie waves back, but instead of staying put, she follows my path around the bar.

Joe holds his arms out like he's waiting for a hug. But Jessie slaps his hands out of the way and pulls Kendra into a hug instead.

Kendra lets out a little oomph before she returns the gesture, patting Jessie on the back.

"What's this?" Joe furrows his brows.

With one arm still wrapped around Kendra, Jessie backhands Joe in the chest. "You should've told me."

It takes a second, but then Joe's shoulders slump, and I watch his eyes get glassy. "Oh."

Jessie smacks him again. "Yeah. Oh."

"I'm fine." Kendra lifts her chin so she can speak over Jessie's shoulder. "In case everyone forgot that part."

"Let us love you," Joe says, then he steps into the girls, encasing them in his own hug.

Kendra turns to me with playfully pleading eyes. "Luther, save me."

I shake my head. "You heard the man." Then I step up opposite Joe, and we trap the girls between us.

Kendra sighs, pretending defeat.

But I feel the way she leans her head against my chest.

And while Joe is busy closing his eyes, I press a quick kiss to Kendra's hair.

Then I bite down on a laugh when I see Doug, a regular, walk up and press his body against Joe's back as he tries to join the hug.

Joe jolts.

Doug wraps his arms around Joe's neck, not touching the women. "What're we hugging for?"

Joe tries to shrug him off. "Dammit, Doug. You need to be invited for stuff like this."

"Aw, come on, man." Doug drops his arms and steps back. "I never get hugs."

Our group breaks apart, and Joe groans as he turns to face Doug. "Fine, you want a hug, you can have one."

Joe opens his arms.

Doug smiles as he steps into my friend and takes it.

Kendra turns to watch them but leans back against me as she does.

Jessie shakes her head, but I don't miss the way she wipes at her eyes. "Doug, you have a wife and seven kids. You get plenty of fucking hugs."

Joe drops his arms. "Seriously?"

Doug hugs him for another second. "So *never* might've been an exaggeration."

Joe shoves Doug off him. "Jessie, put my beer on his tab."

"Tell me what you're all hugging each other for, and I'll pick up the whole tab," Doug offers, and I swear, old men are the biggest group of gossips ever.

Kendra straightens, taking her weight off me.

I hate it. But it's just in time because Joe turns and holds his arm out toward his daughter. "Just celebrating that everyone is in good health."

Doug looks to Jessie, like she's the only one of us who wouldn't lie. "That true?"

She nods. "It's true."

Doug sighs. "Fine, I'll pay. But I'm sitting at the bar with you guys."

As Joe agrees, I place a hand against Kendra's back and guide her to the seat at the end of the bar. Then I take the stool next to hers as my own.

Joe takes the spot next to me, like I expected, and Doug sits next to him.

Jessie will eat with us, but she'll stay on the other side of the bar. And with this setup, Kendra's only option will be to talk to me.

And I know Doug—he talks just as much as Joe does. So they'll distract each other until the end of time.

Kendra looks up at me with a smirk. "Shall I assume you're a regular here?"

I swallow as I dip my chin. "And are you new to the area or passing through?"

"The plan was to pass through." Her eyes light with something. Something good. "But I think I might stay."

Chapter 150

Kendra

Luther is standing behind the bar, shaking his head.

Dad points at him. "You did too."

"I've never eaten a live minnow in my life." Luther holds up his hands. "Your mind is slipping, old man. Time for some fucking supplements."

Dad scrunches up his face. "Huh. Maybe that was someone else."

Luther looks at me. "How do you put up with him?"

I snort. "Noise-canceling headphones."

"Hey!" Dad spins his seat toward me. "You said music helps you concentrate."

I nod seriously. "It does."

Dad narrows his eyes on me as Doug cackles from his other side.

Luther's phone rings, and he steps away from our noisy group to answer.

Resting my elbows on the bar, I smile as I listen to Dad and Doug bicker.

When Dad suggested going out for lunch, I suggested coming to the Inn.

I debated telling Luther we were coming, but I knew from his text this morning that he'd be here, and I wanted to surprise him. And I'm so glad we came.

Aside from the group hug, this was exactly the levity I needed.

Buddy is doing good.

Work is going well.

But not having Luther sneak into my bed every night has been... lonely.

We text all day.

And I know he'd be with me if he could get away with it.

But I still miss him.

I might be healthy now. I'll hopefully be healthy for the rest of my days. But life is short.

And I'm sick of spending time apart from the man I love.

My eyes trail over the man himself.

His back is to us. His shoulder muscles flex under the fabric of his shirt as he takes a deep breath.

I watch him nod. Then he lowers the phone and slides it back into his pocket.

"Everything good?" I ask when he steps back up to the bar.

"It's fine. I just agreed to dinner with Ashley tonight." Luther puffs out his cheeks. "And her boyfriend."

My brows jump.

I wonder if he knows that her boyfriend is... older.

Luther tilts his head, watching me. "What do you know that I don't?"

I hold my hands up. "Nothing."

He narrows his eyes. "Why don't I believe you?"

I laugh. "I'm sure I have no idea."

Luther crosses his arms, and I can't stop myself from watching the way his biceps bulge.

"My angel would never lie." Dad defends me. And I somehow manage not to make a face.

Luther turns his attention to my dad. "Don't you have a couch to go sleep on?"

Chapter 151

Luther

Sitting at the table, waiting for Ashley and her *boyfriend* to show up, I wish for the hundredth time that Kendra was with me.

Ashley had it right the first time she mentioned her boyfriend—a double date would be nice.

Not that I need a buffer between me and my daughter. It would just be nice to not feel like a third wheel.

Purple hair catches my attention, and I stand as Ashley approaches the table.

"Hey, Dad." She beams at me.

The luckiness hits me all over again.

Lucky that I got to have her.

That I got to keep her.

That I managed not to fuck up my relationship with her.

I take her offered hug, squeezing her tightly.

She laughs as she pulls away. "Miss me?"

"Always." I reach for her head to ruffle her hair, but she dodges my hand.

"Dad, this is Kurt. Kurt, this is my dad. People call him Rocky."

I eye the man standing beside my little girl.

He's not quite my height, but he's tall. Lanky. Nerdy. And looks to be almost fucking forty.

I hold my hand out.

His handshake is solid.

"How old are you?" I ask as I let go.

He keeps his eyes on mine. "I'm thirty-six. Sir."

Ten years older than Ashley.

My daughter clears her throat.

When I look at her, she lifts a brow. "Kendra couldn't join us?"

Kendra, my girlfriend, who is twenty-four years younger than I am. And the daughter of my best friend.

I drag my tongue over my teeth as I shake my head.

"Maybe next time." She smiles as she reaches for a chair.

Kurt beats her to it, pulling the seat out for her.

I shake my head again as my lips pull up into a reluctant smile, and I accept defeat.

Chapter 152

Kendra

"How was dinner?" I answer the phone quietly.

I know Dad's still awake in the living room, and I don't want him to hear me talking.

"Fine."

"Just fine?" I snicker.

I can hear Luther's huff over the background noise as he drives. "It was good. Kurt is nice."

I flop onto my back, crossways on my bed. "That's good."

"Did you know he was ten years older than her?"

I bite my lip.

"That's a yes."

"Sorry." I can hear the smile in my voice, so I know he can too.

"Uh-huh. You sound super sorry."

"I would've told you, but she told me in confidence." I think about what else Ashley and I talked about during that conversation. *Do you love him?*

My heart skips.

"She's a mature twenty-six." I try to reason.

Luther snorts. "That's good because he's a mature thirty-six. The man's temples are as gray as mine, and his hairline is eroding faster than the shorelines."

That makes me laugh. "Not everyone can be as good looking as you."

He hums. "True."

"And you're so humble too."

"I need these looks to catch younger women."

"Women, huh?" Irrational jealousy fills my tone.

"Just one," he says softly.

I close my eyes.

Just one.

Just me.

"I wish you could've been there tonight." Luther's tone is full of honesty. "I know I got to see you at lunch, but... I miss you."

Emotion blankets me.

"I miss you too," I whisper back.

"Maybe this weekend we can try again for a sleepover at my place."

I swallow. "I'd like that."

"Is Joe still sleeping on the couch?" Luther asks like he already knows the answer.

"Yeah. But Buddy is doing fine, so hopefully, he'll stop soon."

Luther hums. "You'll let me know." It's not a question.

"I'll let you know."

"That's my girl."

Warmth blooms in my chest.

"Now tell me to have a good night, Baby," he demands.

"Have a good night," I breathe.

"Good night..." he prompts.

"Good night, and I love you."

My eyes open.

I didn't...

Shit, I didn't mean to say that.

Luther stays silent.

The only thing filling the line is the sound of the highway.

I sit up.

My heart is racing.

That's not what he was trying to get me to say.
I didn't mean to...
And he...
He doesn't say it back.
I pull the phone from my ear and end the call.
The screen goes black, reflecting my horrified expression.
I stare at myself with wide eyes.
I told him I loved him.
And he didn't say it back.
He didn't say anything.

Chapter 153

Luther

I can't breathe.
　My chest aches, and I can't fucking breathe.
　She loves me.
　After everything.
　She still loves me.
　My Baby.
　My Kendra.
　I open my mouth and force my lungs to fill.
　And then the line goes dead.

Chapter 154

Kendra

I sit with my phone in my lap.
Waiting.
But it doesn't ring.
He doesn't call back.
And when twenty minutes pass, I accept the truth.
He's not going to call.
I said it too soon.
I ruined what was growing between us, just like I was worried I would.
Something splashes against my phone screen.
But I don't wipe it away.
I don't close my eyes.
I stay where I am. And I feel the bad.

Chapter 155

Luther

I don't park down the road.

I don't hide.

I drive right up to the house.

It's time.

My strides are steady as I take the front steps two at a time.

And my hands are steady as I use my spare key to unlock the front door.

I let the door slam shut behind me.

Joe bolts up from the couch, the glow from the TV illuminating his messy hair.

"Rocky?" He slaps a hand to his chest. "Fucking hell. What's—"

I don't answer him.

I cut across the main room and start down the hall.

"What's going on?" I hear Joe scramble to his feet. "What are you—"

I ignore him.

And I don't pause when I reach Kendra's door.

Chapter 156

Kendra

I stand at the foot of my bed.

I can hear my dad calling after someone.

My heart pounds in my chest, and my pulse roars through my ears because I know who it is.

Who it has to be.

Then my door swings open.

And Luther steps into my room.

He kicks it shut behind him. Then he reaches back, locking the handle a second before it rattles.

"I love you too."

He doesn't waver.

He doesn't hesitate.

He holds my gaze in his as he says it again. "I love you, Kendra. I have for so long."

The air freezes in my lungs.

"What did you say?" my dad shouts through the door.

We both ignore him.

"You hung up too fast, Baby." Luther takes a step toward me. "You didn't give me time to catch my breath." He takes another step. "Because that's what you do to me. You take my fucking breath away. Every damn day."

He takes one more step. And then he reaches for me. With both hands.

Tears roll down my cheeks.

Luther shakes his head as he rests his palms against the sides of my neck. "No more tears. Even if they're happy ones." His thumbs brush away the dampness. "Even if they're because you love me too. I still can't stand to see you cry."

I reach up and grip his forearms.

"Now say it again." He leans down, pressing his forehead to mine. "Tell me you love me again."

I close my eyes and do the easiest thing in the world.

I tell him.

"I love you, Luther." I inhale his exhale. "I have for so long."

His grip on me shifts, and he tips my head back. So our eyes meet.

"Again." His voice is so gruff.

So demanding.

I smile through the tears that keep streaming down my cheeks. "I love you. I think I will forever."

Luther's throat works. And his fingers flex as they circle my throat. "That's good, Baby Doll. Because you're it for me. Until my heart stops beating. And even then…"

I let go of his forearm with one hand and reach up, catching a teardrop on my fingertip. "And even then."

His mouth pulls into a devastatingly sweet smile. Then it crashes down against mine.

He tastes like tears.

I kiss him back.

He tastes like home.

I open for him.

He tastes like forever.

Chapter 157

Luther

She smiles against my lips.

My girl. My Kendra. My Baby.

She's mine.

I slide a hand around to the back of her head, my fingers sliding through her hair.

She's all mine.

Forever.

A throat clears loudly in the hallway.

Kendra's smile grows.

I pull back just enough to look into her sparkling eyes. "Guess we should tell him."

She gives me a tiny nod. "Guess we should."

I keep my hold on her for another heartbeat. "I love you."

Happiness radiates off my girl. "I love you too."

I loosen my grip on her and let my hands slide over her shoulders and down her arms before I step back.

Then I take a deep breath and straighten my spine before I turn, keeping my body between Kendra and the door.

There's a click as I turn the handle, releasing the lock. And I slowly pull the door open.

Joe is standing on the other side of the threshold in boxers and a white T-shirt, hair askew, arms crossed over his chest.

"Here's the thing—" I start.

He steps forward and punches me in the chest. "That's for... whatever you've done with my daughter."

"Dad!" Kendra tries to step past me, but I catch her around the waist and shove her back behind me.

Joe punches me again. Landing this hit next to the first. "And that's for keeping it from me."

"Dad," Kendra sighs.

I keep her behind me and rub at my chest with my free hand. "Shit. When'd you learn how to punch?"

"I didn't." Joe grimaces and shakes out his hand. "What are you made out of? Fucking rock?"

I make my own face as I press my hand over my pec. "You smashed my nipple."

Joe drops his hands to his sides. "Good."

Kendra snickers behind me, and I feel her drop her forehead against my back.

I try not to smile.

Joe points at me. "This isn't funny."

My nipple throbs.

I bite my cheek as I shake my head. "It's not funny."

"That's my daughter."

I nod. "I know."

"And you didn't tell me."

I nod again. "I'm sorry."

His jaw works. "How long—You know what? Don't answer that."

Kendra grips the arm I have against her and slides her hand down until our fingers twine together.

This time, when she moves to stand beside me, I don't stop her. "I'm sorry, Dad. We didn't mean to... I didn't know who he was when..."

"Nope. I don't want to know." Joe shakes his head as he lifts his hands and rubs his palms against his eyes. "I really don't want to fucking know."

Kendra looks up at me.

And I can feel it in her gaze.

I can feel her love.

I can feel her trust.

And I wonder how I ever doubted it.

I wonder how I didn't see it.

I squeeze her fingers.

She squeezes mine back.

And because I can't stop myself, I bend down and press a kiss to her forehead.

Joe lets out a loud, annoyed groan.

I don't bother apologizing for kissing her.

I know I'll do it again.

Joe props his hands on his hips, looking back and forth between Kendra and me. "Any other life-altering surprises you'd like to share with me?"

I feel Kendra's shoulders slump against my arm, and I know she's thinking about the cancer conversation. "There's nothing else. I swear. I'm sorry."

Joe sighs. "No, I'm sorry. I shouldn't've said that. You told me when you could."

"No, don't apologize. It's fair. But...you're okay? With... us?" Kendra asks hesitantly.

I hate that she's nervous, but I understand it.

This is a big deal.

Not just because I've been friends with Joe. But because *we're* a big deal.

There's no going back, not for either of us, so Joe had better learn how to be okay with it. Because Kendra and I... we're each other's person. Until the end of time.

Joe lets out another heavy groan. "There are no two people in this world that I love more than the two of you. And if you can love an ugly man like him..." He jabs his finger into my chest.

"Then yeah, I'll be okay with it."

Kendra sniffs.

Joe shakes his head. "No crying."

Kendra lets out a watery laugh, and I let go of her hand so I can wrap my arm around her shoulders and hold her against my side.

Joe turns his gaze on me. "You better mean to marry her. Because if you break my daughter's heart, I will kill you."

I grin.

"I'm serious. I will literally fucking kill you." He jabs me in the chest again, and I flex my pecs, making him jerk his hand away.

I keep grinning. "Oh, I'm going to marry her. And I'm pretty sure you just gave me your blessing."

Joe lets out another long sigh. "Fine. But no touching each other in front of me."

"Dad."

He points his finger back and forth between us. "I mean it. When we're watching TV, you aren't sitting on his lap or anything like that. Not in my house."

"Oh my god, Dad." Kendra sounds both horrified and amused.

I look down at Kendra. "You can move in with me—"

"You can move in with him when you're officially engaged." Joe talks over me.

Kendra rolls her lips together and nods. "That's reasonable."

I nod too. Because I plan to get *officially engaged* as soon as fucking possible.

Joe steps back out into the hallway, pointing toward the kitchen. "Now get the fuck out of my house. I need to sleep, and you aren't staying over." Kendra and I glance at each other, and Joe presses his palms to his eyes again. "Nope. I don't want to know!"

Feeling happier than... I ever have, I lower my mouth to Kendra's.

"Night, Baby." My lips brush against hers. "I'll come over for breakfast tomorrow."

Her lips smile against mine.

But before she can reply, Joe grips my shirt and drags me out of her room.

"Love you!" I call out as I let myself get manhandled down the hall.

Kendra peeks her head out of her bedroom. "Love you too."

Joe shoves me all the way out the front door, and I grin the whole time.

Chapter 158

Kendra

The Inn practically glows red as the sunset paints it with color.

And I smile.

I've been doing a lot of that lately.

Ever since Luther stormed through the house a week ago, declaring his love for me.

Dad sighs from the driver's seat.

I should've known he'd be cool about it. And he really has been. But in typical Dad fashion, he's teased me every day since about *being in love*.

I'm still glad we waited to tell him.

To be fair, we hadn't exactly decided to tell him when we did. It was all a bit more dramatic than what I'd originally envisioned. But it was actually pretty perfect.

How can anyone argue with love?

Now, if we'd told him sooner, and if he'd been aware of the breakup and the heartache... that would've been a nightmare. And I can only imagine how much he would've complained about his make-believe heart issues.

"You can quit with all the smiling. You'll see *Luther* in just a freaking moment," Dad grumbles as he parks the truck.

I smile even wider as I undo my seat belt and slide out of the passenger seat.

I feel giddy.

Luther's been out of town the last two days, and that's two days too long.

I smooth down the skirt of my dress.

It's the same one I wore to the welcome party. The dress I wore when we snuck off to the laundry room. And now that our luck is no longer cursed, I'm hoping to go home with Luther tonight so he can have his way with me in it all over again.

I'm rounding the front of the truck, hurrying toward the front door, when Luther steps out of the bar.

My smile widens. "Luther."

"Hey, Baby."

Dad groans.

Luther gestures to the door behind him. "Head inside. We'll be there in a moment."

Dad mutters something, making a point to bump his shoulder against Luther's as he passes.

Luther doesn't react; he just keeps walking. To me.

"What do we need a moment for?" I flutter my lashes up at my man.

"This."

With one hand, he grips my hip, while the other palms the side of my neck as he lowers his mouth to mine.

I melt into him.

Melt into his kiss.

Soak in the taste of him.

"Love you," he whispers against my lips.

"Love you," I whisper back.

He presses another kiss to my mouth, then he steps back, holding his hand out to me.

I place my palm in his, excited to have dinner together.

But he doesn't lead me to the bar.

"Where are we going?" I ask as we circle around the building.

"I want to show you something."

His hand is warm against mine.

And I hold on tight as he leads me down the little alley between the back of the bar and the motel.

We stop in front of room two. The room where it all began.

Butterflies swirl in my stomach as Luther pulls a keycard out of his pocket with his other hand.

I want to ask him what we're doing.

But I think I know.

And when he opens the door.

When I smell the flowers.

When I see the glow of twinkling lights.

I know.

When I follow him inside.

When I see piles of pretty blue pots overflowing with blossoms.

I know.

When he stops at the foot of the bed.

When I see the tray of brownies on the bedspread.

I know.

Luther's hand slips free of mine, and he picks up a small wooden box from the center of the tray.

I press my hands to my mouth when he faces me.

And a tear rolls down my cheek when he lowers to one knee.

But when he opens the box.

When I see the pretty blue enamel band and the large square diamond...

I know.

I know this man is it for me.

"Kendra." Luther's eyes shine up into mine. "My girl. My everything. I didn't know there was something missing in my life. I had no idea. Not until I met you." He pulls the ring out of the box, holding it gently between his fingers. "You took my heart that night. Right here. You took it, and I don't want it back. I just want you. All of you. Forever." He holds his other hand out for me.

My fingers tremble as I rest my left hand in his.

He lifts the ring, holding it at the tip of my finger. "Be my wife. Be my forever. Be mine. And I'll be yours."

Tears drip from my lashes. "Promise?"

"Yeah, Baby. I promise." His voice is thick.

"Then, yes." I slide my hand forward, the ring cool against my skin. "I'll be yours if you'll be mine."

Luther slides the ring the rest of the way down my finger.

I step closer. And the ring glints as I raise my hands to the sides of his neck, holding us both steady as I lower my lips to his.

He wraps his arms around my waist.

And when he kisses me back.

When he holds me like he'll never let me go.

I know.

Chapter 159

Luther

With my future wife's hand in mine, I push open the back door of the bar, and we walk in together.

Ashley lets out a squeal as she bounces over, throwing her arms around Kendra.

"Ashley?" Kendra hugs her back.

"I'm so excited!" Ashley keeps bouncing. "Can I be your flower girl?" She finally lets Kendra go but only steps back a few inches.

Kendra looks stunned.

I rest a hand on Kendra's shoulder. "Ashley, give your new mother some room."

That snaps her out of it.

Kendra gapes at me.

Ashley cackles.

And Jessie calls for a round of shots.

I watch Kendra take it all in. Watch as she realizes.

Jessie on the customer side of the bar.

Ashley's boyfriend.

Courtney, Sterling, and their baby.

The guys from Black Mountain Lodge.

The guys from Joe's Furniture.

Doug.

Kendra tips her head back, locking eyes with me. "You did this?"

I pull her into my side. "You won't get a long engagement, but I'll make it a good one."

She grins. "Promise?"

I snag a shot of tequila and hand it to her. "Promise."

We tip our drinks back together. And we take the matching bottles of beer when Jessie hands them to us.

We make our way through the crowd.

We take the drinks handed to us.

And with her hand in mine.

I know.

I know this is what I've been waiting for.

I know Kendra is all I'll ever want.

I know she's all I'll ever need.

Hours later, Kendra leans against my side as I lean against the bar.

I grip her hip, holding her there, and press a kiss to her hair.

Food has been eaten.

Drinks consumed.

Brownies shared.

The room sways pleasantly around us.

I kiss her hair again. "You ready to go to our room, Baby?"

She turns into me, pressing a hand to my chest. "Yes, Daddy."

Heat pulses down my spine.

"Nope!" Joe yells loudly from close by.

Kendra slaps a hand over her mouth.

"Nope. Nope. Nope." Joe holds his hands up as he walks away from us, shaking his head.

I can't help it.

I laugh. Loudly.

"I can't believe he heard me say that." Kendra pokes me in the ribs. "I didn't know he was standing there."

"It was bound to happen." I capture her hand. "Now come on, future wife, it's time for bed."

We wave our goodbyes.
We walk out the door together.
And I smile.
We enter the room.
We reach for each other.
And I'm still smiling.
She takes off my shirt.
I pull off her dress.
And I can't stop smiling.
She comes undone beneath me.
I lose myself above her.
And I know.
With her.
I'll never stop smiling.

Epilogue 1

Kendra

Dad holds his arm out for me, and I take it.

My dress is cream. The skirt is fluffy with tulle. And colorful flowers are embroidered from the bodice to the hem.

It's perfect.

Dad lets out a breath. "Ready?"

I nod. "Ready."

Ashley gives me a big smile, then she starts to walk.

We follow her down around the side of Luther's house.

Our house.

The leaves have changed color.

The bright yellows and oranges and reds stand out against the bright blue sky.

And it's perfect.

When we reach the corner of the house, we turn, and it doesn't feel real.

The white chairs sit in neat rows, and Ashley starts down the aisle ahead of us, tossing flower petals with each step.

Buddy darts across the yard, a black bow tie askew on his neck as he snaps a mouthful of petals out of the air.

It's so perfect.

Dad chuckles beside me, then reaches up with his free hand to wipe at his eyes.

I think Buddy moving over here was even harder for him to deal with than me moving out.

Buddy lets out a shout, then runs back to his house.

A tiny home.

That my dad built.

Just for the fox.

And just like the yard, it's decorated with string lights and bouquets of flowers.

It might not be a zoo, but it's not the wild.

And then we're there.

Standing before Luther.

And he's perfect.

He holds his hand out for me.

And my fingers don't tremble as I take it.

Because this is exactly where I'm meant to be.

Because we're perfect.

Luther

I wrap my fingers around hers, and I look to my best friend.

He dips his chin. "Take good care of her."

I nod. "I promise."

Joe looks between us, then he lifts a hand to my shoulder. "Welcome to the family, son."

A laugh pops out of Kendra.

I roll my eyes. "Go sit down."

He grins. "Also, I lied. There's a third person I love just as much as I love you two."

Kendra tilts her head, then we both watch as Joe goes to the front row. And sits next to Jessie.

Leaning back in his chair, he puts his arm around her shoulders, pulls her into his side, and presses a fucking kiss to my sister's temple.

She blushes. But she doesn't pull away. Instead, she rests her hand on his thigh.

I narrow my eyes.

Joe smirks at me.

And when I think about it.

When I really think about it.

I realize they're perfect.

I turn back to my soon-to-be wife. And the smile on her face... it's all I need.

Kendra squeezes my fingers.

I squeeze hers back. "Want to get married?"

She lifts her brows. "Now?"

My mouth pulls into a grin. "Now's good for me."

Happiness radiates off her as she keeps smiling. "Now works."

Epilogue 2

Luther

"Luther," my wife hisses.

"Nah, Baby." I lower the tailgate of the truck. "Take off your shirt and call me Daddy."

She shakes her head, but she can't hide her smile. "You're bad, Daddy."

Then she proves she likes me bad because she grips the hem of her shirt and pulls it up over her head.

I drag my tongue across my lip. Her tits look delicious in that thin white bra.

"Pants."

She reaches for her jeans. "What if we get caught?" she asks as she pulls her zipper down.

I start to unbutton my shirt. "I called in a report of illegal hunters. On the other side of the park."

Kendra pauses, then laughs as she shoves her pants down her legs. "You're going to end up with a fine when they catch you."

I think about all the money I've already given this park and figure I've already paid my dues.

Then she steps out of her shoes and jeans and stands before me in nothing but her bra and panties. And the sun glistening off her skin is the only thing I'm left thinking about.

The surprisingly warm day turned out to be the perfect opportunity to give Kendra the outdoor sexy time I promised her months ago.

We'll get even more outdoor sexy time next month when we take our honeymoon in the tropics, but for now...

She tucks her fingers into the band of her thong, but I shake my head. "Leave it on."

I throw my shirt to the ground.

I undo my jeans. But before I can shove them down, Kendra places her palms on my bare stomach. "Let me do it."

As she drags her fingernails down my abs, she lowers to her knees.

Looking up at me, she parts her lips in that way I like.

I grip her hair, tilting her head back farther. "Undress me."

She curls her fingers around the waistband of my boxer briefs and tugs them and my jeans down.

My cock is painfully hard and bobs free, inches from her face.

She releases my pants, and they drop to my ankles. "What now, Daddy?"

"Now you practice for our honeymoon, Wife." Using my hold of her hair, I tip her face forward until her lips are level with my dick. "Open your mouth."

She does as she's told. And when her lips wrap around the head of my cock, I groan.

She sucks.

She licks.

She moans.

And I work myself deeper.

"Such a good wife." I drag her mouth off my length.

Kendra blinks up at me with tears of lust on her lashes.

Then she smirks. And I notice the hand between her legs.

My smile is full of teeth. "Good wife, but what a slutty little girl. And slutty girls don't get fucked in the back of a truck." I loosen my hold on her hair and drag my hand around to the front of her throat. "They get fucked on the ground. In the grass." I release her. "Get on all fours."

She pulls her fingers free of her panties, and they shine in the sun as she turns and reaches for the ground.

I drop to my knees behind her.

My feet are still trapped in my jeans, but I'm not taking the time to remove them.

I pat the inside of her thigh, and Kendra widens her stance.

I slide a finger up her slit, feeling the soaked fabric. "Eyes open." I pull the fabric aside. "Mouth shut."

Kendra moans.

She can't hide how much she loves following orders.

And—gripping my dick—I can't hide how much I love giving them.

I line my cock up with her entrance.

"Ready?" I grit my teeth.

My wife nods.

My fingers dig into the soft skin of her hips. Then I pull her back as I thrust forward, filling her.

And I'm *not gentle*.

My head falls back as her heat surrounds me.

And we aren't quiet.

We're loud.

Our moans fill the forest.

The sound of my hand connecting with her ass echoes through the valley.

And when I reach around. When I rub her clit. When she clenches her core around me. I fill my wife to the brim as she cries my name.

Ten minutes later, I pull the truck up to the public restrooms near the visitor center at the entrance of the state park.

"I'll just be a minute." Kendra opens her door as soon as I stop.

"No hurry, Baby."

She grins at me before she slides out of the truck and shuffles across the sidewalk.

If I were a good husband, I would've pulled out and come in the grass.

But knowing that I'm dripping out of her always fills me with too much smugness to do it any other way.

Deciding I could probably stand to wash my hands, I turn off the engine and climb out of my truck.

The brick building looks new. The sign mounted to the wall designating it as the *Public Restroom* is shiny.

And there's another sign below it. More of a plaque.

I step closer so I can read the stamped metal plate.

Building dedicated to Rocky and his Buddy.

I stare at it.

Then I shake my head.

Fucker.

Help Protect Buddy and His Friends

You can't bring Buddy inside, but you can help save him and his canine friends.

Every day, the world turns into a more dangerous place for our wildlife. Between the loss of habitat and human stupidity, they need our help now more than ever.

You can help by donating money or spreading the word about the important work being done at the Colorado Wolf and Wildlife Center. And if you're ever in the area, stop by and visit so you can wave to Buddy and his friends.

https://www.wolfeducation.org/

Acknowledgments

Thank you, dear reader, for joining me on this Rocky Mountain adventure. I'm having such a great time in this part of Tilly World, and I hope you enjoyed Daddy as much as I did. We have one more Mountain Man left in this series, and I promise he's going to be a grumpy good time. (There are two animals in that book... and I dropped mention of them in this book... any guesses?)

Thank you to the actual Rocky Mountains for inspiring this whole series. Minnesota, I miss you, but Colorado, you're where I'm meant to be.

Thank you, Mom, for always being down with whatever I write.

Thank you, Nikki, for your mac and cheese GIFs. They give me life.

Thank you, Kerissa, for always keeping me on task, even when I don't want it.

Thank you, Gabby, for always having words of encouragement.

Thank you, Sam, for always being awake when I need to complain.

Thank you, Liz, for listening to me talk endlessly about these characters.

Thank you, Mr. Tilly, for feeding me and keeping me caffeinated when I literally always find myself behind on my deadlines.

Thank you, Jeanine and Beth, for being such great editors.

Thank you, Lori, for always making me such amazing covers.

Thank you, Wander, for not only your stunning photography but also for doing this custom photoshoot for me. It's perfect.

Thank you to my ARC readers and to all of you who take the time out of your days to make such brilliant content to help me promote this book.

And thank you to everyone who rates and reviews this book. Being an indie (independent) author is amazing. But it's a lot of work. And the likes and shares and reviews make such a huge difference to authors like me. It takes a village, and you're my village.

About the Author

S. J. Tilly was born and raised in the glorious state of Minnesota but now resides in the mountains of Colorado. To avoid the snowy winters, S. J. enjoys burying her head in books, whether to read them or write them or listen to them.

When she's not busy writing her contemporary smut, she can be found lounging with Mr. Tilly and their circus of rescue boxers.

To stay up to date on all things Tilly, make sure to follow her on her socials, join her newsletter, and interact whenever you feel like it!

Links to signed books, merch, events, and everything else on her website www.sjtilly.com

Also By S. J. Tilly

The Alliance Series
(Dark Mafia Romance)
NERO
KING
DOM
HANS

The Sin Series
(Romantic Suspense)
MR. SIN
SIN TOO
MISS SIN

The Darling Series
(Small Town Age Gap)
SMOKY DARLING
LATTE DARLING

The Sleet Series
(Hockey Rom-Com)
SLEET KITTEN
SLEET SUGAR
SLEET BANSHEE
SLEET PRINCESS

The Bite Series
(Holiday Novellas - Baking Competition)
SECOND BITE

SNOWED IN BITE
NEW YEAR'S BITE
The Mountain Men Series
(Hot guys in flannel)
MOUNTAIN BOSS
MOUNTAIN DADDY
MOUNTAIN MEN #3

www.ingramcontent.com/pod-product-compliance
Lightning Source LLC
LaVergne TN
LVHW052319250825
819574LV00032B/722

This book is dedicated to all my girlies who love a book daddy.

You're welcome.

Mountain Daddy

Copyright © S.J. Tilly LLC 2025
All rights reserved.
First published in 2025
No part of this book may be reproduced, stored in a retrieval system, or transmitted in any form or by any means, without the prior permission in writing of the publisher, nor be otherwise circulated in any form of binding or cover other than that in which it is published and without a similar condition, including this condition, being imposed on the subsequent purchaser. All characters in this publication other than those clearly in the public domain are fictitious, and any resemblance to real persons, living or dead, is purely coincidental.
Cover: Lori Jackson Design
Model Image: Wander Aguiar Photography
Editors: Jeanine Harrell, Indie Edits with Jeanine
& Beth Lawton, VB Edits

Mountain Daddy

Mountain Men Book Two

S.J. Tilly